Mustafa and the Multicoloured Koran

Other books by Mark Frew

Mauritian Creole in Seven Easy Lessons
Michael and the Multicoloured Gospel
Farewell My Pashtun
A Right To Love

Mustafa and the Multicoloured Koran

Mark Frew

Mustafa and the Multicoloured Koran

Copyright © 2019 Mark Frew

ISBN: 978-0-6487124-0-4 (paperback)
ISBN: 978-0-6487124-1-1 (hardback)
ISBN: 978-0-9954440-9-6 (ebook)

 A catalogue record for this
book is available from the
NATIONAL
LIBRARY National Library of Australia
OF AUSTRALIA

Indeed, the worst of living creatures in the sight of Allah are...those who do not use their intellect.

Surah Al-Anfal 8:22

Foreword

Quotations from the Koran and chapter and verse numberings were taken from the English translation of the Koran by Abdullah Yusuf Ali and the *Word-for-Word Translation to facilitate learning of Quranic Arabic* compiled by Dr Shehnaz Shaikh and Ms Kausar Khatri.

Quotations from the Bible were taken from the New International Version.

Chapter 1

The story of Lut, or Lot, and the cities to which he was sent is a curious one. Lut, a righteous man and a messenger of Allah, was sent to certain towns inhabited by men to whom Lut had some kinship, as he is described as being a brother of these inhabitants.

The sin that the people of Lut committed is quite clear in the Koran. They committed "lewdness", "abomination", that which is "shameful", a sin which transgressed all bounds. The actual sin is made clear when Lut questions his people in An-Naml 27:55 by asking them, "Would you really approach men in your lusts rather than women?", the assumption, of course, being that Lut was addressing a men-only audience. What further incites Lut to anger is when the inhabitants of the city come to Lut's house because he has guests there. The Koran doesn't explain who these guests were, where they came from nor what they were doing at Lut's place. The Koran doesn't even say what gender the guests were either. But it can be safely assumed that the guests were in fact men as, on account of the guests, the people of Lut came rejoicing.

There were many cities at about this time and no doubt the inhabitants committed sins that according to reasonable people would be transgressing all bounds, such as squandering large amounts of money from elderly people, reducing people to a life of abject slavery, and torturing and murdering innocent people, including innocent children. But Allah simply sat there idly and allowed these cities to continue to exist without His intervention. However, the very thought of men having sex with other men even when they mutually consented to it was just too abhorrent for

Allah to tolerate which is what stirred Him into action to destroy Lut's brothers and the cities they inhabited.

And this is the message which is brought out in the story of Lut and his people, at least, this is what is often highlighted as evidence against homosexuality. The story of the people of Lut leaves us in little doubt that this is testimony to God's abhorrence of this sin.

But this is not the entire story. When we examine the story closely, we find that this is not the only message to draw from this lesson. When the men of these cities came rejoicing because of Lut's guests, the inference being that they wanted to have sex with them, Lut tells them in Al-Hijr 15:71

Here are my daughters, if you must act so

In other words, Lut considered very strongly protecting his guests from having sex with the men of these cities but had no difficulty handing over his daughters in their place. Lut was willing to allow his daughters to be gang raped by each and every male inhabitant of this city in order to protect his guests. What the complete moral of the story of the people of Lut is that sex between men is evil indeed, but raping women, or girls, is okay, even if it is committed against your own daughters. Further, this righteous man, Lut, a messenger of Allah, was prepared to allow these men to commit fornication with his daughters, which subtly implies that there are times when fornication is allowed. This in itself was striking because committing what we call in Urdu, *zinna*, that is, sex outside of wedlock, was punishable by stoning to death, yet righteous Lut, a messenger of Allah, actually was about to engage in promoting this crime. Because the crime of *zinna* deserved a similar punishment to the crime of homosexuality, it is striking that the people of Lut were punished so severely for a crime that carried a punishment similar to that for which Lut was encouraging them to commit with his daughters, and yet Lut was delivered from the punishment while the men of the city were condemned.

There are other problems with this story. The story is recounted in several different chapters, or *surahs*, of the Koran and in each case the account has irreconcilable variations but in all a complete disregard towards women. In Al-Araf 7:80 – 84, Lut was sent by Allah to these people whereas in Adh-Dhariyat 51:31 – 37 unnamed messengers were sent to deliver the only righteous people living in the city who lived in only one house, and it is made clear in Hud 11:77 – 82 that these unnamed righteous people were Lut, his wife and his daughters. However, despite the righteousness of this family, we learn in Al-Hijr 15:60 that Lut's wife was condemned to suffer the same fate as the inhabitants of the city simply for lagging behind, this lingerer not being Lut's wife in Ash-Shuara 26:171 but rather a nameless old woman, and hence she was destroyed along with the inhabitants of the city. This implies that lingering, which appears to us as quite a mild misdemeanour that Lut's otherwise righteous wife – or an unknown old woman – committed, is a sin in the eyes of Allah as heinous as the abominations that the people of Lut were engaging in. It is further assumed that all the women and children who inhabited these cities were unfortunately condemned to suffer the same fate simply because they were human collateral.

As for the names of the cities which the people of Lut inhabited, Muslims are aware that these were Sodom and Gomorrah, and the unnamed guests were actually angels impersonating men. But not because it says so in the Koran. Rather, Muslims only know the name of the cities and the true nature of the guests because it says so in the Bible, the Judaeo-Christian Scriptures, to which Muslims hold a vague and unclear respect for.

If the Koran is therefore our moral compass, the conclusion we can draw from this story is that, if the Koran speaks clearly and evidently against homosexuality in these accounts, we must also draw the conclusion that the Koran also allows for women to be expendable sex objects to be used as men see fit, even if it means committing *zinna*.

But they don't preach this in the mosque. Although I have heard them preach against the sins of the people of Lut, not once did I ever hear them mention Lut's "righteous" acts. There is no hint of accusation against Lut as he remains a righteous man, a man sent from Allah, a man as it says in Al-Anbiya 21:74 to whom Allah gave judgement and knowledge. But are we really supposed to accept this account as an example for us to live by?

This was how I was raised to view the Koran. After many years as a Muslim, I came to the realisation that the Koran was not what I was originally told that it was. However, there are not many people I can tell this to because to admit this openly to the general Muslim public is a death sentence. However, for the few Muslims to whom I can be honest about my apostasy without serious reprisal, this question is difficult to answer: why did I leave the faith?

Where do I start? There are so many factors which led to my decision. It was not something that happened overnight. I did love the Koran and cherish it as Allah's holy Word for many years but I cannot view it in this way today. The Koran is, in a way, a significant and influential work of poetry, but it is impossible to claim that it is perfect.

The story of how I became a Muslim is rather mundane. I was born in a country where Islam was the state religion. Hence Islam was all around me. In particular I was reminded of Islam five times a day when I heard the muezzin call for prayer so it was impossible to ever be out of Islam's reach. However, although the religion was all around me, it became a standard understanding that people only observed those aspects of the religion that were of benefit to them, but when there was no benefit, there was no need to take the religion seriously.

In any case, for me, Islam was the only life I knew. Ever since I left the womb, I was surrounded by an Islamic environment and didn't know anything different.

But my seriousness to the religion really started with my father's approach to it. My father grew up in a family which, as he later discovered, he was actually not born into but rather into which he was adopted. For all his childhood and adolescence, as far as he was concerned, the people he lived with were his biological parents. However, their approach to Islam was rather loose. His mother often wore a sari, which by conventional Islamic thinking is considered, as we say in Urdu, *nanga pehnawa*, that is, "naked dress", because the sari allows the skin of certain areas of the body of the wearer to be exposed. She also played cards and chess which, according to one of the Hadiths, is anathema for Muslims. His father was also rather lax regarding his practice of Islam. He didn't attend Friday prayers regularly. And worst of all, he went around clean shaven, which is considered as a total disregard towards the prophet. Because the prophet Muhammad had a beard, then all his male followers have to have a beard. This requirement to imitate everything the prophet did and said is known by Muslims by the Arabic word *sunna*, that is, anything the prophet said and did is *sunna* which means all followers must do the same thing.

So, my father grew up in a household which did not hold to the Islamic religion tenaciously. Because my father was brought up by Muslim parents who only held to the religion moderately, my father also held a moderate attitude towards the Islamic faith.

What set my father's heart to change was the day he discovered that the man and woman who had raised him were not his real parents. How he found out remains a mystery as he never let on to anyone how he had made this discovery. However, once he did find out, that's when things started to change. His relationship with his adopted parents became strained and he eventually lived in isolation but still under the same roof as his parents, only coming out of his room to partake of meals and then hiding back in his room to contemplate. This knowledge that he was adopted was very unsettling for him and so in order to find some peace, he started attending the local mosque where he met a visiting Mulvi, a person who dedicates his life to Islam and who wanders about and proselytises. This Mulvi took an interest in my father and preached to him Islam. The Mulvi insisted that my father attend his classes after the last prayer of the day, or *isha* prayers. My father attended a few classes as a trial and pretty soon was attending the classes regularly. Because of my father's dedication to the Mulvi and his version of Islam, eventually the Mulvi arranged for my father to marry the Mulvi's daughter. The Mulvi's daughter was a very observant Muslim woman, obedient to her husband, who spent more of her time on a prayer mat than doing household chores, chores that were eventually left for my grandmother to do. My grandmother accepted this fate because this was the only way that she could ensure that her son would not abandon his childhood home. Hence my parents lived in the home of my grandparents, and it is from their union I was born.

I grew up in Alekh-Jahan, a small suburb some distance from the centre of Karachi, the largest city of Pakistan. The inhabitants of this suburb were middle class, a mixture of people from different backgrounds, but all relatively educated and well-to-do. It was a normal middle class suburb of Karachi in which neat and clean streets meandered around concrete buildings within which the locals all lived.

It was a troubling time to grow up in. At this time, the nation was in turmoil because of the political conflict between two great leaders vying for power, Benazir Bhutto and Nawaz Sharif, two of the most prominent politicians of the time, who were caught in a struggle to take control of the country. Karachi being the most happening city of the

14

country suffered the brunt of this struggle. Because we had an unstable government, life itself was somewhat unstable. Whenever Benazir Bhutto lost power to Nawaz Sharif, supporters of Benazir would take to the streets and set fire to the city. This meant that it wasn't safe to be outdoors or far from the family home.

I remember during my childhood that there were frequent curfews. We had to be indoors by a certain time of the evening. A particular memory that remains prominent in my mind is of spending time with my grandmother and waiting for my grandfather to come home after working the night shift. These regular curfews occurred during changes in regimes and hence at these times we could not go out. Rather, I would sit with my grandmother on the balcony waiting for my grandfather to come home. That was at a time when there were no mobile phones so all we could do was sit and wait for a sign that my grandfather was coming home on his Vespa.

I lived with my sister, my parents and my grandparents. It was an unusual relationship. Traditionally, the grandparents live a somewhat relaxed lifestyle while the daughter-in-law does all the housework as respect towards her elders and as a way for the son to requite his parents for all the work the parents have done to raise their son. However, the situation in my house was the reverse. It was the daughter-in-law, my mother, who lived a rather relaxed life, freely able to devote herself totally to Allah, while my grandmother was left with the responsibility of looking after the less holy and yet more practical aspects of life, the looking after the family home.

Every Friday my father took me to the mosque. Traditionally, it is the grandparents who pass on the teaching of the Koran to their grandchildren. However, in my home, because my grandparents were too moderate for my parents' liking, my father organised for a Mulvi, a different one from my mother's father, to visit every day and teach me to read the Koran.

It was from this Mulvi that I learnt much about my religion. What I learnt was that there was once a man called Muhammad who lived about 1,400 years ago. This man received revelations from Allah through an angel called Gabriel, revelations which eventually formed the Koran. Muhammad was no ordinary man. He was very special, so special that we pray what is called *doorood shareef*, a type of prayer to ask Allah to bless Muhammad, so that Muhammad will intercede on our behalf on the Day of Judgement should Allah be tempted to send us to hell, or *Jahannam*. It is this same *doorood* for Muhammad that even the Almighty Allah Himself prays because of Allah's total adoration, respect and devotion towards this created messenger. This devotion of Allah for His messenger is supported by what it says in the Koran, in Al-Ahzab 33:56, that "Allah and His Angels send blessings on the Prophet".

It was from Muhammad that we learnt that the Supreme Being of the entire universe was Allah. Allah was omnipotent, omniscient, omnipresent, and all the omnis you could think of. An example of His omnipotence was the fact that He created the entire universe. Because He was omniscient, He knew everything from the smallest quark to the largest galaxy. That He was omnipresent meant that He was all around us. I remember in my curiosity asking the question as to whether or not Allah was under the table, in the pencil case, in the cupboard, in my shoe, and the Mulvi answered affirmatively, and commended me on how well I had grasped this concept. However, this also created a little bit of confusion that needed clarification. I had also been told that there was one place in which I should never say the name of Allah and that was the toilet because the toilet was an unclean place, and hence I had assumed from this that Allah would never be found there. This led me to ask quite innocently, and to clarify a misunderstanding, that if Allah is everywhere, isn't He also in this unclean place, and hence what deleterious effect would it have on Allah if His name were mentioned there, since Allah not only created the uncleanness, His presence was already in it and among it? Instead of a logical explanation by the Mulvi to satisfy my young curious mind, I received a hard slap across the face and a severe reprimand that I should not be so blasphemous. I was later to learn that this is a common reaction against those who question the religion, even when the question is a legitimate one, in some cases the reaction being a lot more severe.

But not only was Allah everywhere and all-knowing, He was also all-compassionate and all-good. In fact, according to a hadith entitled *Mount of Glory, Lessons on the Month of Ramadan*, there is a story of someone observing a mother bird tending to her chicks when that same person had it explained to him that Allah loves His creatures, the human being, seventy times more. This showed in a picturesque way just how compassionate Allah was. This meant that although Allah is almighty, He was not a despot, as He has infinite compassion for His earthly representatives, us humans, or us *caliphs*, as the original Arabic describes us in Al-Baqarah 2:30. And therefore everything Allah did and said was beneficial for all creation.

With such a wonderful picture of this Almighty Being, the obvious question came to mind: why, then, is this good and wholesome world that Allah created so full of suffering, pain, sickness and death, and why are His creatures, His *caliphs*, capable of committing atrocities against their fellow humans? This was when we were introduced to Satan.

After completely ruining it for us in the Garden of Eden, Satan continued his rule of evil. He was the opposite of Allah, the anti-god, for what Allah was, Satan was not: where Allah was all good, Satan was all evil, where Allah was all love, Satan was all hate, where Allah was all truth,

Satan was all lies. Satan, although he was merely a created being, appeared to have about as much power as Allah.

Allah and Satan were in constant conflict, the battle ground being the earth, the spoils of war human souls. Because Allah loved humankind, He was fighting so that humans could be holy enough so that they could live forever with Him in paradise, whereas Satan, who hated humanity as much as he hated Allah, only wanted men and women to be sent to eternal torment because of his spite towards Allah's goodness and love.

Because of our fallen state, we were refused direct communication with Allah because Allah could not associate with sinful beings. And this was where the Koran came into the picture. The only means of communication Allah had with us was through His Word, the Koran. Although written by men, the men who wrote down the words of the Koran wrote down exactly what had been revealed to Muhammad, words Muhammad had received from the angel Gabriel, who in turn had received from Allah. Because the Koran had come from Allah, the Koran contained neither mistake nor contradiction between its covers.

However, because Satan hated Allah, he added to the temptations he inflicted on humankind the temptation to doubt the Koran and question its infallibility. Anyone, therefore, who denied the infallibility of the Word of Allah was in danger of hell fire. Anything in the Koran that did not make sense, or seemed untrue, or if one verse of the Koran was contradictory to another, these were merely mirages as there were no problems with the perfect Koran but rather anything that appeared problematic with the Koran was in reality Satan trying to tempt us away from this holy text in order to entice us away from believing any of it at all, and thus paving the way for our eternal damnation. Wow! Who'd want to doubt the Koran with this type of understanding of it?!

But what is the Koran? To fundamental Muslims, this is an absurd question. They would pull a book off the shelf with *The Holy Koran* stamped on the front in beautiful Arabic script and wave it in your face! Indeed, I remember the imam at our local mosque waving it in the air before all of us to convince us of its divinity.

The problem was that what we were told about the origins of the Koran ran contrary to what revered Islamic scholarly writings actually say about it. What we were told about the origin of the Koran was based on what is written in Al-Buruj 85:21, 22 that

This is a glorious Koran, in a tablet preserved

written, as it says in An-Nahl 16:103, in

Arabic, pure and clear

This meant, so we were told, that the Koran had been forever preserved in heaven, co-existing with Allah and never changing, and that the tablet it was written on was a pure tablet that exists in the heavens together with Allah. This, of course, implies that if the Koran has forever co-existed with Allah, then the language that Allah speaks is therefore Arabic.

We were further told, even though it doesn't say so in the Koran itself, that the Koran was revealed to Muhammad by the angel Gabriel. The entire Koran was revealed to Muhammad orally for him to recite and memorise, and then Muhammad got friends to write down the recitations as Muhammad himself was illiterate. Just before Muhammad died, the entire Koran had been revealed to Muhammad and faithfully transmitted to his scribes.

The problem is that, for a start, the verses in Al-Buruj do not tell us that the tablet on which the Koran was written is a tablet co-existing with Allah. It merely says that the Koran is on "a tablet preserved". This preserved tablet could simply be an earthly tablet, similar to the rock on which in around 1700 BC the Law Code of Hammurabi was written, a large block of rock which has been preserved for millennia and can still be viewed today at the Louvre Museum in Paris, or as the Jews and Christians claim about the Ten Commandments, that The Ten Commandments were written on tablets of stone, not some spiritual or transcendental stones but on stones that form part of the physical earth on which we live. In fact, this mention of "a tablet preserved" and the story of Moses eventually led to my suspicion that it was originally the Ten Commandments written on tablets of stone that this verse was actually referring to, especially as it says in Surah Al-Araf 7:145 that Allah ordained for Moses, and not for Muhammad, "the tablets regarding everything, an instruction and explanation for everything."

Further, the Koran itself also states on many occasions that it is equal to the Judaeo-Christian Scriptures, being sent down after and in the same way as The Old and New Testaments as it says in Al-Imran 3:3, and that Allah Himself swears by The Old Testament, the New Testament and the Koran, all three as one unit, as He clearly states in Al-Taubah 9:111. This association of the Koran with the Holy Bible implies that the Bible has to also have co-existed together with the Koran if the Koran has forever existed and is in unity with the Judaeo-Christian Scriptures. Not only so, on many occasions, the Koran instructs its readers to remember accounts found in the Judaeo-Christian Scriptures, such as what had been said about Moses and Abraham.

Also, the Koran speaks about events that occurred in a time before the Koran itself, such as when the Koran tells unidentified readers in Al-Imran 3:44 that "you were not with them when they cast their pens as to which of them should take charge of Maryam; nor were you there when they were disputing". If the Koran itself tells readers to recall certain past events, this implies events which took place before the writing of the Koran, which inevitably means that the Koran simply cannot be eternal.

In fact, much of the Koran relies extensively on historical figures, people who the Koran itself acknowledges lived prior to its existence, and who the Koran uses as examples for us to follow, such as Noah, Abraham, Moses, Lut, Zakariah, and Issa. An eternal document cannot logically refer back to people of history because an eternal document predates, is contemporaneous with and postdates the existence of these people.

The Koran also talks of times "before", that is, in the past. An eternal document logically could never use the word "before" or any words like it because an eternal document cannot by definition have a "before". In fact, an eternal document can never use the past tense ever in its text seeing the use of the past tense fixes the text to a particular point of time. And yet the Arabic equivalent of the past tense is used much throughout the text.

Not only does the evidence show that the Koran is time dependent, the Koran gives hints of the timing and location of its composition. Because the Koran talks about how the universe was created, the Koran was composed after the universe had come into existence. And because the Koran mentions Jews and Christians, then the Koran was composed after these religions had been established. The Koran mentions the defeat of the Romans in the surah called Surah Ar-Rum, which therefore means that it was written some time after Rome's fall. And it was composed before modern technology came into being because it talks of cows, horses and donkeys as transport vehicles in An-Nahl 16:7, 8 but not ships, trucks or trains fuelled by oil or electricity. And it describes the stars as a means of guiding people in An-Nahl 16:16 but mentions nothing of the use of satellites and GPS systems. In fact, the Koran's composition, or at least its final compilation, can almost be given an exact year. In Al-Baqarah 2:142 - 144 the Koran

21

talks about the changing of the direction of prayer, or as it is known in Arabic, the changing of the *qibla*. Once we know the exact timing of the *qibla* change, we can determine the precise timing of the composition of the Koran - or at least this portion of the Koran.

As well as hinting at the timing, the Koran also provides hints about the location of its composition. The fact that it was written in Arabic tells us that it was written in the Middle East. This is further confirmed with its mentions of places once located in the Middle East, areas such as Thamud and Iram. By contrast, there is no mention of ancient civilisations such as the Sumerians, the Assyrians, the Olmecs, the Aztecs and the Incas, nor of modern states such as the USA, China, Australia, Iceland, New Zealand and even Pakistan.

Not only so, the Koran further hints at an evolution in its formation. In An-Nahl 16:101, 102 the Koran has Allah saying, "And when We substitute a verse in place of a verse...Say, 'The Holy Spirit has brought it down from your Lord in truth'". If the Koran were eternal, it would be impossible that one verse could replace other verses if all the verses were always there all the time. Rather, this suggests a text in evolution which started out in one form and went through various revisions before the final form was accepted, the final version we read today.

Further, the entire subject matter of the Koran makes it evident that the Koran is not eternal. The entire Koran is about the relationship between Allah and humans, the humans being divided into two groups, the unbelievers or *kaffeers*, and the believers. This means that the Koran only makes sense in the lifetime of humanity. The Koran gives dictates on how humans, and humans alone, need to conduct their lives. It talks of marriage and who can marry whom and how many. It talks about divorce. It talks of what to do to suckle children. It talks about how property is to be distributed when people die. Outside the lifespan of humanity on earth, before the creation of this world and after its destruction, the Koran makes absolutely no sense and has no meaning because the subject matter of the Koran is purely about humans and about the world on which these humans inhabit. If the Koran were eternal, then it would require that the existence of humans also be eternal. But according to the Koran, humans only made their appearance at Creation and they will no longer continue in this form after Judgement Day.

And, of course, if the Koran were eternal, and Allah wanted all humanity to know about the contents of the Koran so that all humanity knew how to conduct their lives in the way that pleased Allah, why is it that Allah waited thousands of years after Creation before He decided to reveal the Koran to us humans? As the Koran clearly states, Allah sent many Messengers, Adam, Ibrahim, Moses, David and Issa, hundreds to thousands of years before the advent of Muhammad, but waited till He had created and sent Muhammad before He revealed the eternal book to all humanity.

What became further revealing was what was said about the Koran in the Hadiths. The Hadiths are collections of sayings and doings of Muhammad beyond what is written in the Koran, and for many Muslims they are held in high esteem and almost on an equal footing with the Koran. The Hadiths have been reverentially preserved, copied and passed down through the centuries by Muslim scholars. However, the Hadiths surprisingly relate a completely different story as to how this supposed holy book was compiled. According to the collection of hadiths called Sahih Bukhari, the Koran did not appear in its current book form until the reign of Abubaker. Abubaker was the ruling Caliph who took over leadership of the Arabian Empire after the death of Muhammad. At that time, Muhammad had passed on the Koran by oral recitation only and hence when Muhammad died, the Koran had not as yet been compiled together as a book. The task to preserve the Koran in written form was, as it says in Sahih Bukhari, Volume 6, Book 61, Number 509, given to a man called Zaid bin Thabit, a friend of the prophet, who was ordered to do so by the Caliph Abubaker. Zaid bin Thabit was assigned this task because many of those who could recite the Koran from memory had died in battle and it was feared that if all of these reciters were killed off before passing on the recitation, the entire Koran would be forever lost. Zaid bin Thabit at first was resistant to carry out such a project, especially as this was something that Allah's Apostle, Muhammad, had never done, as Muhammad's means of passing on the Koran was by oral recitation, not as a written record. In other words, what Zaid bin Thabit was being commanded to do by Abubaker was not sunna. However, eventually Zaid bin Thabit confesses, as it says in the hadith, that "Allah opened my chest for it" – which implies that we should view Zaid bin Thabit as a prophet, and as a greater prophet than Muhammad as Allah spoke to Zaid bin Thabit directly, but to Muhammad indirectly, because Allah spoke to Muhammad through an intermediary, the angel Gabriel. In answer to Allah's chest opening, Zaid bin Thabit went out in search of the different sections of the Koran which had been written on palm stalks, on flat white stones and from men who had memorised the Koran, and put the Koran together in book form. The problem with this is that Muhammad was now dead and unable to supervise the project and tell Zaid bin Thabit which of all the writings that Zaid bin Thabit had collected were in the original Koran and not simply verses invented by other people who wrote them down and convinced Zaid bin Thabit that these were also part of the Koran. So, from this hadith, we could say that the Koran really was composed by Zaid bin Thabit.

But then, in the same Hadith, and directly after this account, there is a different and in some ways contradictory story as to how the Koran was put together. In the same Hadith, Sahih Bukhari, Volume 6, Book 61, Number 510, we read how it wasn't Abubaker who ordered the compilation of the Koran but rather the Caliph Uthman. Uthman was the ruling Caliph some years after Muhammad, coming after the Caliphs Abubaker and Omar. Uthman noticed that there were differences among the recitations of the Koran. Uthman then commanded all current manuscripts of the Koran be brought to him and given to four men: Zaid bin Thabit, Abdullah bin Az-Zubair, Said bin Al-As and Adbur-Rahman bin Harith bin Hisham, who were then instructed to compile the final perfect copy. If there were any discrepancies between the different manuscripts, these men were ordered to write the final manuscript in the Quraish dialect of Arabic as it was in this dialect that the Koran was revealed – which further implies that not only was the Koran originally preserved in heaven in Arabic, it was preserved in the Quraish dialect of Arabic and hence this is the dialect of Arabic in which Allah speaks. Once this project was completed, Uthman ordered all variant copies of the Koran and variant fragments of manuscripts which did not match the final versions compiled by these four men to be burnt. I was shocked to learn this because if anyone burns a Koran these days, this incites a riot. But also, not only did this last story contradict the earlier story about Zaid bin Thabit and the compilation of the Koran under the caliphate of Abubaker, it also indicated that there was a time when the original written Koran actually existed with variant readings for several years and not in one pure form sent down from heaven by the angel Gabriel to Muhammad and then written down by Muhammad's scribes. This raises the question as to how variant readings existed in the first place if the Koran had originally been sent down perfectly.

This means that those who believe that the Koran is the infallible Word of God do not put their faith in Allah or Muhammad, but in Zaid bin Thabit who under the command of Abubaker or in confederacy with three other men under the auspices of Uthman, compiled this book and decided what should and shouldn't be in the final Koran.

Even further, those who believe in the Koran put their trust in the writers of these hadiths.

But not only were variant versions burnt, other hadiths admit that whole sections once existed but have subsequently been left out of the final Koran. In Sahih Bukhari, Volume 8, Book 82, Number 816, there is mention that the command to stone to death those who commit illicit sexual intercourse was originally a verse in the Koran whereas in the Koran that we read today, this verse does not appear. If this verse initially appeared in the Koran, it has subsequently been taken out, which means that the Koran that exists today is not complete as there are verses missing in today's Koran which existed in the first versions. Which further begs the question: are there any other verses which were originally in the Koran which have subsequently been left out?

But the most shocking thing to learn was that, according to the hadith in Sunan Ibn Majah, Volume 3, Book 9, Number 1,944, not only was there a section of the Koran which no longer forms part of this perfect book, the seemingly careless way in which it was lost completely horrified me. According to this hadith, an entire section of the Koran was under Aisha's pillow, Aisha being one of Muhammad's wives, when a sheep came into Aisha's tent, rummaged under her pillow and unceremoniously munched into and devoured this section, and hence these verses no longer form part of the modern day Koran. What was further extremely troubling about this story was that today, if a human being damages a copy of this book in any way, even accidentally and unintentionally, Muslims go totally berserk and kill that person in indignation for the damage to this lifeless collection of paper and ink, of which there are multiple copies around the world anyway so nothing of the content of the book is lost. In fact, there is a horrific story of an illiterate Christian man and his five-month pregnant wife some years ago living in a small village quite far from where I lived who were brutally murdered for allegedly destroying parts of the Koran. This young couple were throwing out rubbish, mainly in the form of paper, and among the rubbish were, so it was claimed, pages of the Koran. Being illiterate, the Christian couple were totally unaware of what was written on the pages. However, somehow, others in the village supposedly recognised verses of the Koran written on this paper being thrown out and as a result a large mob was incited to attack the young couple, the mob cruelly torturing and finally incinerating them in a local kiln while the couple was still alive, in a similar way to how the Nazis placed Jews and other dissidents against the Nazi regime into furnaces. Yet, by contrast, Allah, the Creator of the universe, looked on quite benignly while an animal munched into a portion of His holy book, resulting in an entire section no longer forming part of this supposed perfect text. And Allah did not seem to care in the slightest nor show any interest in restoring this missing section and having it replaced back into His book. And for all we know, this sheep lived out its life quite contently.

However, at this time, I didn't know all this. On the contrary, I was comfortable with this image of Allah, the Koran and the universe presented to me by my Mulvi until I reached my teen years, the age at which I discovered my homosexuality. But the word "discovered" is quite incorrect. I was always aware of my homosexuality from as early as I can remember. When I was about eight years of age, I can recall my fascination for the male body. I remember seeing in the local newspaper advertisements for the body building championships with colour photos of well-built men wearing only speedos. Seeing these photos of men almost naked did marvellous things to my metabolism that I could not explain in words at the time. I used to secretly remove these pages from the newspaper when these newspapers were being thrown away and keep them in a secret place in my room to look at privately.

At about this age, although I couldn't put my finger on it, I knew I was different to other boys. Pairing up of men and women in fairy tales, movies and cartoons, all these troubled me for some reason as I felt that I did not belong.

It took a long time before I realised that the society in which I lived abhorred men who loved men. This all started when I was introduced to the word "heejrah". At first, I didn't know what the word meant but I did know that whoever called you this was not paying you a compliment. There was something uglier, more hateful, more evil about these people because the term projected forth from the lips with such venom. And this word was used against the scrawny, nerdy, effeminate and more childish boys of our age group. This was because the word "heejrah" carried the idea of transgender, that is, a boy who wanted to become a girl, who somehow was a girl living inside a boy's body and wanted to further this by making the outside body reflect what the girl inside the boy felt of herself, which is what made him - or her - behave in such an effeminate way, and why he – or she – was interested in having sex with boys and not girls.

Eventually, somewhere down the line, I discovered what the term meant, or moreso what it implied about the sexual attraction a man has for another man, but I did not equate it with my own sexual feelings. A heejrah was, after all, something negative, and none of my friends would tolerate a heejrah as part of their group. Heejrahs were men who had sex with other men, not in any beautiful sense, but only in some slimy, sleazy sort of way, in desolate places, such as in a deserted park or in a vacant parking lot, forcing it onto some senseless victim who just happened to be innocently lured there by some dirty old man. And there was a feeling that it was contagious. You got the feeling that once you had sex with one of these men, you would want to have more sex with this man and indeed with other men and pass on the contagion.

It was when my male friends began showing greater interest in the opposite sex that I noticed the vast chasm that separated us. Women became a constant obsession: breasts, vaginas, backsides, all these constituted a part of every conversation. Boys managed to secretly get their hands on heterosexual pornography recorded on CDs and readily exchange them with other boys in school and in the neighbourhood. But the more they talked about women and the female anatomy, the more I realised how unappealing women's naked bodies were to me.

It took a much longer time before the Muslim view of the practice became obvious. Homosexuals were sickly, perverted people, committing acts that could only come from *Shaitaan*, or Satan, and when Muslims mentioned such people, which they hardly ever did, there was a sort of "them" attitude, as if no Muslim could possibly have homosexual tendencies because it was so evil.

Because of the negative light thrown on homosexuality, even though I was aware of my physical attraction towards men, it took a long time for me to realise that I was in fact a homosexual. But when and how I finally associated my sexual feelings with these people whom the Muslims and general society had taught us to hate I can't remember exactly, but I do remember that when I finally made this connection I became completely disgusted with myself. I didn't feel twisted, and deserted parks and vacant parking lots did not take on a new appeal. But the conflict between the external portrayal of homosexuality and how I felt within created a lot of anxiety.

Relief came to me when I became aware that sexual urges were actually common to all humans and not just me. We learned nothing formally about sex, not at school, not at home, and definitely not at the mosque. The only way we became aware of sexuality was in discussion amongst our friends. When we reached the age that boys begin to have wet dreams, there began a competition as to who had had their first wet dream and then who had the most wet dreams in a given period. There was a certain prowess about having wet dreams as this proved one's manhood. Of course, the content of the dream so it was assumed would be women. How relieved I felt at the time, knowing that when I had my first wet dream, the proper, clean, heterosexual orientation would at last be awakened in me and I would be like the rest of my friends.

But that didn't work either. I can still remember my first wet dream as vividly as if it were yesterday. There was a boy at my school who was in the senior years, whose name like me was Mustafa. He was in fact my first boyhood crush when I was still a junior. This senior Mustafa was very athletic and I often admired him from a distance when I saw him in shorts and T-shirt when he competed in certain sporting activities. One night, I had a dream that this same Mustafa and I were somehow in a hotel room. Mustafa had gone to the bathroom while I was sitting on the bed. When he came out of the bathroom, he was completely naked. Then I realised I was completely naked as well. I can still see that picture of a man, that well-built body, his healthy dark skin, his hairy chest and his sturdy legs. Soon we were together on the bed having sex and right in the middle of it I woke up. The dream, of course, was true to its name!

Naturally, you can imagine how disgusted I felt about myself, and these feelings of disgust towards myself continued because I had many more wet dreams after that and not a single female was ever in them. I couldn't understand what was wrong with me but simply excused it with the thought that it was a phase I was going through that I would eventually grow out of. But, as you can obviously tell, I never did.

Chapter 2

When I was about twelve, I remember my parents decided that the first Mulvi who had been teaching me about the religion was really not for me. I can't remember the details but there was some dispute between my parents and the Mulvi, and something to do with my sister, accompanied by a chance encounter between my father and another more popular and highly favoured Mulvi in the area.

I was happy with their decision. The first Mulvi my parents put over my tutelage was a cold, prickly sort of man whose whole approach to Islam was unquestioning obedience. And this was punctuated by violence, even towards a young boy like myself. Despite having a few black eyes, a bruised cheek and a sore back on several occasions, this was not the reason for my parents making the decision to terminate this Mulvi's services. In fact, I found my parents' silent approbation of this Mulvi's violent instruction was quite unnerving even for my young child's mind. It was rather this Mulvi's unusual interest in my sister and what appeared to be my sister's complicit responses to this Mulvi that caused my parents to dispense of this rigid man. As I grew older, I found this to be an underlying theme amongst my fellow religionists, that violence was always given complicit approval, but anything that involved or appeared to involve human affection was seriously frowned upon, and everything was done to disallow its occurrence.

This first Mulvi had been so ruthless and cold in his teaching approach that I really was only going through the motions of learning about my religion in order to satisfy my parents, not because I particularly felt any conviction for the truth of the religion.

This first Mulvi also had an obsession with hell and I was constantly fed with the horrors of this awful place should I ever doubt the religion in any way or deviate from the requirements of the Koran. This Mulvi successfully impressed on me the horrors of hell so much that this fear remained with me for many years afterwards. I can still see the Mulvi's terrifying grimace and the formidable strength in his arms whenever he held the collar of my shirt at the neck and told me of the horrors of hell, and how Malik, the angel who will preside over hell on the Day of Judgement, would grab me in a similar way. All my pleadings for forgiveness for doubting the Koran and the veracity of the religion would not dissuade this angel in any way from throwing me headlong into the fires of Jahannam. And this Mulvi was not backward in telling me what would happen to me in hell if I did not obey the Koran implicitly. As it says in An-Nisaa 4:56

Those who reject Our Signs,
We shall soon cast into the Fire:
As often as their skins are roasted through,
We shall change them for fresh skins
that they may taste the penalty

and, in Al-Mu'minum 23:104, how

The Fire will burn their faces,
and they will therein grin,
with their lips displaced

Not only will those who disbelieve in Allah and His Holy Book suffer this unimaginable torture for all eternity, Allah will make the righteous see the torture He inflicts on those in this murderous place, for He says to the righteous in Ibrahim 14:49, 50

you will see the sinners that day
bound together in fetters
their garments of liquid pitch,
and their faces covered with Fire

What a gruesome image of life after the grave for simply questioning anything in the Koran or anything about the religion in general. It certainly left a great impression on my young mind. Even so, as impressionable as all this was, for many years, I found it hard to equate these horrific, chilling descriptions of hell being orchestrated by He who was called the Compassionate and All-Forgiving. Further, I wondered what the righteous would think of Allah when Allah paraded them past the gates of hell to allow them to see what Allah was doing to those in this horrific place all because of the simple sin of thought-crime, that is, for entertaining in their minds doubts about the infallibility of the Koran and all we were taught about Islam when Allah could have avoided all this horrific torture by dispelling all doubts of His existence by simply making His existence completely obvious.

But it even further troubled me to think that the righteous in heaven would be shown those suffering in torment in hell. Could anyone with any human feeling and empathy seriously say that this would be eternal paradise when they were forced to look on at the horrific torture Allah was administering eternally to those whose only earthly criminal act was simply what was going through their minds? What was further disturbing was, how were the righteous supposed to react when they saw with their own eyes the horrendous torture these souls in hell were suffering? If the righteous were moved with feelings of repulsion and terror while they witnessed what the thought-criminals were suffering, and then began to question how the Almighty could carry the epithet of the Compassionate while He sadistically and with unfeeling glee orchestrated this entire hellish affair, would Allah then force the righteous standing there with Him into this hellish world to also suffer? And if this is what the righteous were forced to witness in the next life, could the life after the grave really be called paradise?

All this information about hell is a complete tragedy. The tragedy is that I can understand why many today fear to question the faith, not only out loud and vocally, but even in their own minds, as this incessant fear of eternal torture hijacks any thoughts of sense and reason, thoughts which may actually lead to critical thinking about the belief system. I also realized years later how these constant threats of hell forced those still in the faith to commit doublethink, that is, to hold two opposing and contradictory thoughts and maintain that these contradictory thoughts could both be true, such as Allah being extremely compassionate and at the same time a ruthless monster, simply in order to avoid this eternal torturous place.

My new Mulvi was a lot different. His devotion to the belief was just as passionate as my former Mulvi but his approach was a lot warmer. This new Mulvi told me that I should clear my mind completely of everything I had learned before about Islam and just let the Koran speak to me. He taught me that I shouldn't wait till Friday prayers to hear what the Koran had to say from the imam. The Koran was, after all, our daily bread, and we should read it as regularly as we ate a meal.

And so I did. Even though the Mulvi came regularly to teach me to read the Koran, I made it part of my daily routine to include a reading from this book.

But also, this Mulvi was a passionate man. His recitation of the Koran was mesmerizing, awe-inspiring, hypnotic. He had a mastery of reciting the Koran that captivated me like a snake charmer charms a snake with his wind instrument.

I so admired this Mulvi that I wanted to be like him. He created within me the burning desire to love the prophet Muhammad and to cherish Allah's holy book more than anything else in life. In fact, this Mulvi made me love the Koran so much that I wanted to become a *Hafiz-ul-Koran*, that is, someone who commits the entire Koran to memory.

I thought the Koran contained such a wonderful message and I wanted to tell the world.

One of the first steps in becoming a good Muslim is the learning of Arabic. In fact, the entire religion relies heavily on the proficiency of the Arabic language as this is the language in which the Koran was written. As a result, learning to read the Koran meant learning the Arabic language. What struck me as odd even then, although I knew at the time the consequences for questioning this out loud, was that more stress was placed on getting the pronunciation of the Arabic correct than understanding exactly what the text actually said. It soon came to the point that I was able to recite the Koran well in the Arabic language even though I did not know what it was I was reciting. Although it sounded melodic, and in particular when the Mulvi recited the Koran for me in his beautiful, mellifluous voice, it was poetry without meaning, a song being sung in a foreign and incomprehensible tongue.

Apart from learning about the Koran, this Mulvi taught me about the five pillars of Islam. These five pillars are central to the entire belief system and it is upon these pillars that Islam precariously rests.

The first most important pillar of Islam is the belief that there is no God but Allah and Muhammad is His Messenger. A very simple belief indeed. There isn't much more to this pillar than this simple belief.

Another of these pillars and a much more complicated one are the prayers. It was never explained why all these prayers needed to be said, except that this is what Allah wanted of us. I could never really work out what it was that Allah derived from all these prayers, nor what benefit it gave to us humans. But as with much of the religion that made no practical sense, I believed it had to have some benefit as Allah had demanded it of us. As an incentive, each prayer carried a reward, something like reward points when using a credit card, and all these reward points could be collected together on the Day of Judgement and be of benefit somehow in paradise for the person who had prayed all these prayers all throughout this life.

I was told that there were five prayers throughout the day and they were regimented as to what time they should be said. The first prayer was called *fajr* prayer. This prayer was said before the rising of the dawn. Then there was *duhr* prayer which was offered just after the sun had reached its zenith in the sky. The next prayer was *asr* prayer. This prayer was said in the afternoon at the time when the shadow of an object was about double the length of the object itself. Then there was *maghrib* prayer. This was said just after sunset, after the sun had disappeared behind the horizon but the sky was still light. The final prayer was *isha* prayer. This prayer was offered straight after it had become completely dark.

However, because the practicalities of life tended to get in the way of the observances of these prayers, especially as our modern lives go on twenty-four hours a day unlike back in the seventh century when there was no artificial light and businesses only operated diurnally, sometimes people simply were unable to say these prayers at the prescribed times. As compensation, people could then pray compensatory prayers, called *kaza* prayers. For example, just say someone missed saying the *fajr* prayer at the prescribed time, that is, before the rising of the dawn, this person could simply wait until the time of saying the *duhr* prayer and then say both the *duhr* prayer and the missed *fajr* prayer, this missed *fajr* prayer being a *kaza* prayer. However, although the *kaza* prayers were compensation for prayers missed, *kaza* prayers only earned half the reward of prayers said at the time they were meant to be said.

When the call to prayer was made by the muezzin, all the devotees congregated in the mosque and then the prayers were said. And the prayers were always said at precisely the same time, so much so that you could set your watch to the timing of the prayer. At the time, I marvelled at the precision of the eternal clockwork of Allah's prayer timetable. I was awestruck at how Allah had set the prayers at precise times and how the designated prayers acted like a universal clock for all humanity.

Another pillar is *zakat*. Zakat is money that Muslims should give voluntarily to help the poor. The whole system of how much one should pay is quite a complex system, analogous to a complex national tax system.

Then another pillar is fasting. There are a number of different fasts prescribed for Muslims. The major fast, and the one that is now familiar internationally, is during the month of Ramadan, the 9th month of the Islamic lunar calendar. Fasting is obligatory in Ramadan during the daylight hours, and is a requirement if Muslims want to avoid the fires of hell. So it is important for devotees to abstain from solid and liquid consumption during the daylight hours of this holy month. However, there are times when for practical reasons people simply are unable to fast every single day of this holy month. As a result, for every day that Muslims don't fast during Ramadan, they can fast on other days on other months as compensation, these substitutionary fast days being called *kaza* fasts.

One less well known fast is the fast during Shawal, the 10th month of the Islamic calendar. Once completing the 29-or-so day fast during Ramadan, Muslims, if they choose, can fast for a further six days in Shawal, the only exception being that they cannot fast on the first day of this month, because to fast on the first day of Shawal is *haram*, that is, forbidden. However, for those who do not diligently and faithfully complete the fast during Ramadan, even when they complete the *kaza* fasts on other days in the year, these people are not permitted to do the six day fast in Shawal.

Another not so well known fast is the fast during Eid-ul-Adha. Eid-ul-Adha is a commemoration of the time when Ibrahim was going to sacrifice Ishmael to Allah but just before Ibrahim plunged his knife into Ishmael's body, an angel appeared and provided Ibrahim an animal to sacrifice as a substitute, and hence Muslims commemorate this event with fasting.

The final pillar is the Hajj, that is, pilgrimage to Mecca. It is a requirement for all adult Muslims who are physically and financially capable to do this pilgrimage at least once in their lifetime. Although this could be done at any time of the year, I was told that it was specifically important to make the pilgrimage on the last month of the lunar calendar, Dhu-al-Hijjah, and even more specifically, from the 8th to the 12th day of this month.

For a long while I believed that all these pillars were quite well explained in the Koran. Further, I was convinced that this Mulvi observed not only all these pillars but that he did everything else according to the Koran no matter what. I had the impression that my Mulvi was as close to being Allah's Messenger as any human can attain.

My fervent zeal towards Islam grew on me gradually so it is difficult to pinpoint an exact time when my average, moderate approach to the religion ended and my strict, zealous Islam began. Like all my friends at school and in my neighbourhood, I did what boys normally did. Living in a built-up area, we used vacant areas, usually car parking lots between buildings when there were no cars there, as our own personal playground. We played sport, in particular cricket, and we rode our bicycles in these enclosed areas. I was also a fan of the latest pop groups and knew all the words whenever we played music on our cassette recorders.

However, I was unlike my friends in that I didn't swear. My parents had told me that swearing was a bad thing to do, that Muhammad would never have allowed such vulgar language pass his lips and that swearing was a grave sin.

It was at about this age that my friends were showing signs that they were extremely sexually turned on when boys were discovering girls and girls, boys. Every opportunity was exploited to talk about sex, so much so that any object which resembled genitals was something of a playground delight. Swearing, too, was very much a part of the school ground vernacular, and of great interest at the time were the latest rock groups like Vital Signs, String, Junoon and so many others. I personally only had a particular interest in these groups when they sang patriotic songs on the 14th of August to celebrate Pakistan's independence.

My growing zeal to the religion occurred gradually. Initially I only felt strong religious fervour at certain times, particularly during the important festival days and on Friday. By contrast, I was much more relaxed towards my Islam at all other times, as was the case with all my friends and, really, moving in and out of these two worlds was quite normal for me. At school I was a school student, but at home, particularly in the presence of the Mulvi and at the mosque for Friday prayers, I was a strict, zealous Muslim. I never thought these two worlds were supposed to collapse into one but they did and the results were disastrous.

There were three boys who used to sit at the back of the class: Parviz Chamelee, Wahid Fikraha and Taheer Khan. All three were unusually large for their age and appeared to be older than the rest of the students in my class. They were all into sport and this was evident in their bulky physique. They were a rough mob, always untidily dressed and very vulgar in everything they said and did. They were also somewhat aloof, strangers to everyone else, and it became obvious that they didn't want to associate with anyone apart from themselves and no-one in return wanted to associate with them.

Parviz was tall and athletic-looking with a central part in his hair and he was always pushing his hair back to make it look neat. Wahid was bulky but in a solid, masculine, physically fit sort of way. I remember also that he had a good set of teeth and a mischievous smile.

Then there was Taheer. Taheer was a bit shorter than both Parviz and Wahid, somewhat physically fit and robust, and with his hair cut back almost to the scalp. Taheer was also a Hafiz-ul-Koran. I found this strangely incongruous, Taheer, this large school boy, terrifying in appearance and weird in behaviour, yet he was a Hafiz-ul-Koran. I had always associated Hafiz-ul-Korans with Muslim saints and Taheer simply did not fit this image at all.

One particular morning, before the teacher had arrived in class, Taheer strolled up to my desk and sat right on my exercise book in an intrusive manner, picked up a pencil and started playing with it. This act obtained the attention of the rest of the class and a semi silence fell over the room which only highlighted my embarrassment. Taheer half turned his body towards me and staring me straight in the face he asked, "Hey, Mustafa, do you swear?"

It took me by surprise. I had grown accustomed to hearing others using swear words that I had no longer noticed it. I suppose Taheer was expecting to hear me say, "Of course, I *expletive* swear!" But I didn't. To me, the mark of a good Muslim man was his clean speech and impeccable conduct. For the love of Muhammad, I could not use a word that would be offensive to his holy ears. Because of the question, by the suspended atmosphere that had built up around this moment, by a sheer gut feeling, something made me balk at replying. Being zealous towards my faith was all of a sudden a shame because I wanted to be like everybody else, to be an accepted part of my peer group. I was thinking of using a swear word to get rid of him, or to be accepted by him, or both, when an image formed in my mind of my first Mulvi, like the angel of hell, grabbing me by the shirt collar and with that evil grimace he pulled telling me of the horrors of Jahannam for those who disobey the Koran. The fires of hell burned furiously before my eyes and I could feel the heat of the flames that would roast my skin, the same skin that Allah would continue to replace and replace and replace forever and ever. I told Taheer that I would not swear because good Muslims simply don't use such language. Taheer just leaned back and laughed out loud, and the class joined in unison with the laughter.

And so the mocking against my extreme approach to my religion began. There was one time when Taheer and his two friends grabbed me and held me fast while Taheer pinched my skin and would not allow me to go unless I swore. I made an attempt at using a swear word but what came out was an inarticulate garble and so it didn't come out the way I wanted it to, the sound I made being a compromise between the fear of what these boys would do to me if I didn't swear and what the angel of hell would do to me if I did. To them, this in itself was amusing and they relaxed their grip which enabled me to get away. But I was again and again subjected to this horrible behaviour until these boys finally gave in to my firm resolution.

When I told my Mulvi of my ordeals at school, he told me not to let it bother me. It was between me and Allah what I did and I should ignore what these boys were trying to do, and continue to strive to be a good Muslim in the best way I could regardless. This was, after all, a test. As it says in Al-Ankaboot 29:2, 3, "Do men think that they will be left alone on saying, 'We believe', and that they will not be tested? We did test those before them" and in Al-Baqarah 2:155 "And surely We will test you with something of fear, hunger, loss of wealth, lives and fruits". Allah had promised that we would be tested for our faith and so these awful experiences were simply my tests.

Even though these verses helped me to understand why I had to succumb to this humiliation, it still was a rather awkward time for my thinking. These school friends of mine were Muslim and I was Muslim, and yet I was mocked for being more Muslim than they were. This seemed to indicate that there was a spectrum in Islam from those who only observed a little of the religion at one end to

41

those who observed it completely at the other. The thought did go through my mind though: is it possible that Islam is a spectrum religion? And was there a dividing line along this spectrum which separated those Muslims going to paradise and the others going to hell?

My zealousness towards the religion may have created difficulties but looking back on this now my zealousness actually ended up being my protection. My zealous religious beliefs gave a reason as to why I wasn't interested in sex in the same way as my school friends were.

Like my friends at school, I had natural sexual urges. To help assuage these urges, there was a constant exchange of CDs of pornographic material, even though we knew looking at this pornography was a bad thing. But what struck me even then was the contradictory attitude towards women. On the one hand, these male friends of mine would be enflamed with hot rage if one of their female relatives had sex outside of wedlock. For some reason, it was a shame not only for the woman herself but for her entire family, her parents, her brothers, her uncles and the entire extended family if a woman had sex while she was still single. If a woman committed *zinna*, she was to be stoned to death. This was also known as honour killing. It was well understood amongst my male friends that if any of their sisters or female cousins or any of their other female relatives were caught having sex when they weren't married to the man in question, my male friends in hot dispute would definitely be ready to put her to death. On the other hand, these same friends were quite happy to watch women they were not related to having sex with men these women were obviously not married to in order for my friends to derive their own sensual pleasure. These women on these CDs after all had to have been the sister or cousin of male relatives somewhere in the world. The attitude, therefore, was that it was not okay for their direct blood relatives to have the freedom over their own bodies to have sex with whom they wanted to, but it was okay for women to whom they weren't related to to do so because my friends gained a sexual benefit out of it.

What was further strange for me was that there was not the same indignation towards male relatives who had sex outside the marital state. In fact, there was an undertone of approval towards such men for their sexual competence. The more women he had, the greater the stud he was. Instead of heated indignation leading the family to kill this man, there was a sort of contented appreciation and undercurrent of pride for his sexual prowess. Somehow it wasn't a shame for the entire extended family if he had sex outside the marital state, even though it also raised the question as to how he could do so because the woman he did it with would either have to be married, and therefore he was committing adultery, or she was single, and therefore he was committing *zinna*.

These thoughts about protecting women was my first explanation I provided myself as to why I had homosexual tendencies. I would not have liked my sister to dishonour the family by having sex when she was not married. I certainly would not have liked to have accidentally seen her on one of these pornographic CDs. Thus I felt uncomfortable looking at these incognito women in these sexual poses. While trying to dam my sexual energy for women in order to protect women, my sexual energy, so I reasoned, needed an outlet and hence as a result it began to be directed towards men.

While at this stage of my life I was becoming more and more aware of my homosexuality, at the same time I did not associate myself as being a heejrah. I was a man, albeit an adolescent one, but I had no desire to be a girl, to wear girls' clothes, or to act like a girl in any way. I totally knew that I was a young man who was happy to be a man and I enjoyed my male body, but at the same time I knew that I would enjoy the company of another male person during the sexual act. This was another reason why I didn't consider my homosexuality a bad thing.

Although illegal in Pakistan, I managed to get my hands on gay pornography. There was an undertone that homosexual acts were bad, although it wasn't explicitly said out loud because it was generally assumed that no Muslim had homosexual tendencies, especially in an Islamic country. However, this didn't stop me. It is amazing the lengths a young man will go to when driven by his sexual energy. Also, the men in these pornographic materials were definitely not heejrahs at all but were good, solid, well-built men, very much like the men in the pages I had removed from newspapers when I was younger. This only further helped me to justify that my homosexuality was not a bad thing. After all, because these men were men, they were not heejrahs, and ultimately they were not defiling women. This explanation helped me for a while to carry me through this troubling time.

Until one Friday at the mosque.

On this particular day, the imam had chosen to read a passage from Surah Al-Araf. When he got to the part in verse 81 where it says

You approach men lustfully instead of women

there was a lot of venom in his pronouncements. Here the imam expounded that homosexuality was a terrible sin and it was because of this sin more than any other that caused Allah to destroy the cities of Sodom and Gomorrah. The imam further used this as an attack on the West. In the West, homosexuality had become legalized and homosexuals were now granted the right to engage in this sexual act when these same men should be obliterated instantly from the planet. And because homosexuality had become accepted in the West, this was why Western societies were collapsing into decadence. Because all the men were now free to have sex with men and all the women were free to

44

have sex with women, marriage laws were disintegrating which would ultimately lead to the entire collapse of these societies.

I could almost feel the imam salivating as he related how homosexuals were doomed to hell. As it was with my first Mulvi, I once again could feel the bitter hatred coming from those who believe that Allah is the Compassionate, the Almighty who loves His creatures, the human being, seventy times more than a mother bird loves her chicks.

But I was terrified. While the imam was presenting to me this new revelation, I heard for the first time the most dreadful curse against my very person from the book I had been brought up to love and cherish. I can remember other men around me saying things like, "I can't imagine approaching men lustfully! How disgusting!" and yet I knew my feelings were the opposite of theirs. I couldn't imagine lustfully approaching women because to me sex with a woman was a disgusting thought.

But there were further issues that were raised in my mind about this verse that the imam had quoted. Allah seemed to be saying in this verse that we all have lust that has no particular direction. It is we who control the direction of this lust. The men of Lut had lust but instead of directing it in the "proper" way towards women, the men of Lut chose to direct it towards men. The implication was that lust or sexual desire was in our control, something like a bicycle. If while riding I wanted to turn left, I simply turned the bike and it went left, or if I wanted to turn right, I steered the bike and I turned right. But I knew that this was not the reality. Sexual attraction is more like sitting in a small boat or on a raft without oars or anything that can be used to steer the boat in the middle of a flowing stream and being led by the current. Even if I wanted to go right, if the boat veered left because that was the way the stream was directing it, there was nothing I could do but simply allow it to do so, irrespective of whether or not I wanted it to go in that direction. And I could tell that this was so when I heard the other guys' comments. These guys didn't say something to the effect of, "Mmmmm! I'll have to keep this in mind when I'm walking down the road and I happen to see a man and a woman coming in my direction that I make sure that I don't steer my lust towards the man". They already knew that their lust was firmly and fixedly directed towards women like the north side of a magnet is fixed in its attraction towards the south. And I knew that my attraction towards men was just as firm and fixed.

What troubled me further about this verse was that it was as if Allah was not aware of what was going on inside me nor that my sexual proclivity was fixed. If Allah did not like me having lust towards men, who was to blame for my lust? After all, who created my sexual desires? As it says in An-Nisaa 4:78 "All things are from Allah" and hence my sexual desires could only have been created by Allah in the first place. I certainly did not have any control in the slightest as to the direction of my sexual attraction, my sexual attraction towards men occurred within me despite what I thought about it. Therefore, Allah, who is supposed to be omniscient, should surely have been aware of this Himself. So why did it come across to Him as some sort of mystery as to why the men of Lut like me had sexual attraction towards other men? Why did Allah find these men's obsession with fulfilling their lust on other men and not on women so mystifying when He cried out through Lut in An-Naml 27:55, "Would you really approach men in your lusts rather than women?" This mystification was shared by my male compatriots who asked themselves the same question while shaking their heads in disgust as to why any man would want to have sex with another man. While I could appreciate the attitude of these guys around me and their total inability to comprehend how a man could find another man physically attractive, Allah in His omniscience should already have known and understood the physical attraction homosexual men have towards the naked male body and hence He would never have made such a pronouncement. I therefore reasoned that since whoever wrote this portion of the Koran was totally unaware of how a homosexual man can be sexually aroused by the naked male body, this implied that this portion of the Koran could not have been written by someone who is omniscient.

But then the first Mulvi came to mind of him holding me by the shirt collar and with an evil grimace telling me what would happen to those who questioned the Holy Koran. Hence once again I was forced into doublethink, on the one hand realizing that this verse logically was not written by an omniscient being, on the other hand, in order to avoid Jahannam, believing in full fervour that it was.

What further created complications in my thinking was that the Koran does not within any of its verses explain the source of homosexuality nor what men are supposed to do to redirect their sexual energy to the opposite sex. All that is mentioned in the Koran is that Allah cannot understand how a man can be physically attracted to another man, and therefore He simply wants such men destroyed. Even at that young age this thought was strange. If Allah hates homosexuality, why did He create men with a sexual drive towards other men in the first place, and then, instead of redirecting this sexual drive back to women, why did He rather destroy the men?

Because the Koran provided no explanation for the source of my homosexuality, I had to invent one. I tried to maintain the reason I had these feelings towards men was simply because of my respect towards women and my lack of desire to see these pornographic CDs of unknown, unmarried women freely giving their bodies over to these unknown men to exercise their lusts. Yet, the evidence kept indicating to me that this really was not the case. When I tried to look at heterosexual pornography, the view of a woman naked was ghastly and repugnant to me that I

47

couldn't continue watching. The view of the naked woman on the naked man made me feel so uncomfortable as if I had some disgusting object on my body which I wanted to immediately remove. The idea of engaging in sex with a woman and hence even seeing a woman naked was just too horrible a thought for me. In the end, I went back to secretly watching homosexual pornography both gaining deep physical pleasure out of it and yet at the same time feeling extremely guilty for the enjoyment it provided me.

I decided to become even more religious at this point in my life. If Allah hated men approaching men with lust and He planned to throw such men into eternal torment, then my sexual proclivity had to have come from somewhere and there was a way to redirect my sexual energies back to women. The great problem was, I couldn't ask anyone about this because anyone I told would want to kill me.

The only place to go for the answer, therefore, was the Koran. The Koran was delivered to the inhabitants of earth through the angel Gabriel and the prophet Muhammad, and it contained the answers to all the problems of the world.

And, after all, the Koran could not be wrong for it was co-eternal with Allah who is also perfect, therefore there were no mistakes nor contradictions within its pages.

Chapter 3

It was a glorious sunny day, a glorious Friday, the holiest day of the week according to the Islamic reckoning of time. Friday afternoon prayer was the most important prayer of the week and it was important not to miss it.

This particular Friday was the first Friday of Ramadan. It was a tradition on Friday during the month of Ramadan for the imam to ask young boys, madrassa boys as they were called, to work as volunteers to collect money from the worshippers. Money collected from the congregation generally went to the maintenance of the mosque. Sometimes, those at the mosque used this time to pay zakat. However, while zakat was an obligation and could be paid at any time of the year, in Pakistan, zakat was often collected during Ramadan. This was because we were told that every good deed done during the month of Ramadan had the worth of a thousand times more than good deeds done at any other time of the year. Hence, zakat paid during Ramadan earned a thousand times the reward points than zakat paid in any other month.

Because Pakistan is a Muslim country, zakat is automatically deducted from bank accounts as an automatic governmental deduction. I was later to learn that this automatic deduction of zakat only applied to Sunni Muslims. Shiite Muslims were exempt. The way Shiite Muslims became exempt from this governmental zakat deduction was by obtaining a zakat declaration form so Shiites were free from governmental intervention and could pay zakat when they chose to. However, even though the government automatically deducted zakat from Sunni Muslims' accounts, there was a perception that this automatic governmental deduction went into the hands of corrupt politicians – who were themselves Muslims – and hence cancelled the worth of the payment of zakat and ultimately nullified the effect of this good deed, and ultimately reward points would not be collectable in the life after the grave. To get around this, many Sunni Muslims, despite their utter contempt towards Shiites, obtained a zakat declaration form by claiming that they were Shiite in order to get their money reimbursed, and then they took that money to the mosque and paid zakat to the madrassa boys.

Being especially zealous for my faith, I was eager to be one of the madrassa boys to show my devotion towards Allah. Along with the other boys who chose to be volunteers, I went out the front to the imam. The imam then gave each of us a white bag that we were to carry around amongst the devotees in the mosque to collect money. The imam then told us that we were not to put zakat money in the white donation bag because money that went in the white bag was for the house of Allah, that is, for the upkeep and maintenance of the mosque. If anyone in the congregation gave money for zakat, we were to keep this separate.

Once I had received my bag, along with the other madrassa boys who had volunteered for this task, I walked among the other devotees to collect money. It wasn't long before this stroll among the devotees was interrupted when one man stopped me, grabbed my arm and then said to me, "Don't put this money in the white bag. This money is for zakat."

I took the money and hesitated for a moment as to where I was going to put this zakat money before finally shoving the notes into one of my side pockets. This occurred a few more times during my round, some men insisting that I keep a certain amount of money separate, that it was for zakat, others giving me two lots of money, some to put in the white bag for the House of Allah, the other to be separated and used for zakat.

For some reason, as a result of the day's events in the mosque, I became somewhat puzzled by zakat and so I asked my father about it. As I had been told earlier in my childhood, my father explained that zakat was money collected and used to help the poor. But my father then went into greater explanation about how much zakat was to be paid. Back when this system began in the early 600s, people were only required to pay zakat if they had at least 21 *tolas* of gold, which in the metric system is about 250 grams of gold, or if they had at least 52 *tolas,* that is, about 625 g of silver. However, in our modern times when not everyone possesses gold and silver as exchangeable currency but rather the national currency, Pakistani Rupees, my father explained to me, although without giving any particular evidence for it, that every thousand rupees a person possessed, that person was obligated to pay ten rupees in zakat. Further, zakat had to come out of other forms of possessions of value. For those who owned land, for example, there was a further obligation to pay a portion of the land value as zakat. My father went on to explain an entire complex percentage scheme where for each valuable object that a person possessed there was a certain amount that this person had to surrender as zakat. I was later to ask myself the question: what is the difference between the payment of zakat and paying tax, and why do we have both systems in Pakistan?

This complex system sounded admirable and ensured that the rich carried out their obligation towards the poor in society. It made me question, though. Pakistan has a large population and in particular my parents and those who inhabited Alekh-Jahan were well-to-do. Why then were there so many poor people in Pakistan still living in abject poverty with nothing to eat if a great many of Pakistan's inhabitants were paying zakat?

Being a zealous Muslim, I wanted to read first hand where it said in the Koran about zakat and this wonderfully complex monetary system.

The next time my Mulvi came to teach me the Koran, I asked him about the practice of zakat, and what the Koran said about it.

"Yes," my Mulvi explained, "it is written in the Koran in several places. For example, in Al-Baqarah 2:43 Allah says to 'be steadfast in prayer, give zakat, and bow down your heads with those who bow down'."

I was waiting for the Mulvi to continue reading and bring out much of the extensive detail my father had told me about zakat. But the pause indicated that what my Mulvi had just read was the completion of the passage.

"But it doesn't say," I then said, "that zakat has to be paid in the month of Ramadan in this verse. Nor how much someone has to pay as zakat. Is that the only verse that talks about zakat?"

"No, my child," my Mulvi replied. "It is mentioned in several surahs." My Mulvi then quoted other verses that mention the giving of zakat, yet in each case there was no mention of when zakat needed to be paid, how much needed to be paid, who must pay and who was exempt, nor the time of year or to whom zakat was to be paid. The verses only mentioned that zakat needed to be paid. But even this wasn't quite correct either. In Arabic it doesn't read this way. The Arabic reads *wa aatoo alzakata*, that is, "and *give* zakat", not *pay* zakat. Further, there was nothing in these verses which suggested what zakat actually was, even though we had been taught that zakat was a form of charity. Why this particularly troubled me was because there is a verse in Al-Baqarah 2:177 which reads "it is righteousness...to spend of your substance" – or *maala*, as the word is in Arabic for "substance" – "for your kin, for orphans, for the poor, for the wayfarer" and then later in the same verse it says "to give zakat". If we are to give *maala* to family members, orphans and the poor, then what is the purpose of zakat if we have already spent our *maala* on the poor? Also, in Al-Taubah 9:60 it says "The charities" – or in Arabic, *asadaqaat* – "are only for the poor, the needy" that is, charity and not zakat is for the poor and needy. In fact, there is not one mention in the Koran that explains what exactly zakat is and why we need to give it.

However, I didn't let this trifle bother me. But what intrigued me was what I later read about what it said in other verses about zakat. In Al-Baqarah 2:83 Allah tells us to "remember We took a covenant from the Children of Israel: worship none but God; treat with kindness your parents and kindred, and orphans and those in need" and then later in the verse as a separate idea, "give zakat". Although once again the giving of something to those who need it was stated separately to the giving of zakat, what interested me about this verse was that Allah said that the giving of zakat was something He had told the Jews to do. And later, in Surah Maryam 19:31, Allah says through the prophet Jesus, or *Issa*, that Christians were also given the command to give zakat. This should mean, or so I understood it, that in synagogues and churches around the country, those who attended these holy places also gave zakat. Zakat was therefore not only a Muslim practice, it was a Judaeo-Christo-Muslim practice.

When I mentioned this to my Mulvi, I was astonished at his reply.

"No, Jews and Christians are exempt from zakat," my Mulvi explained. "Rather, they are under obligation to pay *jizya*."

My Mulvi no doubt could tell from my facial expression that jizya was a new word for me and had no meaning. My Mulvi then showed me the verse from Al-Taubah 9:29 where it is written

Fight those who believe not in Allah

> *nor the Last Day, nor hold that which is forbidden*
> *by Allah and His Messenger*
> *nor acknowledge the religion of truth*
> *(even if they are) of the People of the Book,*
> *until they pay the jizyah*
> *with willing submission*
> *and feel themselves subdued.*

What this meant, so my Mulvi explained, was that the People of the Book, that is, Jews and Christians, were actually required to pay something else, something called *jizya*. My Mulvi explained that jizya was a type of protection money non-Muslims of the Jewish and Christian religions had to pay in order for them to remain safe under Muslim dominance. Not only were Jews and Christians required to pay *jizya*, when they paid it, they had to show that they understood that they were inferior to Muslims, and that they accepted this subordination willingly. The expression translated "with willing submission" is in Arabic *an yadin*, and literally means "according to the hand", that is, the actual implication of the verse was that Jews and Christians had to make this payment themselves, in person, by hand, and not via an intermediary or have money deducted from their accounts as it was in the case of Sunni Muslims with zakat. And like zakat, there was no specified amount that Jews and Christians were required to pay. When I thought about it, it was totally up to the clemency of the ruler of the Islamic state to decide how much Jews and Christians were required to pay in the form of jizya.

Because of this and in my zeal to follow the Koran, I told my Mulvi that I would be happy to carry out this duty as a madrassa boy and collect the jizya from the Jewish and Christian communities within our area. It would also be an opportunity, I added, to actually preach to these people and try to get them to see the error of their ways so that they would finally leave their faiths and follow the one, true faith of Islam.

"You are a very zealous young man," my Mulvi replied and patted me on the back as reinforcement of my unwavering dedication. "However, these days, we don't practise this anymore."

"But it says to do so in the Koran," I replied emphatically.

"Yes, yes," my Mulvi laughed and leant back in his chair. "I understand why you think that. But you have to remember that we live in different times. You have to understand the context in which this verse was written. At that time it was a custom for Jews and Christians living in an Islamic State to pay jizya. But Pakistan is not an Islamic State. To be an Islamic State, Pakistan has to be ruled by a caliph. Yes, it is true that the state religion of Pakistan is Islam but Pakistan is not an Islamic State because Pakistan continues to follow the parliamentarian system that it adopted from the British. And, in any case, Jews and Christians already pay income tax. So, they are in a way paying jizya."

I thought about it for a moment. But this explanation didn't satisfy me. Jizya, so the verse in the Koran stated, was to be paid *an yadin*, in hand, not deducted electronically, indirectly and impersonally through the state system.

"Young man," my Mulvi explained. "Sometimes you have to look deeper into the verse and not just skim the surface. The Koran is no ordinary book but comes from the heavens. So, sometimes we need to read much deeper into the meaning of the verse. Yes, the words may say *an yadin*, but this is a surface reading. When Jews and Christians pay income tax, it is money coming out of their hands in an allegorical sense. It is like the hand of Allah. The Koran talks about the hand of Allah in Surah Al-Fath 48:10 and says in Surah Ya-Sin 36:71 'Do they not see that We have created for them from what Our hands have made, the cattle, and they are their owners?' and then a few verses later in verse 83 'Glory be to the One Who in Whose hand is the dominion of all things'. But does Allah who fills the entire universe have literal hands in the same way that we have hands? Well, of course not! This is simply allegorical. So when Jews and Christians are called to pay jizya *an yadin*, in the same way as with the hand of Allah, this can mean that they need to pay using an allegorical hand."

I understood what my Mulvi was trying to say and I had to accept that he was, after all, more learned than me. But still, when I read the verses for myself, the natural understanding of the verse to me meant that Jews and Christians were literally required to pay jizya by hand so that they could "feel themselves subdued". Jews and Christians were required to do so in order for them to recognize that their religious persuasions were inferior to the superior religion directed by the glorious light of the Koran and, by doing so, this should eventually lead them out of the darkness in which their religions held them into the glorious light of Islam.

However, that evening while I was alone in my room, I read again the verse from Al-Taubah 9:29, first in English and then in the original Arabic. There was a problem with the way the verse was written in Arabic and how it was translated. I had an English translation of the Koran by Abdullah Yusuf Ali that my father had given to me as a young child which I sometimes used to help me when I had difficulty reading the Arabic. The English translation of this verse reads as "Fight those who believe not in Allah nor the Last Day, nor hold that which is forbidden by Allah and His Messenger nor acknowledge the religion of truth (even if they are) of the People of the Book". The English adds the words "even if they are" in parentheses. When I read this portion again in the original Arabic, that is, *la yadiinoona diina-lhaqi mina alladhina ootoo lkitabi*, I noticed that this literally translated as, "do not acknowledge the religion of truth of those who were given the book". Without the added words, the portion which says "those who were given the book" implies Muslims as Muslims were those who were given the book, that is, the Koran. However,

56

by adding the words in parentheses, the passage reads as "even if they are those who were given the book" and this changes the meaning to imply Jews and Christians because then this book refers to the Bible. I could understand the additional words in parentheses because everywhere else in the Koran, the expression "the People of the Book" refers to the Jews and the Christians. If the expression "those who were given the book" was synonymous with the expression "the People of the Book", this implied that the true religion according to Al-Taubah 9:29 was that purported by the followers of the Bible. At the time this struck me as strange. And of course extremely preposterous. In any case, my Arabic wasn't perfect so I surmised that maybe the English rendition was a truer reflection of the original meaning of the Arabic.

But this wasn't the only time that what I read in the Koran and the actual Muslim practice in our country were not the same. During this month of Ramadan, I was reading the longest surah of the Koran, Al-Baqarah, when I came across the verse in Al-Baqarah 2:187, talking about Ramadan, where it is written

Eat and drink,
until the white thread of the dawn
appears to you distinct from its black thread;
then complete your fast till the night appears…
thus does Allah make clear His signs

It was the first time that I read in the Koran the precise timing of the fast. Prior to this time, I had naturally been fasting at the prescribed time stated by the leaders of the mosque. In fact, what we used as an indicator of the timing of the fast was displayed on calendars that people could stick up on their walls in their homes.

I remember waking up very early, long before sunrise, and having the first early morning meal, what we call in

Urdu *sehri*, coming from the Arabic, *soohoor*. While looking at the calendar, a thought went through my mind, that these calendars are not mentioned in the Koran. As the Koran says, it was by the use of the black and white threads that Allah makes "clear His signs". Needless to say, at the time, I had simply assumed that those in the mosque and the Muslim scholars knew what they were doing when they made these calendars. In fact, I imagined that to decide what times to put on the calendars, there were imams in special rooms, totally enclosed by four walls to prevent any light from the street or lights from the neighbouring homes from interfering, and without a roof so that only the light of the sun could enter the room. The imams had two threads laid out on a table like holy relics, and with a bag of dates in one hand and a cup of tea in the other, they munched and sipped continuously, eyes transfixed on the threads in readiness to stop eating and drinking at the first moment of distinction, and then announce this to the Muslim community.

But lots of thoughts kept churning out of this verse and into my head. This verse from the Koran implied a few things. It first implied that wherever Muslims were in the world, they had at their disposal black and white threads, and if they didn't, it was necessary to ensure that they did. It also assumed that those who observed the threads were away from any light, the burning campfire light from a Bedouin encampment, or away from artificial electric light as it was in our modern time. It also assumed that they had good vision, as someone who had to wear glasses to read and further a blind man or woman would be totally incapable of knowing when to stop eating. Further, I was perplexed when I thought more on it, how the imams were able to prepare calendars before Ramadan started and show on the calendars the exact timing of the fast for every single day throughout this holy month, knowing at precisely what time they would be able to distinguish between black and white threads long before the month began.

This being my first Ramadan after having read this verse, in my diligence, I was determined to follow this precept to the letter. The trouble was that my entire neighbourhood was lit up with electric lighting from street lights and from lights pouring out of all the buildings in the neighbourhood. The only way I could carry out this verse as it was stated in the Koran was to find somewhere in downtown Alekh-Jahan which was not influenced by twenty-first century modernity. There was a park some blocks away from my parents' place and so I made my way down to it in my diligence to fulfil the bidding of this verse. As a result, I stood outside with food and drink, having a chew here or a glug there while nursing the black and white threads in the palm of my other hand.

But there was something else that puzzled me on this particular morning of Ramadan. The call to prayer was moved back 15 minutes and used as a signal to mark the end of eating sehri. People then got ready and went to the mosque and waited for the imam to start leading the *fajr* prayers. Usually the timing between the call to prayer by the muezzin and the commencement of the prayer was about 5 minutes. However, during Ramadan, when the worshippers were called to prayer, the time between the call to prayer and the actual beginning of the saying the prayers was extended to 15 minutes or more. For all the other months of the year, the timing of the prayer was always at precisely the same time. How was it that during Ramadan, this timing could be altered so readily when Allah had initially set the prayers at a precise time on His universal clock?

Soon I heard the muezzin call for prayer. There was movement throughout the neighbourhood of boys and men dutifully answering the call and making their way to the mosque to say the morning prayers. I slipped the two threads into my pocket and made my way to the mosque with all the other devout Muslims. However, once prayers were said, when I left the mosque, it was still dark. I removed the two threads and tried in the darkness to distinguish between them but for all honesty could not. The general practice was that when the *fajr* prayers had ended, fasting had to begin. But according to the Koran, this was too early. Allah's timing of the beginning of the fast was clearly in the black and white threads. I marvelled at how the entire Muslim community had changed the timing for when the fast began. Further, I wondered according to what criterion the Muslim authorities used as the gauge as to when the fast should begin because to me it was obviously not from the Koran.

This puzzled me all day. Fasting is difficult enough, but with this clash between what the Koran actually said and what the Muslim community did filled me with anxiety. But the problem of timing once again became an issue at the end of the day. The completion of the verse is that we were to fast "till the night appears". I remember watching with anticipation the sun slowly approaching the western horizon and knowing that in some time soon, I would be able to satisfy my solid and liquid desires. I just had to wait till it was night time. To me, this meant that when it was completely dark in the sky and there was no sign of sun at all, it was then that we could break the fast.

Once again, the timing of the prayers was adjusted simply to facilitate the believers. Usually, the time between the call to prayer and the commencement of the prayer was about 5 minutes. However, during Ramadan, *maghrib* prayers were set about 5 minutes earlier than usual and the timing between the call to prayer and the commencement of the prayer was extended to 15 minutes to allow for people to grab some food that they could then carry with them to the mosque and eat on the way.

Further, to my surprise, as soon as it was the time displayed on the calendar when the fast could be broken and we could start eating, I took a good look at the sky. It was still light. It was dusk but it was still light. According to my definition at least, it was not night time because night is when there is no sunlight at all. What struck me even further is that I noticed this as clear as the nose on my face. Yet the entire Muslim community, including the Muslim authorities, seemed to be following a timing that was different to what was written in the Koran.

Once again, I had to ask my Mulvi about this. So the next time he came to teach me about the Koran, I posed the question to him.

"Sir," I asked. "According to Al-Baqarah 2:187, we are to stop eating as soon as we can distinguish between a black thread and a white thread. This morning, after *sehri* and after the call to *fajr* prayers, I stood outside and observed these two threads in the darkness and simply thought that we would have to stop eating when I could tell the two apart. However, *fajr* prayers were started 15 minutes earlier than during the other months of the year. Not only that, I noticed that the fast started when it was still dark and I could not as yet distinguish between the two threads. The verse then says that we are to complete the fast till night. However, everyone started eating and drinking this evening when it was still light."

"My goodness," my Mulvi replied. "You definitely are a diligent student of the Koran. And it's good to see that you are diligently reading and studying it."

The compliment was well received. But it didn't answer the question.

My Mulvi continued.

"My son, do you seriously believe that the religious authorities are out to deceive the entire Muslim community here in Karachi?"

I didn't know how to answer this question. In any case, it was no doubt meant to be rhetorical. But it caused further problems with my thinking. I was told by the Muslim authorities that I had to follow the Koran. I suddenly found myself looking at the world with double vision. The Muslim authorities told me to follow the Koran implicitly. When it came to observing Ramadan, the Koran was clear in indicating the beginning and ending of the fast, but the religious authorities began and ended the fast at a different time to what it said in the Koran. So who was I supposed to obey: the Koran, or the religious authorities who said I must obey the Koran? I posed this question to the Mulvi in the most respectful way I could. The Mulvi laughed gently in his fatherly way.

"You have to remember," my Mulvi continued, "that at the time that this was written we didn't have the technology we have today to precisely know exactly when the sun rises and sets. Back at that time, this was the only sure way to determine the precise moment fasting should start and end. But today we have advanced technology and the Muslim authorities can determine with precision the timing of the fast even weeks in advance which is why we have calendars prepared long before the first day of Ramadan. Can't you see how wonderful Allah is in making it easier to know when to start and end the fast so we don't all have to be wasting our time standing outside in utter darkness looking at threads, but we can be better planned and can concentrate on other things?"

As much as I respected this Mulvi with great devotion, to me what he was saying in effect was, follow the Koran as Allah's pure word, but then in another breath, we don't have to take Allah's word to the letter. The look on my face must have said it all.

"My son, think of it this way. We live in a community where there is electric lighting so it is difficult to find places these days where it is dark enough for us to determine the timing when we can distinguish between a black thread and a white thread. And in any case, notice further the wisdom of Allah, in that now people with poor vision and blind people are also able to know precisely when to start and stop the fast. If we needed to literally continue to use the test of the black thread and white thread, how would these people ever know when to start fasting and when to stop?"

This did not clarify the situation in any way but only further exacerbated the confusion. While my Mulvi's explanation supposedly showed the wonder of Allah's wisdom in that myopic and blind people now had the ability to know when the fast should start and end, wasn't Allah aware that there were myopic and blind people long ago when this surah was revealed? So why did Allah inform people the use of the black thread and the white thread as an indicator of when the fast should start when He was aware that those with poor or no vision simply could not follow this injunction?

This put me in a bind in so many ways. I was told that the Koran was the venerable Word of Allah and I had to obey it implicitly. Now I was being told that we didn't have to follow the Koran so precisely, and further we could rely on modern technology to interpret the commands of the Holy Book.

In another way, this put me in a never-ending cycle of confusion. I was told that I had to obey those in authority when they told us to follow what it said in the Koran about fasting during Ramadan. However, in order to follow the Koran faithfully, I would have to go against what the entire Muslim authorities, the scholars, the imams, and my Mulvi told me about the timing of the Ramadan fast. This confusion was never resolved. I ended up following the timing brought down to us by the authorities even though it sat uncomfortably in me that this timing was different to what it said in the Koran.

Then there was another occasion which caused me to further question this entire view of how we viewed our Holy Book. There was a guy in my class called Saleem. He was a nice guy. I wasn't actually a friend of his but he was a good acquaintance and a really nice fellow student. Saleem was from a very wealthy family and this came out because of the nice possessions he often brought to school.

There was a time when Saleem had a special pencil box. It was a wooden box, delicately carved in ornate design no doubt by a major craftsman who had a passion for his work. Saleem obviously loved this pencil box. The problem was, this pencil box was also the envy of pretty much all the other students of my class.

This became obvious the day the pencil box went missing. The only explanation was that the pencil box had been stolen. The school authorities had to do something. After repeated warnings in order to reveal the identity of the perpetrator, eventually when his identity was not forthcoming, the school had no other recourse than to actually interrogate and strip search all of the students and fossick through their belongings. Even after this embarrassing ordeal that each of us had to go through, the pencil box was not found.

After undergoing this humiliating process, we were sent home. On my way home, I happened across Taheer and his two mates huddled together in admiration of a particular object. And it was obvious what the treasure was that they were admiring. It was Saleem's pencil box. And it was Taheer who was holding it, the new possessor of the stolen pencil box, Taheer the Hafiz-ul-Koran.

I stood there frozen in terror. I just couldn't believe my eyes. I couldn't move. And as a result, this enabled the boys the time to turn around and see me standing there looking at them, catching them in the act. With that, Taheer's facial expression changed from delighted glee for the capture of his booty to frightening, almost satanic terror as he

64

made a dash at me. The look on his face was extremely terrifying and so I turned and ran as fast as I could. I was, unfortunately, not as fit as Taheer and it wasn't long before I felt Taheer's talons clasp the back of my shirt and cause me to stop. He then dragged me down into a vacant lot. He was puffing and panting but I could feel the strength in his grip as he held a handful of my shirt shoved against my throat. His facial expression changed from a terrifying diabolic grimace to a terrifyingly demonic grin.

"Yes, I stole the pencil box," he said through gasped breath. "That Saleem doesn't deserve it. And anyway, his father is rich enough to get him another one."

Taheer then brought the pencil box to my face and rested one of the corners on the crest of my nose, digging it in enough to make it hurt.

"And if you tell anyone I stole it, I'll do more than just drive the corner of this box between your eyes."

Allah was on my side, or so I thought, as I still had enough fighting spirit in me to say something against him.

"But, Taheer," I gasped. "It is wrong to steal. And the Koran makes it clear the punishment for those who steal. If you give the pencil box back to Saleem, or make out that you found it somewhere and restore it back to Saleem, no-one will ever have to know."

But this was obviously the wrong thing to say. Taheer then gripped my throat with his left hand and pinned me against the wall. I could barely breathe. But I was also amazed, as well as frightened, by the strength in his left hand and his ability to hold me firmly in place.

"If you even suggest to anyone to have my hands chopped off for stealing this pencil box, I'll make sure that you have your head chopped off for denouncing a Hafiz-ul-Koran."

The wildness in his eyes was terrifying. And I could feel his warm breath against my face. It felt as if I were looking directly into the face of Satan and feeling the warmth from the depths of hell coming up through his body and out through his mouth.

"Is that clear?" Taheer snarled.

He emphasized this with a stronger clench on my throat to the point that I could barely breathe. His actions told me that he was willing to carry out what he had threatened with his very words. He held onto that grip for some time, short enough not to kill me by asphyxiation, long enough for me to get the message to keep my mouth tightly shut.

"In any case," Taheer concluded after releasing the grip on my neck, "Allah has allowed for getting booty. As He says in Surah Al-Anfal 8:69 'So consume what you got as war booty, lawful and good'. Saleem is a Shiite and therefore an enemy of Allah and so Allah has given me the right to take booty from His enemies. And this is my booty."

Taheer looked once more down at the pencil box and then back at me.

"Okay, chum?" he said as a concluding note, gave me a light slap over my right cheek with his left hand, turned around and left.

I stood there for a moment and then slowly slid down the wall to sit at its base. I just wanted to cry. It took me some time to finally gain the strength and composure to get up off the ground and make my way home.

Not long after this event, my Mulvi took me through the fifth surah, Surah Al-Ma'idah, verse 38, where it is written

As to the thief, male or female
cut off his or her hands:
a punishment by way of example,
from God, for their crime:
and God is Exalted in power.

Who, I asked, is given the right to carry out this punishment?

My Mulvi looked at me a little perplexed.

"Did you have anyone in particular in mind who should have their hands cut off?" he asked.

Although I particularly did, there was no way I was going to tell my Mulvi, especially when I remembered what Taheer had said he would do to me if I told anyone else about his theft, and he said this not only with words but also through his brute strength.

"In any case, Mustafa," my Mulvi interrupted my thoughts, "we now have a judicial system to deal with thieves. The chopping off of hands is not a practice for today. You have to remember that in those days when thieving was rife, this was the only way to deal with thieves. These days with our intricate system of law and investigation, we don't need to follow this practice to the letter. What you have to understand is that sometimes what is said in the Koran is allegorical and not literal. As Allah says in Al-Imran 3:7, 'He it is Who has sent down to you the Book; in it are verses basic or fundamental; they are the foundation of the Book: others are allegorical'. This means that there are verses in the Koran that are allegorical and no doubt this verse about cutting off the hands of thieves is allegorical. Allah would not seriously want His people to follow such a barbaric practice. Here in Pakistan, the punishment for theft is a term in prison. This allegorically is the cutting off of the thief's hands as the thief is now cut off from his or her freedom which is what the hands in this verse represent. And if you read the verse which follows, Allah says, 'But if the thief repents after his crime, and amends his conduct, God turns to him in forgiveness; for God is Oft-Forgiving, Most Merciful'. If we were to literally cut off the hands of a thief, and then the thief repents of his or her crime, does Allah then sew the hands back onto the thief? If not, then what does it mean that Allah turns to him in forgiveness? So this verse cannot be talking about the cutting off of literal hands but the cutting off of something that the hands represent, in this case his or her freedom. After all, when thieves have served out their crime, they are then granted their freedom, that is, their hands allegorically are restored to them."

Once again, I tried to follow the argumentation presented by this Mulvi. After all, he was a learned man and had studied the Koran in detail. By contrast I was young and still learning about what was written in Allah's book.

But even so, these events and my Mulvi's explanation of these verses in the Koran created more questions. To a point I could understand what my Mulvi was telling me about the literal understanding of these verses and how these verses became relievingly humane when provided with an allegorical interpretation. I could understand his allegorical explanation about the cutting off of the hands of a thief because the literal understanding of the punishment was not only barbaric and in some ways blasphemous in its requirement to mutilate the perfect human creature that Allah had created, but also it was an over compensation for the actual crime. But if some of what was written in the Koran was basic and fundamental and some allegorical, how were we to know which verses were fundamental and which were allegorical? And then I thought further: who decides which parts of the Koran are allegorical and which ones are to be taken literally?

But further, the commandment to cut off hands looked at literally or allegorically rubbed against my feelings about how to deal with thieves. Deep within my heart, I just knew that a more just way to deal with thieves was to carry out a punishment equal to the crime. In the case of Taheer, he stole a pencil box. The pencil box could readily be returned and Taheer could be further punished by having to pay the value of the pencil box as well as for the inconvenience of losing the pencil box. Further, there was nothing in Al-Ma'idah 5:38 which made any reference or suggestion as to what the thief stole or how often the thief committed the crime. And further, why the thief committed the crime in the first place. If a young, poor child living in a poor neighbourhood who had not eaten for two days stole an apple, would any reasonable person with a heart seriously feel that this young thief's hands should be cut off in the same way as a regular cat burglar who enters homes and steals gold and jewellery simply to fulfil his or her own greed? In the case of the poor child, the better solution was to create a social environment in which he or she was not forced to steal in order to survive in the first place.

But this question of literal and allegorical interpretations of the Koran also made me ask this question: if the Koran says that Allah destroyed the cities of the people of Lut because of their abominations, was this to be understood literally or allegorically? Further, the Koran does not talk about punishment for homosexuality. The Koran only says that it was Allah who destroyed the cities of the people of Lut. It makes no statement to call on anyone on earth to do so. This meant to me that the only one with the right to punish homosexuals for their sins according to the Koran is Allah Himself. Anyone on earth who believes he or she has the authority to punish homosexuals in this way was implying that he or she were Allah.

But these were not the only issues that made me question whether what I was reading was to be taken literally or allegorically. The Koran says the sun sets in a spring of dark mud in Al-Kahf 18:86, that it orbits the earth in Fatir 35:13 and Ya-Sin 36:40, the stars were put in the sky to "to guard against every rebellious devil" as it says in As-Saffat 37:7, that Allah created earth flat like a carpet in Nuh 71:19 and made the mountains pegs to hold the earth down as it says in An-Naba 78:7, and through the centuries, different commentaries were written regarding these verses, the earlier ones saying that these verses were to be understood literally, the later ones that they were merely allegorical.

Further, in the verse in An-Nisaa 4:34 which reads

> *Men are the protectors and maintainers of women…*
> *As to those women on whose part you fear disloyalty*
> *and ill-conduct, admonish them…and beat them*

were men to follow this commandment literally or allegorically? And if allegorically, how does a man allegorically beat his wife?

And what about the verse in Al-Taubah 9:5 where it is written

> *Kill the polytheists*
> *wherever you find them*

and seeing Hindus are polytheists, was it our duty to literally or allegorically kill any Hindus who were living in our community? And if allegorically, how does one allegorically kill a Hindu?

What also made it difficult for me was, what were the repercussions if I confused when to take a verse literally or allegorically? If I were to follow the precept of a verse literally when it was meant to be taken allegorically, or allegorically when I was meant to take it literally, would I be doomed to a painful, fiery eternity as a result? I often thought that it would have been more helpful if Allah had simply colour-coded His holy book, having the allegorical portions written, say, in blue ink, and the literal ones in black. Or that He could have made it easy for everyone by not using any allegories or metaphors at all and simply writing the entire Koran in plain speech.

Further, the completion of the verse in Al-Imran 3:7 was that "those in whose hearts is perversity follow the part thereof that is allegorical". So, according to my understanding, to play on the safe side, I should always be erring on a literal understanding of the Koran to avoid eternity in Jahannam.

This problem of trying to determine whether or not passages from the Koran should be understood literally or allegorically continued to create confusion. For years

I agonized over many of these issues myself because I witnessed or at least heard about those who argued hotly and venomously with each other, almost fighting to the death, over whether verses in the Koran should be taken as literal commands or merely as allegories – until I realized that this controversy showed the humanness of the Koran.

Chapter 4

The rest of the years in the earlier part of my school days passed uneventfully and I really don't have many memories of this time. I can't even remember what I did during the holidays that separated my years at school and the last two years, the two years of college.

Starting my college education began a new phase in my life. The two college years themselves were a demarcation from the earlier years at school and, although still part of my secondary education, in a way they were a foretaste of tertiary education that was to later follow. It was during these final two years that I would attempt to achieve the highest mark possible in the final exam.

We had two systems we could follow, the Cambridge system and the local Pakistani system. I chose to follow the Cambridge system, studying for the final 'A' Level Exams, which meant that it was obligatory to study English and mathematics as two major subjects.

Beginning these final two years created a transformation in my life and in the life of my peers. We were elevated in status because we had a section of the school dedicated to us away from the rest of the other school students, an area which was better kept, had park benches, trees and a well-kept lawn, almost like a miniature reflection of an elite British university campus.

This transformation into the college years of our secondary school education brought about some dramatic changes in the last leg of our adolescence. We felt older, more mature and better respected. It did not feel like eight weeks had passed since we had left school the year previous, it felt more like an eternity. Those in the earlier years seemed so much younger in comparison, the gap was so vast. It was as if we had blossomed out of a cocoon to begin a new development in our person.

During the earlier years of my secondary education, I had made no close friends and so the first day back left me a little lost because I didn't know anyone well. But within a couple of weeks, I managed to get mixed up with a group of ten students. They were a great bunch of students and surprisingly tolerant. I had known them in the junior years but now they seemed different, older, wiser, more mature and more accepting.

Our group sat on a couple of benches that we squeezed together. We laughed, joked and had a great time. Another group formed not very far from us but their group required four benches to seat everyone comfortably. However, there were only five benches on the lawn section. So, whenever the recess or lunch bell rang, whoever was the first in either group to get to the lawn section grabbed as many benches as was required for the group and clung to them with all their might until the rest of the group arrived. There were tug-o-war matches over the benches until the strongest won the bench and it was hilarious fun to watch or be a part of the battle. There were some very imaginable means of keeping all the benches in one group together that often had us in stitches of laughter.

But studying for the 'A' Level Exams itself was the most trying time of my school life, probably because so much hinged on the final result. In my earlier years in secondary education, I studied for about one or two hours an evening maximum, but for my 'A' Level Exams, I was up to all hours trying to keep abreast of homework, assignments and study. The relief, then, at recess and lunchtime of laughter, joking, talking and philosophizing that my friends and I involved ourselves in was just priceless.

But my Islam had to spoil it. At home a new fervour had developed because of what my Mulvi had been telling me – the return of the Mehdi. My Mulvi often spoke about the imminence of Mehdi's return and the need to keep urging my friends and relatives to fervently follow the teachings of the Prophet. Mehdi's return, so my Mulvi told me and showed me from the Hadiths, would be heralded by increasing natural cataclysms such as earthquakes, plagues and famine, an increase in human unrest leading to more and more wars, and the increase of false prophets and of people falsely saying that they were the long awaited Mehdi. These were occurring at this time which meant that the return of Mehdi was near.

It is difficult to remember the names of all the people in our group and what they looked like. I remember a girl called Sameen. She was a rather large girl, pleasantly plump, and a very hyperactive person who tried to be smart in class. She sat next to me in my English class and often drew hearts and arrows in my exercise book, and wrote poetry about her intimate love for Allah, but in the same fashion as a heterosexual woman would write deeply and intimately about the love she bears towards her male sweetheart. I guessed she was really writing these poems for me. In some ways I found this somewhat disturbing yet at the same time I got a secret pleasure out of the attention.

Then there was Tanveer. Tanveer was a tall, thin guy with smooth, silky, black hair, so smooth it almost looked artificial. He was a serious student, quite smart, but not given very easily to joviality. He was excellent in the sciences and mathematics but was reluctant to help anyone who may have been able to benefit from his ability.

There was another guy, Dawood, who I vaguely remember, who was tall with short, dark hair. From memory he was an excellent football player and had represented the school in a series of competitions. About the only other thing I recollect about him was that he was also in my physics and chemistry classes and I sat with him there.

Then there was Ambreen. She was a very small girl, so small that she earned herself the name Mouse, a name which she hated! There were times when we thought she was sitting when in fact she was standing fully erect. Ambreen was an excellent artist, in particular in painting, and I remember one day when she had brought with her to the break a painting she had done for one of her assignments in which she had painted a bowl of fruit with sunlight falling on it from an angle, and the artistry was so amazing because it looked as if she had simply taken a photo and enlarged it on a sheet of canvas.

Then there was Keeran. How Keeran ever was a member of anyone's group is anyone's guess. Unlike the other girls in our group, she wore a scarf to cover her hair but not completely as she allowed her fringe to remain exposed. She was tall and thin, with an awkward physique. She was extremely arrogant and opinionated although she could afford to be because she was one of the most intelligent students in the school, possibly because she had added assistance as her parents hired a private tutor to help her. I don't know why she ever condescended to be amongst such average students that made up our group but in a strange sort of way, she ended up blending in and becoming a part of us.

I enjoyed this group of students. It would have been better for me when I reflect back on that group if I had just remained a normal, teenage school kid. Really, I liked these people very much. I suppose this is what created the urgency in me to bring them back to observing the Islamic faith in its entirety and with intensity.

I can almost remember distinctly how it all began as if I were still sitting there on the bench. One particular morning, Sameen was late to join us at recess and she came bolting towards our group like a horse gone mad, bubbling with excitement. But as she approached our group, she tripped and in full velocity hurtled onto Tanveer's lap. At first, Tanveer reacted to her with raised hands as if some extremely huge and dangerous animal had landed on his lap. He began gesticulating in a manner to get Sameen off him but at the same time not wanting to touch her as if the mere touch of the skin of this animal would be fatal. Sameen struggled to her feet with great effort. Once she was back on her feet and was dusting herself down, Tanveer let out an exasperated "Allah kheir karey", an expression which roughly translates into English as "God will look after this".

But I was shocked. Sameen and Tanveer had committed a sin. According to us, boys and girls are not allowed to touch each other, even in a co-ed school where boys and girls intermingle, because for a boy and a girl to touch when they are not related is a grave sin according to Islam. Sameen and Tanveer, although initially affected by the contact, didn't seem too much bothered by it. But to me they had committed a serious sin and there were serious consequences for committing such a sin, and so I prayed out loud in full solemnity a *Taubah*, a type of prayer for forgiveness, in order to prevent something terrible happening to either of the two for committing such a heinous crime in the eyes of Allah, such as lightning striking them out of the cloudless sky or the sky itself falling on top of them and crushing them to death.

For a moment there was some silence from the rest of the group. Then Tanveer looked at me and said, "Mustafa, it was an accident."

"It was more than just an accident," I replied. "Boys and girls are not allowed to touch each other when they are *naa-mahram*."

Everyone knew what was meant by *naa-mahram*, that is, a relationship between a man and a woman where it was possible for them to marry.

"Mustafa, don't take this so seriously," Tanveer said by way of what sounded like consolation, but what I understood as a luke-warm, wishy-washy approach to our religion. I then looked up at Sameen.

"And you should be wearing a veil," I said quite condescendingly. "And why can't you walk womanly?"

Sameen paused from brushing herself down and stared at me through her deep brown eyes.

"What business is it of yours anyway to tell me what I should and shouldn't wear?" Sameen spat out. "It's a hot day and that's why I'm not wearing a veil. It's too hot to wear one anyway. In any case, I'm covering enough of myself so that the mandatory parts of my body are covered."

"But the Koran says in An-Noor 24:31 that believing women should cover their heads as well as their bodies."

At that moment, the bell went and put an abrupt end to our discussion. We all got up and began walking to our prospective classrooms. I felt that my friends in our group all knew that I was right but they just did not want to admit it. Everyone kept a safe distance from me for the rest of the day. Sameen, who as always sat next to me in my English class, this particular afternoon was rather reserved and continued to pout. There were no Valentine hearts and love poems added to the collection that afternoon.

Then there was another occasion. This particular lunch period, the girls of our group were talking about the latest famous Indian actor, Hrithik Roshan. I remember that Hindi movies and Hindi songs were all the rage, movies which I would never watch and music I would never listen to because neither of these forms of entertainment was in honour of Allah, not to mention that they came from India. What was particularly shocking was that a lot of these singers and in particular the Bollywood male actors were displayed in explicit detail, completely shirtless and baring their manhood shamelessly.

On this particular day, Sameen had brought along a magazine with upcoming reviews of the movie *Kaho Na Pyar Hai*, that is, *Say You Are In Love,* and the girls all began examining and talking about the details in the magazine and in particular about the main actor, Hrithik Roshan. Soon everyone was involved and giving their feelings about certain events in earlier movies that this actor had been in. But also it became evident that it was not so much the movies that impressed the girls but the main actor himself. Suddenly, Sameen dropped her magazine on the ground and I instinctively picked it up. But as I looked at the photo of Hrithik Roshan in his beautiful pose, wearing what looked like a leather vest which was open and revealing his amazingly rippled muscular chest and stomach, I was overwhelmed by two different feelings. The first was one of total attraction to this beautiful specimen of a man. My hormones started going into overdrive. However, this was mixed with pious anger at these girls who were unabashedly looking at these photos of this man in almost total undress and they were not worried or ashamed for doing so. Further, what horrified me was that these Muslim girls were looking at the naked torso of a Hindu man.

"This is totally un-Islamic!" I retorted indignantly.

The guys started laughing. Sameen, obviously offended, snatched the magazine out of my hand.

"Who cares what you think anyway, Mustafa," she snapped.

I didn't care that she was offended. Sameen and all the girls in our group were committing a grave sin. These Muslim girls were looking at the naked torso of a non-Muslim man.

"This is un-Islamic?" Tanveer commented with half a laugh. "So, we are committing a sin?"

"Yes, the girls are," I said in all seriousness.

The whole group began telling me off as if I were an idiot and continued to look at the magazine.

"So, what pictures do you look at?" Tanveer then asked. "The calligraphy of verses from the Koran?"

Everyone started laughing while I sat there, except for one of the girls, a beautiful, dark-skinned girl who was the quietest of us all. Her name was Rubasha Hussain and she seemed to smile with the rest of the group out of shyness. Something in her eyes told me that she smiled not because she saw the joke in Tanveer's comment but out of sympathy.

"He probably sits alone in his room," Tanveer said, "copying out verses from the Koran with plugs in his ears so he can't hear the sound of the neighbours' televisions!"

Everyone laughed at that.

"No," I replied quite embarrassed but to defend myself. "I also sometimes watch television. But I'm careful about what I watch. And so should you all. After all, we are Muslims, are we not?"

There was a moment of silence and then Tanveer spoke up again.

"Yes, we're all Muslims. But we're not fanatical like you. Why don't you just lock yourself away and sing *naat* to Muhammad?"

It was obvious on the face of everyone in that group that all agreed with Tanveer's loose view of Islam. Sameen looked up at me and the expression on her face was as if she were telling me where to go with my strict view of Islam.

I turned away frustrated but caught in the corner of my eye Rubasha watching me intently. But when I turned to look at her, she turned away and looked at the ground to avoid direct eye contact with me.

Suddenly the bell went and lunch was over. We made our way back to class. My friends always kept a slight distance from me after my outburst of religious zeal. But what was even stranger, and I admit quite comforting when I look back at it, was that these friends of mine were a lot more understanding and tolerant than I could ever be. Eventually Sameen returned to her illustrations and short love poems in my exercise book, Tanveer and Dawood talked about the cricket. But Rubasha, whom I knew the least in my group, stared at me across the classroom. But I only noticed this from the corner of my eye because each time I looked to see her staring, she looked away.

The events of that day troubled me for some time and so the next time I saw my Mulvi, I asked him the question.

"Sir, you have taught me a lot about our religion, how we are to follow the five pillars of Islam, and say the prayers at the prescribed time, observe the fasts with reverence, and to lead a clean and holy life. Is this what we are required to do to make it into paradise?"

"Well, yes, my son," my Mulvi replied in his soft voice. "Why do you ask?"

"For the past number of years I have been made fun of by my friends at school because of how serious I take my faith and yet we are all supposed to be Muslims. My friends say that they believe in Allah and that Muhammad is Allah's prophet. But at the same time, these same friends listen to un-Islamic music and watch Bollywood movies with non-Muslim actors. And some of the girls actually look at these famous actors in Bollywood movies when these men are almost naked and they see nothing wrong with this."

My Mulvi gave me a condescending smile.

"My son, you have to remember that at the Resurrection, what actually will save us on the Day of Judgement is not our actions but the intercession of the Prophet, peace and blessings of Allah be upon him. Even if you follow everything that is necessary for a Muslim to do, we still need the Prophet, peace and blessings of Allah be upon him, to intercede for us. So perhaps these friends of yours may in their hearts love the Prophet, peace and blessings of Allah be upon him, even though they are not as conscientious in their faith as you are, but they will probably still make it into paradise when the Prophet, peace and blessings of Allah be upon him, intercedes for them."

It took me a moment to digest this information. My Mulvi had explained in detail the five pillars of Islam and

I had been doing everything to follow these tenaciously. After all, why had my Mulvi gone into such detail as to what formed the five pillars on which the Islamic faith rested if all one really had to do was rely on the clemency of the Prophet?

"So, it is not necessary to follow the five pillars after all?" I asked perplexed.

"Do you mean to say that you think I'm contradicting myself?" my Mulvi asked in his normal gentle tone but there was an undertone of anger in his voice which made the answer to this quasi rhetorical question evident. As such, I did not provide an answer verbally but looked back at my Mulvi without saying a word. My Mulvi's facial expression relaxed and I guess he decided that my question actually wasn't a full-on attack but a sincere desire to understand the complexity of what he had just been teaching me.

"Okay," my Mulvi then went on to explain. "It says in the Koran in Surah Bani Israel 17:79 in reference to the beloved Prophet, peace and blessings of Allah be upon him, 'Soon will your Lord raise you to a Station of Praise and Glory'. This Station of Praise and Glory, the *Makaam-e-Mahmood*, as it says in the original Arabic and literally means the Praised Place, is the place where the Prophet will intercede on behalf of his followers. As this shows, although it is important to follow all the precepts of the faith, ultimately what will get us into paradise is the intercession of Muhammad, peace and blessings of Allah be upon him, on our behalf."

I looked at my Mulvi for a moment in reflection before continuing.

"So, even if we follow everything precisely as the faith teaches us," I asked a little confused, "the Prophet, peace be upon him, may decide not to intercede for us? In other words, we may not make it into paradise after all?"

"Think of it more in the reverse," my Mulvi replied. "It says in Surah Al-Baqarah 2:217, 'If any of you turn back from their faith and die in unbelief, their works will bear no fruit in this life and in the Hereafter; they will be Companions of the Fire and will abide therein'. So, even if you have spent your entire life observing every tenant of the Islamic faith, you have prayed the five daily prayers every day at the prescribed times, you have observed all the fasts faithfully, you have paid zakat and even if you have faithfully committed the entire Koran to memory, without the intercession of the Prophet, peace and blessings of Allah be upon him, you will not make it into paradise."

I was quite stunned by what I had heard. And it still needed some clarification.

"So, what use is it, then," I questioned, "of following all these precepts of the faith?"

"These precepts were given to us because they are good for us," my Mulvi replied. "Allah wants us to follow these precepts for our benefit. But He knows that not all of us can faithfully keep these precepts. Only special people can really observe all the precepts faithfully. But don't you see the mercy of Allah in that, even if we are unable to observe all His precepts tenaciously, we still have a chance of getting into paradise, simply by the intercession of the Prophet, peace and blessings of Allah be upon him?"

My Mulvi continued his explanation about how entry into paradise ultimately depended on the clemency of the Prophet but that this didn't mean that the other requirements of the religion, prayer, fasting, pilgrimage and paying zakat, were meaningless. Our sincerity in observing the five pillars naturally would weigh in our favour and no doubt the Prophet would strongly intercede on our behalf as a result. However, at the end of the day, our entry into paradise relied on the Prophet's mercy.

Later that evening in the privacy of my bedroom, I contemplated what my Mulvi had said to me. The way it came across, our entrance into paradise really depended merely on the clemency of Muhammad. So all this information about the five pillars of Islam seemed completely irrelevant, except, of course, for the first pillar, the belief in Allah and that Muhammad is His prophet. All this reading and studying the Koran to ensure that I was observing the prayers, the fasts and the zakat exactly as Allah had prescribed in the Glorious Koran seemed, in the light of my Mulvi's explanation, a total waste of time. Even trying to accumulate reward points for saying prayers exactly when they needed to be said and paying zakat during Ramadan to earn the thousand times more reward than paying zakat at any other time of the year in the end meant nothing if Muhammad did not show any clemency on our behalf.

I decided to read the verse that my Mulvi had quoted to explain the source of this belief. I flicked open my Koran to Surah 17, Surah Bani Israel, verse 79, where it was written, "Soon will your Lord raise you to Makaam-e-Mahmood". I glanced at the verse before it and then read the verse again in context:

> *Establish regular prayers at the sun's decline*
> *till the darkness of the night,*
> *and the recital of the Koran in morning prayer*
> *for the recital of dawn is witnessed.*
> *And as for the night keep awake a part of it*
> *as an additional prayer for you:*
> *Soon will your Lord raise you to Makaam-e-Mahmood.*

On my first reading, what went through my mind was that I simply could not see in these verses what my Mulvi had told me. However, once again, I took my Mulvi on trust because he was very learned. And if he knew for sure that this is what this passage meant, then obviously it meant this.

But it just set my head once again into a never-ending cycle. Were we to keep the five pillars of Islam or did it matter? And to what extent should I observe these precepts? Should I keep any of them at all? But isn't keeping all these precepts a way of showing my belief in Muhammad? Then why didn't my Mulvi explain to me that Muhammad will not simply make intercession on my behalf but he will actually go into detail and explain to Allah how I had kept to the best of my ability and with as clear a conscience as possible all the precepts Allah required of me and therefore I should be granted entrance into paradise?

But then I had further questions. How did Muhammad know all this seeing he has been dead for all these years and knew nothing of me? Where did he get all this knowledge about my life? And why did Allah have to depend on Muhammad to gain this knowledge of me? Didn't omniscient Allah already know everything about me?

As for the explanation of the *Makaam-e-Mahmood*, I read the verse again and again, and the verse before it to get the idea in context, but it didn't matter how many times I read it, I could not for the life of me see where my Mulvi got the idea that the Station of Praise and Glory, or the Makaam-e-Mahmood, was the place of intercession where Muhammad would be on the Day of Judgement interceding on our behalf. Rather, it came across to me that the two verses were directed at us, the readers. We, the readers of the Koran, were being told how often to offer prayers and when to accompany these prayers with the recital of the Koran. How I understood the termination of this verse was that, if we keep saying the prayers at these prescribed times and recite the Koran, Allah will eventually raise us to the *Makaam-e-Mahmood*. I understood this to mean that all these prayers we said would elevate us to a higher state of consciousness, like I had heard about those who meditate and enter some sort of trance. I read the verses again and again, hoping in some way that the meaning that my Mulvi had provided for the last portion of verse 79 would suddenly be revealed in me and I could finally say, "Ah, yes, now I get it." But I didn't. For all my agonizing over these verses, I just could not get the verse to say what my Mulvi said it did.

I thought of my school friends, of Tanveer, Dawood, Sameen, and all the others, and my Mulvi's explanation. If my school friends were able to get into paradise through the intercession of Muhammad, why was I delving further and further into my religion to be the best Muslim I could and trying to follow all the precepts to the nth degree?

And then I thought of the photo of Hrithik Roshan. Once again I caught a glimpse in my mind's eye of that sinewy body in explicit detail in the photo in that magazine. This began to engender fantasies in my head that I really didn't want to entertain but which ran through my mind whether I wanted them to or not. What on earth was wrong with me? Why was my lust directed so strongly towards the male form when I so desperately didn't want it to be?

Chapter 5

Going on Hajj, or pilgrimage, to Mecca is one of the five pillars of Islam, and my aging grandmother, my mother's mother, wanted to fulfil this obligation before she died. Her husband, my mother's father, had already managed to do the pilgrimage at an earlier time, being a very dedicated Mulvi, but was unable to take his wife at the time because she had fallen ill and couldn't travel. Now her husband, my grandfather, was dead and she knew that she would probably die soon and so she wanted to take the opportunity to travel there before she died. My father, in his full dedication to the faith, finally had the means to make the trip to Mecca and offered to take his mother-in-law along.

My father began making all the arrangements for both him and his mother-in-law to travel to Mecca to fulfil one of the requirements of the Islamic faith. But my Mulvi pointed out a problem with this trip: my grandmother and my father were *naa-mahram*, that is, they didn't have a blood relationship so it was possible for them to marry. Or, to put it in more concrete language, they were according to the rules of Islam a man and a woman who could form a marriageable couple and they were going to travel together unchaperoned, the implication being that while in each other's company during this trip to and from the holy place they could accidentally end up having sex together and committing *zinna*.

Those in countries unfamiliar with the idea of *mahram* and *naa-mahram* don't understand the complexities of interrelationships between people of the opposite sex. In Muslim countries, at least this is the situation in Pakistan, men and women cannot even touch each other unless they are blood relatives or married. It is true that I attended a co-ed school, but while I interacted with girls in the school, even when girls and boys sat next to each other, they were still forbidden to touch each other. Even Sameen who wrote erotic poetry in my exercise book was careful to ensure that her skin and my skin never came into direct contact.

Mahram is an Urdu word and means "blood relationship" and describes the relationship between a man and a woman which makes it impossible for them to marry, such as the relationship between a boy and his sister, or a woman and her son, or a man and his daughter. Because it is forbidden for such couples to marry, it is naturally assumed that Muslim men and women who have a mahram relationship simply would never even be tempted to have sex with each other. The opposite is called *naa-mahram*, or simply, "not mahram", that is, the relationship between a man and a woman which can lead to marriage. A man and a woman who have a naa-mahram relationship are forbidden to be in a situation where they find themselves alone with each other when they are unmarried because the idea is that in this situation, this man and woman may actually end up having sex together. This creates the overall impression that human beings are insatiable sex machines without any control over their sexual desires which is what causes the tensions to exist in our societies between the sexes.

My father had already started to make the preparations for him and his mother-in-law to go on Hajj and my grandmother had become quite overwhelmed with joy that she was finally able to go. But now, two conflicting views of the faith raised their ugly heads: on the one hand, they were going on Hajj to fulfil one of the obligations of the Islamic faith, but on the other hand, they shouldn't be going, or at least, they shouldn't be going together, because the relationship between mother-in-law and son-in-law was *naa-mahram.* I know this is a terribly disrespectful thing to say but I just couldn't imagine my father, a good-looking, middle-aged man still in his prime, wanting to have a sexual relationship with a frail, old woman like my mother-in-law. Further, although she was his mother-in-law, my father viewed his wife's mother almost in the same way as he viewed his own mother and, as a result, would he really fall into the temptation of wanting to have a sexual relationship with his mother-in-law?

My father must have had the same thoughts because he decided to consult another Mulvi. Eventually he found a Mulvi who said that a mother-in-law could in fact accompany her son-in-law on Hajj. This Mulvi produced a Hajj application form which showed that the son-in-law can accompany the mother-in-law even though they were *naa-mahram*. My Mulvi, however, was not impressed. He still maintained that this relationship was *naa-mahram* and hence my father and his mother-in-law could not travel together like this. This created a contentious issue between my Mulvi and my father even long after my father had returned. I often wondered if my Mulvi in his discontent entertained the idea that at some time during their trip to and from Mecca my father and his mother-in-law secretly indulged in a bit of pleasure of the flesh.

Not long after my father and grandmother had returned from Mecca, my sister, Maryam, got married. Maryam's wedding was rather troubling for me. Although the wedding ceremony was filled with the usual pomp and fantasy, the reception, or as we call it in Urdu, *valima*, brought out the earthy and base nature of what really happens when a man and woman marry. The parents of both bride and groom made constant comments about awaited grandchildren, and the tones and innuendos in their voices brought out the obvious implication of what was required of Maryam and her new husband, Musa, in order for grandchildren to make their appearance.

Maryam and Musa's wedding troubled me a lot because I knew this would be expected of me in the future. Weddings were supposed to be joyous occasions and everybody looked forward to them, not only the couple that was being joined, but the entire extended family. What was worse for me was that marriages in Pakistan were often arranged by the parents, especially if the son or daughter did not get the ball rolling themselves, and there was no possibility of getting out of such an arrangement. While I watched on at the wedding, inside I was filled with horror, knowing that one day I would have to be standing in Musa's position, and it would be expected of me to participate showing all the exuberance and delight that every heterosexual man has when entering the married state, because heterosexual men in this situation know that they will soon be able to participate in one of the most fundamental urges of our humanity that is supposed to be a thrilling experience. What heterosexuals fail to understand, and what they do not care to try and understand, is that while the sight and touch of a naked woman is an extreme delight for a heterosexual man, for a homosexual man, the sight and touch of a naked woman is vulgar and repugnant. I certainly did not want to look at a naked woman, and further, while naked, I certainly did not want to touch her or have her touch me.

When a homosexual is under compulsion to marry a heterosexual, this is cruel for both partners. The homosexual man is totally repelled by his wife's naked body and does everything to avoid having to touch it. The woman surely must notice the repugnance her homosexual husband has towards her body even if he does not divulge to her the reason for his lack of physical attention, and this must make her feel terribly unwanted. I can only imagine what it is like for a homosexual woman to be forced to marry a heterosexual man. Men play a dominant role in Pakistani society on the whole and in the marriage in particular, and I can only guess what she has to go through each time her husband forces himself onto her and how she as a dutiful wife can do nothing else but comply.

What made it even more problematic was that the only view of homosexuals, at least male homosexuals, in the Koran is that of the men of Sodom and Gomorrah. There was nothing which mentioned how a man may actually fall in love with another man and want to marry him in the same way as Musa wanted to marry Maryam. Homosexual attraction, as it is implied in the koranic narrative, is purely physical. And worse, it is animalistic, cruel and demonic, where such men only forced it onto other men without ever considering how the victim of their lust felt about it.

But this was not how I felt within. Yet again I was forced into committing doublethink, on the one hand required to believe the koranic view of homosexuality as nothing more than an evil lust, whereas on the other hand, my whole reasoning bore out that my physical attraction towards a man was no different to Musa's towards Maryam, that my desire to have sex with a man could be coupled with the desire to fall in love with a man and spend the rest of my life together with that man. And the situation was soon to arise when I would become aware of this and realize from firsthand experience the realities of it.

As for discoveries, I began to notice how Taheer had abruptly changed in character. He had been a cold, sadistic, selfish little horror in the earlier years of school, but he had since changed somewhat in the years of our 'A' Level exams. Taheer sat across from me in my mathematics class. One afternoon in summer, after we had returned from the lunch break, I was sitting at my desk with perspiration sprinkled all over my face. Taheer looked at me and at first laughed, thinking that I had washed my face and left my face wet without drying it. I commented that it was sweat. Taheer by contrast was as dry as a desert as if the oppressive heat didn't affect him. When he realized that I was serious, Taheer pulled out a handkerchief from his pocket and passed it to me. He assured me that it was clean. I thought at first it was a joke but then Taheer unfolded the hanky and openly displayed it to show the evidence of the truth of his statement, something like a woman on her wedding night proving that she had entered the marriage a virgin, in Taheer's case conversely showing that there were no unsightly patches on the cloth. Eventually I took the handkerchief and removed the surplus water from my face. I made a comment that I would have the handkerchief cleaned and returned to him the following day but Taheer insisted I give it back to him laden with my sweat. It was the oddest of feelings. After passing Taheer back his hanky now with a part of me in it, on the one hand it was a disgusting thought that Taheer wanted his now sweat-filled handkerchief, sweat that came from someone else's body, returned, yet on the other, it felt as if some sort of close bond had formed between the two of us because a part of me was now in his possession.

But this was not the only time that Taheer showed that he actually possessed human feelings and in fact he had begun to open up towards me. Over time I ended up with pens, pencils, exercise books, pencil sharpeners and other paraphernalia that had originally belonged to him and from someone who was willing to share and give.

And it was around this time that eventually Saleem got his pencil box back. When I asked Saleem who returned it to him, he told me that it was Taheer. Taheer, however, had not admitted to the theft. Taheer had simply said he had found it hidden in some hard to find place in the school.

And it wasn't long after Taheer returned Saleem's pencil box that Taheer apologized to me. One afternoon before I made my trek home from school, while about to exit the school premises, I felt an arm wrap around my stomach from behind which naturally hindered my progress. I was expecting this to be Dawood or one of my other school friends, but when I turned to see who this person was, there was Taheer. Taheer removed his arm from me and then smiled. He then took a quick glance around to ensure there was no-one else in close proximity to hear our conversation.

"Hey, Mustafa," he began. "Look, I just wanted to say sorry for the way I treated you when you saw me with Saleem's pencil box."

I was deeply amazed by his apology. But I was also rather suspicious.

"Here," he then said and shoved something in my hand. "I want you to have this."

It was a handkerchief. I wasn't sure if it was the one he had allowed me to use earlier but it was definitely clean and fresh.

"You know, Mustafa," Taheer continued, "I admire how you didn't tell anyone. Really, a strict Muslim would have done so but you obviously have a good heart."

I just looked at Taheer in confusion, unsure what to say. However, I had no time to give a response if I wanted to because Taheer suddenly turned and ran off.

Taheer appeared to have changed. However, he still remained strange and erratic. Parviz and Wahid had left this school, one moving to another part of Pakistan, the other to the UK, which meant that Taheer was now alone. Taheer, the erratic character that he was had obviously not made any other friends since then which made his unusual change in behaviour even stranger. However, he hadn't totally changed. He still often made sarcastic quips to me, but now there were times when he said things about what I did which really touched my heart.

Taheer's comments about my good heart and how this went against the strictness of the faith had a strange effect on me. This made me think that maybe I was becoming too soft in my approach to the religion and this could have dire consequences in my life beyond the grave. Although my Mulvi had explained to me that in the end it was merely the clemency of the Prophet that assured us entry into paradise,

I reasoned that the Prophet would have greater clemency towards us if we had done our utmost to uphold all Islamic practices to the best of our ability. As a result, I decided I had to become stricter again in my approach to the religion and hence had taken it upon myself to be our school's upholder of Islamic principles. During the lunchbreak, I used every opportunity to speak about the religion. It must have been really annoying for my school friends because at the best of times, Islam was constantly in our faces, and I was further keeping this religion all-invasive even during this time of relaxation.

I remember many times getting into conversations about Islam. If the subject of the conversation hadn't started there, I would have carefully and courageously steered it in that direction. One lunchbreak I managed to do so when Keeran blurted out, "Mustafa, why do you always have to bring up Islam at the lunchbreak? Can't you give it a rest?"

"No," I replied. "Because Allah wants us to keep remembering Him and be reminded of everything about Him so that we will enter into paradise."

"So, you mean that only Muslims will make it into paradise?" Keeran asked.

"Yes," I replied emphatically.

"That's not true," Keeran spat out. "Virtuous people will go to paradise despite their beliefs. If we do good works, this is what Allah wants of us."

"That may be so," I replied, "but believing in Allah and His Messenger is a major good work. Refusing to believe in Allah and His Messenger is a great sin, a great misdeed."

"Then why does Allah say that Jews, Christians and Sabeans will also go to paradise?" Keeran retorted. "Jews, Christians and Sabeans do not believe that Muhammad is Allah's Messenger and yet these people will enter into paradise. And they will enter into paradise because Jews, Christians and Sabeans like us Muslims follow a code of ethics, a set of principles that requires people to do good."

"If that is the case," I replied, "then why is one of the pillars of Islam, and indeed the first pillar, the belief that there is only one God and Muhammad is His Messenger? Like in a building, if you remove one of the pillars holding up the roof, the building will become unstable and it will eventually fall. So it is with Jews, Christians and Sabeans. Perhaps they follow a good set of principles, but they are not following the fundamental and basic principle of believing in the Prophet."

There was a moment of silence and then Tanveer took up the challenge.

"But how can you say that? I heard during a Friday sermon that Muhammad said that Allah has appointed to everyone rites they must follow, even if they are not the same rites as we as Muslims follow. And if the Jews, Christians and Sabeans follow different rites, they are following those rites that were given to them from their Messengers, none of whom were Muhammad, because Muhammad only delivered one set of rites and he delivered these to Muslims. But although the other religions follow different rites, they are still following rites that were once given to them by Allah through their messengers."

Everyone agreed with this but I was not convinced.

"Tanveer, yes, what you heard from that Friday sermon comes from the verse in Al-Hajj 22:67. But you need to read the entire verse and not only quote a part of it to fully understand what Allah is saying. The entire verse states that 'to every People have We appointed rites which they must follow: Let them not then dispute with you on the matter, but invite them to your Lord. For you are assuredly on the Right Way'. The Jews, Christians and Sabeans may have been appointed rites in the past and these rites differ to the rites observed by us Muslims. But now that Muhammad has come, He has appointed the best of rites, the 'Right Way' to which we need to invite them if they wish to enter into paradise. Muhammad was the last Prophet sent by

Allah and he has brought us the best religion and the best rites which accompany this religion."

"But how do you know Islam is the best religion?" Tanveer spluttered. "How do you know these other religions are not better than Islam?"

I was quite surprised that Tanveer asked the question. Tanveer was Muslim, so why did he even consider asking something so absurd. But I knew I had the right answer.

"Because Islam is a comprehensive religion. More than all the other religions of the world Islam has answers to all the questions about life," I replied in all confidence. I made this statement when I really knew very little about Judaism, Christianity and the religion practised by the Sabeans, or any other religion such as Hinduism.

"Does it explain how to deal with a father who is abusive to his wife and children?" I heard a voice behind me more state than ask. I turned around to see the source of the voice and saw Taheer towering behind me. The question he posed was an odd one, and quite sinister. It was even creepier the way he had suddenly appeared out of nowhere.

"Yes, it does," I replied. "The wife can resist him getting in bed with her or resist doing other things. And if this goes on for a long time, she can ask for *hoola*."

Everyone understood that *hoola* was what a woman does when she wants to divorce her husband.

Taheer laughed and leant back.

"And where in the Koran does it say that?" he snickered.

I didn't have an answer. This was something my Mulvi had once told me or I had heard about it at the mosque. It wasn't something I had actually read in the Koran, at least, not in the parts I had become acquainted with.

Taheer then commented. "No, but the Koran teaches that a man can abuse his wife!"

There was something in Taheer's voice which expressed pain and grief. But I was shocked that he made such a comment. The Koran, Allah's holy book, could never condone such a thing.

"Where does it say that?" I cried out emphatically.

"Hahaha!" Taheer gave out what sounded like a demonic laugh. "As it says in Surah An-Nisaa 4:34", and Taheer first said it in Arabic then translated it into English, "'as to those women on whose part you fear disloyalty and ill-conduct, admonish them, refuse to share their bed and beat them...for Allah is Most High, Great'. And this verse doesn't say that the man has to *prove* that his wife is disloyal or of ill-conduct, he simply has to *fear* that his wife is, and led by this fear, he has the right to beat her."

I was not familiar with this verse. But I was incensed at the implication from Taheer.

"That may be what that verse says on its own. But you cannot distort the words of Allah to suit your own desires. If a man truly loves his wife and is compassionate as Allah Himself is compassionate, he would only take to beating his wife as a very last resort if there was nothing else to prevent his wife from being disloyal or having ill-conduct. It is up to a man to show love to his wife."

Taheer waited a moment and then asked, "And what does the Koran say about a man who falls in love with another man, not falling in lust but in love?"

I was completely shocked by the question. There was snickering among the group so it was obvious that they all thought Taheer was saying this as a joke. But I felt as if Taheer could read my soul and knew where my sexual proclivity really sat. However, I was not going to allow his statement to remain unchallenged.

"A man can love another man," I replied measuredly. "That's what creates friendships among men. But a man falling in lust with another man, that's impossible, because it is *haram*, so at least a Muslim man would never fall in lust with another man. A man would never fall in love with another man like a man falls in love with a woman. When a man falls in love with a woman, that love, as well as the intimacy that goes with that form of love, is natural, it is from Allah. That a man can fall in love with another man in just as intimate a way is not supported by the Koran and is simply a distortion created by Satan. If a man wants to be intimate with another man, it is purely a lust thing, as the example of the story of Sodom and Gomorrah tells us."

I made this last statement in confidence but I knew I was also committing doublethink. I knew on the one hand I had to maintain this view in support of the Koran that a man having sex with another man was merely some sort of evil attraction and men only did this to other men in the same way as a sadist inflicted pain and humiliation on his victim. In fact, the way it was taught in the mosque, that's all homosexuality was, simply a form of sadism. But I also knew that this was incorrect from my own feelings. My sexual desires towards men were not to put the target of my attraction into a humiliating position where the other guy would suffer and be humiliated while I gained twisted pleasure from this. I had entertained the thought that the person I would be intimate with would enjoy the moment with me as much as I did. But I had to believe the koranic view was correct because I would go to hell if I even thought that the koranic view was wrong, even though I knew completely that the koranic view was unjustified as my own feelings and experience dictated. What troubled me further was that Taheer raised this point and I felt that he had sussed me out and knew deep down what was truly going on inside of me. This filled me with great fear and so to further dissuade him, I added, "and such men will definitely go to hell along with all those who do not follow the Prophet."

"And they're going to burn in hell, I suppose?" Taheer replied without missing a beat. Taheer then gripped my left shoulder firmly and then I felt something rub on my face which caused me to close my eyes.

"Just checking that you're not burning!" Taheer stated. "I want to remove the sweat that you're developing because of the fires of hell making you hot."

I heard the guys in our group laugh which confused me as Taheer was making a mockery of the concept of hell.

Taheer finally removed the handkerchief, put it to his nose and took a sniff.

"Mmmmmm! You smell so nice," he commented, a vision of reverie appearing over his face as he closed his eyes and smiled. Everyone else in our group just laughed at Taheer's charades.

Taheer then returned to the discussion.

"Yah Mustafa, do you seriously believe that Allah is compassionate and that Allah will put people in hell? How can a compassionate God throw His creatures in hell? Isn't that totally inconsistent?"

"Yah Taheer," I replied in confident defiance, even though I was shaking within. However, I felt as if Allah was guiding me in my words. "No, it is not inconsistent. You have highlighted one aspect of Allah but ignored other aspects of Him. It is true that Allah is Compassionate. But Allah is also Justice. You have to understand the totality of Allah to appreciate the full story. Now, if Allah were all Compassionate, He would allow all people into paradise despite what type of people they were, even if they associated others with Him, that is, they committed sheerk. There would have therefore been no reason to send the Prophet Muhammad to be born and then send the angel Gabriel to reveal to him the Koran. But Allah is also a God of Justice. When people commit sin, they have to pay for the sin. Again, if Allah were purely justice, He would have sent everyone to hell because everyone has to pay for the crime. But Allah again sent Muhammad as the instrument to reveal the Koran to the world so that people know what is right and wrong, and in any case, it is in the end through the intercession of Muhammad that we will make it into paradise.

If we deny the Prophet, we are insulting Allah and making a farce out of the entire history of Muhammad. There would have been no reason for having the Prophet. But because Allah sent the Prophet, it is a requirement of entrance into paradise the belief in this prophet. Those who don't believe in the Prophet, despite their good works, they will simply not make it into paradise. It is our duty to tell everyone so that at the end of the world those who have heard about the Prophet and not believed in him cannot say they were ignorant of his message."

"You're not saying that you believe in the end times?" Taheer sneered. It struck me as rather odd that Taheer, a Hafiz-ul-Koran, actually was questioning the faith. However, I took it to mean that he was not questioning the faith as such but simply challenging me for the sport of it. So I took up the challenge.

"Yes, as a Muslim, I believe so," I replied in all confidence.

"But they've been saying that for years," Taheer sneered again.

I took a deep breath to inflate my confidence.

"Yes, that may be so. But Allah told us the signs that would show that the end times are coming and these are starting to occur while we speak. In particular, never before have all these signs been coming to pass as they are today. Allah prophesied that in the end times, there would be frequent earthquakes, there would be wars, there would be famines, there would be floods, and there would be more solar and lunar eclipses. And look around us. The number of earthquakes around the world has increased, there are more and more wars, there are many places experiencing famines and there are more and more floods even in our own country, and there have been more and more eclipses."

Taheer looked at me and replied, "But there have always been earthquakes. We cannot tell whether or not the number of earthquakes is increasing when considering the age of the earth because the world was not completely populated like it is today thousands of years ago, and people didn't monitor and record earthquake activity like they do today. As for wars, this is almost like a self-fulfilled prophecy. The more people there are, naturally the more wars there will be because people are always vying for space on earth to occupy and no doubt this will continue as the population of the earth increases. This then explains why there will be more famines because the more people there are, the more resources we need in order to be able to feed everyone, and our resources are limited. As for floods, at least here in Pakistan, there have always been floods in all recorded history. And there have always been eclipses. We just have been witnessing more of them simply because of the media."

"This may appear," I replied off the cuff, "as a self-fulfilled prophecy but no-one really knew that the world would become so overpopulated that wars and famines would ensue as a result."

"So, the end of the world could come today?" Taheer asked.

"No, not yet," I replied now in full confidence. "It is prophesied that there are yet other signs that need to be fulfilled. It was prophesied that people would see women dancing in their own houses which is now coming to pass because people can now see women dancing in their own houses on television. It was prophesied that the sun will rise from the west and set in the east and this is yet to happen. And even before that, there will be a great, global dust storm, a great dust storm of red dust which will sweep over the entire globe. When that happens, all true Muslims will vanish. All moderate Muslims and the non-Muslims

100

will remain to suffer the consequences of what will happen next on earth."

"A large dust storm of red dust? Maybe that will happen when you fart!" Taheer explurted and everyone just broke out into laughter. I was on the one hand embarrassed and on the other perplexed. I was embarrassed because Taheer had made of me a laughing stock in the argument. But I was perplexed because everyone in our little gathering was Muslim, yet they laughed at me about a belief that was a part of the Islamic faith.

The boys in my group then started to make farting noises by putting their forearms to their lips and blowing raspberries onto their skin, each time making comments such as, "Whoops! Is that the beginning of the dust storm of red dust?" or "Wow! Now that was a relief! That will definitely start off the end times!" and everyone just laughed while I sat there humiliated. It was also perplexing that these people around me shared the same faith as me and yet they were making fun of me for believing in what I knew was a part of our religion.

That afternoon we had a chemistry class. Like always, my friends continued to befriend me but they also continued to blow raspberries into their arms and then laugh at my expense.

During our chemistry class, we broke up into our prospective groups and set up the equipment to perform the experiment. I had gathered the glassware and accompanying apparatus and walked back to my bench. Rubasha was standing nearby.

"How can I help you?" I asked.

Rubasha looked down shyly and then back up at me.

"I don't know how to set up the experiment. My chemistry partner is away and I can see yours is too. Would it be okay if I did the experiment with you?"

"Yeah, sure," I replied and gestured to Rubasha to come closer.

I began setting up the experiment and explaining to Rubasha what we were supposed to be doing. I got Rubasha to help me set up the apparatus as well so that she was somewhat involved. Once the Bunsen burner was lit, we simply had to wait for things to happen before we could begin recording results from the experiment. Rubasha then abruptly turned the conversation back to what we had been discussing at the lunchbreak.

"All that you were saying at the lunchbreak, is it true? Do you believe that?"

"Well, yes, I do," I replied.

"How do you know all about that?"

"It's in the Koran."

"You've read the Koran?"

"Yes, I've read the Koran. Well, I've read it in Arabic. I don't understand everything in the Koran at the moment because I'm still trying to improve my Arabic. But I do understand parts of it."

"And you read it on your own?"

"Yes, I do. I have a Mulvi who helps me but there are lots of times when I also read it on my own."

"Oh," Rubasha said by way of quiet shyness, "I have always wanted to read the Koran. I study the Tafseer by a scholar of my sect, but I haven't actually read from the Koran directly, it is such a complicated book."

Rubasha mentioned a scholar from her sect. Her full name was Rubasha Hussain and Hussain is well-known to be a typical Shiite Muslim surname. So, because she had talked of a scholar of her sect and that her surname was Hussain, I immediately realised that she was Shiite. This immediately put me on guard because we had grown up to believe that the Shiites had corrupted the Islamic faith and they were, for all intents and purposes, not really Muslims. It immediately set up a barrier between her and me, and the fact that I had read from the Koran directly and not via the intermediary of a Tafseer, that is, a commentary on the

Koran and an explanation of the verses within this holy book, I felt a sense of superiority over her. Nonetheless, Rubasha and I chatted for the rest of the time we performed the experiment, at times making casual references to religion, at others discussing the progress and results of the experiment.

Eventually the final bell went. It was the first time I felt disappointed going home because I was just getting interested in this conversation. We began packing up.

"Oh, Rubasha," I commented. "I wish you lived near me so we could continue this conversation."

"Why? Where do you live?" Rubasha asked me. I told Rubasha that I lived close to Utility Store, on the south side of it. When I mentioned that, Rubasha beamed with delight.

"I also live close to the same Utility Store, but a couple of blocks on the north side."

"But you catch the bus to school," I commented.

"Yes, of course. How do you get to school?" Rubasha asked.

"I walk."

"Three kilometres?"

"Yes, it's about a half hour walk and it's good exercise. And it's pretty safe at this time of the day to walk. Why don't you walk home with me?"

Rubasha went into deep thought for a moment and then replied.

"It's a bit far. But, yes, I would like to continue this conversation. But I will have to tell Ambreen that I'm not going to catch the bus with her. Oh, okay. Meet me at the side gate. I'll be there in about ten minutes."

Rubasha rushed off while I made my way to the side gate. I was so excited. Finally someone at school was interested in Islam as much as me and didn't just go through the motions of the religion as part of the general routine.

Soon Rubasha was back, walking at a fast pace but puffing.

"What do you do when it rains?" she asked.

"I get wet," I replied, and we both laughed and set off.

Rubasha and I made our way through the streets of Alekh-Jahan. Around us were the usual concrete buildings that made up the skyline of this suburb. We were able to make ourselves heard over the clamour and clatter of the traffic that passed by, of cars, buses and motorcycles vying for space on the roads as they moved around. We passed various street hawkers selling a variety of foodstuffs.

We finally made it to a park near Utility Store. The park had four small paved avenues which radiated out from a central pavilion which marked the centre of the park, with an array of bushes covered in colourful flowers lining the paths and other bushes dotted about throughout the park grounds. We found a bench and sat down.

"Wow, it's so lovely here," Rubasha said freely.

"Yes, it's beautiful, this park. I often come here to meditate on Allah and the wonderful things He has done for us."

"Yes, I like to find a quiet spot to meditate about Allah."

I was touched by Rubasha's outlook on life, especially as she believed in contemplating and meditating about what Allah has done for us in the same way as me.

"Tell me, Rubasha. Do you believe that there is only one God and Muhammad is His Messenger?"

"Yes," Rubasha confirmed.

"And do you believe in the other pillars of Islam, that we should fast, pray, pay zakat, and go on Hajj?"

"Yes, of course, I do! I'm a Muslim!" she stated, this time with a little bit of suspicion in her voice.

"And do you believe that only those who believe in Allah's Messenger will go to paradise?"

"Yes!" Rubasha said and looked at me a bit impatiently. "Why are you asking me these questions?"

"Well," I replied, "you're a Shiite, and my parents and my sect believe that the Shiites corrupted the Islamic faith and are really not Muslims. But so far, you have told me that you believe in those things which are fundamental to my faith."

Rubasha chuckled at that.

"That's funny because we were brought up to believe that you Sunnis were led astray. But after listening to you at school talking about the Koran, I've grown quite curious to know what you believe. You have some strange beliefs but I asked my scholar about some of the things you've said in the past and he agreed with what you say. Also, you speak so confidently and assuredly about what you believe."

"Your scholar agreed with me?" I asked.

"Yes, sure. Why do you ask in such a manner?"

"No reason," I replied quietly.

But there was a reason. For all my childhood and growing up, we had been indoctrinated with the belief that a Shiite was a weird person, with weird beliefs who had rituals which were different to ours, and for all intents and purposes were not Muslim at all. But from all the questions I had asked Rubasha thus far, she believed the same things as I did. And not only that, her scholar agreed with what I had said in the past at school. I was a little perturbed but also excited at the same time. Shiites are Muslims after all, I thought, and because of this, Rubasha was very much an equal in the faith.

But while I thought on this, my mind was diverted when Rubasha moved her hand and the ring she was wearing caught my attention. The ring was worn on her right middle finger and it reflected in the sunlight a beautiful blue.

"Wow! That's a beautiful ring!" I commented.

"Thank you. Yes, I wear this ring because it contains a neelam stone, similar to what some of our imams wear."

I had heard somewhere before that a neelam is a gemstone and how certain Shiites wore rings with neelam stones or other precious stones in them but I didn't know if they had any particular religious significance.

"I wear this," Rubasha continued, "because it reminds me of Allah and the declaration of my faith."

I looked at the ring and then back at Rubasha.

"And what is your declaration of faith?" I asked.

"Our declaration of faith is just like yours, I'm sure. You know, in the Shahada, where we proclaim that 'there is no God but Allah and Muhammad is His messenger, Ali is the *wali* of Allah'."

I felt an uneasiness when I heard Rubasha's version of the Shahada. The Sunni version of the declaration is that 'there is no God but Allah and Muhammad is His messenger' and that part at least is common to both faiths. But the Shiites add the reference to Ali being the *wali* of Allah, *wali* meaning among other things "friend", and in a way bringing Ali up to the same level as Muhammad. It was troubling because on the one hand Sunnis and Shiites acknowledge the belief in only one God and only one Messenger, but then the Shiites add to this belief the acknowledgement of Ali as a significant person worthy of an acclamation of some sort in a similar way to Muhammad.

Rubasha then changed the subject rather abruptly to the conversation I had with Taheer at the lunchbreak.

"All that you were saying today about what will happen in the end times, do you believe that?"

"Yes," I replied in all confidence.

"Did you read that also in the Koran?"

"No," I replied. "A lot of this is found in the Hadiths. As a Shiite, you believe in the Hadiths as well, don't you?"

"Well, yes," Rubasha replied affirmatively. "Of course, I do."

Rubasha then began providing me an inventory of Hadiths but also Tafseers that she was familiar with. However, the Hadiths and Tafseers she mentioned, some I had heard of, others were completely new to me. Once she had told me all these commentaries of the Koran, she asked me which of these gave the best accounts of the events that

106

were going to occur in the end times. But because she had mentioned quite a number of unfamiliar ones, I told her that I would have to speak with my Mulvi and then I could relay back to her what my Mulvi had recommended.

With that, we looked up at the sun and decided to make a move to go home. Rubasha invited me to accompany her to her place.

Rubasha lived in a modest apartment in one of the concrete structures that lined the streets of the suburb of Alekh-Jahan. We made our way up the building to her apartment. Rubasha knocked on the door and soon Rubasha's mother opened, looked at both Rubasha and me, and then welcomed us inside.

Rubasha's mother greeted me and then invited me to sit down in the livingroom. In this central room was a modern décor lounge set, very cubic and angular, covered with green material. This faced opposite a relatively large television screen set atop a TV table made of glass and very lovingly polished. But what caught my attention were the religious items scattered around the room. On one wall hung a wooden *alam*, the characteristic object that was in the form of a right hand held up like a student desiring to ask the teacher a question, with a crescent moon surrounding it. There was another alam made of brass on the CD player cupboard in another corner of the room. On another wall was a *Panjatan Pak*, the characteristic plaque with the name of Allah in the centre and then surrounding Allah's name the names of Muhammad, Ali, Fatima, Hassan and Hussain, all written in beautiful Arabic script. Above this hung a sword which streamlined to the end with a forked tip similar to that of a snake's forked tongue, the characteristic *Naad-e-Ali*, that is, the sword of Ali.

Rubasha's mother fussed over me, offering me tea accompanied with cream and plain biscuits. She then asked me about my family and about school.

Eventually it was time for me to go. I thanked Rubasha's mother for her hospitality. Rubasha accompanied me downstairs and onto the street.

"Thank you for accompanying me home and for inviting me to your place," I said to her.

"I had an enjoyable chat!" Rubasha replied with a pleasant grin.

"Rubasha, I'd like to learn more about your version of Islam."

"Well, why don't you come to my imam bargah for Friday prayers?"

"Mmmmmmm. I'm not quite sure if my parents would allow me to attend the imam bargah and hence miss attending my local mosque for prayers."

Ruth looked at me with a strange expression on her face.

"We are after all praying to the same God," she said almost in the form of an apologetic.

"I guess so. I'll speak with my parents and see if I can organize a day to come with you to the imam bargah."

With that, I said good-bye and went home.

That evening, I decided to ask my parents about Rubasha's version of Islam. It had puzzled me all that afternoon because of the conflict between the negative light Shiites were viewed by us Sunnis juxtaposed by what Rubasha had said were part of her beliefs, especially those aspects that were fundamentally the same.

It was later in the evening. I had spent quite some hours doing my homework and so I decided to take a break. My parents and grandparents were drinking tea. I came into the livingroom and sat down. My grandmother asked me if I also wanted tea, and then got up and poured some into a cup before I had answered in the affirmative. Once my grandmother had placed the cup in front of me, before taking a sip I simply opened the conversation.

"Are Shiites Muslims?" I asked.

"Why do you ask that?" my grandfather asked.

"Well, there's this girl at school, Rubasha Hussain, and she's a Shiite. I walked home with her today and we chatted about our versions of Islam. Rubasha believes in the five pillars of Islam and that those who follow these five pillars will go to paradise."

"Well, if they believe that, they're going to paradise," my grandfather replied in his soft grandfatherly voice.

"No, they are not!" my father retorted immediately.

I looked at my father with surprise.

"But why not?" I asked.

"Because Shiites follow a distorted version of Islam. They say the Koran has been corrupted and so they don't take the Koran as seriously as they should. And they commit sheerk. Not only do they acknowledge that Muhammad is the prophet of Allah, they add to this their adoration for Ali, almost as an equal of Muhammad. Anything that gets mixed up with the adoration of Allah and His Messenger, Muhammad, is of *Shaitaan*!"

Shaitaan is the Arabic-cum-koranic version of the English *Satan*, and my father, because of his religiosity, preferred to use the Arabic epithet probably with the thought that the real enemy of Allah is better recognized in the Arabic of the Koran than in a translation into a European language.

"But Rubasha said that in her Shahada, she acknowledged that there is only one God, Allah, and that Muhammad is His messenger."

"Yes, I know," my father replied gruffly. "But you can't mingle belief in Muhammad with the adoration of another person. Allah says that we should not commit sheerk, that is, associate others with Allah. In the same way, we should not associate others with Muhammad. Shiites acknowledge Ali very much in the same way they adore the Prophet and this is in a way verging onto committing sheerk."

I sat there for a moment and then changed the perspective on the argument slightly.

"But Rubasha seems like a nice girl and an example of how a Muslim should live as well as believing in Allah and Muhammad. Rubasha is not like my other friends because she doesn't swear, or tell dirty jokes, she dresses moderately and appropriately, and is dedicated to practising her faith."

"Son, what Shiites teach is unfortunately heresy," my father replied. "Shaitaan deceives us subtly. He doesn't appear with neon signs saying, 'Here I am! I am Shaitaan sent to you to mislead you!' Shaitaan presents the truth mixed up in falsehoods. And that's why we have the Koran so that we know what the truth is. Does the Koran teach us to acknowledge Ali?"

I just sighed. No, I could not think of any verse in the Koran which I had become familiar with which acknowledged or even mentioned Ali. Also, my Mulvi had never granted Ali any special mention or directed me to anywhere in the Koran which indicated as such.

"No," I replied. I then added. "Rubasha has asked me to attend her imam bargah one Friday for prayers."

I was expecting my father to become violently angry but I was quite surprised by his much more self-controlled reply. "If you go to the imam bargah, you will not find the truth there."

"I wasn't planning on going to the imam bargah to find the truth," I immediately replied in defence. "I wanted to go to find out what makes the Shiite version of Islam corrupt and, if it is, show Rubasha and her family so that they can turn to the correct path to paradise."

There was a moment of silence and then my father's face relaxed. He then became quite complimentary for my noble reason for attending the imam bargah and how that in this way I could become a witness to Rubasha and her family.

After drinking tea, it was time for me to retire to bed. But while lying in bed, I went back over the conversations I had had with Rubasha earlier in the day and the conversations with my Mulvi and my father. We had been brought up to believe that Islam was the perfect religion and we had to maintain the five pillars to assure our place in paradise. But when I told my Mulvi that some of my classmates weren't totally dedicated to the Islamic faith, my Mulvi said that in the end it was really up to the clemency of the Prophet that enabled us to get into heaven.

Now I was hearing more of the lengthy Terms and Conditions required to get into paradise. Even though someone believed in Allah and His Messenger, observed the five pillars of the faith, and was overall a virtuous person, dressing appropriately, acting appropriately and speaking appropriately, the thoughts one entertained in one's mind about certain historical characters who had been in association with the Prophet may be the wrong thoughts to have about these people. The thoughts we entertained about these supposedly significant historical figures who were instrumental in getting the Islamic faith to become a firmly established religion may be the wrong thoughts to have about them and could ultimately be the cause for us entering an eternity in hell alongside all the other really bad people who one would think would be more deserving of this awful place.

But I knew very little of the Shiite sect. Apart from what Rubasha had told me that day about certain aspects of her faith, I realized how I knew almost nothing about the Shiites except that Sunnis believed that Shiites had corrupted the Islamic faith.

But Rubasha had shown in our conversation earlier that day that she believed in very much the same things that Sunnis believed in, especially those things that were fundamental to the Islamic faith. So, I was at a forked road. Was Rubasha really a Muslim because she believed in the same fundamentals as I did and was a well behaved young lady? Or was she not a Muslim and therefore going to hell simply because of these seemingly small differences between the Sunni and Shiite faith? And if she were following a corrupt version of Islam, therefore she would be condemned in the next life to live eternally in the fires of hell. And I didn't want that. Rubasha was a lovely young lady and a fellow student. I certainly would not like to see her burning in the fires of Jahannam. But the only way to prevent her from entering this evil eternity was to find out more about the Shiite sect and, once I knew more about it, show Rubasha the error of her ways and bring her back into the light of the truth of the pure form of Islam so that Rubasha could live eternally in paradise with me.

Chapter 6

It wasn't long after my conversation with Rubasha that I decided to accompany her to Friday prayers at her local imam bargah. Before I left, my father gave me strict instructions to pray the way I had been taught at the mosque as a child, something that sounded quite strange at the time but had great significance later in the day.

I walked around to Rubasha's place, walked up the stairs to her apartment and was warmly greeted once again by her mother who answered the door. However, she greeted me ever so much nicer than the first time I had come around. It took me by surprise but I simply put it down to mere Pakistani hospitality.

As it happened the last time I went to Rubasha's place, I was invited to take a seat on the sofa. Once seated, Rubasha's mother asked me if I wanted a cup of tea and something to eat.

At this time, a young man who looked a little older than me and who resembled Rubasha entered the room and introduced himself as Reza. This was Rubasha's brother. He approached me with an extended arm and I stood up and grabbed his hand with a solid handshake. We had barely made our acquaintance when suddenly Mr Hussain entered the room. Once again I stood up and shook his hand although this time with greater reverence seeing he was the master of the house. Mr Hussain was a tall man, quite handsome, with dark skin, and salt-and-pepper hair that continued down to his well-trimmed moustache and beard. He was well-dressed as would be expected of a man of his calibre and background. Mr Hussain welcomed me to resume my place on the sofa in a very gentlemanly way as if he were a member of the English aristocracy.

"So, you must be Mustafa Faakhtaa," he followed with almost a regal voice in beautiful polished English. "I'm really pleased to meet you. My daughter has spoken a lot about you and I'm finally delighted to meet this Mustafa I've heard so much about."

Mr Hussain then settled back in his chair. Mrs Hussain poured tea into a cup, placed it before him on the coffee table and then disappeared out of the room.

"So, you study at school together?" Mr Hussain continued.

"Yes, Rubasha is in a number of my classes."

"And she tells me you are a very bright student. And she tells me that you are very religious."

When he said this, the blood rushed to my head. I was aware of the antagonism between Sunnis and Shiites and so now I was a little unsettled.

"I guess you could say that," I said by way of respectful reply.

"That's good. It's good that a young man like you takes his religion seriously. We live in a country where the state religion is Islam but a lot of people only pay lip service to the religion and don't take it terribly seriously."

Mrs Hussain returned with a plate on which were various biscuits and cream crackers elegantly spread around the plate, first offered me one, then to Mr Hussain and Reza, and then placed the plate on the coffee table before once again disappearing out of the room.

"Rubasha tells me that you are of the Sunni sect and that you know the Koran well."

I could feel the heat in my face after Mr Hussain made that comment.

"I wouldn't say I knew it well," I replied as humbly as I could. "I have read all of the Koran but in Arabic only. I only understand parts of it at the moment but I'm doing my best to master it."

"You're a good man," Mr Hussain continued. "Not many young people your age apply themselves to reading the Koran in the Arabic or even reading the Koran at all. Most young people these days only hear about what is written in the Koran and the teachings of Islam at Friday prayers. Very few have ever read it for themselves and hence have no idea what is actually written within."

I really didn't know what to say to that. I was struck completely off balance by such a complimentary comment.

Eventually, Rubasha entered slowly and sedately into the room. She was wearing what was traditionally the correct religious apparel for a woman entering an Islamic holy place. It was the first time I had seen her so religiously attired, wearing a black veil to cover her head with only her face exposed. I looked on aghast at her. Rubasha had completely transformed from a regular school girl into a pious, religious saint. She did not sit down though but remained standing over on the side of the room. Soon after, her mother appeared similarly attired. With that, Mr Hussain made a move to stand up which was the signal for all of us to go.

We all made our way to the imam bargah on foot. It was a good distance away and in an area of Alekh-Jahan I had never been to before. The walk there was no different to my usual stroll to the mosque with my father except that I was going in a different direction. Among the street hawkers of Alekh-Jahan's major roadways was the normal haphazard traffic of downtown Karachi.

Along the way, a group of people mingled amongst Rubasha's family and it was obvious that they knew each other. Among them I met a young man called Afghar who looked about the same age as Reza. He was a rather average looking guy, certainly not blessed with features that would make him the most desired man in the suburb. Afghar,

Reza and I entered into conversation, and exchanged pleasantries and small-talk while we made our way to the place of prayer.

Once we had arrived at the imam bargah, the women and men went to separate sections. Reza, Afghar and I entered together while Mr Hussain went off to mingle amongst a group of men of his age.

This was the first time I had actually seen an imam bargah in real life. What struck me about the imam bargah was how the structure to some degree looked like our traditional mosque. However, on the grounds of the imam bargah was a large model of a mausoleum. This mausoleum was an exact replica of the main mausoleum in Karbala, the original mausoleum housing the last resting place of Ali, Muhammad's son-in-law and the fourth caliph after the prophet Muhammad, but also Ali's son Hussain, and Ali's sister Zainab, and here in this place of prayer was a replica of it. In other words, there was a tomb in the precinct of the house of the eternally living God.

The internals of the imam bargah, however, were much the same as in the mosque I attended, with the mithrab, an elaborately decorated enclosure in one wall showing the direction or *qibla* of prayer, and prayer mats scattered over the floor. In fact, I would never have known I was in a house of prayer belonging to a different sect of the Islamic faith.

Until it came to actually performing the prayers.

For me as a Sunni, during the ritual of prayer, once the imam has said *Allahu akhbar,* our hands are raised to our ears, and then we cross our arms across our navel. By contrast, the Shiites, after they have placed their hands at their ears, they drop them down to their sides and then extend their hands out, palms raised as if they were beggars begging for alms. Then, when they get down on their prayer mats, they prostrate with their forehead touching a clay tablet called a *turbah.*

I noticed that it was quite crowded in the imam bargah, but then I remembered that it was the month of Muharram. This is a holy month for Shiites. Shiites venerate this month because it is during this month that they commemorate the Battle of Karbala. This is a battle during which the grandson of the Prophet died along with all his male heirs.

Once the ritual inside the imam bargah was complete, all the devotees went outside into a large courtyard where a certain ceremony I was unfamiliar with took place. This ceremony is called *azadari*. I had heard of this ceremony and this was the first time I saw it happen before my very eyes. I stood against a wall in the courtyard together with Reza and watched on while Afghar and a number of other dedicated Shiites flogged themselves while they recited prayers and chanted in ecstasy. Some of them flogged themselves using merely their hands, hitting their bare chests. Others, however, flogged themselves with a lethal looking thing made up of metal chains and what looked like blades of small knives on them, beating their chests and back. It didn't take long before these men in total ecstasy were drenched in their own blood. But it was horrific to watch. What drove these men into such ecstasy to cause so much harm to themselves? Further, I was not acquainted with any of this from the Koran nor from my Mulvi.

This went on for quite some time and I can only guess that with such a loss of blood these men would have eventually met their deaths had it not been for the attendance of medical staff to administer first aid. I found this quite disturbing, both from the point of view that these men inflicted such horrific pain on themselves so willingly, and further that there was no call in Islam as far as I was aware that required them to do so. It was difficult and gruesome to watch and yet at the same time I was compelled to observe this horrific ritual till its conclusion, with puddles of blood forming on the ground beneath them.

Eventually we were escorted to another area on the grounds of the imam bargah where there had been no blood spilled, to another type of courtyard, on the ground of which blankets and place mats had been placed. Reza chose a place to sit down together with a group of other men that he was obviously acquainted with. Reza, the honourable person that he was, introduced me to all those amongst our group and each shook hands with me in welcome. Not long after this, volunteers came around bringing bowls of food, placing them in the middle of our groups and soon we began to eat.

Reza eventually turned to me. "Rubasha said that you had some questions about our version of Islam you'd like to ask."

I began to feel a little uncomfortable. My back stiffened while I thought about it. There were so many things that the leaders and other members of my sect had criticized the Shiites of observing that I thought if I started expressing these views it would cause some friction. But Reza had asked the question and it sounded as if it were open for me to discuss any point I so desired and how I viewed these points irrespective of how it sounded to Shiite ears. There were so many things I wanted to ask and as I looked around I saw some calligraphy elegantly written on the building wall which called to mind the Islamic Holy Book.

"Reza, Shiites believe that the Koran has been corrupted. But the Koran says quite clearly that it has never been changed. As it says in Al-Anaam 6:34, 'there is none that can alter the Words of Allah'. Again, later in the same surah, in Al-Anaam 6:115, it says 'none can change His words'. If the Koran is the Word of Allah, then it hasn't been corrupted. Otherwise this is a contradiction."

Reza looked at me with a strange expression on his face. "Who told you that Shiites believe the Koran has been corrupted?" he asked quietly and gently. Just the fact that he had met my brazen accusation gentlemanly was very striking to me and really showed up his character. "We Shiites also acknowledge that the Koran has never been corrupted and for the same reasons as you Sunnis. We also acknowledge that this is the Book of Allah and how that Allah protects His Book from any additions or subtractions, from any distortions and corruptions of any kind. Allah would never send down His Book and then allow it to be corrupted or changed at all."

This was rather perplexing. Why, then, had my father said that the Shiites had corrupted the Koran when Reza acknowledged to the contrary that the Koran had never been changed in any way? Reza's friends in our little gathering also acknowledged that they also accepted that the Koran was Allah's holy book, complete and without adulteration. I didn't know what to say and so I didn't make any further comment to that.

Reza's friendliness and gentlemanly composure was quite striking. I realized the sincerity of his belief and no doubt if he were misguided, it was not due to a total desire to believe the wrong thing. However, Sunni and Shiite versions of Islam were not the same and so it was important to determine who was right and who was wrong.

"I stand corrected," I said as a respectful comment to meet Reza's gentlemanly composure. "However, there are some differences between our sects. One thing different between us Sunnis and you Shiites is that you recognize Ali as a great figure and in particular the rightful heir to the caliphate after Muhammad and as a result he deserves our reverence almost as much as the prophet. You call this leadership through Ali an imamate and not a caliphate. However, being a Sunni, I recognize him merely as one of the rightfully guided caliphs and that the caliphate fell first to the rightful caliph, Abubaker."

Reza smiled, grabbed a small handful of food, placed it in his mouth, chewed a bit, swallowed and then sat up.

"Ali was the rightful caliph after Muhammad. This is true. Haven't you read about the life of Muhammad and what occurred just before he died, all recorded in the venerable Hadiths? On his last pilgrimage, in the same year that the Prophet died, Muhammad taught all the Muslims of the time how to perform the pilgrimage correctly. It was the largest gathering of Muslims on pilgrimage in the time of the Prophet. After completing the pilgrimage and on his way back to Medina, Muhammad stopped at a place called Ghadeer Khumm. At this place the verse in the Koran from Al-Ma'idah 5:67 was revealed to him which says, 'O Messenger! Convey what has been revealed to you from your Lord, and if you do not, then you have not conveyed His message. And Allah will protect you from the people.' Muhammad then ordered a high platform to be constructed. It took hours to construct. Once completed, the Prophet mounted the platform and spent more hours reciting to the people from the Koran. Muhammad knew that he would soon be taken to paradise and so in part of this sermon he declared to the people, 'I am leaving you two things: the Book of Allah and my *Ahlul Bayt*', the Ahlul Bayt being the family of Muhammad, through his son-in-law, Ali. Muhammad then said to the people, 'Don't you know that I have more right over you than you have over yourselves?' to which the people agreed. Then the Prophet called up Ali to mount the platform with him, grabbed the hand of Ali and held his hand so high in the sky that the Prophet's garment fell so you could see his armpit, and then declared, 'he of whom I am the *mawla*, of him Ali is also the *mawla*'. Muhammad was the mawla, the spiritual leader of the Muslim community, and Muhammad knew he was soon going to die and so he ensured that the people knew who they should recognize after his death as the new leader, the new mawla. To seal the completeness of the handing over of the mawla-ship from Muhammad to Ali, the verse from Surah Al-Ma'idah 5:3 was revealed to Muhammad where it says,

'This day have I perfected your religion for you, completed My favour upon you and have chosen for you Islam as your religion'. This shows that Islam was perfected and completed with the announcement of Ali as the rightful successor after Muhammad. This is unequivocal evidence that Ali was the rightful successor of leadership as the new mawla.

But when Muhammad died, Abubaker took leadership of the caliphate unlawfully. Ali could have fought for the rightful place as the successor of Muhammad. But he knew that his supporters were of small number in comparison to the supporters of Abubaker, and this would have led to the true Islam being extinguished.

The problem with the majority of Sunnis is that they do not explore deeply into historical matters but only believe their religion superficially. The few Sunnis who actually do explore deeply into historical matters only look at those things that justify their point of view or manipulate what is written to support their own selfish desires."

This last comment about the Sunnis sounded like a personal affront against me. I could not speak on behalf of all Sunnis but I knew as it was for me, what I believed was because of my total devotion to Allah, irrespective of what I desired. However, I listened on to what Reza had to say.

"There are few Sunni Muslims who are even aware of what happened at Ghadeer Khumm. But those who do simply say that Muhammad was declaring Ali's virtue. What they say is that there were murmurings amongst the groups of people against Ali so Muhammad had to get everyone to respect Ali. But there are quite a lot of documented sources, not just Shiite sources but even Sunni sources, that show that what happened at Ghadeer Khumm was more than a declaration that Ali required respect.

Many Sunnis downplay the word 'mawla', not only what it means but also why the Prophet chose this word. Many Sunnis claim that the Prophet could have used the Arabic word *khalifa*, that is, 'caliph', if he had intended to nominate Ali as the successor caliph after Muhammad had died. But what Sunnis don't quite get is that Prophet Muhammad was not simply talking about a temporal leadership. I mean, there are earlier documented histories which already claimed that Ali was nominated caliph prior to the events at Ghadeer Khumm and of course both Sunnis and Shiites acknowledge that at some point in history Ali did become caliph. But at Ghadeer Khumm, the proclamation that as Muhammad was the mawla so Ali was the mawla who succeeded him was a divine proclamation made by the Prophet Muhammad himself. Are Sunnis going to declare that Prophet Muhammad was wrong? Those who took the caliphate after Muhammad died, Abubaker, Omar and Uthman, were never declared to be the mawla, not by the Prophet, nor by any other prophet. This declaration of mawla-ship was uniquely given to Ali."

Reza then paused and finally concluded with, "Don't take my word for it. Look it up and read it for yourself in your own histories and Hadiths."

Reza answered my question extremely well. The difficulty was that he explained historical detail and quoted the Hadiths, details of which I was totally ignorant of. My Mulvi had said nothing of this piece of what sounded like very important historical detail. I was not familiar with these hadiths but Reza quoted them with confidence. I was quite taken aback by this. Was it possible that I was following the wrong sect by not acknowledging Ali in the same way as the Shiites did but rather believing that Abubaker was the rightful successor to the caliphate after Muhammad, especially as this proclamation that Ali was the mawla came straight from Muhammad?

I didn't know what to say to that. Not once in my learning about the Islamic faith had I heard or given any dedication to Ali. All veneration was given to Allah and to His direct Messenger, Muhammad. But the information that Reza had provided me, the sincerity in its delivery and the acceptance by his fellow Shiites around me gave me the impression that what Reza was telling me was true and therefore justified. If this were the case, could it be that I was observing the wrong sect of Islam? Would my entrance into paradise be jeopardized as a result?

I really didn't know what to say to that. Seeing throughout all my religious instruction I had never heard of the reverence for Ali or that he was specifically made Muhammad's successor as the replacement mawla, although Reza had justified this thoroughly, what he said had to be wrong if Sunnis believed it to be wrong. But I had nothing to counter his argument and so left it for a later time when I had time to research this further.

"Another question," I then asked, "is, why do you pray in an imam bargah? And why do you have a mausoleum on mosque grounds? Why do you have a house for the dead on the grounds next to the house of the living God? The mosque is the most holy place for Muslims and it should not be defiled with other things on the grounds. A mosque, or as it is in Arabic, a masjid, is a place of prayer, a place for 'sajada', that is, a place for prostrating before Allah."

Reza laughed gently. It sounded as if he had heard this before from a thousand Sunnis before me.

"Yah Mustafa. Yes, this is an imam bargah. We use an imam bargah for ceremonies like this azadari, the one we had today. But, no, an imam bargah is not a masjid and we Shiites have never said that it was. We also pray in mosques, mosques that are reserved solely for prayer, and we keep these holy. However, we also have other holy buildings, imam bargahs, as a place, yes, also for prayer, but also for other religious ceremonies.

Again, Sunni Muslims ignore the significance of the imam bargah. The imam bargah contains a replica of the mausoleum in Karbala. Again, Sunni Muslims do not know their history or only skim the surface and only recognize those things that suit their own desires. The Battle of Karbala is recognized by both Sunnis and Shiites alike in our histories if Sunnis cared to read them in full. This was a time when Ali's son, Hussain, was killed for not swearing allegiance to the caliph Yazid I. Hussain was the rightful caliph at this time, especially as he was the son of Ali to whom Muhammad passed on the mawla-ship and who was part of the Ahlul-Bayt, the House of the Family of Muhammad, that Muhammad had left as his legacy. Yazid usurped this and demanded Hussain to recognize him as caliph but Hussain in his devotion to Allah refused which is why Hussain preferred to fight and die to follow Allah. Hussain's death is not simply a tragic part of Islamic history. It is the symbol of sacrifice in the struggle between right and wrong, the struggle for truth and justice against wrongdoing and falsehood. But further, Hussain was beloved of the Prophet so much so that in the Hadith Tirmidhi 5, Chapter 48, hadith 3775, Muhammad said that 'Hussain is from me and I am from Hussain. Allah loves whoever loves Hussain'. So reverence for Hussain once again is not baseless but comes from the mouth of the very Prophet that both Sunnis and Shiites recognize as the Messenger of Allah. Therefore, our reverence for Hussain, Muhammad's own grandson, and the place where he was buried is a very deep symbol for us Shiites. It doesn't replace our reverence for the Prophet, nor for Mecca, the holiest of all places. In a way, our reverence for Hussain is reverence to the holy Prophet because, again, the Prophet said, 'Hussain is from me and I am from Hussain' and so our reverence for Hussain is still reverence for the holy Prophet. But like you Sunnis, we also have mosques and these mosques are places purely for prayer."

Again, Reza gave an explanation for his version of his faith. However, he quoted from a hadith I had never heard of. Even so, I was aware that there were Hadiths and so it was up to me to go and read all this myself to see if what Reza was saying was really backed up from the commentaries.

Reza's confident speech and his gentle and thorough explanation made me feel less that he was an enemy and more like a co-religionist that I began to feel that my questions about the Shiites were less antagonistic and more the genuine search for truth. I did get a little offended when he made statements that Sunnis only believe their versions of events because of their own evil desires because this implied that I only followed the Sunni understanding of Islam merely because I wanted to. At least as it was for me, I had grown up in a Sunni family and hence this was all I knew.

However, I was now emboldened in my quest for truth to ask questions about those things that were foreign to my understanding of the faith.

"I noticed," I began on a new topic of conversation, "that when you pray, you and all the other Shiites in the imam bargah placed your foreheads on a turbah. Why do you pray on a turbah and why do you pray on a rock that has the inscription of names other than Allah? When you prostrate yourself on this rock, doesn't this mean that you are committing sheerk and praying to others apart from Allah? Isn't this some form of idolatry?"

Reza leaned back holding his legs and smiled. "Yes," he replied, "I've heard many Sunnis say that. For a start, the turbah is not a rock but it is soil from the grounds of Karbala where Hussain and his family were murdered. So to us this is holy ground. When we pray, we must pray on natural things, not on artificial objects. This turbah is a portion of the soil from Karbala so it is natural. Again, we use the turbah to rest our foreheads on while we pray and this is sunna. In Sahih Bukhari Volume 3, Book 33, Number 244, also cited obliquely in Sahih Al-Bukhari, Vol 1, Book 12, Number 798, there is a story where the prophet was praying in a mosque that was made of date palm branches. One day while inside this mosque, it was raining heavily so that the rain penetrated through the roof onto the floor of the mosque. The Prophet led the congregation in prayer regardless and as a result the devotees saw the marks of mud on his forehead, obviously caused by the rain which had mixed with the soil they were praying on. In the same way, we have something made of soil on which our foreheads touch when we are led in prayer just as it was with the Prophet."

Again, I was amazed at Reza's extensive knowledge. But still there was something that didn't quite make sense.

"But Reza, why do you have the names of Ali, Fatima, Hussain and the like inscribed on your turbah? Doesn't that mean that you are praying to these people? And these people were after all only people. Isn't this idolatry?"

Reza smiled and touched me on the shoulder.

"Yah Mustafa," Reza replied. "Don't you, as a Muslim, pray towards the black rock in Mecca when you pray five times a day? Why do we pray to the black rock? Does that mean we are committing idolatry five times a day when we pray towards the black rock? We pray *in the direction of* the black rock, not *to* the black rock. In the same way we pray *on* the turbah, not *to* the turbah."

I was stunned by the comparison. I had never thought of this before. I had always prayed towards Mecca, towards the black rock and had never thought twice about it. But now this was called into question. But with further complications when Reza added, "haven't you read what it says in the Holy Koran, in Al-Baqarah 2:144 'We see the turning of your face to the heavens: now shall We turn you to a Qibla that shall please you. Turn then your face in the direction of the Sacred Mosque: wherever you are, turn your faces in that direction'. Even Allah Himself commands us to pray towards the black rock in Mecca. So if Allah commands us to do that, how can this be idolatry? We are not praying to the black rock as an object of adoration but simply as a direction towards which our prayers are to be made. In the same way, when we touch the turbah with our foreheads, we are not worshipping the turbah nor are we acknowledging that the names inscribed on the turbah are worthy of our worship. All our worship is towards Allah."

What could I say to that? If I said that the turbah, an object made of dirt on which the Shiites prostrated, was a form of idolatry, I had to admit that Muslims praying towards the black rock in Mecca was also a form of idolatry and that Muhammad through the Koran had instructed us to be idolatrous. But I believed Muhammad was the Prophet of Allah. But also, Reza had justified the use of the turbah from what was written in the Hadiths which I couldn't deny. Yet, it had never been a practice within the Sunni sect to pray on such objects. We simply prayed on a prayer mat and our foreheads touched the floor on the mat we prayed on. Were we supposed to pray on a turbah?

Afghar came past and he was all bandaged up from his self-flagellation. He sat down on the far side of our group and those on that side began passing food to him. This diverted my thoughts to a new topic and therefore a new question.

"Reza, why did these men flagellate themselves today?"

Reza gave out a deep sigh. "They do this in commemoration of the sacrifice and martyrdom that Hussain and his household suffered at the Battle of Karbala. These people cause themselves to suffer in the same way as Hussain and his household suffered on the battlefield. It is a way of showing their respect to Hussain so that we don't forget the suffering he went through so that such a massacre is never repeated."

"Then, why didn't you flagellate yourself today?" I asked.

Reza smiled, leant back holding his legs and then straightened up. "Yes, I know it's a way to commemorate the terrible tragedy of the battlefield and to remember Hussain and his suffering, but I personally don't feel it's necessary for me to do it. It's not sunna as there is nothing in the literature which supports this type of behaviour but at the same time I don't see a problem with it. It is their way of empathizing with Hussain and his household's suffering. I personally think it is enough to actually dedicate time in reflection and setting time aside as we do in this month to remember what happened at the Battle of Karbala. Maybe self-flagellation is an extreme way of showing one's solidarity. It's not something I'd personally do but I don't see any harm in it."

When Reza said this, I couldn't help noticing the oddness in his choice of wording when he said that there was no harm in self-flagellation. These guys actually drew blood and some used that awful metal whip-like contraption which drew a significant amount of blood, and there were, after all, medics on site to administer treatment.

"Hi, there, Mustafa," we heard a voice say behind us which completely interrupted my thoughts. We turned to look up and there was Reza's father standing imposingly behind us like a regal figure. "I hope you enjoyed yourself here and learned something about our version of Islam."

"Yes, thank you, sir, I did. Your son was most hospitable," I replied and then scrambled to stand up as did the others in our group.

"Okay, son," Mr Hussain then said after turning towards Reza. "It looks like Michael is bringing forth a storm so we should start making a move to go home."

It is amazing how a mundane comment can be the cause of a cascade of thoughts. Michael was bringing forth a storm? Reza and I looked up at the sky and could see in the distance the oncoming rainclouds. But it was the fact that Mr Hussain had attributed the coming storm to Michael the Archangel that sent my thoughts flowing.

Michael the Archangel, so I had been taught, was the angel of rain and storms, and hence when a rainstorm or thunderstorm raged it was through the power of Michael the Archangel. Angels play a prominent role in Islam, and in fact, we are required as Muslims to believe in the existence of angels as the Koran commands us to do so. But for the first time, the question came to me. Why does Allah need angels? Wasn't Allah the All-Powerful and the All-Wise and He just has to say "be" and whatever He commands happens? So why did He need angels?

When I thought longer on it, I thought of the other angels. There was the angel Gabriel, the messenger angel who spoke to Muhammad as well as to other prophets such as Issa. There was the angel Raphael who held the trumpet ready to blow to bring on the last days of earth and summon all those who have ever lived to Judgement Day. There was the angel Israel who takes out the souls from the dead. There was Malik, the terrifying angel of death, who will cast the unbelievers into Jahannam on the last day. There were hundreds and thousands of angels which carried out many a duty on behalf of Allah.

What struck me was how similar this was to Hinduism, the prominent religion in our southern neighbour, India. Hindus believe in many gods, each god carrying out its own function. I knew very little of Hinduism but at least I knew a little bit because there were Hindus within our community. According to Hindus, the god Indra is the god of storms. I could imagine that in the local Hindu temple, the Hindu equivalent of Mr Hussain was saying, "Okay, son. It looks like Indra is bringing forth a storm so we should start making a move to go home." Which made me ask internally the question: how different really was Islam from Hinduism? In this particular case I saw a striking similarity: what we call angels in Islam, they call them gods in Hinduism. And the similarities were strong. There was a cognate god in Hinduism to the angels in Islam. First there was the comparison between Michael and Indra as the controller of storms. And then there was Krishna, the messenger god who spoke to the chariot rider, Arjuna, who was like Gabriel, the messenger angel who spoke to Muhammad. And there was the Hindu god, Naraka, the god of hell, similar to the angel Malik, the chief guard of hell as mentioned in Surah Az-Zukhruf 43:77.

Further, the Koran says quite explicitly in Al-Baqarah 2:98 that "Whoever is an enemy to Allah and His Angels... and Gabriel and Michael, then indeed Allah is an enemy to the disbelievers". Because we had been told that the Koran is eternal, this means that this statement is eternal, which therefore implies that all the angels including Gabriel and Michael are eternal, just like the Hindus believe about their gods. The Hindus, as far as I was aware, believed in one overarching god, Brahma, and all the lower gods came under Brahma's authority. But what made all the lesser gods in Hinduism gods was their much greater power than humans and moreso their immortality. These lesser gods may have been created and therefore were subordinate to Brahma, but they were still considered gods because of their immortality and divine powers. I couldn't help but notice that the koranic view of Allah and His angels looked exactly the same.

For the first time I noticed how Hinduism and Islam weren't too different after all. Further, I wondered to what extent one could really call Islam a monotheistic religion. It was true that in Islam we were supposedly ferociously believers in purely one God, Allah. However, I could see that instead of completely getting rid of the entire concept of polytheism, Islam had simply changed the word "gods" and instead used the word "angels". But apart from a name change, the angels' god-like nature and functions remained intact. In this particular instance, Michael the Archangel had to be a powerful entity much more powerful than any human as he had control of the rain and storms. His power only became even more powerful when we considered how large the world was. For all the rainclouds and storms that rage over the entire globe to be under the power of the one angel, this Michael the Archangel must have great divine powers indeed. And it was implied that Michael had always been doing this ever since the creation of the world, so while many generations of people were born, lived, then died, Michael continued and would continue to live on.

What further made the idea complicated was that it said in the Koran that it was Allah who took command of the rain and the storms, scattering the clouds around and causing the rain to fall as it says in Surah Ar-Rum 30:48 and Surah Luqman 31:10. If this is the case, why did Allah actually need Michael at all? When Allah created Michael the Archangel and delegated to him the responsibility of controlling these meteorological phenomena, was this so Allah, who never slumbers, could rest from this duty and occupy His time playing on His smartphone or doing some other more enjoyable and pleasurable task?

I further imagined myself standing together with a Hindu counterpart of myself observing this climatic phenomenon and the two of us arguing over who was the real cause of the storm. I would argue that it was Michael the Archangel and my Hindu counterpart would insist that it was Indra. The difficulty was that it would be impossible to prove who was right and who was wrong simply by observing the development of the storm. We now have powerful telescopes to observe the sky and planes fly up through the clouds within Michael's or Indra's domain, but these so-called invisible yet powerful entities defy our observation. If they are beyond our perception and detection, how on earth do we know they really exist except that it says so in our respective sacred texts? When it came down to it, I only knew that it was Michael who caused the storms because Islamic literature said that it was and my Hindu counterpart would argue it was Indra because he believed what it said in Hindu literature. And my Hindu counterpart and I only believed our respective bodies of literature were true because someone had told us that this was so.

And once again I found myself in the throes of doublethink. We believe in one God only. And I must believe this to make it into paradise. At the same time, I need to believe in the existence of these godlike creatures, which were simply the lesser gods in a polytheistic belief system but just not called gods to maintain this idea of monotheism.

Fortunately, Michael or Indra or Allah or whoever was the commander of the clouds managed to hold the reins on the storm for some time. Rubasha's family and I made it back to Rubasha's place while the rainclouds hung ominously heavy from the sky but the potential storm was held at bay. I thanked Mr and Mrs Hussain for allowing me to accompany them to the imam bargah and become acquainted with this alternate branch of Islam. I particularly thanked Reza who had provided me a greater insight into what the Shiites believe and the basis for their beliefs. All the family members then went into the building but Rubasha stayed outside just a little longer.

"Thank you so much for coming," Rubasha said shyly. "I was really pleased you came. And I can see that my parents and my brother like you a lot."

"Well, I really like them too," I replied. "Your brother was particularly hospitable and I greatly appreciated that."

I took a furtive glance up into the heavens. What was happening in the sky was in a way an exteriorization of what was occurring within the world of my mind.

"I guess I'd better go," I then concluded.

Rubasha smiled in silent agreement and then entered her building. With that, I turned and went home.

During my stroll back, all that kept going through my mind was, what an experience! It was completely taxing on my entire thought system. I thought about the Hussain family's wonderful hospitality but moreso how Reza was able to answer my questions to support his beliefs using Islamic literature, the Koran and the Hadiths. But at the same time I couldn't agree with him. But why couldn't I when we both used as the source of our beliefs the same sacred texts?

It wasn't long before I got home. When I reached the entrance to my apartment block, I stopped and sighed. Gentle drops of rain began falling on my head and a gust of wind passed by and whipped up the dust. The rumblings of an impending storm could be heard which were an ominous foreboding.

When I got inside my unit, my grandmother and mother were there. My grandmother asked me if I wanted tea to which I replied in the affirmative when at that moment my father and grandfather walked in the door. They greeted us, and my father commented about just getting into the building in time, while the two men took off the appropriate excess clothing they had been wearing, and then came and sat down around the coffee table. My grandmother soon came to the table with tea and biscuits.

"So, how was it, son?" my father asked.

"It was interesting," I replied cautiously. I took a slight pause. The storm outside had begun to make its presence felt. I looked towards the window and then back at my father.

"Father, why aren't Shiites Muslims?"

"Because they have corrupted the message delivered to us by Muhammad," my father replied militantly. "They believe in things that are not part of the Islamic faith."

"But I spoke with Reza, Rubasha's brother," I replied hesitantly, "and he demonstrated quite clearly the basis of the Shiite version of their beliefs and I could not answer him or find fault in his basis."

"Such as?" my father asked.

"Well," I began, swallowed, and continued, "Let's start with Ali. We believe that Ali was one of the rightly guided caliphs, one of the four after Muhammad, that is, after Abubaker, Omar and Uthman. But the Shiites believe that Ali was more than that, that he deserves special status because he was specifically nominated as the new leader of the Islamic community after Muhammad died. Reza explained to me that on Muhammad's last pilgrimage, on his way back to Medinah from Mecca, he arrived at a place called Ghadeer Khumm. Allah sent down the verse from Al-Ma'idah 5:67 which says, 'O Messenger! Proclaim the Message which has been sent to you from your Lord. If you do not, you will not have fulfilled and proclaimed His mission. And Allah will defend you from men.' As a result, Muhammad built a platform which took hours to complete. He then sat atop the platform, held Ali's hand and declared, 'he of whom I am the *mawla*, of him Ali is also the *mawla*'. Reza further explained that when Muhammad had finally made this claim, another verse from the Koran was revealed to him, from Surah Al-Ma'idah 5:3 where Allah said, 'This day have I perfected your religion for you, completed my favour upon you and have chosen for you Islam as your religion'. It seems from this explanation that the Shiites have a point when they claim that Ali was the rightful mawla and therefore caliph after Muhammad and not Abubaker, Omar and Uthman."

My father sat up erect and let out an exasperated sigh.

"That's not what that means!" my father spurted. "You have to read that declaration in the context of the time and not construe the declaration like the Shiites do to suit their own perversity and corruption. Ali had just completed a victorious conquest in Yemen and he wanted to hand all the spoils of war over to the Prophet and not distribute the spoils immediately. As a result of seeing Ali's continual fidelity, the Prophet declared to the people not to become Ali's enemy. Rather, they were to remain Ali's friend. And as the Prophet Muhammad was their friend, their mawla, so Ali was their friend, their mawla. After all, 'mawla' here means 'friend' and not 'Lord' as the Shiites like to interpret it according to their own wilful desires. Why didn't the

Prophet announce this at Mecca, the centre and font of the Islamic religion? Rather, why would the Prophet announce the succession of leadership to Ali at this strange out-of-the-way place, a place where there was no water and most inconvenient for people, and most certainly not all Muslims were there anyway because some no doubt had left Mecca to go in a different direction to return to their home cities?"

I listened to my father's explanation while the rain beat down and the distant thunder serenaded us.

"Further," my father continued, "as for the verse from Surah Al-Ma'idah 5:3, Muhammad did not proclaim this verse at Ghadeer Khumm. He proclaimed this verse at Mecca during the last days of the Hajj. It makes more sense that he proclaimed the completion and perfection of the Islamic faith at the centre of the religion during Muhammad's last pilgrimage to Mecca in order to begin the continual link between Muhammad's last pilgrimage and the continual line of pilgrimages observed by Muslims from that time ever since, a continual line that leads us back to Muhammad."

I didn't have an answer to this. I didn't know any of this history. However, my father took a sip of tea I guess for lubrication so that he could continue.

"Not only that, when Muhammad died, Abukaber was the best candidate for the caliphate to replace Muhammad, and not Ali. First, consider the age difference. Ali was a young man whereas Abubaker was much older. Abubaker was also wiser and more composed. Abubaker was the best friend of the prophet and had helped the Prophet when the Prophet needed him the most. And he continued this help once the Prophet had died. The entire Muslim community was traumatized that the Prophet was dead and no-one was able to speak. Only Abubaker was the strongest in soul to be able to console the people and get the people to function once again as a community. During a Friday sermon, Abubaker declared that those who worship Muhammad should acknowledge that Muhammad is dead. Those who worship Allah should know that Allah is still there and worthy of our worship."

My father paused, took a deep breath and continued. "By contrast, Ali was too traumatized after hearing the news of the death of the Prophet to function properly. In fact, when Ali heard the news that the Prophet was dead, Ali almost cut off the head of the person who had brought him the news. This shows that at this time Ali was not the best person to take on the leadership of the Muslim community. He was too young and emotionally weak. Abubaker was more experienced and much more emotionally strong."

Once again, I was at a loss. I knew none of this history. If what my father had said was true, then I could well follow his argument. But Reza had also explained in depth why he and all the Shiites gave reverence to Ali. My father did agree with the proclamation of Ali as the replacement mawla but he gave a different interpretation of the word. As for the verse from Al-Ma'idah 5:3, my father agreed that it was revealed during Muhammad's last pilgrimage, but at Mecca, not at Ghadeer Khumm.

I was at a loss of what to say. I did not have the depth of knowledge to provide myself a definitive position either way. Both Reza and my father had provided a depth of background to back up their arguments and yet they both came up with different conclusions.

My father sat back on the sofa but he was still restless and fidgety.

"And I hope you prayed the proper way, the way you were taught to at the mosque," my father grunted.

I nodded in confirmation. "Yes," I then worded my confirmation, "I noticed that the way they pray is a little different to the way we pray. But I prayed the way I have always done even though it was different to the Shiite way of praying."

"Good!" my father replied. "And I guess you saw all those Shiites praying on those idolatrous turbahs!"

"Are they really that idolatrous?" I asked. I then explained what Reza had told me about the reasoning behind the use of the turbahs from the hadith that Reza had quoted about Muhammad leading a small community in prayer while it rained through the roof of the mosque which made the floor muddy, so that there was a patch of mud stuck to the Prophet's forehead. I then went on to explain what Reza had told me about there being no difference between praying on the turbah and praying towards the black rock. If we were to accuse the Shiites of being idolatrous for praying on a turbah, we were also at the same time being idolatrous for praying towards the black rock in Mecca.

"What nonsense!" my father exclaimed. "I don't believe his explanation of this hadith. Why would Muhammad tell us to do ablutions and wash ourselves, our hands, our feet, our heads, and wear clean clothes before we enter a mosque to pray and then pray in the mud? This is not sunna! This is merely the Shiites making up stories so they can follow their corrupt and perverse desires!"

I found what my father had to say quite offensive because it made out that Reza had simply made the claim because he wanted to use the turbah for no other reason than that that's what he wanted to do. But Reza showed by his argumentation that he was well-versed in Islamic literature and it sounded as if he was just as determined to follow the Islamic faith as strongly as my father.

"As for praying to the black rock," my father continued, "this is not idolatrous. After all, the Prophet Muhammad kissed the black rock in veneration, so it is sunna. When questioned about this, the second caliph, Caliph Omar, who was a close friend of the Prophet, once stood in front of the black rock and said that he knew kissing and worshipping the black rock was idolatrous but he had seen the Prophet kissing it so now it had become sunna and therefore can no longer be considered idolatrous. The Prophet said nothing about turbahs!"

That last comment hit me with aghastness. The kissing as a form of worshipping the black rock was sunna? As a part of sunna, we were now required to give adoration to a rock, something that is not Allah? What struck me about this was that the second caliph actually recognized quite clearly that this act of kissing the black rock just like those of idolatrous religions kiss and worship objects made of stone was an act of idolatry. But what changed this act from idolatry to not being idolatry was not the actual performance of the act but the person who had performed it. Further, because Muhammad had done it, it no longer was merely acceptable, it was actually sunna, a requirement for all Muslims to do it. The reality was, this act was not changed from idolatry to no longer being idolatry, it simply meant that this particular form of idolatry went from being a sin to a righteous act.

I was completely stunned by what my father had said. Yet, I had nothing to say in way of reply. I was later to find out that there are Muslims who still consider the kissing and worshipping of the black rock a sinful act. In fact, the members of ISIS threatened that if they ever made it to Mecca, they would destroy the black rock because it had been turned into an object of adoration. They could clearly see that this was an idolatrous act. And so could I. So why couldn't my father?

Those who maintain that the black rock is important but its adoration is not idolatrous make the claim that in reality the black rock is simply a marker to help us know where the centre of our worship lies. That's the only function it plays. One has to ask, then, why it needs to be this particular black rock? And why did Muhammad kiss it?

The reasoning behind the choice of this rock as the marker so it is claimed is that the black rock came from paradise. This is no doubt based on a belief from a time in the past when the universe was divided into two, things that were earthly and things that were heavenly. Anything from earth was imperfect, but all things from outside the earth, that is, in the heavens, including the sun, the moon, the planets and the stars, were perfect. Anything that fell out of the sky, in particular, meteorites, because they were of heavenly origin, were believed to be holy. Hence the veneration of the black rock, a meteorite, a rock that had come from the heavens.

I really didn't know what to say to my father's last comment. There was obviously a lot of research I needed to do to be able to get to the truth.

"Apart from that," I then said, "Rubasha and her family are good people. And as Shiites, they believe in one God, Allah, and His Messenger, Muhammad. They also believe that the Koran is perfect. They don't believe it has been corrupted but that it has remained intact, without additions, subtractions or any forms of change. They believe in all the other pillars of Islam that we also believe in. Doesn't that mean that they are Muslims?"

"No!" my father snapped and sat up on the sofa. "They are not Muslims! They might be good people and they might believe in Allah, His Messenger and the Holy Scriptures. But they commit sheerk by giving unnecessary veneration to Ali and his household almost as if they were prophets equal to Muhammad when they were simply ordinary people. Until they turn from their corrupt ways, they will burn in Jahannam with all the other kaffeers! As it says in Al-Taubah 9:67, the hypocrites enjoin what is wrong to that which is true, and this is what the Shiites are doing simply so they can follow their own evil desires."

There was nothing more I could say to that. At this stage, I could see what my father was saying but I could also see things from Reza's angle as well. And I could see that I needed to do a lot of reading to further get to the underlying truth of my religion.

Later that evening in the privacy of my bedroom I thought about Rubasha and her family, and what my father had said. Were Shiites Muslims or not? What did it mean to be a Muslim?

But what was further driving my mind into overdrive was what had caused the rift between the two versions of Islam. What had been borne out in these discussions was that history was important. I had earlier thought that it was only important to know that the angel Gabriel appeared to Muhammad and told him to recite the Koran which eventually was made into a book. Now I had discovered that it was important to know and understand the events that had occurred well after the Prophet had died, the Battle of Karbala being a good example. This additional history gave greater depth in understanding of the Islamic faith. And the hadiths about the Prophet and his relationship with Hussain showed there was a solid link between the Prophet and these later historical events.

The thought then went further than that: if we required a detailed knowledge of history after the advent of the Prophet to understand Islam better, what about the history before the advent of the Prophet?

The point was that it was the Hadiths that were the source of all this history. But how well could we trust the Hadiths? What struck me about the argument presented to me from Reza and my father was that they both acknowledged the proclamation that was made about Ali as the mawla. But the same could not be said about the revelation of the verse from Al-Ma'idah 5:3. Reza claimed that this verse was revealed at Ghadeer Khumm but my father claimed that it was made at Mecca. But if this extremely important verse about the perfection and completeness of Islam was revealed at an extremely pivotal moment in Islamic history concerning a person that both Sunnis and Shiites revere more than any other person in history, how could there possibly be any doubt and therefore dispute as to when, where and why this Koranic verse was revealed? The issue was that both hadiths could not be right. Either one was right and the other wrong. Or worse – and this thought caused a shudder to go up my spine – both of them were wrong.

I decided to look up the verse from Al-Ma'idah 5:3 and see what it says to see if this verse in the Koran enlightened me as to the real meaning of the proclamation. I looked up the verse and this is what it says in its entirety:

> *Forbidden to you are dead meat, blood,*
> *the flesh of swine, and that on which*
> *has been invoked the name of other than Allah,*
> *that which has been killed by strangling,*
> *or by a violent blow,*
> *or by a head-long fall,*
> *or by being gored to death;*
> *that which has been eaten by a wild animal;*
> *unless you are able to slaughter it;*
> *that which is sacrificed on stones;*
> *also is the division by raffling with arrows:*
> *that is impiety.*
> *This day have those who reject Faith*
> *given up all hope of your religion;*
> *yet fear them not but fear Me.*
> *This day have I perfected your religion for you,*
> *completed My favour upon you,*
> *and have chosen for you Islam as your religion.*
> *But if any is forced by hunger,*
> *with no inclination to transgression,*
> *Allah is indeed Oft-Forgiving, Most Merciful*

This verse starts off by talking about what Muslims are allowed and not allowed to eat. But then it jumps to talking about those who reject faith, and then it contains the proclamation that Muhammad made about the completion of the faith, the Sunnis claiming it was made at Mecca, the Shiites claiming it was made at Ghadeer Khumm. But then it goes back to talking about diet. There was nothing in the proclamation, according to what both Reza and my father had said, that the statement Muhammad made about the completion of the religion also mentioned dietary laws. So why was this proclamation inserted here?

In fact, I noticed that when I removed from the verse the statements about rejecting faith and perfecting the religion, this verse reads seamlessly and sensibly as

> *Forbidden to you are dead meat, blood,*
> *the flesh of swine, and that on which*
> *has been invoked the name of other than Allah,*
> *that which has been killed by strangling,*
> *or by a violent blow,*
> *or by a head-long fall,*
> *or by being gored to death;*
> *that which has been eaten by a wild animal;*
> *unless you are able to slaughter it;*
> *that which is sacrificed on stones;*
> *also is the division by raffling with arrows:*
> *that is impiety.*
> *But if any is forced by hunger,*
> *with no inclination to transgression,*
> *Allah is indeed Oft-Forgiving, Most Merciful*

Further, I noticed the subject matter in this verse was mentioned in other Surahs, such as Al-Baqarah 2:173. In fact, when I compared the verse from Al-Baqarah with the verse from Al-Ma'idah, it became clear that Muhammad's proclamation didn't really belong in this verse.

Al-Ma'idah 5:3	Al-Baqarah 2:173
Forbidden to you are dead meat, blood, the flesh of swine, and that on which has been invoked the name of other than Allah, that which has been killed by strangling, or by a violent blow, or by a head-long fall, or by being gored to death; that which has been eaten by a wild animal; unless you are able to slaughter it; that which is sacrificed on stones; also is the division by raffling with arrows: that is impiety. **This day have those who reject Faith given up all hope of your religion; yet fear them not but fear Me.** **This day have I perfected your religion for you, completed My favour upon you, and have chosen for you Islam as your religion.** *But if any is forced by hunger, with no inclination to transgression, Allah is indeed Oft-Forgiving, Most Merciful*	*He has only forbidden you dead meat, and blood, and the flesh of swine, and that on which any other name has been invoked besides that of Allah. But if one is forced by necessity, without wilful disobedience, nor transgressing due limits, then he is guiltless. For Allah is Oft-Forgiving, Most Merciful.*

This message also occurred in Al-Anaam 6:145, again, telling Muslims what they were forbidden from eating but then adding the caveat that if they were forced by hunger to eat these forbidden things that Allah would forgive them. But the message about those rejecting faith and the perfection of the religion was absent. This message to me was a glaringly obvious insertion into this verse which made me ask the question: How then was the Koran compiled? Earlier in my upbringing I had been told that Muhammad received revelations from the angel Gabriel which he recited to his companions to memorize. It appeared to me that the revelation about the prohibition of certain foods was first made to Muhammad at an earlier time and then the revelation about those who reject faith and the perfection of the religion came later. And from what both Reza and my father had said, this declaration definitely had nothing to do with dietary laws and hence was completely independent of what was written before and after it in this verse in Al-Ma'idah. This then meant to me that the declaration of the perfection of religion was received at a later time to that of the dietary laws, and then Muhammad altered the way he recited this verse by inserting the revelation about the faithless and the perfect faith within this verse. But then why in the middle of this verse when it probably would have made more sense to insert it at the beginning or the end? Further, I thought, is this how Al-Ma'idah 5:3 reads in the eternal Koran written on the eternal tablets in the heavens and therefore Muhammad knew to insert this here? And why was it inserted only in this verse and not the other two verses which talk of the same subject?

And because the verses from Al-Baqarah 2:173, Al-Ma'idah 5:3 and Al-Anaam 6:145 pretty much said the same thing, was this revelation made once to Muhammad but ended up in three different surahs with slight variations, or was it actually revealed three times on three different occasions, in these three slightly different ways? And if so, wouldn't Muhammad have said to Gabriel on the second and third time he received the revelation something like, "Yeah, I know. You've said that before" or would Muhammad simply have accepted the revelation given to him three times on three different occasions and received them each time as if they were fresh and new? And if they were revealed on three different occasions, had there been three different contexts for why they were revealed at these times? In what situation would you need the exact same message revealed more than once about what you can and can't eat when the declaration by its nature is universal and applicable in all contexts?

And my mind kept thinking. I thought more about the explanation Reza gave for the context of this passage which was completely different to what my father gave. When I thought long and hard about it, I tended to favour my father's explanation. I reasoned that Reza's understanding of the context of this passage didn't ring true because his explanation was supposed to have been made in conjunction with the declaration that Ali was the new mawla. But this connection was not apparent in the Koran. If they were intricately linked, why didn't the declaration of Ali as the new mawla appear here in the Koran as well? What I discovered later was that this whole statement about Muhammad, Ali and the mawla-ship was not in the Koran at all. Yet considering the importance the Shiites weighed on the connection between the perfection of Islam and Ali being the mawla, to me this should have been evident in the very Koran.

And my mind kept on thinking. The statement about the perfection of Islam being made "this day" was in the Koran but not the context. Anyone who read the Koran but had never read nor had access to the Hadiths would have no idea what this declaration is talking about. Further, the statement on its own makes absolutely no sense without a context. To know which day was "this day" required background material. I tried to imagine walking up to an inscription written on stone in my local park beginning with "this day" but there was no date on the inscription. Further, I knew nothing of who wrote it and for what occasion it was commemorating. The first question that would go through anyone's mind would be, "which day?" And possibly a second, "Why on this day? What happened to establish this day in this way?"

This led to another problem. Because the proclamation began with "this day", this meant that there was a focus on a particular day in all eternity and it was on this specific day that Islam was perfected as a religion. This means that before this day Islam was not perfect. So there is a specific time in all eternity that held significance because it was on this day that Islam became complete. How, then, could this particular proclamation be an eternal statement in the eternal Koran when it speaks of a specific moment in time, a specific day? It is totally impossible to have the statement "this day" on an eternal document.

Further, if written on this eternal document co-existing with eternal Allah it was on "this day" that Islam was perfected, does this mean that prior to this day Islam was imperfect? I thought of time before "this day" and then continued further and further into the past, way back to a time when Allah had not yet created the universe and when He existed alone. Was it possible that there could be a time when a perfect God co-existed with an imperfect Islam?

For a moment I was overwhelmed by a great wave of doubt. But then suddenly the evil angel Malik came to mind. I could see his burning eyes and feel his strong grip on the collar of my shirt and feel the flames licking against my feet. Yes, I had been warned. I shouldn't doubt. I should not entertain these thoughts because they will lead me to an eternity in hell. Satan was misleading me. And he was showing me just how powerful his deception was. And this was a major attack. I just had to block all these doubts out of my mind and just accept the truth of the Koran in blind faith. Eventually there would be clear, logical explanations to resolve all this.

Chapter 7

At school the next day, while sitting in our group at the break, I looked at all my friends seated there. What amazed me was that everyone in our group claimed to be Muslim yet I wondered just how much of Islam they really knew about or really cared to know. From our earlier conversations, it was made clear that their knowledge of the religion was quite shallow. They knew very little about what it said in the Koran and no doubt knew even less about what it said in the Hadiths. And none of this concerned them. Further, from our earlier discussions, it had become clear to me that their whole concept of Islam was a combination of what they had heard at Friday prayers and what they wanted their religion to purport such as the idea that moral people will go to heaven irrespective of their religious background, a belief that sounded reasonable and one they defended, yet was not backed up by the Koran. But even when I pointed this out, instead of acknowledging that their belief was erroneous because I was able to show that the Koran taught otherwise, my school friends considered me as somewhat of an oddity.

Even the Sunni-Shiite divide didn't seem to concern them. The Sunnis amongst our friends simply considered Shiite Muslims, if not with the same contempt that my father appeared to have for them, as something like three quarters of a Muslim, people who were Muslims to a certain degree with whom Sunnis could associate but they still weren't Muslims to the fullest. And the Shiites amongst my group had the same attitude towards the Sunnis. Yet neither side really had the depth of knowledge nor the understanding as to why the two sects differed. And yet they were completely sure of what they believed. What amazed me more was how confident they were in their religion even though I knew they knew so little. By contrast, the more I delved and probed into the intricacies of what constituted the Islamic faith, the more I realized how uncertain I was of what it meant to be a Muslim.

In a way, I was quite envious of my school friends. It was enough for them to hear what they were told at the mosque or the imam bargah about what they were supposed and not supposed to believe and do. I could only guess that although the religion placed some inconvenience on their lives such as having to attend the mosque on Friday, having to stop and bow towards Mecca a number of times a day, having to avoid pig meat and alcohol, and not being allowed to consume food and drink during the daylight hours at least one month of the year, the religion really didn't interfere with their lives enough to question it. They had been told that they would go to hell if they didn't follow these aspects of the religion, so they went along with these, possibly grudgingly, but these were a minor inconvenience to their everyday lives. They also were told that they had to believe that the Koran was the venerable Word of Allah without error and if they didn't believe this, again, they would go to hell in the next life. As a result, they maintained this belief in the Koran and were quite sure of the veracity of this statement, even though it had become obvious that they really didn't know what was written between the pages of this supposed holy book.

But I had read the Koran in its entirety. I had to admit that my knowledge of what it actually said was still somewhat shady because my knowledge of the contents was through the prism of the Arabic language. Even so, there were already parts of the Koran that I had begun to understand which had caused earlier disputes both within my own mind and also among my school friends.

But the most unsettling was what we had been told and what I had read in the Koran about the cities to which Lot had been sent to. According to the universe of the Koran, my physical attraction towards men was a mystery to Allah but still a grave sin. And because the Koran said it was a sin, so it had to be. But because of my very nature, I couldn't just nestle into the comfort of this belief. This negative outlook of homosexuality affected me greatly especially because I was strongly attracted towards men and there was absolutely nothing I could do about it.

Further, what the Koran didn't explain was how our sexuality, both heterosexuality and homosexuality, actually governed our relationships. Because I was physically attracted to men, I had totally no idea of how a heterosexual man interacts with the woman he loves. My relationship with Rubasha was definitely developing into a strong friendship. I certainly liked Rubasha a lot. She was a lovely girl. Our friendship was becoming strong and hence my friends began assuming we were going steady, including, so I later judged looking back at Rubasha's parents' interaction with me, Rubasha's parents and mine. My father was not particularly pleased and made comments that if something serious developed between Rubasha and me, Rubasha would have to abandon those aspects of her faith my father found repugnant. However, I couldn't see what the issue was. Why couldn't I simply have a close friendship with someone of the opposite sex without it being more than a simple friendship?

But there was a deep-seated reason that I simply did not want to accept. I wasn't in love with Rubasha. I was in love with her brother, Reza. I didn't have it in me to make my relationship with Rubasha go any further than a simple friendship. But where Reza was concerned, I could have given him my very soul.

It had become a commonplace going to Rubasha's place to study. Rubasha's parents welcomed me very specially.

However, it was customary that we were chaperoned whenever we studied together, and it was most often Reza who took on that duty. The irony of it was that in the end, although I went to Rubasha's place to study, it gave me the real excuse to go to Rubasha's place, not to see Rubasha, but to see Reza. Reza, like his sister, was good-looking, he was fairly intelligent as he was studying IT at university, and he was a gentleman. My natural instinct guided me towards him. I was blind to any attention that Rubasha was giving me to show me that she liked me a lot. But how was I to know? It did not come naturally for me to fall in love with a woman. It came naturally for me to fall in love with a man. But while on the one hand it felt beautiful these feelings I had for him, at the same time it made me feel guilty and evil. These feelings that had developed inside me towards him were, so I had been taught, guaranteed to send me to eternal torment in the next life if I allowed myself to be led by my natural instinct.

I would never have made my relationship with Rubasha any more than a simple friendship. In fact, I thought I was quite safe from anything happening between us because my father would definitely not have approved. But I think my mother loved Rubasha enough and saw her as a potential daughter-in-law, despite her religious background. Although my father was pleased I did not express any strong interest in Rubasha, my mother realized that there was nothing in my words which spoke of future lives together or of preparing for a future wedding. And so, because she was a little anxious to help me along the way, my mother decided to give me a little push.

"You know, the Prophet used to show his love to Khadeeja by visiting her often and bringing things for her," my mother once said to me one afternoon just after I had arrived home from school and was sitting having a cup of tea with her. The comment was made without any context so I looked at my mother perplexed. My mother obviously could see I had no idea what she was talking about.

"Well," she then elucidated, "you should do the same with Rubasha. When you visit her, take a small something for her."

This struck me like a blow in the face.

"Mother, I really like Rubasha, but I'm not in love with her."

My mother smiled gently.

"Rubasha is very much in love with you. And I can see you are in love with her. But men usually have the habit of being slow to show their affections to their true love. And Rubasha is a lovely, intelligent girl, and I can see that Allah is working through you to finally win her over to the truth."

I just stared at my mother speechless.

"Don't worry," my mother concluded. "I know what girls Rubasha's age like. I will buy some little inexpensive but treasure-like things that Rubasha is sure to like and these will definitely win her heart over to you."

I was dumbfounded. I liked Rubasha a lot. But I didn't love her. I knew that. There was no magic. I enjoyed her friendship, talking to her, learning about the differences between our Muslim sects, talking about life in general. But as for loving her and doing things for her to win her over to me, I didn't have it in me.

When I had a chance to think about it later, I guessed this was Allah's way of curing my homosexuality. Of course, it all made sense. Satan was using Reza to lure me away from Allah and the pure version of Islam because my mind was enraptured in thoughts about him. Allah's real plan was for me to present to the members of the family the truth of Islam, to show them the errors of their sect and bring them into the true light of Allah, and in turn help me to have the right attraction for the gender I was supposed to have. Satan may have been trying to get me to be attracted to Reza and then become entangled in the corrupt Shiite

151

version of Islam. But Allah knew what He was doing and I began to recognize the plan myself. By getting to know the family, this was an opportunity for me to learn more about the Shiite sect and show up the errors, and somehow eventually my sexuality would finally become redirected towards Rubasha.

I really tried my best. My mother bought little trinkets to give to Rubasha and it was obvious that Rubasha liked the things that I brought for her. However, I was doing this all robotically, clinically, mechanically. As much as I tried to convince myself to the contrary, I didn't love Rubasha. She was a lovely girl and I liked her. But this is something that heterosexuals just don't understand nor do they care to even try to understand, that my sexual proclivity was not directed towards Rubasha which meant that I could never love her as deeply as my mother or Rubasha's parents wanted me to. Heterosexuals in our society just don't appreciate nor do they want to admit that love, the affection towards a special person, is heavily intertwined with the physical attraction, the sexual attraction. Towards Rubasha in particular and to women in general, I had no such physical attraction.

The way I interacted towards Rubasha was simply an attempt to please Rubasha, my mother, and, of course, Allah, but inside I had no feelings for Rubasha. I knew my true feelings lay with Reza. I tried to suppress my feelings and pretend they did not exist, but the more I tried to suppress them and to bury them, the greater my love for him became and it made me all the more frustrated and miserable.

One afternoon after school, I accompanied Rubasha home with the intent purpose of working on some school assignments. When we arrived at Rubasha's block of units, we saw two young men playing cricket in the spare block adjacent Rubasha's home, one figure who I recognized, who called out to me once he saw me.

"Hey, Mustafa," Reza called out. "Why don't you come over here for a bit and play a round of cricket?"

Rubasha and I looked at each other.

"Don't worry!" Reza called out. "It will be thirty minutes maximum. I promise."

Rubasha once again looked at me.

"Go on!" Rubasha encouraged me. "I'll see you in thirty minutes!"

I can only guess that Rubasha was pleased that Reza wanted me to participate in this sporting activity to improve the friendship developing between Reza and me so I would fit well within the family. Little did she realize that my desire to spend a moment with Reza without her was for a totally different reason.

Rubasha took my school bag and then disappeared into her block of flats while I made my way across the street to join Reza and his friend. Cricket wasn't a sport that I particularly liked. But it was a popular sport in Pakistan and at least it created a reason to spend some time with Reza on his own.

Reza introduced me to the other person I didn't know. It was Reza's cousin, Faisal. Once Reza had mentioned my name, Faisal went into retrospection at first and then, as if he had had a revelation, he asked me, "Are you Mustafa Faakhtaa, Taheer Khan's friend?"

I was quite taken aback by the connection. How was it that Reza's cousin, Faisal, not only knew about Taheer but he also associated Taheer with me?

"Taheer is a school friend," I replied. "I wouldn't say that we were particularly friends. I know him and he is in some of my classes but I wouldn't say that I was a close friend of his or even a friend at all."

Faisal said nothing more. He made a move which was the signal for us to begin playing a round. We began to get into the game. Faisal was bowling and Reza was batting while I played wicket keeper. Faisal bowled the ball to which Reza gave a good whack and the ball disappeared down the street.

All three of us just watched the ball hurry away.

"You hit it," Faisal yelled, "so you get it!"

Reza dropped the cricket bat and then bolted down the street in pursuit of the ball. While we waited, Faisal came up to me. He crouched down next to me and pulled a strange face.

"That Taheer talks a lot about you," Faisal then said. "He seems to like you a lot. He definitely admires you."

This hit me with a start. I didn't know what to say.

"You know his father used to abuse him," Faisal continued. "He was a violent man. He often beat his wife. And he abused Taheer. And Taheer's brother. Taheer must have told you that, seeing you and he are close. It must have come as a shock and perhaps in a way a relief to find out that his abusive father had died."

The news hit me like ice water being splashed in my face. But what further intrigued me was the choice of words used to describe how Taheer's father treated his wife and treated his sons. Faisal did not elucidate the type of abuse Taheer and his brother were subject to and I wasn't sure I really wanted to know.

"I really don't know Taheer very well," I replied.

"You know," Faisal then said after a slight pause and then lowered his voice to ensure that only I was the recipient of what he had to say. "That Taheer is somewhat unstable in character." He paused, looked left and right, then back at me. "Mmmmmmm. I'm not sure how to say this, but Taheer has an unusual infatuation for you, if you know what I mean. He seems to have been the most affected by his father's abuse." He then deepened his furrow. "There isn't anything going on between you two?"

Faisal's last statement caused a shiver to go up my spine and my mouth to go dry. This is not information about oneself that anyone wants broadcast in Pakistani

154

society. The repercussions if anyone suspected two men of being intimate together were quite dangerous, in some cases lethal. It was heard that heterosexual male members of our community would take these two men into some secret location and torture them, rape them – ironically – or disfigure them. And worse, the police would do nothing about it because it was considered that the two men had brought this on themselves.

"No! Definitely not!" I stated emphatically.

"Good, then," Faisal then said as he stood up, his face relaxing. "Just be careful with him, though," Faisal concluded. "Taheer has become somewhat erratic in behaviour."

Reza could be heard running and puffing. Faisal abruptly changed expression and his body language dictated that he didn't want to talk any further in the presence of Reza.

This continued to be a mystery as to how Faisal knew Taheer and his family and how he knew so much about Taheer. Warning me to be careful about Taheer obviously meant to make sure I kept my distance from him. But the irony was that by mentioning to be careful about Taheer led to a strange set of circumstances in which I ended up being together with him alone.

During the week, our classes finished around 3.30. But on Friday, classes finished at 1.00 so that we could attend Friday prayers. Usually at 1.00 we could go home, but I had a lot of work that I had to do so I decided to work in the project lab. The project lab was a special room dedicated to the seniors. It was called a lab but it was not a science lab but a room full of computers all linked up to internet with free Wi-Fi. Usually there were a number of students occupying this room but this particular day, when I got there, there wasn't a soul. That was great. I could work on my assignments in peace. I pulled out my work and began working furiously on one of my mathematics assignments. I had been there for about half an hour when I heard someone enter the room and interrupt the tranquillity of the moment. I looked up to see who the intruder was, and there was Taheer. When he saw me, a big grin spread over his face.

"What are you doing?" he asked as he walked over to the desk I was seated at. "The mathematics problems?"

"Yeah," I replied cautiously.

Taheer came over to the desk adjacent mine and stood really close to me. With that my heart started pounding and I was scared he could hear it. He looked at my work uninvited which embarrassed me. I was expecting to hear his cynical laugh and to hear him say how stupid I was. But instead he pointed his finger at a problem I was doing and commented, "No, you've done this wrong."

With that, Taheer grabbed a chair and placed it right next to me, sat down and began explaining what I had done wrong. While he spoke, I listened. But his calmness terrified me. Faisal had warned me that Taheer had become erratic and so I felt as if he were a time bomb sitting there waiting to explode at any moment. But also, Faisal had said that Taheer had an infatuation for me. This befuddled me and made me ask the question as to what were his real intentions for helping me out with problems in mathematics.

Taheer went through the list of questions, pointing out that I had actually made the same error in all the questions. He then showed me how to do the first few a different and more efficient way. I was amazed at his intellectual stamina. This only increased my feelings of reservation. Emotionally erratic people are even more dangerous when they have the additional dimension of great intelligence.

Eventually he finished his explanation and then looked up at me.

"Do you understand?" he asked.

"Er...yes," I replied cautiously.

"Any other questions?" he asked and then stretched himself back with his hands behind his head very casually.

"No...no. That was all," I replied.

There was a momentary pause. Taheer's facial expression changed slowly from one of a friend trying to help out to a rather sinister look. He removed his hands from his head and slowly sat forward.

"So," Taheer said ever so quietly, "have you and Rubasha done it?"

I felt as if all my blood had gone to my face. I paused for a moment but then finally gave an answer to his question.

"No, we haven't," I replied with almost a squeak.

"Why not?" Taheer asked. "Is she not your type?"

Again I felt a flush in my face. Boys of our age would have used this moment as an opportunity to boast about their sexual prowess. But I knew that I couldn't lie even about this because I would probably have choked on my words in disgust trying to explain what I had done sexually with a woman. At the same time, I had a religion to uphold.

"No, because I'm not married to her. And so I won't commit zinna."

Taheer leant back and once again put his hands behind his head.

"Tell me, seriously, Mustafa," Taheer began. "Do you seriously believe all this stuff they tell us about our religion, about Islam and the Koran?"

"Well, yes," I replied and nodded in affirmation. "Don't you? Don't you as a Hafiz-ul-Koran also believe and acknowledge all this?"

"Hahaha!" Taheer laughed and then stood up from his chair. "A Hafiz-ul-Koran! Yes, I'm a Hafiz-ul-Koran. I believe in Allah and that Muhammad is His messenger and whosoever believes in this will not be harmed."

Taheer began to walk around the room wringing his hands in agitation. Faisal's warning of Taheer's erraticism made me afraid. The only relieving aspect was that I knew we were in the school and if he did something drastic, he would get in trouble.

Eventually Taheer walked back to me, stood behind me, grabbed my shoulders and began massaging me.

"And how do you know the Koran is the venerable Word of Allah?"

The massage was both pleasurable and disturbing. And rather distracting, not allowing me to answer right away. Taheer must have sensed this because he stopped which brought me back to his question which I answered.

"Because it says at the beginning of the Koran, in Al-Baqarah 2:2, 'This is the Book, there is no doubt in it'. The Koran makes it clear right from the start that it is the Book from Allah."

Taheer began digging into my shoulders again.

"Hahaha, yes," he said and then quoted the verse I had said in Arabic and then offered his own translation. "*That* is the Book, there is no doubt it in. *Dhalika alkitabu*, 'that is the book' not *hadha alkitabu*, 'this is the book'. Have you ever wondered what book this verse was referring to when it introduces us to 'that' book?"

I pondered on this verse again in the Arabic and was amazed by what Taheer had said. Yes, the Koran begins with *dhalika*, "that", not *hadha*, "this". What book, then, was the Koran referring to when it said "that book", the one over there, not the one the reader is holding in his or her hand?

"So you believe the Koran is perfect," Taheer interrupted me and began grabbing my shoulders again, "because the Koran says it is. There are other books out there that claim that they are the Word of God also. Will you believe those books as well?"

"No," I replied.

"And why not?" Taheer asked.

"Because the Koran doesn't say they are."

"Hahaha!" Taheer once again gave out his demonic outburst. "Be honest with yourself, Yah Mustafa. The only reason why you believe the Koran is divine is not because the Koran says it is but because your parents say it, our teachers say it and our government says it. And with our blasphemy laws, who is going to question this belief?"

I took a quick glance around to see if there were any other students who had inadvertently entered the room. That last statement Taheer made struck me. Yes, this conversation we were having where Taheer, a Hafiz-ul-Koran, was questioning the Koran was a crime against the state.

"And how do you know," Taheer continued unabashedly, "that the Koran has been faithfully transmitted down through the centuries intact without any additions and subtractions? I mean, how do you know that what we call the Koran today is the same as what was revealed to Muhammad and written down by Muhammad's companions?"

I looked up at Taheer with the thought that he should already know the answer to this question.

"Because Allah wouldn't allow His Word to change through time. As it says in Al-Anaam 6:34, 'none can alter the words of Allah'."

When I quoted that verse, like Taheer had done, I quoted the verse in Arabic, then translated it into English.

"Also," I added, "you should know as well as I do that if you compared any Koran against any other in all history, they would all be exactly the same."

"Are you so sure of that?" Taheer more exclaimed than questioned. However, he let that question hang in the air without offering any reason why he called such a statement into question. He then began massaging my shoulders again.

"None can change the words of Allah," Taheer echoed my statement somewhat mockingly. "So, then, why did Caliph Uthman have variant copies of the Koran burnt if Allah's Word never changes? What need would there have been to burn the variant copies except to remove the evidence that changes had been made in the earlier manuscripts?"

Taheer must have felt the shock this statement sent through me because he stopped abruptly once he had made this statement. I could almost feel without looking up the smirk that had formed across his face. Taheer then began massaging my shoulders again and continued. "Yes, they don't preach that at Friday prayers, now do they? But Uthman's burning of the Korans with variant readings is mentioned clearly in the Hadiths."

Again, the Hadiths were mentioned. Which Hadiths Taheer was talking about he did not elucidate but I was to find out later when I began my own research.

"It may have been written in the Hadiths," I replied as a form of defence. "But the Koran doesn't say so. And the Koran is more important than the Hadiths. The Hadiths can make mistakes but not the Koran."

"Ah, so the Hadiths can make mistakes," Taheer mocked. "But not the Koran. So, let's listen to the Koran. So, tell me, why does it say in Al-Baqarah 2:106, 'Whatever we abrogate of a verse or cause it to be forgotten, We bring a better one or similar to it'? If the Word of Allah cannot be changed, then how can verses be 'abrogated' – replaced – or verses can be forgotten and then similar ones or better ones brought into the Koran to replace those that had been abrogated and forgotten in this unchanging Koran?"

The feeling of a cold electric shock moved up through my spine, up through my chest and into my head. This was a verse I had recited many times but this was the first time that I understood Taheer's inference and what this verse was implying. This verse overtly implied that the Koran that we read today was actually a final version but not the original. Earlier versions of the Koran had verses in them but these verses had since been removed and alternate verses put in their place. And the reason why we don't know this is because Allah caused us to forget them.

What was further shocking was Taheer's overt questioning of the Koran. He was discussing the Koran as if it were a book open to debate. This was an approach to the Koran which had never entered my consciousness before. I had always axiomatically accepted the Koran as divine. There had never been any reason to go right back to first principles and start with questioning the very foundation stone on which my beliefs were based. Suddenly here I was engaging in a discussion which called into question the very reliability of the foundation stone of my belief system, the perfection of the Koran. From my childhood I had been taught that this was an extremely sinful thing to do. Further, as Taheer himself had pointed out, this was also a crime against the state and someone could get jail time for raising such doubts. So I could not understand why Taheer could comfortably and unabashedly treat the Koran in this way, and further, especially as he was a Hafiz-ul-Koran.

"The Koran is fourteen hundred years old, Mustafa," Taheer continued. "The Hadiths hint at variations being in the earlier manuscripts and the Koran itself suggests that changes were made to make the final version that we now hold. So, think about it. Why has there been so much effort put into trying to convince everyone that the Koran is perfect and that there have been no changes, and why are we threatened with imprisonment or death for raising doubts about the supposed unchanging nature of the Koran if it is certain that the Koran has remained unchanged from its inception?" There was a slight pause and then Taheer added as a coda, "After having burnt all the evidence of variant copies that once existed?"

This was frightening on various levels. If someone else in this room heard what Taheer was saying, Taheer and I could be in serious danger of being accused of committing a crime. And then I saw the angel Malik with those burning eyes stoking the flames.

"No, the Koran is perfect!" I stated emphatically. "It's Satan who makes it look like the Koran has been changed."

"It's the fault of Satan," Taheer said somewhat mockingly, then moved away from my shoulders and walked between the rows of desks. "Satan, Shaitaan, Iblis," he then said, as if to ensure that I was certain that these were the different names we knew Satan of having.

"And where did Iblis come from?" Taheer asked.

I looked at Taheer walking back and forth before answering.

"Allah created him as He did all the other angels, out of smokeless fire."

"And why is Iblis misleading us into believing that the Koran is not perfect? Why isn't Iblis, like all the other angels, worshipping Allah and giving Him all the praise? Why is he so adamant to mislead humans?"

"Because," I replied, "when Allah created man, He told the angels to bow down to the man. But Iblis refused because man was created out of clay but Iblis and the angels were created out of smokeless fire, and so Iblis felt he was superior to man, being made from a purer substance than man. Because he refused to worship the created man, Allah cursed him and sent him out of heaven."

"And Allah, the All-Wise and All-Compassionate, knowing the suffering and destruction that Iblis would cause to Allah's creation, in particular, to the descendants of the man He had created, Allah destroyed Iblis there and then?"

I looked at Taheer. "Well, no," I replied. "As it says in Al-Hijr 15:36 to 38, Iblis asked Allah for respite and Allah granted Iblis this respite till the day the dead are raised back to life on Judgement Day."

"And then in verse 39," Taheer continued, and said this first in Arabic, melodious and mellifluous, and then in English, "Iblis said, 'O my Lord! Because You have put me in the wrong, I will make fair-seeming to them on the earth, and I will put them all in the wrong'." Taheer then paused before adding, "Iblis told Allah that Allah had done Iblis wrong, that is, Iblis said that Allah *aghwaitani*, Allah 'misled me'. And Allah didn't deny this. According to the Koran, Allah remained indifferent to the statement made by Iblis. And so Iblis said that in the same way as Allah had misled Iblis, Iblis would mislead all in the world. And Allah said nothing and did nothing to stop Iblis. So according to the Koran, not only did Allah create Iblis, Allah deliberately misled Iblis, who in turn misleads us humans. So who really is the one doing the misleading?"

I gasped in horror at Taheer's rhetorical question. What Taheer inferred I could see was correct: according to the Koran, indirectly, it is Allah who misleads humanity, for Allah misleads humanity through Iblis.

What was worse was that it said in Ash-Shuara 26:94, 95 that Iblis and all his armies would be thrown into eternal Fire after the Final Judgement. If Allah had intended to destroy Iblis in the end, why didn't He destroy Iblis in the beginning and prevent Iblis from misleading all humanity? The implication of the verses in Al-Hijr 15 was that if it wasn't for Iblis, humans simply would never have even entertained the thought of questioning Allah and His holy Book. So if Allah intends to destroy Iblis in the end, why didn't He simply destroy Iblis in the beginning and prevent humanity questioning and disbelieving in the Koran and in Islam and leading them to their destruction in eternal fire in the next life?

What was Allah really doing? Did Allah gain some sort of pleasure out of misleading both the angels and the humans? Was Allah some sort of sadist who gained pleasure out of human suffering especially as He had the power to do whatever He wanted? Did Allah get a kick out of this game He played with Iblis, allowing Iblis to exist and mislead humanity, knowing full well that in the end He will destroy Iblis and worse destroy all those innocent people who were helplessly misled by Iblis when Allah could have destroyed one being, Iblis, and spared all humanity from being misled by this powerful being?

I thought I was going to pass out. The whole implication of these verses gave a totally opposite image of the Allah I had been taught about and which was presented in other places in the Koran, that Allah was the Compassionate, the All-Forgiving.

Taheer came back and sat down in the adjacent chair. He looked at me with a disturbing expression on his face and then let out an evil laugh as if he were Iblis himself sitting in front of me. But even if he were Iblis incarnate, he had the tacit approval of Allah to do what he was doing to me.

"So, that's why we can't really trust that the Koran is the venerable Word of Allah without error because it does not hold consistent beliefs. It is a book of people's views at a particular time in history but views change."

I was horrified. Even though I knew that Taheer could justify his position, he was merely a school student. He wasn't an Islamic scholar.

"But the Koran is applicable to all time," I gasped. "What the Muslims believed when Muhammad received the revelations of the Koran and what Muslims believe today is still the same. That's why we can be confident that the Koran is the venerable, unchanging Word of Allah. Muslims still believe in the same Koran that was revealed to Muhammad without having to update it. It has remained constant."

Taheer just gave me a cynical smile and looked around the room. He then stood up, and while wringing his hands, walked back and forth close to the desk I was sitting at.

"Not only does the Koran admit that there have been changes made to it," Taheer continued, "it is obvious that the Koran was written in a milieu when the idea of the universe was different to what we actually understand it to be now. Don't you remember what we learnt in science about the workings of the universe? Don't you remember that we learnt that the earth is a sphere and it orbits the sun, and the sun is simply a large star, no different to the other stars? And the other stars are no different to our star at the centre of the solar system, simply large fiery balls that don't do anything more than just sit there burning in space?"

Taheer then stopped and looked at me.

"Yes," I replied. "We learnt that in Class 3."

"And how does the Koran describe the universe? In the same way?"

Taheer gave me a sinister grin. There was something awful in the way he grinned at me. He was misleading me. He was Iblis. But then it would be Allah indirectly misleading me because Allah gave Iblis permission to do the misleading.

"I don't recall," I spluttered, "reading about the workings of the universe in the Koran but I'm sure that the Koran would describe the universe in the way we were taught in school. Otherwise this would mean that even our science teachers were blaspheming if they taught the universe contrary to how it is described in the Koran."

Taheer started walking again. "How well said! And how much they blaspheme in the science classroom."

Once again, an electric shock went up through my spine, up into my head. I hastily looked around the room to see if anyone else was there because this comment by Taheer would have got him and possibly me in serious trouble. However, undeterred, Taheer continued his anti-koranic exegesis.

"As it says in Al-Baqarah 2:22, Allah 'has made the earth a couch for you', in Taha 20:53 it says about Allah that He is 'the one who made for you the earth as a bed', in Qaf 50:7 it says, 'and the earth, we have spread it out', in Ash-Shams 91:6 it says 'by the earth and its expanse'. Tell me, Mustafa, how many couches and beds do you know in the shape of a ball? And how many times have you in the mosque spread out your prayer mat into the shape of a sphere?"

"But these verses are simply allegorical," I said by way of defence. "Allah is not speaking literally here about the actual shape of the earth."

"'As for those in whose hearts is perversity – they follow what is allegorical from the Book'," Taheer quoted from the Koran.

I sat motionless for a moment not knowing what to say. As I had learnt before, taking the allegorical angle was stifled by this troublesome verse from Al-Imran 3:7.

The pause was broken with Taheer continuing with his exegesis.

"And Allah says in Al-Anbiyah 21:33 that He 'is the one who created … the sun and the moon, each floating in an orbit', in Al-Fatir 35:13 it says that Allah 'has subjected the sun and the moon, each running its course for an appointed term', in Yaseen 36:38 it says, 'And the sun runs to a term appointed to it'. The Koran talks of a moving sun, floating in an orbit and running a course. This is not what they teach in science, now, do they? In fact, every science teacher who teaches a spherical earth orbiting a stationary sun should serve jail time for their blasphemy."

I was absolutely stunned. I didn't dare move. My mind oscillated between what we had been taught in science and what Taheer had quoted from the Koran. Yet again I was caught in the throes of doublethink: I had to entertain the thought that the earth was a round, spherical object and orbited the sun as it had been clearly shown through scientific observation and by what astronauts have actually observed and photographed of the planet from a distance, and at the same time hold the thought in my mind that the earth was also a stationary, flat, spread out expanse around which the sun floated, to ensure that I did not burn for an eternity in hell.

Our discussion was abruptly interrupted when another classmate walked into the room. It was a fellow student called Muhammad who I knew vaguely and at least I knew he was a Shiite. Muhammad smiled and greeted us politely.

"Have you seen Mr Ismail?" he asked.

Taheer and I first looked at each other and then back at him, admitting that we didn't know where he was. With that, Muhammad left the room.

Once the door was closed and it was assured that Muhammad was out of earshot, Taheer made a comment.

"Another Shiite!" he said quite gruffly. "When will they ever turn away from committing sheerk?"

This entire statement was completely incongruous with what Taheer had been arguing earlier. He had been putting the Koran in question and hence the entire Islamic religion, and then just as abruptly he changed completely, becoming completely hostile towards the faction of the faith which opposed his Islamic world view.

"You know, Mustafa," Taheer then said. "You are a Sunni and therefore on the right path. And I've watched you over the years. You're a good Sunni Muslim, devoted to the faith. I have admired how you have diligently followed the faith. So, why do you waste your time with Rubasha, a Shiite woman? Those Shiites are unbelievers, *kaffeers*. They associate Ali with Allah hence committing sheerk. And what does Allah demand of us in Al-Baqarah 2:191 to do? 'Kill them! Such is the reward of the disbelievers'."

Taheer once again took a grab on my shoulders and started to massage me, this time in earnest.

"And I know you are like me," Taheer more gasped than said. "And I know why you are really making friends with Rubasha. It's not going to work. The only way to escape is by a martyr's death. All our earthly filth will be burnt up. Then all our sins we will be forgiven and we will make it directly into paradise."

That last comment sent an ice cold chill up my spine and into my hands and feet. I stood up, forcing Taheer to release his grip on me. I then grabbed my things, threw them hastily into my bag and then left the room. Of all the strange occasions I had had with Taheer, this was the strangest of them all.

Taheer's whole character disturbed me. But so did his argumentation. And his argumentation, although it came from someone with erratic behaviour, was a sound argument. He had quoted from the Koran and hence shown that the Koran suggested that it was not the infallible perfect book from Allah that I had been taught.

Seeing my father was such a devout and dedicated Muslim and that he was much older than me, I naturally thought that he no doubt had been confronted with these issues and had resolved them with logical explanations that ironed out all these questions. Hence that evening I decided to question him.

I had been working for hours on schoolwork and decided to take a break. I heard that my grandmother had just prepared tea so I came out of my room and sat down with my parents in the livingroom.

"How are your studies going?" my father asked me after taking a sip of tea.

"Oh, okay," I replied.

I paused for a moment and then asked the question that was foremost on my mind.

"Father, I know the Koran is the venerable, unchanging Word of Allah. But how do we know this? How do we know that the Koran that we have today is the same Koran that was revealed to Muhammad fourteen hundred years ago?"

My father looked at me with a perplexed expression on his face and then answered me.

"Because it is. It is the unchanging Word of Allah. As it says in the Koran in Al-Kahf 18:27, 'Recite what has been revealed to you of the Book of your Lord: None can change His Words'. The Koran is quite clear that it is the unchanging, venerable Word of Allah." My father then paused and then asked, "Why do you ask this question?"

"A friend of mine at school, a Sunni Muslim like us and a Hafiz-ul-Koran, told me that it says in the Hadiths that there were a number of different Korans with variations, but under the rule of Uthman these variant copies were destroyed which implies that there originally were Korans with changes in them."

"You know that we can't always take the Hadiths entirely seriously," my father stated but there was a hint of anger in his voice. "Even though the Hadiths are helpful, they are not always reliable. You know that."

"Yes, I know," I replied cautiously and swallowed. I paused for a moment and then continued. "However, my friend quoted the verse from Al-Baqarah 2:106, 'What we abrogate of a verse or We cause to be forgotten, we bring a better one or similar to it. Do you not know that Allah has power over everything?' If the Koran has remained unchanged, then what does this verse mean?"

"This verse doesn't mean what you think it means," my father replied with an air of hostility in his voice. The fact that he denied the meaning of the verse the way I understood what it was saying overtly implied that my father fully understood that this was what the verse was actually saying. "What this verse means is that sometimes we read one verse in the Koran and then we read another verse in the Koran, and they may sound like a contradiction. For example, Allah says in Al-Baqarah 2:256 'There is no compulsion in religion' but then He says in Al-Taubah 9:5 'kill the polytheists wherever you find them…but if they repent, and establish regular prayers, and pay Zakat then open a way for them'. The verse from Al-Baqarah says that there is no compulsion in religion but in Al-Taubah it says that polytheists, such as Hindus, should be forced to follow the pure, Islamic faith. This may sound like a contradiction

169

but it is in fact an abrogation. Allah first allowed for others to follow different religions but now He wants all to follow the true religion."

I can still remember the shock when I heard my father give this explanation. Had he really heard what he had said? Did this really sound logical to him? Even so, I knew it had not answered my question and my curiosity was still too strong to allow this question to hang in the air.

"But, father, the verse in Al-Baqarah 2:106 not only says that better verses are brought in to replace the earlier verses but that some verses have been brought in and replaced earlier verses that Allah has then allowed us to forget. If there are verses that Allah has caused us to forget, this implies that there were other verses in an earlier form of the Koran which have subsequently been taken out which implies that the Koran has, in fact, been changed."

My father exploded at my comment. "Are you saying that the Koran is contradictory? Are you saying that the Koran has been changed?" The look in my father's eyes was reminiscent of the angel Malik and I could see the fires of hell through the windows of his soul. My father rebuked me severely and told me I would need to pray the prayer of Al-Taubah, the prayer of repentance, to ensure that Allah did not decide to cast me there and then into the pits of Jahannam.

I was frightened. I desperately wanted an answer to this question so that I could be satisfied that what I was believing was the true religion. But no logical explanation was provided. Instead, I was provided with my father's wrath.

There was a long moment of silence in the room. In the end, I took this as a sign that I should leave the battlefield quietly and hence retired to my bedroom. I sat on the bed and stared at the opposite wall not really knowing what to think. I heard further discussion in the livingroom and soon a soft knock was heard on my bedroom door. My father then entered the room rather calmly and sat on the bed next to me. He placed his arm around my shoulders and then pulled me towards him.

"Son," he said quietly. "I realize that what you were asking, you were sincerely looking for answers to doubts about the Koran. I don't know if I answered your question. If I haven't, please understand that I want the best for you. Shaitaan is very powerful and he manipulates our thoughts, making us question the Koran. We need to have faith in Allah and resist Shaitaan's ruses. We don't want to go to Jahannam – well, I don't want you to go to Jahannam. Just be careful not to let Shaitaan deceive you."

I really appreciated my father coming into the room and telling me that. We hugged and this showed that our relationship had not been impaired by my honest questioning about the Koran and what it said.

But once my father had left and I had finally got into bed, while staring up at the ceiling in the dark, the conversation between Taheer and me kept going over in my head, followed by the outburst of my father when I raised questions about the faith. Allah misled Satan who in turn misleads humans, which simply means that if we cut out the middleman, Allah misleads humans. Allah might not be doing this directly, but by allowing Satan to mislead humanity, Allah was giving Satan's deception His tacit approval. This means that Allah is not the Compassionate that we had been brought up to believe. But was this view of Allah in reality Satan misleading me? And how does one know?

And what about the Hadiths and the verse from the Koran which implied that there had been earlier versions of the Koran and that the Koran that we have in our possession is actually the final unchanging Koran but only after changes in earlier versions had been made? This means that Allah's Word has changed, even though the Koran states in effect to the opposite. Even my father's attempt at an explanation

171

to iron out the issue only made the matter worse. If there is one verse in the Koran that states one thing, such as there being no compulsion in religion which therefore means we should leave people to follow any religion they wish, and then there is another verse which says we should kill polytheists such as Hindus in our neighbouring country unless they convert to Islam hence meaning that there is compulsion in religion after all, even though these words in the Koran have remained unchanged through the centuries, there has been a change from there being no compulsion in religion in one verse to there being one in another. Anyway I looked at it, contrary to what the Koran said about there being no changes in Allah's Word, there had been changes. And although my father was noble enough to soften the blow of his anger by coming into my room to make peace with me, it was obvious that he himself did not have a satisfactory answer to the question.

Thus, if the Koran is true, then Shaitaan was misleading me. But then I thought further on that, on what it meant to mislead someone. I had always thought that someone misled you when they only presented you with some information but not all of it. Politicians and con artists misled people simply by presenting information in a particular form. Those people who weren't misled were those who could see the inconsistency in the presentation of this information or they actually had more information that countered the misinformation presented by these deceivers. If Shaitaan were misleading me in this situation, all Allah had to do was present information that showed that Shaitaan was deceiving me because Shaitaan had only presented me with some information or distorted information. But I had received this information directly from the Hadiths and more importantly from the Koran. And the information wasn't distorted. It was what was written. And my father did not come up with any verses in the Koran to contradict the way I understood the verse from Al-Baqarah 2:106

172

but rather he actually supported this understanding by showing examples using yet again verses from the Koran.

This confusion continued to swim inside my head without resolution for some hours. If Allah caused verses to be forgotten as He claimed in Al-Baqarah 2:106, I could not see any other way than that this logically meant that there had been verses in an earlier version of the Koran and these have disappeared to be replaced with similar and better ones. Which means there have been changes in the Koran. And if the Koran itself states that there have been changes made to the Koran yet the Koran also states that 'none can change the words of Allah', then the Koran is contradictory and therefore cannot be Allah's Word.

This very conclusion caused a great overwhelming shudder to pass through my body and once again I could see the angel Malik grabbing me by the collar and ferociously casting me into the blazing fires of Jahannam.

I had to stop doubting. Which meant I had to stop thinking. Shaitaan was obviously trying to deceive me. The Koran was the unchanging Word of Allah. I just had to accept it. That's just the way it was. I had to believe it by faith.

Chapter 8

My feelings for Taheer since that afternoon in the computer room remained rather mixed. There was a terrible feeling of fear towards him as if there were a bomb inside him ready to explode at any time. In one sudden moment, Taheer completely changed character from being an iconoclast of the entire Muslim religion and then, like removing a program from a computer and replacing it with another, he abruptly became a completely different person, hostile to any dissidents to the faith, in particular, those who followed the corrupt Shiite version of Islam and not the pure version proposed by the Sunnis. This was very incongruous behaviour and in a way revealed the contradictory nature that made up Taheer's character, as if he were suffering from a split personality.

But it was what Reza's cousin, Faisal, had told me about Taheer's infatuation for me coupled with the comment Taheer made to me which made me want to get away from him that Friday afternoon which gave me some pity for the guy. These subtle indications meant that Taheer's sexual proclivity was on par with mine. Further, his sexual energy was directed towards me for some unknown reason. I often looked at myself in the mirror and considered myself a rather average looking guy. That Taheer took an interest in me was somewhat of a compliment. However, even though I also had sexual energy directed towards men, I was not particularly attracted to Taheer. Perhaps it was because of the negative associations with him in the past that I was unable to see anything positive in his physical attributes. Or probably there was an even simpler, more mundane reason, that Taheer simply was not my type. Unlike the men of Sodom and Gomorrah, I noticed that I had a preference for certain men and not for others which showed that my desires were not powered indiscriminately towards all males of the human species.

There still persists within me a feeling of guilt for not doing anything to help avert what was later to happen to Taheer. Perhaps if I had been more aware of and more alert to the imbalances obviously going on in his mind, I may have been able to provide him with at least the solace that he was not alone. But there was no way I could open up to him. Although all indications pointed that way, I was not one hundred percent certain that this was what was really going on in his head and hence there was no way I could reach out to him. After all, the consequences would have been disastrous if I had been wrong about him. But also, how would he have reacted if I had said that I really was not interested in him even though he was a fellow Sunni but I had feelings for Reza, a member of the opposing camp Taheer obviously despised? In fact, I feel that deep down he already knew this and this is what led to his final tragic demise.

And then I thought of Rubasha. Poor Rubasha! If she ever found out that I simply was not in love with her, I wonder how this would have made her feel. Worse, I wonder how she would have felt if she discovered that if I could have had it, I would have married her brother.

And I wonder what would have happened if Reza discovered my true feelings for him. Would he have continued to be the open-minded, gentle guy that he appeared to be or would he have reacted violently against me as many Pakistanis do to such men who are discovered to enjoy the secret, intimate company of another man?

But my strong feelings towards Reza troubled me. We had been told that they were wrong. After all, the All-Wise, All-Knowing Allah was perplexed by the direction of my sexual energy towards other men when through

Lut He cried out in despair, "Would you really lust men more than women?" So despite the beautiful feelings that flowed through me whenever I was in the company of this absolutely handsome and gentlemanly creature, Allah was going to throw me into hell for eternity because of these feelings. Which, as I already knew and I continued to realize, were completely beyond my control.

This in itself fuelled further the doubts about my religion on top of the fuel Taheer had thrown into the fire. It created a lot of confusion within me. Allah, the All-Wise and All-Compassionate, wanted the best for His creatures, and did not want people to "spread corruption" but only that which was good. Hence my feelings for Reza, in what way was this corruption? This sexual energy, this human electromagnetic force which directed itself towards Reza was considered by the world around me, and Allah who created this world, to be evil, wrong, perverted, pure lust of the flesh. But if Rubasha was put in the place of Reza, these same feelings became good, right, normal, a pure form of love. The nature of the attraction remained the same, but by merely changing the gender of the object of this attraction decided whether this sexual energy was of Allah or was from another source.

This made me think of the splitting of hairs of definitions that religious people go through to justify certain aspects of their religions. In particular I saw a similarity in my situation with what was discussed about the adoration of idols and our adoration of the black rock. While bowing down to a rock or objects made of rock in other religions was idolatry, when we did the same to the black rock, this was good. Further, it was sunna. The only thing that was different was the end object of this act. In the same way, a man having sexual energy towards another man was evil but towards a woman it was good. The only thing that changed was the final focal point towards which this energy flowed. Yet had I been able to express it, if Reza was in a situation to reciprocate my feelings, despite some people in our society considering it disgusting, what we did together in privacy out of public view would not have changed the workings of the universe in the slightest. And no corruption would come out of it. The world would go on regardless with no-one affected by the act. Rather, for Reza and me, we would simply have derived pleasure from it.

This orientation came from within. It was something I had no control over. In a way, I felt as if there were two parts of me, a part of me which I could control, the thoughts that went through my head and the movement of my body. Then there was another part of me, separated from my mind but still attached to it but with a mind of its own. I had absolutely no control over this part of me despite how much I wanted. I so desperately wanted this other part of me to be under my control so that I could decide in which direction my sexual energy flowed. But I didn't. And what was worse, the same strong sexual feelings I had towards men in general and to Reza in particular had the flip side of the strong sexual repulsion to women in general and towards Rubasha to whom I was trying so desperately hard to orientate them.

But I was determined not to give up. Allah was perplexed by my sexual orientation and if He didn't like it, then in my total admiration and devotion to Allah and His Prophet, Muhammad, I was determined to find a way to work against this repulsive sexual energy. The problem is that the Koran does not provide any assistance in finding a way out of these feelings. And worse, because the Koran states emphatically the total abhorrence of this sexual orientation, there is no way I could come out and ask anyone, my parents or my Mulvi, about my feelings in order to receive guidance out of it.

As a result, I had to find my own guidance. I did pray even more fervently to Allah to help me. The only answer I had was to ensure that my righteous acts far exceeded my sinful ones and also my sinful thoughts. I often entertained sinful acts with Reza in my thoughts in the privacy of my bed, both just before I went to sleep and when I first woke up in the morning. And worse, he was often the object of my wet dreams. This fact that I had sexual energy directed towards men and in particular towards Reza totally against my will was absolute torture. And this is what drove me to immerse myself totally in the religion. To ensure I did not burn in hell in the next life, I made sure that I followed as many of the tenets of the religion as possible.

In desperation and in order to find a reason for having homosexual tendencies, I entertained the thought that I needed to prove to Allah definitively that I would implicitly obey Him no matter what and sacrifice everything for Him, even that which was dearest to me, in exactly the same way as Ibrahim was willing to sacrifice Ishmael. In this case, Reza had become my Ishmael. My resistance to further proselytising to him was because I didn't want to lose him as a friend. I therefore invented the reason for my association with Rubasha and hence meeting Reza that it was a test that Allah was presenting before me. Which would I ultimately choose: Reza or Allah? As reluctant as I was, eventually I resolved to accept Allah over all things.

But I needed a moment to speak with Reza alone. I had the impression that he held an important position in the family, being the eldest son, but also because of his indepth knowledge of the religion. So converting him out of Shiite Islam would have the flow-on effect of converting the rest of his family out of this corrupt version of Islam into the glorious light of Allah and the correct Islam purported by the Sunni sect. From this, I would eventually marry Rubasha and despite my sexual repulsion to the female form I would honour Allah by having sex in the way that pleased Allah and maybe, I reasoned, this would finally adjust my sexuality in the correct direction. But I needed

178

to find a moment to be with Reza on his own so I could accomplish this task.

One afternoon after school as I walked across the park near my home, to my amazement I saw Reza sitting on the grass cross-legged with his eyes closed completely motionless. Just the presence of Reza was enough to draw me to him but I was further drawn to him because of this unusual activity he seemed to be engaging in. As I approached, he suddenly came to life, kissing what looked like from the distance I was from him a coin suspended from a chain which he then tucked down through his shirt collar.

Reza began to stand up and while doing so looked in my direction. As soon as his eyes met mine, he signalled me over to him with a wave of his hand even though I was already walking in that direction. He then greeted me warmly in his usual ebullient way with a solid hug which just filled me with indescribable joy.

These beautiful feelings evoked by Reza's warm gesture made me further ashamed of the evil person I felt I was, and this is what became the driving force which led me to venture into the conversation I believed was necessary for me to have. I really didn't want to do it because I didn't want to spoil the pleasantness of the moment and overall the good relationship that had formed between the two of us. But at the same time, I didn't want to go to hell because of these feelings I had towards him and I certainly didn't want Reza to go to hell for following his corrupt version of Islam and committing what I perceived as sheerk.

Reza and I first exchanged pleasantries. I then asked him about the object that he had kissed and placed inside his shirt. Reza removed the object to show me. It was a gold medallion with an image of Muhammad on one side and Ali on the other. This just horrified me. Why was Reza carrying this object that to me was simply a form of idolatry?

This further prompted me to enter the conversation I felt I needed to have with him.

"Reza," I began. "You believe in the Koran and how that it is the venerable Word of Allah."

"Yes, of course!" Reza replied. "I am a Muslim. I believe that wholeheartedly."

"And do you believe that everything we believe in must first be based on the Koran, the holy book that came from Allah, to the angel Gabriel and then revealed to Muhammad?"

"Yes, of course, I do!" Reza replied.

I gulped and took a breath before continuing.

"I am troubled by how you Shiites venerate Ali. Ali was a man like everyone else, like any Muslim man. Your veneration of him borders on committing sheerk. The Koran is so clear in saying in Al-Imran 3:80 that we should not take angels or prophets as our lords. And the way you venerate Ali, you have made him your lord in contradiction to the Holy Koran."

Reza laughed a hearty laugh.

"Please," he beckoned with a motion of his hands, "let's sit over there on that park bench."

We strolled over to the bench Reza had indicated and sat down. Once settled on the bench, Reza grabbed my hands and held them with earnest.

"Yah Mustafa, like you, I also believe in the holy Koran and confess that it is the venerable Word of Allah. Now, yes, we Shiites acknowledge Muhammad and the Ahlul-Bayt, in particular, Ali. And we acknowledge Ali as the mawla after Muhammad. However, we do not venerate Ali as our Lord. Like you, we confess that there is only one Lord, that is, Allah. And it is for this reason that we do not take anyone else as Lord. So we do not respond to Ali as Lord. He is a mawla. Because Ali is on the pendant I showed you with Muhammad on the reverse side doesn't mean that we acknowledge Ali as a lord. We are simply showing respect towards him as the successor mawla after Muhammad died. I'm sure you're familiar with the concept of *tawasool*, you know, the use of a *waseelah* to reach Allah."

I had never heard of such a thing and replied in the negative. Reza released my hands to enable him to gesticulate in order to emphasize the argument he was about to make.

"It says in the Koran, in Al-Ma'idah 5:35, 'O you who believe! Fear Allah and seek the means to Him'. This word 'means' in the original Arabic is *waseelah*. Not only do we pray to Allah, we use 'means', 'waseelahs', to seek Him. And one of these means, these waseelahs, is Ali, the successor mawla after Muhammad. But we don't look to him as a lord as there is only one Lord, Allah."

I had to think about that for a moment before replying. "But, Reza, we are not to pray to anyone but Allah. The waseelah, or means to Allah is not through intermediaries or other people. The waseelah, or means, is through the prayers and other rites and practices of the Islamic faith. Praying five times a day, reading the Koran, fasting during Ramadan, conducting our lives in accordance with the precepts of our religion, these are the means to Allah. Don't you agree?"

Reza laughed and moved. "Yah Mustafa, I appreciate your insight. But you have to understand the origin of the word. The word *waseelah* comes from the Arabic triliteral root *wsl* which among many things means 'to plead' or 'to ask for help'. From this we get the related word *tawasool*. In Classical Arabic, a tawasool described a person who held a position of power close to the king, meaning someone who had the ability to speak directly to the king on behalf of someone lower down in society. The word *waseelah* which also comes from the triliteral root *wsl* carries the concept of an intermediary, a go-between, in the form of someone, rather than an action. In other words, the concept of tawasool is to seek Allah through an intermediary, a means, a waseelah.

In the same way, Muhammad, the prophets, the Ahlul-Bayt and the imams, all these people are waseelahs through whom we can gain access to Allah because the waseelahs speak on our behalf. So, although I have Ali on my pendant and I respect him, I respect him as a waseelah. I don't view him as my lord for there is only one Lord, Allah."

I had to take a moment to digest this information. Reza obviously had a deeper understanding of this verse and the original Arabic meaning of the words used in this verse than I did. However, his explanation still didn't quite gel when I thought of what it said elsewhere in the Koran.

"But Allah is close to all of us," I objected. "As it says in Al-Qaf 50:16, 'And certainly We created man, and We know what his soul whispers to him, and We are nearer to him than his jugular vein'. This means Allah is closer to us than any waseelah could ever be, if the waseelah were a person. Further, Allah says to us in Al-Baqarah 2:186 that 'I am near. I respond to the invocation of the supplicant'. In this verse, not only does Allah acknowledge that He is close to us, closer than our jugular vein, when someone prays directly to Allah, Allah answers that person's prayer. There is no need for an intermediary. I mean, right at the beginning of the Koran, in Al-Fatiha 1:5, part of the prayer that both Sunnis and Shiites pray daily, it says 'You alone we worship and You alone we ask for help'. If this is what we pray daily, then the waseelah to Allah cannot be an intermediary to speak on our behalf because then we would be asking someone else for help and not from Allah alone. If Allah is so close to us, closer than our jugular veins, this means Allah is much closer to us than any intermediary could ever be, whether it be Ali, the Ahlul-Bayt or even Muhammad himself. So, this means that if we go to Allah through an intermediary, a waseelah, we are actually taking a longer route to Allah seeing Allah is closer to us than our jugular veins, but Ali, the Ahlul-Bayt, the imams and Muhammad are not that close and are in a specific time and place in the universe."

Reza leaned back, looked up in the air and then back at me. "I can see your confusion," Reza replied, "and I totally understand it."

I was quite taken by Reza's reply to me at this point. At first I felt rather insulted and my shackles went up when he said that I was confused. The verses in the Koran which I had quoted were quite clear. However, I was more taken by the fact that he did not attack me and say that my argumentation was wrong or flawed. Rather, I could see he was opening up his mind and sincerely trying to see things from my perspective in order to see if we could reach a common point of view. This was so unlike my father or my Mulvi who, without actually trying to see things from the point of view of the Shiites, adamantly said the Shiites were wrong whenever the Shiites proposed any argument. By contrast, Reza was trying to see things from my perspective in order to see if we could both arrive at the same general consensus.

"If what you are saying were true," Reza replied, "then we would have a contradiction in the Koran. Now, it says in An-Nisaa 4:64, 'And We did not send any Messenger except to be obeyed by the permission of Allah. And if, when they wronged themselves, they had come to you and asked Allah's forgiveness and the Messenger had asked forgiveness for them, surely they would have found Allah Oft-Forgiving, Most Merciful.' Notice how Allah sent messengers and these messengers were sent to be obeyed but only by the permission of Allah. So even when we ask a waseelah for help, we still are asking Allah alone, but simply through an intermediary who Allah set up. Further, notice how at the end of the verse it says that 'the Messenger had asked forgiveness for them'. Here there were those who could have asked not only Allah but also the Messenger for forgiveness. But because they asked the Messenger

183

for forgiveness, this didn't mean that they were seeking forgiveness from the Messenger. Rather, the Messenger was simply an intermediary who spoke for them on their behalf. I mean, both you as a Sunni and me as a Shiite, we both depend on the clemency of the Prophet both now and on the Day of Judgement to intercede for us, just as it is implied in this verse. But we both acknowledge that this really means that we are asking Allah indirectly.

The Koran shows that Muhammad, the Prophet, the great waseelah, is not the only waseelah. In Yusuf 12:97, 98, we read how Joseph's brothers asked their father, Jacob, to ask Allah for forgiveness. Joseph's brothers didn't speak to Allah directly and say, 'Allah, please forgive our sins'. Rather, they said, 'O our father! Ask for us forgiveness of our sins' to which Joseph's father replied, 'Soon I will ask my Lord for forgiveness for you'.

Even in the Hadiths we have yet other waseelahs. In Sahih Bukhari Volume 5, Book 57, Number 59 we read how Umar bin Al-Khattab said to Allah that they used to pray through the Prophet Muhammad for rain but when Muhammad died they prayed through the uncle of the Prophet for rain and Allah answered their prayers. The Prophet's uncle became the intermediary, their waseelah.

And, I mean, be honest with yourself, Mustafa. How many times have you asked someone to pray for you? I know I have often asked my father to pray for me such as when I'm about to sit for an exam. As soon as I ask my father to pray for me, he becomes my waseelah. But when I do this, am I asking someone else for help? No, of course not! I'm asking Allah, indirectly mind you, but I'm seeking help from Allah and Him alone."

I sat there speechless for some time. I simply didn't know what to say. What Reza had said made a lot of sense and further was supported by both the Koran and the Hadiths. However, the difference was that Reza could see unity in his argumentation but all I could see a blatant contradiction. If Allah is closer to us than our jugular veins and Allah answers the prayers of the supplicant who calls on Him and it is to Allah alone that we seek help, then all these other means, these waseelahs, are simply redundant. Further, to me it was all sheerk. However, Reza appealed to both the Koran and the Hadiths themselves for support and even to our own daily practice of asking others to pray for us to show that seeking help from Allah indirectly through a waseelah was clearly supported in the Koran and the Hadiths.

But what struck me even further was all my argumentation to show the redundancy of waseelahs could also apply to Muhammad. As Allah alone had the power to forgive, what need was there for the Prophet? Further, the Koran says many times such as in Al-Baqarah 2:107 that we will not find from anyone else but Allah as protector and helper, and in verses such as Al-Imran 3:38 it says that Allah only is the "All-hearer of prayer". And Allah warns in Ar-Rad 13:14 "And those who invoke besides Him", that is, Allah, "they do not respond to them with a thing". As these verses indicated, we did not need nor was it useful to go through any waseelahs to Allah as we could go straight to Him directly, bypassing everybody, including Muhammad.

Further, my argumentation to show Reza his veneration for Ali was in a way sheerk only highlighted to me how our veneration of the prophet Muhammad is also sheerk. It may be true that Muhammad was the greatest prophet, but the fact still remained that he was only a man and a created being no different to all the other prophets, the Ahlul-Bayt, the imams, the mulvis, as well as all the angels to whom we were not to take as lords, as there was only one Lord, Allah.

I then thought of Reza's pendant again. Reza's pendant had a figure of Muhammad on one side and Ali on the other. This made Ali appear equal to Muhammad. My initial thoughts had been that this was blasphemous that Shiites made Ali equal to Muhammad, a mere man brought up almost to the equal status of the venerable Prophet. But for the first time, I felt as if Allah were trying to show me through the Shiites that this pendant showed the opposite, that the pendant brought Muhammad down to the level of Ali, showing that Muhammad should not be exalted as highly and uniquely as we tended to make him, and to show us that, like Ali, we should not take Muhammad as a lord but view him merely as a human.

But this further created confusion in my head. The first pillar of the Islamic faith was that there was only one God and Muhammad is His prophet. I had simply assumed that this meant that Muhammad alone was the intermediary between us and Allah. But according to what Reza had explained to me and had explicitly supported as evidence from both the Hadiths and from the very Koran itself, there were other intermediaries, waseelahs, through which or through whom we could and further we were required to use to communicate with Allah. Any arguments against these waseelahs by their very nature included the Sunni veneration of the holy Prophet, Muhammad.

I simply had no answer at this time. What further surprised me was that Allah was not providing me with guidance while I was trying to convert Reza out of the corrupt Shiite version of Islam to the pure Sunni sect. Rather, Satan was creating more confusion inside of me. That was the only explanation I had. Satan was misleading me, creating the false understanding of these Koranic verses so that Reza could continue to follow his evil desires in venerating Ali as equal to Muhammad which almost brought him equal to Allah.

"You know, Mustafa," Reza then said and held my shoulders in his hands. "I totally admire you, you know? You're not like other Sunni Muslims who just accept their religion superficially. You really enquire into your faith to ensure that what you believe is true. Further, the fact that you go so far as to associate with Shiites and actually ask questions about the faith is a great admirable quality about you. If more Sunnis could be like you, there would be a lot more unity within the Muslim community and this would break down the wall between us. I really like you a lot, Mustafa."

This last comment by Reza engendered wonderful feelings inside me. Reza holding my shoulders and telling me that he liked me was simply beyond description. If ever I had deep feelings for him it was at this moment in time.

And this moment in time also created great confusion within to which I attributed all to Satan. Reza was being nice to me and saying these wonderful things about me. And I had wonderful feelings for him. But this was not because Reza was a really nice, open-minded guy, trying to establish peace between our two divided sects. Satan was using Reza, both through his beautiful character and through his physical attractiveness to lure me away from the pure version of Islam into the corrupt Shiite sect of the faith.

For the first time since I had known him I wanted to get away from him as quickly as possible. During this sudden pause in conversation, I abruptly got up, giving Reza an excuse as to why I needed to go so suddenly. Reza stood up with me. We went through an elaborate farewell and then I turned to leave. But just as I was about to head off in the direction of my home, I saw Taheer over in the distance of the park sitting on another park bench. I wondered how long he had been there and if he had noticed me talking with Reza. He wasn't looking in our direction but staring at the ground in front of him so I didn't know for sure if he was aware that I was in this park. My mind was going into further chaos. Everything about Taheer, about Reza, about all the questions about the religion was suddenly swimming around in my head that I just wanted to turn off all thought processes.

When I reached home, I must have had a distraught look on my face because my mother's first question after I had arrived was to ask what had happened to me and if everything was alright. I simply summarised my conversation with Reza in vague terms, explaining that I had had an argument with Reza over a great difference between the beliefs of the Sunnis and those of the Shiites. I realized that I must have come across as a lot more upset by the discussion than I really felt about it when I heard what my mother had to say in reply.

"Don't let it worry you too much," my mother sighed. "Allah knows what He's doing. Maybe Rubasha is not the right girl for you." She added a deeper sigh which I guess was simply her expression of disappointment that a potential wedding was no longer in the wind and she was accepting this as a despondent acceptance of the will of Allah.

"In the end," she continued in a tone of determined optimism, "it is important to honour Allah, even if people don't want to hear the truth. After all, how many of the prophets in the past met with resistance? As the Koran teaches, many were killed. Even the Prophet himself risked his life when he presented the truth to the people. Allah is no doubt training you to stand up for what you believe no matter what."

From then on, my relationship with Rubasha was rather awkward. Rubasha was the brother of the man who I both felt extremely close to but who also had been the cause of seeing further gaping flaws in my perfect religion, and so even though I had not had this conversation with Rubasha directly, I knew that she no doubt shared these same views. I tried hard to maintain some cordiality with her but I could tell that she knew that something had broken between us. Eventually I provided an excuse that was easy for her to swallow, that trying to keep abreast of schoolwork with the

188

final exams looming over us was affecting my mood, an excuse which she fortunately readily accepted.

Not long after my discussion with Reza, I was on my way home from school and once again walked through the same park that I had always done. Suddenly a white pigeon flew down in front of me. It then looked up at me as if it hadn't realized I was there and then flew up in the air over my head. I turned to watch it fly off in the distance and with that, I saw behind me about a hundred metres away Taheer walking in the same direction I had come. I instantly froze. But then so did he. He then smiled and continued in my direction. Although my natural instinct was to immediately run away, I knew I couldn't do this without providing an explanation later to Taheer for such behaviour and so I just waited for him to reach me.

Taheer extended out his arm and we greeted with a handshake.

"I didn't know you lived in this area," I said somewhat surprised.

"No, I don't. I came this way to see someone," was Taheer's reply. My intuition was telling me that he was stalking me. And then I further thought, how many other times had he followed me home like this?

"Well, I don't want to keep you," I then said as a means to get away from him without it coming across as rude.

Taheer looked around in the park.

"Your friend isn't here today?" he asked.

I stood there for a moment, not sure what to say. I knew who he was talking about but I didn't understand the full meaning of the question. But then Taheer's tone changed from friendly to somewhat of hostility.

"Why are you associating with that guy anyway? He's a Shiite. And the Shiites follow a corrupted version of Islam. They commit sheerk and follow other innovations brought into the religion. Like all infidels, they are not fit to live!"

That last comment made me shudder. My mouth went dry and it felt as if I needed to run. But I had to say something. But this last comment of his also made me somewhat angry.

"Taheer, whose business is it of yours to say who I should be friends with and who not? And in any case, isn't Reza and his family and all Shiites free to investigate the faith and find out what is true and what is not? And do you think it's your decision who goes to paradise and who doesn't?"

There was a moment of silence and to me this signalled that it was time to part. I turned to continue my journey home when Taheer grabbed my right arm with both hands. This made me stop and turn to face him. There was an earnestness in that grip. However, Taheer just looked me in the eyes with an intent I cannot explain nor could I read in his eyes what he was trying to non-verbally say to me. It appeared that he was about to say something but then he just released my arm, turned and left. I watched Taheer walk to the other end of the park before I made my final journey home. This strange event troubled me. But from that time on, Taheer became completely aloof at school and I no longer saw him at the park.

It was finally time for our final school exams. Both Rubasha and Taheer sat for the same final school exam that I sat for. One thing struck me that day that I had never realized until this moment: once this exam was over, I would have no real reason to visit Rubasha and hence see Reza, except if I were to continue the charade that I was in love with Rubasha.

When we left the examination hall, a number of my friends and I hugged and cheered about having completed school studies forever. While in our jubilant state, I heard Rubasha call my name and so I turned to see her come rushing over to us with Sameen and Ambreen close behind.

"It's over! We've finished!" she said full of elation, and Sameen and Ambreen supported this statement with expressions of absolute relief and delight on their faces. We spent a moment asking each other about questions in the exam and what each of us had answered, yells of delight mixed with humphs of frustration when one of us discovered we had probably answered certain questions with similar answers hence correctly and others completely differently and possibly incorrectly. But there was nothing more we could do now except wait for the results to come out and determine the destiny of our adult life.

Eventually we began to disperse. As my friends started to walk down the stairs from the examination hall, I saw over in the distance Taheer staring at me. I cannot be sure what was going through his mind at that moment but the expression on his face was very troubling. We looked at each other eye to eye for what seemed like an eternity.

This was interrupted by Rubasha calling for my attention.

"Can you wait for me?" she asked after having said goodbye to the others in our group. "I just need to pick up some of my assignments and then we can have one last walk home from school together for old times' sake."

"Yeah, sure," I replied, half with my attention on Rubasha, half with my mind on Taheer. "I'll meet you over on one of the park benches."

Rubasha ran down the stairs and disappeared. I looked up to see Taheer but he had completely vanished. I scanned the area but he had completely disappeared as if he had been vaporised, almost like a premonition of what was soon to really happen to him.

Rubasha and I set off on our walk back home. We finally made it to the park. So many memories were wrapped up in this park. We went and sat down on one of the park benches. For a moment there was silence as we watched the birds come down and feed. There were different types of birds of different species feeding harmoniously together. This put a thought in my mind.

"Rubasha, meeting you and your family has opened my mind somewhat. I know we hold different views of Islam but after speaking extensively with your brother, Reza, I've realised that there is a lot more of my religion I need to learn."

"What do you mean?" Rubasha asked perplexed.

"We have been told to view the Koran and the tenets of our religion in only one way. But after discussing with Reza and what you Shiites believe, I've come to realise that maybe Sunnis and Shiites can actually find, what can I say, a middle ground that unites us. What supposedly separates us to me appears a lot smaller than what actually unites us."

"That's wonderful to hear that," Rubasha said with delight. There was something deeper in Rubasha's delight than simply the agreement that Sunnis and Shiites could work closer together.

"You know," I continued, "I'd really like to continue to visit you and speak with Reza more on the topic." I gulped when I had finished that last statement because I knew that part of the reason for seeing Reza again was not above board. Rubasha's response to this also showed that her delight also was not totally above board either. She made a comment about how this would bring us closer together although who was involved in the "us" was ambiguous.

We sat for a while in the park, reminiscing about our time at school, laughing about embarrassing and silly moments, teachers we would miss and those we wouldn't, and everything about school life that had finally come to an end. Rubasha eventually made the comment that she had to return home.

Before leaving the park, I took one glance around to see if Taheer had been watching on all this time. But he was nowhere to be seen.

Little did I realise at the time that this was the last time that I would associate with Rubasha and that I would ever see Reza again.

It occurred merely days after our final exam. The explosion was loud enough to be heard in our area. This was soon followed by a plume of dark smoke ascending up into the blue sky and the sound of sirens piercing the air. Like a fallen leaf stuck in the flow of water in a river, I was drawn in to hastily follow the crowd that was moving in the general direction of the explosion. The terrible pain of fear in the pit of my stomach continued to grow as the swarm of people moved closer and closer to the source of the explosion and the familiarity of the place became more and more evident. At some point the crowd stopped and we couldn't go any further but simply observe it from a distance. However, from our vantage point it was clear to see the source of the explosion. There burning furiously, with emergency vehicles and people moving rapidly in chaotic randomness in the vicinity, was the Shiite mosque, the one near the imam bargah in which I had once prayed with Reza.

"Oh, no, God, no," my lips involuntarily pronounced as the reality of the moment overwhelmed me. It was Friday and the hour of prayer. The terrible pain of fear reached a crescendo when the realization hit me that there was a good chance that Reza had been in the mosque when the explosion occurred. The anguish inside pushed me forward to find out if what I was thinking about Reza were true. However, I just couldn't make it through the throng. There was total pandemonium, people pushing here and there, emergency personnel yelling, injured people screaming. The pain in my gut was overwhelming and had spread to my throat. The terrible sound of screams of people, mainly women, was just horrific, moving me to want to be sick and to weep all at the same time.

I stood for quite some time, watching on as emergency personnel attempted to remove people from the burning inferno of the mosque and firefighters attempted to put out the flames. Eventually I realised that there was nothing further I could do but wait till the fiasco had cleared and light could be shed on the situation. With much reluctance I accepted the fact that I couldn't do anything more and decided reluctantly to return home.

At first I thought it had been a terrible accident. However, things turned out worse than I imagined. It came out in the news that the source of the explosion was a suicide bomber who had entered the mosque and in the middle of the moment of prayer, he had detonated himself with what had seemed to be quite a messy bomb, one that could create a lot of immediate damage and continue to burn for some time afterwards, creating the maximum amount of damage to the greatest number of people possible in such a confined space. A Sunni Muslim had become a martyr for the Sunni cause against the rogue, corrupted Shiite version of the Islamic faith.

As a way to take control of the situation, we were required to stay within our homes and only go out when necessary. On occasion I tried to ring Rubasha but the phone was always engaged.

But the worst was to find out the identity of the suicide bomber. About a day or so after the incident, someone knocked at the door. I was sitting in the loungeroom with my grandparents drinking tea. My grandmother got up and opened the door, and there standing at the door was Reza's cousin, Faisal. Faisal stood at the door forlorn. My grandmother looked at me and so I stood up and made my way to the door.

"Faisal?" I asked.

Faisal then entered through the door, hugged me and then cried into my left shoulder. I could feel the warm wetness from the tears. My grandmother gave me a strange, disturbing look and then disappeared, only to return with a freshly made pot of strong tea. By this stage, Faisal was able to get a hold on himself. I led Faisal over to the sofa.

My grandmother offered Faisal a cup of tea. Faisal looked up at her with a sniff and thanked her respectfully while taking the cup. He then placed the cup in front of him on the coffee table. He then pronounced those dreaded words.

"He's dead," he spluttered but this time I could tell that he was holding back the tears and doing his best to maintain his composure. "Reza's dead."

The news hit me like a bucket of cold water being thrown over my body. I could not hold back my emotions and so it was my turn to weep. Faisal held me and we both wept onto each other's tunics. This was the most devastating of news.

Some time elapsed before either of us could talk. When we were able to take control of ourselves, I noticed that my grandmother, my grandfather, my mother and my father were seated in the room looking on disturbingly. Eventually Faisal was able to enlighten us with the events. Yes, there had been a suicide bomber who had blown himself up inside the mosque. Faisal knew the identity of the suicide bomber – it had been Taheer. Taheer's brother, Amin, had been telling Faisal of his concerns about his brother and his erratic behaviour. Faisal and Amin had become suspicious that it had been Taheer himself who had committed this terrible act because of Taheer's rather erratic behaviour on the day of the bombing. Faisal had been at Amin and Taheer's place that morning and there was a time when Amin commented that it had been unusually quiet in Taheer's room. When Amin had entered Taheer's room to investigate, Taheer wasn't there. On the floor were empty packets that had contained ball bearings, a half empty packet of rat poisoning, and a bucket containing part of the rat poisoning that the original packet didn't have. Amin instinctively put all the pieces together and told Faisal that they had to get to the Shiite mosque before Taheer did. But they had barely made it out of the block of units when they had heard the explosion. Although there was nothing left of Taheer's torso, his head and hands had remained intact enough for the authorities to identify the body. The ball bearings soaked in poison which Taheer no doubt had used to bring the casualty count to a maximum to increase his chances of martyrdom had also killed Reza.

When I had heard that, in my mind's eye I saw that image of Taheer in the project lab, his deep brown eyes open widely as he uttered those words, "Those Shiites are unbelievers, *kaffeers*. They associate Ali with Allah hence they're committing sheerk. And what does Allah demand of us in Al-Baqarah 2:191 to do? 'Kill them! Such is the reward of the disbelievers'." And Taheer had obeyed the command from the Koran explicitly.

I felt as if I was going to throw up but somehow managed to divert that sensation and limit it to simply bursting into tears. Faisal held me close and while I wept I could feel Faisal's convulsions and that he was weeping too.

Some time later, there was another knock at the door. It was Amin, Taheer's brother. I had never met Amin before but recognised the resemblance of his brother in his features. Amin had gone to Rubasha's place to look for Faisal, and Rubasha had told him where Faisal had gone. I began to realise that Faisal and Amin were friends and eventually worked out that they were friends from school and had remained friends once they had left. This then explained how Faisal had known so much about Taheer.

Amin was invited in. He came and sat with Faisal and me. He kept repeating over and over again that he was sorry. He apologized to Faisal and me but also to everyone else in the room as if he were directly responsible for this horrible event.

It was my grandfather who brought harmony into the place. He gave words of consolation to Amin, explaining that it wasn't his fault, and to Faisal that it wasn't the end and that we would see Reza at the Resurrection. My grandfather continued his soothing words which helped somewhat to tolerate the pain. Eventually Faisal and Amin were once again self-composed enough to leave, apologizing for their intrusion and thanking my parents and grandparents for their hospitality.

This awful event crushed me deeply for a long time afterward. It was not only the loss of Reza that affected me but also what Taheer had done as his conviction for following Allah as he understood it from the Koran. And this was not an isolated event. Violence perpetrated against people of different religious persuasions continued. We would hear about other Sunni Muslims suicide bombing inside Shiite mosques, Shiite suicide bombers attacking Sunnis, Sunnis bombing Al-Ahmadiyyah mosques, a continual succession of suicide bombers blowing up the mosques belonging to what on the surface really were simply the mosques of fellow Muslims, all because of a variation in their beliefs.

Where, then, will all this lead us? If those of one sect of Islam consider those of another sect as kaffeers, and therefore like Taheer take heed to what Allah commands in the verse from Al-Baqarah 2:191, what future awaits us?

Chapter 9

And that was school. The only memories that I retain of this period of my life are firstly the pleasant and then lastly the tragic memories of Reza. In life, Reza had followed his religion in total devotion and he backed up what he believed from careful study of what is almost universally believed by Muslims to be considered Islamic literature, both the Koran and the Hadiths. Reza greatly influenced the way I thought about Islam and caused me to delve further into the literature associated with the faith.

But what troubled me the most was not knowing where Reza went after he died. Despite the sincerity of his belief and the support he gave to it, I was still brought back to the thought that the Shiite version of Islam was wrong. Had I been given the time to do so, I was sure I would have eventually been able to provide the evidence to show Reza the errors of his belief and bring him round to the true light of the pure version of Sunni Islam. But Taheer had abruptly terminated all this. Instead of sitting down, having a long discussion and providing evidence to show Reza unequivocally that his Shiite version was a corrupt version of Islam and leading him to Jahannam and that if he altered his beliefs to encompass only the pure light of Sunni Islam that this would lead him to an eternity in paradise, Taheer simply killed him.

Both Reza and Taheer affected the way I thought about Islam. Taheer's gruesome proclamation to "Kill them! Such is the reward of the disbelievers" as it says in Al-Baqarah 2:191 was a commandment from the Holy Koran. When I had the strength to read this in the context of the entire passage without bursting into tears at Reza's tragic death because of this verse, I tried to reason that Taheer had taken this small passage completely out of context. So I went back to the Koran and read the verse before it and then the verse in question, Al-Baqarah 2:190 and 191:

And fight in the way of Allah those who fight against you,
but do not transgress. Indeed, Allah does
not like the transgressors.
And kill them wherever you find them
and drive them out from wherever they drove you out,
and oppression is worse than killing.
And do not fight them near Al-Masjid Al-Haraam
until they fight you,
then kill them. Such is the reward of the unbelievers.

I consulted my Mulvi and he said that the context of this verse was this. There was a group of non-Muslims in the area of Al-Masjid Al-Haraam that the Muslims wanted out of there. Al-Masjid Al-Haraam, which literally translates as *The Forbidden Mosque*, and is rendered in some English translations of the Koran as *the Sacred Mosque*, was the Kaaba in Mecca, so my Mulvi explained and which all Muslims understand it to be, although there is nothing in this verse nor in the entire Koran which substantiates this. The Muslims, so my Mulvi further explained, were therefore given permission to strike back at these people, not only to simply get them out of Mecca but to even kill them. Those modern day Muslims who take these verses to mean that it is all-out permissible to simply kill non-Muslims or anyone considered to be a kaffeer willy-nilly were simply taking these verses out of context because these verses related to a specific event in history.

While this explanation was soothing, especially as it had come from an authority figure, I was still left with certain issues I couldn't resolve. If these verses relate to a specific moment in time, what then were they doing in the eternal Koran? This is a contradiction in thinking that

199

Muslim apologetists don't seem to realise, that if verses in the Koran need to be understood within a context, then the Koran cannot be eternal. To make the claim that verses in the Koran need to be undersood within a context, that is, at the time in which these verses were written, then these verses are fixed to a specific moment in time. So for apologists to argue that critics of the Koran take verses out of context, these Muslim apologists are at the same time implicitly admitting that they don't believe in the eternality of the Koran.

Another problem was that I could still see that Taheer had a point. The last portion of verse 191 simply says "such is the reward of the unbelievers". That is, the reward for the unbelievers is death, that they be killed, that this is their reward for being *kaffeers*. I could see that Taheer hadn't taken this portion of the Koran out of context at all. While in this specific example certain unbelievers had been killed by the believers, the believers were given sanction to kill the unbelievers simply because they were unbelievers. This meant that the "reward" for unbelievers in general was that they be killed, for no other reason than that they simply did not believe. It wasn't because of any particular crime they had committed, how they had stolen from believers, raped believers or murdered believers, the reward of death was as this verse indicated simply because they did not believe.

And then there was the issue about martyrdom. Although it wasn't something specific that my Mulvi or my father ever talked about, it was generally understood what it meant to die a martyr's death. That is, Muslims could martyr themselves by killing as many kaffeers as they could and by doing so bypass Judgement Day and get into paradise quickly without having to give an account of any of their earthly misdeeds. All sins were forgiven. But killing oneself is not an easy thing to do. Not everyone has the courage nor the audacity to end his or her life no matter how strongly they believe in the religion, nor how much they claim that they believe that by doing so their next destination is paradise. So why did Taheer do it? What led Taheer to completely destroy himself at such a young age? Taheer, as Faisal had implicated, and as Taheer himself had almost confessed to me, no doubt had feelings for men as I did, and in particular, he had feelings for me. Homosexuality carried a severe penalty in Pakistan. So it didn't matter how natural it was, the ruling body and the laws of the country stipulated that if we allowed our natural proclivity to express itself, we would be condemned severely, even though the sexual expression caused no harm to society whatsoever. What was worse, and this must have been the case for Taheer, was that whether societies which condemn homosexuality realise this or care, along with our sexuality is the love we develop for a special person, as it was with how I felt about Reza, and from what I suspected Taheer felt about me. It was as if Taheer had ultimately decided that if it was against the law, against society and against the religion to love whom he wanted to love according to the dictates of the essence of his being, what point was there for living? Further, if Taheer didn't choose himself a wife to marry, someone in his family would eventually have done so and Taheer would have been faced with the horrid reality of having to force himself to make love to someone he found physically and sexually repugnant. But the religion had provided him with a way out. By bypassing Judgement Day, Taheer wouldn't even have to give an account to Allah for all the sexual thoughts he had had about men which, as it was with the inhabitants of Sodom and Gomorrah, would have condemned him forever in Jahannam. And if the religion promised a blissful hereafter for killing oneself for the sake of killing others, why not take this way out and avoid the obvious awkwardness of this life and the horrors of the next?

But I was determined not to go down this road. It was obvious where my homosexuality would lead me so I was determined not to become a casualty like Taheer. I often thought of where Taheer had really gone.

In the Koran, Allah is puzzled by the people of Sodom and Gomorrah because of their lust for men and not for women. What was implied from these verses in the Koran was that Allah was not only horribly perplexed by the men actually having sex with other men, He was horrified by the very notion that men actually felt sexual attraction to other men. This creates an extremely difficult situation for gay Muslims. Although we can hide from the world our sexual orientation through what we say and do because people cannot see our inner thoughts and feelings, we cannot hide from Allah anything and hence Allah even knows what is going on inside our very thoughts, including our sexual attraction for the same sex and the repulsion for the opposite.

The side effect from this is that it taught me how to tell lies and tell them so convincingly that I could feel that I myself believed them, even when there was no truth in them. In fact, the whole need to commit doublethink as I had discovered earlier in my journey taught me how to lie effectively. I had to lie convincingly enough not only for others but also to myself that I had sexual desires towards women as every heterosexual man has so that Allah could not even detect the very homosexual thoughts that I tried so desperately to suppress.

What was worse was that there was no-one to turn to for answers. Neither a man nor a woman in Pakistan can go to their parents or their mulvi or their imam and say, "Excuse me, sir or madam. I can feel I have strong sexual feelings towards people of the same sex but a total abhorrence towards people of the opposite sex. What is your advice? Can you help me out of this predicament? How do I turn my lust towards the opposite sex and not towards my own?" Religious scholars cannot point to a verse in the Koran nor the Hadiths that says something to the effect of, "if you find yourself in this situation, do this and your sexual orientation will be reoriented towards the opposite sex". Further, the chances were that you would not come out of this meeting alive.

Therefore, I had no-one to talk to. My only answer was to apply myself completely and wholeheartedly to my religion. There surely had to be an answer because Islam was a complete religion.

I had been brought up to believe that the fundamentals of my religion were the Koran and the Hadiths. But from my discussions with Reza and my own reflections, I had come to question the Hadiths. As it was, in earlier discussions with my Mulvi, my father and with Reza, there was no clear consensus about which hadiths were reliable and which ones weren't. It appeared that people held in high esteem those hadiths that supported a particular point of view only because these people simply wanted that point of view to be true. For example, according to one hadith, as Reza had pointed out, the proclamation made by Muhammad about the perfection of Islam was made at Ghadeer Khumm. But my father denied this hadith in favour of a different hadith which claimed that Muhammad had made this declaration at Mecca. Also, one of the justifications Reza made for the use of the turbah while praying was the hadith where Muhammad prayed inside a mosque with a leaky roof, a hadith that my father flatly denied. Another was the hadiths which talk about what Muhammad left behind when he died. According to the Sunnis, one hadith says that before Muhammad died, he said he was leaving behind the Book of Allah and his sunna. By contrast, Shiites support a different hadith which says that what Muhammd really said was that he was leaving behind the Book of Allah and his Ahlul-Bayt.

What further led me to question the Hadiths in total was that some hadiths were considered *sahih*, or reliable, while others were considered *dhaeef*, or weak. But even this had its complications. While certain people held certain hadiths as *sahih*, other people considered these same hadiths as *dhaeef*. So there was no general universal agreement about which hadiths were true and which ones weren't.

But even how the Hadiths came to be in the first place made me question their reliability. The first and greatest of the Hadiths, Sahih Bukhari, was first penned about a hundred and fifty years after Muhammad had died by a man called Muhammad Al-Bukhari. We had been told that Al-Bukhari was aware that there were many *hadiths*, that is, sayings or narrations, of Muhammad the Prophet floating around in the empire and people were using these as a guide in order to conduct their lives and then forced others to live by. Why people believed these hadiths was because each hadith had an *isnad*, that is, a chain of people who had passed this hadith down from the Prophet to the person who finally penned it to paper. The isnads started out by saying that person A heard from person B who heard this from person C who heard this from person D and so on until we got to the person who was, for example, seated at dinner with the Prophet and he had heard the Prophet say something or he saw the Prophet do something. The very idea that the hadiths were originally passed on orally from a line of people and were only written down after they had been passed from one person to another over many years already logically meant to me that the hadiths could not be trusted. From the time of the Prophet down to the person who actually wrote the hadith down, who could be sure that what was written had been faithfully and reliably passed down from its source, especially as it was passed on by word of mouth?

In any case, Al-Bukhari decided to compile all these sayings into a book. Al-Bukhari gathered all the hadiths of the Prophet that he could find. But he realised that some of these sayings seemed to go against the teachings of the Koran. These obviously could not be authentic hadiths of the Prophet and were probably made up. So Al-Bukhari went through all the hadiths brought to him and sifted through them like a gold prospector separating the nuggets from the dirt. If a hadith did not accord directly with the Koran, then that hadith was rejected.

It was a momentous task. If anyone has ever seen the volumes of Sahih Bukhari beautifully displayed as a collection of many volumes in beautiful Arabic script, they would see that this Hadith is the final version of about 7,000 hadiths that Al-Bukhari decided were the authentic hadiths of what the Prophet said and did. What made this task momentous was that Al-Bukhari started out with a collection of somewhere between 200,000 to 600,000 hadiths which he supposedly meticulously read through and compared against the Koran.

But this simply raised more questions. It was Al-Bukhari who decided which hadiths were authentic and which ones weren't. But who gave him this authority? Did an angel from Allah come down and assist him with the task? And because he never claimed to be a prophet, how serious should we take his compilation?

Further, if Al-Bukhari started out with as some say 600,000 hadiths and from these he only deemed about 7,000 as authentic, this means that he found that 99% of all the hadiths going around the empire attributed to the Prophet were unauthentic. Yet people had been living their lives according to these unauthentic hadiths for over a hundred years. Why would Allah allow such a thing to occur, to watch people who believe in Him follow sayings and deeds attributed to His Prophet, yet do nothing to show which were the true and which were the untrue examples of the Prophet believers were to live by for at least one hundred years?

Even further, the 7,000-odd hadiths that made it into Al-Buhkari's collection in Sahih Bukhari were deemed authentic because Al-Bukhari said they were in accordance with the Koran. But is this really what makes a narration authentic? If I wrote a hadith and it was agreed by all to be in accordance with the Koran, should people believe that I heard this indirectly from the Prophet? And if I included an isnad from my time that led back to the Prophet, how on earth could anyone authenticate each person along the line of the isnad?

Further, Allah sends messages to humanity through the prophets, so were we to accept that each person in the isnad was a prophet? If not, why should we believe any of them?

But what really destroyed completely my consideration of Sahih Bukhari having any bearing on my view of my religion was when I read the following hadith from Sahih Bukhari Volume 7, Book 71, Number 590. In this hadith, there were some people from Medina who were unhealthy and so the Prophet Muhammad ordered them to drink the milk and urine from his shepherd's camels. It was the order by the Prophet to drink camel urine that affected me the greatest. We had been told many times that certain bodily fluids, in particular urine, were so unclean that if even a drop fell on our skin, we had to wash ourselves completely. In fact, Muslims have to go through an entire rigmarole each time they go to the toilet to ensure that not even one drop of urine touches any part of their body or their clothes. Urine is so impure that if a few drops land on clothes after one has relieved oneself, those clothes have to be meticulously washed before they can be worn again. And if only a couple of drops end up on the body, say, on one's finger, then there is special washing that needs to be employed before the finger is deemed clean, so impure this bodily fluid, urine, is considered. This idea of the impurity of urine is supported by what it says in the Koran in the verses from An-Nisaa 4:43 and Al-Ma'idah 5:6 that it is a requirement to clean oneself after coming from the toilet, especially if one is going to pray, because any traces of urine need to be removed from the body as this bodily liquid is

206

extremely unclean. This therefore means that the hadith about drinking camel urine is totally not in accord with the Koran. So why did Al-Bukhari include it if his criterion for rejecting hadiths was the dissonance between what the hadith said and what was written in the Koran?

I initially read this hadith online. I questioned a friend of mine about it and he said that it probably was put there by Jews or Christians to insult our religion. If I were to consult an actual physical book form which contained this hadith, I would find it was not there. However, to my dismay, this hadith even appeared in Hadiths in printed book form which meant that they were written by Muslims, and copied and transmitted faithfully from the time of Al-Bukhari in the 700s from generation to generation up to our present time.

What was worse was that the hadith goes on to say that these men who drank the urine from the camel were later punished by Muhammad himself by having their hands and feet cut off, and they were brutally blinded by having their eyes branded with hot irons and left to die in the desert. This made Muhammad look like a complete monster, totally opposite to the way he was presented to us as the perfect, holy man to be imitated. I was absolutely stunned that Muslims actually agreed to carefully preserve and pass on this terrible hadith which was just so ghastly on so many levels. To me, this particular hadith and all others like it which presented Muhammad in this awful light were insults to the Prophet and hence I felt that Muhammad Al-Bukhari and all other authors of Hadiths with similar stories should have been put to death for blaspheming the Prophet, and anyone who continued to maintain these hadiths as authentic should also suffer the same fate.

There was yet another reason why I just didn't accept the Hadiths. Because the Hadiths were a collection of things Muhammad said and did, did this mean that every single word that came out of Muhammad's mouth and every movement that Muhammad made was divine? Muhammad was a human being and he was capable of saying things that were simply his thoughts at the time because of how he was feeling or what was occurring around him, feelings and events which uniquely related to him.

To bring out this idea, as irreverent as the idea was, I thought, what would have happened if, while at the dinner table, Muhammad had burped or farted, and it was known that he was the source of this pneumatic extrusion, yet out of embarrassment he blamed it on someone else at the table or on one of the servants? Would his accusation be a divine revelation because it had simply come from his mouth, or would this be considered the typical thing that any human would do, embarrassed by something considered rude in public and to divert the embarrassment away from him, blame it on someone else? If someone at the table had heard this and then passed this on, and then this was finally written down and recorded in one of the Hadiths, did blaming someone else for one's air eruption from the internals of the digestive tract at the dinner table become sunna? Further, was it a requirement to burp and fart at the dinner table because Muhammad himself had once done so? In fact, the whole idea of making every proclamation and every action Muhammad ever said and did a commandment of Allah came across to me as sheerk. The Hadiths, in their attempt to record everything Muhammad said and did as if every single syllable that exited the mouth of the Prophet or every movement he made was of divine origin implicitly implied that Muhammad himself was a divine being, even Allah Himself.

From this, I reasoned that the Hadiths weren't to be trusted. They might make interesting reading but in the end they were human fabrications to be appreciated in the same way as anything else written by humans.

By contrast, all Muslims believe that the Koran is the Word of Allah because these were the words revealed to the Prophet directly from the angel Gabriel who in turn had obtained them from Allah. So all that was in the Koran was what had been revealed to Muhammad from the supernatural world, the world of the unseen.

At the time, I didn't know that there was a group of Muslims called Koranists who simply reject all the Hadiths like I was beginning to do and only followed the Koran. I was later to find out that not only are there Koranist Muslims, many Muslims consider that the Koranist Muslims are not Muslims at all because they don't believe in the Hadiths. These same Muslims say that we need the Hadiths in order to interpret the Koran for one cannot understand the Koran on its own. This only raised further questions. If we need the Hadiths to explain the Koran because the Koran is incomprehensible without them, then if the Koran is eternal, so are the Hadiths, as the everlasting Koran could never be understood without the everlasting Hadiths to explain it.

As for not understanding the Koran, this was not because by its nature it was not understandable. This was because we had been told that we could not really appreciate the Koran unless we read it in the original Arabic. Seeing Arabic was not my first language, I had to struggle with the learning of this language before embarking in my understanding of this book.

However, at this stage of my thinking, I decided I wanted to not only read but also understand what the Koran said. My Arabic was definitely improving but I felt with the help of a bilingual Koran I could speed up the process in discovering what Allah required of us from His Holy Book.

In a way, it felt as if I were cheating but I decided to read the Koran in my everyday language anyway. In Pakistan, I spoke two languages, Urdu and English. I decided at first to read the Koran through a translation in Urdu but I found the Urdu translation too awkward and difficult to understand. I had an English translation made by Abdullah Yusuf Ali but this was purely only in English. I wanted a Koran in both the original Arabic and in a language that I used in my every day so I could still cross-check back to the Arabic. To my delight, I stumbled across an Arabic-English interlinear Koran, compiled by Dr Shehnaz Shaikh and Ms Kausar Khatri, which contained a word-for-word translation of the Koran, with one line of Arabic text and below each Arabic word the direct translation into English. In the margin was a complete translation of the verses into English. This meant that I could still read the Koran in Arabic through the use of the Arabic-English interlinear and read the corresponding English translation in the margin to aid my understanding.

Before embarking on my reading of the Koran, I first reflected on what we had been told about this book, that the Koran had existed eternally, co-existing with Allah Himself. This already caused problems with my understanding of Islam. We were told that we should not associate anything with Allah for He alone is God. But if the Koran existed eternally with Allah, then this meant that the Koran like Allah was eternal and uncreated, having very much the same attribute of eternal existence we gave to Allah, and therefore in a way the Koran like Allah was a god. Looking at it from a different angle, a book by its very nature needs to be written. It requires someone taking a pen and writing words onto a solid surface. So logically, a book by its very nature simply cannot be eternal.

When I came under the tutelage of my second Mulvi, this Mulvi had told me to clear my mind of everything I had ever heard and learnt about Islam and read the Koran afresh. Thus I took this approach once again and decided to let the Koran tell me if it was eternal or not, and answer all the other questions I had about my religion.

I began with the first surah, Surah Al-Fatiha. Al-Fatiha wasn't only a Surah of the Koran, it was also a prayer that I as a Sunni Muslim said up to 44 times a day. But it was verses 5 and 6 which struck me:

You alone we worship, and You alone we ask for help.
Guide us to the straight path.

I tried to imagine way, way back in the past, before Allah had created humans and even before Allah had created the angels, at a time when there was nothing in the universe but Allah. If the Koran had been eternal, when Allah looked at these verses on this eternal Koran which existed alone together with Him, who would the "we" and the "us" be referring to? For us as Muslims, we knew that whenever we prayed this prayer, the "we" and "us" were us human Muslims who prayed this prayer. But also, it seemed quite clear to me that this surah was also written from our perspective, the perspective of us humans. So, just in this first surah, the Koran itself was telling me that the Koran simply could not be eternal.

What further seemed strange was that this surah told us to tell Allah to guide us. But we had been told all our lives that the Koran was our guide. I felt that this seemed rather incongruous. It was like tourists in the main centre of Karachi holding a map of the city in their hand and then asking some locals, "Excuse me, could you tell us how to get to such and such a place?" The locals would look at the tourists and the map the tourists were holding, and then think to themselves, or if they were rude enough say to the tourists, "What's your problem? You can't read a map? Isn't that why you have a map in your hand so that it will guide you through the city?" From then on, every time I prayed this prayer, each time I said in Arabic, "Guide us to the straight path", I could hear in the back of my mind a frustrated voice saying, "For God's sake! Just read the Koran! This will guide you. Why are you continually asking me for guidance when I have already sent down guidance to you in My book?! Just open it up and read it!" This frustrated voice became further pronounced when I opened the Koran to the second surah, Al-Baqarah, the longest

211

surah in the Koran, to the second verse of this surah which reads "This is the book, there is no doubt in it, a guidance for the God-fearing." This only further puzzled me why we had to pray up to 44 times a day to ask Allah to guide us when the opening of the very next surah tells us plainly that the Koran was this guide, so we no longer needed to keep asking for guidance as we already had it at our disposal.

But also, once again, what Taheer had told me came to mind. The original Arabic says "*That* is the book", not "*This* is the book", which implies that whoever wrote this was not referring to the book in hand but to another book. But which book? What other book could there be beyond the Koran that the Koran acknowledged that could not be doubted and was the guidance that all humanity needed?

I continued through the surah. The first part is dedicated to simply claiming that this is the truth but only the defiantly disobedient refuse to believe this. What I found odd, though, was that in verse seven Allah says that He has put a veil over the hearts of the unbelievers and that this explains why when we try to convince unbelievers of the truth they continue to refuse to believe. But then in verse 28 the question is raised, "How can you disbelieve in Allah?" when I thought verse seven had already answered the question, they can disbelieve because Allah has made them disbelieve by putting a veil over their hearts.

The surah then goes on talking about the story of the creation of Adam, and how Allah tells the angels to prostrate towards Adam. All the angels obeyed except Iblis, that is, Satan. Adam and his wife were then commanded by Allah to live in *Jannah*, that is, paradise. What this paradise was or where it was located is not clearly spelled out in Al-Baqarah. All that Al-Baqarah tells us is that there were trees in this paradise. Adam and his wife were free to eat from all the trees except one, simply designated as "this tree". However, Satan made Adam and his wife slip and the human pair was forced to go down on earth. This implied that the paradise in which they were originally living was up above the earth. They were also to go down "as enemies to one another" and I guessed that the inference was that there would always be constant tension and enmity between men and women which is why Islam has these specific laws about keeping men and women separate. Adam and his wife were then to wait for Allah to send down guidance. Seeing it says in verse two that "that is the book" which is "a guidance for the God-fearing", I simply assumed that Adam simply had to wait till Allah sent down to him the Koran, or whatever "that book" which was implied in the second verse. However, we never find out the true identity of this guidance nor when Adam finally received it because the topic which follows is directed at the Children of Israel.

In this part of the surah, we read about how the Children of Israel were persecuted by Pharaoh, the boys being killed and the girls kept alive. Then we read how Allah parted the sea and created a path. Which sea it was talking about is not specified in this part of the Koran, simply that there was a path through the sea and this was the opportunity for the Children of Israel to escape persecution under Pharaoh. What followed was that Allah appointed Moses for forty nights and then the Children of Israel took a calf – what they did with it was not specified in the original Arabic but the English translation had in brackets that they worshipped it – and this was wrong. After that, Allah gave Moses the Book "that you may be guided."

This made me pause for a moment from my reading. Allah told Adam to wait for the guidance to come, assuming it to be a book as the second verse of this surah implies, and then we read how Allah sent the Book to Moses for this very purpose. I then wondered, was Adam still alive when Allah sent the Book down to Moses? If not, did Adam eventually receive guidance? And in what form? And was it the same as what was sent down to Moses?

The story goes on how Allah forgave the Children of Israel for taking a calf, and that He provided them with food in the form of quails and something called *manna*, although there is nothing that explained exactly what manna was. Then the Children of Israel were directed to enter an unnamed town and eat abundantly, and to pass through an unknown gate and bow humbly. However, there were some among the Children of Israel who changed words that were said into different words and they were punished accordingly, although what words were changed was not brought out in the story.

Then the Children of Israel asked Moses for water and so Allah told Moses to "strike the stone with your staff." Which stone Moses was told to strike and the stone's location and size was not explained in this part of the story. However it must have been a large rock for out of it flowed twelve springs, although I presumed it meant twelve rivers as I understood springs to be like small lakes which don't flow. Why twelve springs were necessary and not simply one wasn't made clear but there had to have been twelve groups of some kind among the Children of Israel because it says that "all the people knew their drinking place". However, despite the miracle, the people continued to complain to Moses, demanding from Moses to provide them with better food than that which they had been eating, assuming it had been the manna and the quails, and that they wanted cucumbers, garlic, lentils and onions. Allah, however, gave in to their complaint and told them to go down to a city and there they would receive the food they were after. I thought, is this the same city they were told to go to earlier or another city?

Even so, despite providing them with the food they wanted in an unspecified city, Allah struck them with "humiliation and misery" and this was because "they used to disbelieve in the Signs of Allah and kill the Prophets without any right."

When I read this last part, I looked up. Which prophets did the Children of Israel kill? In this part of the narrative there had been two people mentioned to whom Allah gave, or promised to give, guidance, Adam and Moses. Although it didn't say in this part of the Koran that Adam and Moses were prophets, we had been told that they were. Were we to later read that the Children of Israel killed Adam and Moses?

I returned to reading on in the surah. Suddenly there was an interruption to the story about the Children of Israel with the statement that Jews, Christians and Sabeans will also have their reward in the next life, the assumption being that they will all enter paradise together with Muslims. This took me back to something Tanveer at school had said about moral people making it into paradise. In a way, I could see he had a valid point. Jews, Christians and Sabeans will make it into paradise despite the fact that they do not follow the first pillar of the faith, that Muhammad is the Messenger of Allah. This is what it said in the very Koran. This puzzled me but I ignored it, thinking that there was an explanation later in the text.

And then we were brought back to the story of the Children of Israel. At this point of the story, Allah made a covenant with the Children of Israel and raised up a mountain off the ground. I wondered which mountain this verse was talking about. However, had I been there and seen Allah lifting a huge mountain and suspending it in mid-air, I would have been frightened out of my wits and would have done anything Allah told me to do. However, the Children of Israel, so it says in the next verse, turned away from Allah and refused to obey. Certainly a group of people with inflated confidence! One of these commandments that the Children of Israel refused to obey was to do with "the matter of the Sabbath" but what this matter was was not explained.

We then read how that Allah commanded the Children of Israel to kill a cow. In fact, it was this part of the story which gave the name to the surah, for *al baqarah* in Arabic means "the cow". The Children of Israel, however, were reluctant to carry out this command and kept asking Allah what type of cow they were to kill. First Allah said through Moses that it needed to be a cow that was middle-aged, not too old and not too young. The Children of Israel then asked what colour cow Allah wanted killed and the reply was a bright yellow cow. The Children of Israel then asked Moses to ask Allah for more information because to them all cows looked alike. Moses returned with a reply from Allah that it had to be a middle-aged, bright yellow cow, that had never been used as a beast of burden to plough fields, and it should not have a blemish on it at all. Finally, the Children of Israel killed the cow.

The story goes on to talk about a man that "you" killed, although who this "you" is is not brought out in this part of the story but in the context I assumed it was talking about the Children of Israel. Allah then commanded them to strike the corpse with "a part of it" – what this "it" is referring to remains a mystery – and this, so it explains, is how "Allah revives the dead".

At this point of the narrative, I looked up and thought about it. If all that was needed was to strike "a part of it" and a corpse would return to life, all we needed was to identify what this "it" was and then perform the miracle by going into every hospital and bringing back to life those who had died from terminal diseases or from the result of a tragic accident.

I then read on. The narrative goes on to say that even with this amazing miracle, there were those who still refused to believe in Allah and their hearts remained hardened. I found this amazing. If I had been a witness to such miracles, there would no longer be any room for doubt. However, then the narrative moves from hearts being hardened like

216

stone to the very nature of stones, those from which rivers gush forth, then others which split open and water pours out of them – although I couldn't see the difference between these two categories of stones – and then a third type of stones which fall down in fear of Allah. From where they fall and where these stones finally land is not explained. It then goes on to talk about the disbelievers in general only to return back to talking once again about the Children of Israel.

At this point, we read how Allah established a covenant with the Children of Israel and this time it is specified what is in the covenant. The Children of Israel were told to worship Allah and no other god, to be good to their parents, to their relatives, to orphans and the needy, to speak well with people, to establish prayer and to give zakat, to not shed blood and not to evict people from their homes.

It was the part which said "do not shed your blood" which spoke to me. During the Shiite ritual of azadari, those who flogged themselves ended up shedding their own blood. To me this was in direct contravention of this verse in Al-Baqarah 2:84 which illustrated that this ritual was in fact haram.

There was a brief interlude about how Allah sent Moses, then Messengers after Moses, including Issa, but the Messengers "you" denied or killed, the "you" I assumed to be the Children of Israel. Then there was a Book from Allah sent to confirm what was with them. What this book was is not clear in the original Arabic but in the English translation it was accompanied with the word "Koran" in brackets. But the earlier narrative had said that Allah gave Moses a book, and I assumed this was the Torah. This next book that came from Allah "confirming what was with them" I felt was in reference to Issa mentioned a few verses earlier and that it was probably referring to the Injeel, that is, the New Testament.

The running narrative returned to the story of Moses and his communication with the Children of Israel, but it repeated what had been said earlier, how Allah made a covenant with the people and raised a mountain above their heads.

This narrative was then abruptly interrupted. There was an accusation against the greedy, followed by a statement about the necessity of believing in Allah and the angels, in particular Gabriel and Michael.

The narrative then changed from talking about "you" to "they" but it was not really clear who these "they" were. Here I read about King Solomon and about two angels, Harut and Barut in Babylon. This was followed by a number of unrelated comments, one being the infamous verse about the abrogation of verses Taheer had raised with me.

The narrative then changed from talking to the Children of Israel to talking to the People of the Book, that is, the Christians and the Jews. There was an accusation against the People of the Book wanting to turn people away from belief. It was not very clear to me what belief these People of the Book were trying to turn people away from. As it was, these people were People of the Book, and thus far along in the narrative the Book that was sent down from Allah was what was given to Moses, that is, the Torah, and then later another book which confirmed this earlier book, either the Injeel or the Koran. But if Allah had sent Jews and Christians the Book, what did it mean that they were trying to make people disbelieve? Disbelieve in what? It couldn't mean that they were trying to get people to disbelieve in the Book because then how could it be claimed that they themselves were disbelievers if they were People of the Book? That's what it meant by definition that they were People of the Book, that they believed in the Book that was sent down from Allah. This came out further in verse 113 when the Jews said the Christians were nothing and the Christians said the Jews were nothing and this puzzled the writer of this verse who then stated the oddity of this because both the Jews and Christians recite the Book. This confusion only became highlighted in verse 120 where it said that the Jews and Christians will never be happy till "you", and it was unclear who this "you" was, follow their religion. The "you" was instructed to say, "Indeed, the Guidance of Allah is the only Guidance". But this guidance, as it was assumed from what I had read thus far in this surah, was the Torah that Jews and Christians follow. And because the narrative returned back to the Children of Israel, it sounded as if this was the "you" to whom Allah had been talking to.

The Children of Israel were then told to remember Ibrahim, how Ibrahim was made a leader for all humankind and how he built the House as a place of return for all humanity. In the original Arabic, it doesn't say what this House actually is but the English had in parentheses the Kaaba, hence it was assumed to be the Kaaba in Mecca, and the "return" had following it in parentheses that this implied pilgrimage. But the original Arabic didn't say this. The narrative went on to say that Ibrahim built this House with Ishmael and then later they both asked Allah to raise up a Messenger from among their offspring who will "teach them the Book". This Book, going on the preceding portion of this surah implied the Torah, the Book given to Moses. The narrative then focused on Ibrahim's grandson Jacob who told his sons to worship the God of their fathers, Ibrahim, Ishmael and Isaac.

The narrative then jumped back to addressing the Jews and Christians, and sounded like an argument proposed against the Jews and Christians on the one hand, and a group of unidentified believers on the other hand who believed in all prophets, Abraham, Ishmael, Isaac, Jacob, Moses and Jesus, and the books that were given to them, at least the latter two, that is, the Torah and the Injeel. And then there was the concluding comment about prophets: "We make no distinction between any of them". At the time,

219

I thought to myself, yes, we as Muslims do that, we believe in all the prophets, including the prophets of Judaism and Christianity. That's what makes Islam a complete religion and superior over the other Abrahamic faiths.

The narrative continued aimed at an unidentified group of believers who were then confronted with the qibla change. We had been told there was a time when Muhammad received the revelation from Allah to change the qibla from towards Jerusalem, in particular, the Al-Masjid Al-Aqsa, to the Al-Masjid Al-Haraam, which we all knew was the Kaaba in Mecca. There was an accusation against the People of the Book who refused to change the qibla, especially as they knew this was from Allah but they knowingly chose to conceal the truth. This was followed later with the symbols of Safa and Marwah, two rocks in Mecca between which the believers run during pilgrimage as the Prophet once did – although it doesn't say as such in the Koran.

This was followed by a collection of random and somewhat unrelated verses, all of them different commandments. It talked about what we should believe, what we should and shouldn't eat, what happens to those who conceal truth, and the legal retribution of an eye for an eye. It talked about the importance of leaving a will and making sure that the testator does not change it. It talked about the fast at Ramadan and when to start and stop the fast. It talked about fighting for Allah and in which months it was prohibited and in which it was allowed. It then talked about pilgrimage and what to do before, during and after it. It talked of the abstinence of alcohol and gambling. It talked of who to marry and who not to marry. It talked of menstruation and avoiding wives in this state. It then went into great depths talking about what to do in the case of divorce.

The text then returned to narrative, talking about people who came after Moses. There was mention of "their

Prophet" but it doesn't name him. This Prophet said that Allah had appointed a man called Talut as king. From the context, these people were the descendants of the Children of Israel mentioned earlier in the surah because when they argued with the Prophet about this man being made king, the sign of his kingship was a remnant from the family of Moses and his brother Aaron. This King Talut went out to fight against a man with the rhyming name of Jalut. However, before going off to fight, King Talut tested the people with a river. Those who drank from the river were not of King Talut's people. Those who didn't drink from the river were from King Talut's people – except those who took water from the river in the hollow of their hands. Then off they went and defeated Jalut.

The text reverted back to random statements, some commandments, others simply statements to observe, with the final one being a detailed description of what to do if people make an agreement and need to write a contract.

The surah ended with a comment about the Messenger, which I assumed was Muhammad but the Arabic doesn't say as such, and then asking Allah to not burden us with any problems that we find too weighty to bear.

I then read the next surah, Surah Al-Imran. This surah begins by talking of three books, two named, the Torah and the Injeel, then a third, called the Book and the Criterion. The Koran goes on to talk about the Book, especially the infamous verse about taking the meaning literally and allegorically. It is assumed that the Book being mentioned is the unidentified Book mentioned earlier in the surah but then in light of Al-Baqarah this Book could just as well be identified with the Torah.

The Koran talks about people who disbelieve in Allah and why they should believe. There is a brief mention of the people of Pharaoh, but nothing in detail as it came out in Al-Baqarah, only returning to warnings and examples of people who believed and those who disbelieved.

We finally come to a running narrative when we read about the family of Imran, after whom the entire surah is named. Imran promised that he would dedicate his child to Allah, this child being Maryam, or Mary, the mother of Jesus. A man called Zakariya, who I later guessed was the biblical Zachariah, looked after Mary and begged Allah to allow his own wife to have a child for she was barren. We then discover that Zakariya and his wife were very old, and so it was a miracle that Zakariya's wife finally fell pregnant. Zakariya was told to call his son Yahya, and I knew this was the John the Baptist of the Bible, and Zakariya was given a sign that his aging wife would have a child when he was made dumb for three days and three nights and could only communicate using hand gestures.

The narrative changes from Zakariya who was looking after Maryam to Maryam herself. Allah told Maryam that she would have a baby boy, even though she was a virgin, and that the name of the child would be *Al-Massikh Issa*, or in English, the Christ Jesus. Maryam asked Allah how it was possible for her to have a child when she was a virgin to which Allah replied that it was a miracle on His part. But not only would the birth itself be miraculous, so would the Messenger who was a result of this birth. Issa as a child would be able to make birds from clay, breathe into them and the clay birds come to life. Issa would also be able to heal people from diseases and even raise people from the dead. What was intriguing was that Allah says in verse 48 that He would teach Issa "the Book and wisdom and the Torah and the Injeel". I thought this quite intriguing because Allah taught Issa the Torah, the Injeel and then a third unidentified Book. I wondered what this third Book was, if it was another book apart from the Torah and the Injeel, and the same unidentified book mentioned at the beginning of the surah.

The text then goes on to urge people to believe the truth, particularly the People of the Book. In particular, there is exhortation to believe in Allah only, and not to take any of the prophets or angels as lords, the implication being in what could be considered the context of this part of the surah that Christians should not consider Issa equal with Allah.

There is then a collection of random, unrelated statements. Believe in Allah. Spend what you have for Allah. The Jews made unlawful foods that the Torah does not say is unlawful to eat. Don't fabricate lies about Allah. The first House set up for humankind is at Bakkah, which is implied to be Mecca, and the requirement to go on pilgrimage there. And only make friends with fellow believers.

Intermingled among these commands are verses about the difference between the believers and the unbelievers and how Allah will treat both groups. There is mention of what to do in times of battle and war, and how the believers will be rewarded and for the believers to not give up. The surah finally ends with an admonition to remain steadfast in belief.

I then read the fourth surah, Surah An-Nisaa, that is, The Women. This surah starts out by talking about orphans and how to treat them and then leads to the laws of inheritance to laws about who one can marry, that is, relationships that a mahram and naa-mahram, and this continues on to how women are to be treated in marriage. The rest of the surah tapers off into a collection of random verses, some commandments, some declarations of what will happen to the believers and to the disbelievers. There is a brief mention of Moses and once again the making of the covenant and the raising of the mountain above their heads. But then, the very last verse is yet again about the distribution of inheritance, a verse that would much more properly belong at the beginning of the surah along with all the other verses in this part which give a detailed description of how the inheritance is to be distributed.

As I read on through the Koran, I noticed that the verses in the surahs became less and less connected to the point that one verse could be talking about one subject and the verse which follows talked about something completely different. What was also perplexing was that the title of the surah often only related to a small group of verses within that surah and the rest of the surah was just an agglomeration of statements, often very similar or exactly the same as verses found in other surahs. There were verses which talked about the description of the earth, the description of the heaven or the heavens, how Allah created the earth and the heavens, how Allah created humans, how that the humans were divided into two major groups, the believers and the unbelievers, that the unbelievers obstinately refuse to believe in Allah, although there were many verses which actually said that Allah Himself made these unbelievers "unbelieve", there were statements that believers were told to say things, although I wasn't sure if we were supposed to say these out loud or simply acknowledge these as part of our beliefs. There were then further commandments, what was prohibited, what was permitted and what was demanded of us. There were passages which talked about the Messengers, sometimes named, sometimes unidentified with only the word "Messenger" or "Prophet", although the translators often inserted in parentheses the name of the Messenger or Prophet with no particular justification for the choice. The Koran has passages that talk about how that the unbelievers in the past refused to believe the earlier Messengers and the brutal punishment that occurred to them as a result, what will occur on Judgement Day, descriptions of Jannah or heaven, and descriptions of Jahannam or hell. There were verses about Allah sending down to humans a Book, the Koran, Our signs, water and clothes. There were descriptions about the jinns and the angels. There were verses which told us to look at nature and see the signs of the existence of Allah in them. There were also many epithets given to Allah, the All-Wise, the All-Powerful, the All-Knowing.

I felt that if I had the inclination, I could collect every single verse from the Koran and then collate them according to their subject matter. In this way I could recreate the Koran without the unnecessary repetitions and also make it easier to find the verses which relate to a particular topic. The Koran in its current state made comprehending its message difficult.

And I would ensure that all pronouns had a definite referent to make it clear to the reader. This was something else that made the Koran difficult to understand. There are copious verses which use the personal pronouns "you", "he", "we" and "they", but there is nothing in the verses which precede these pronouns or sometimes in the entire surah which tells us who the "you", "he", "we" and "they" are referring to. The translators often put in parentheses who they believe the pronoun is referring to but as much as I appreciated their suggestions, often I could tell it was merely a guess. It was particularly the use of "We" to refer to Allah that I found a little troubling. The Koran says often that there is only one God and it is vehemently opposed to polytheists who believe in many gods, and even the Christians who on the one hand say there is only one God but then say that there is a Trinity of three personages who together somehow make one God. Why, therefore, does Allah refer to Himself often in the Koran as "We"? I had heard that the use of the plural pronoun was used as a sign of respect, and Allah being the ultimate power, He deserved the ultimate respect, hence the use of the plural form. But I didn't fully understand this because there were other occasions when Allah referred to Himself in the singular, using "I". Further, sometimes within a surah, the "We" was assumed to be Allah speaking about Himself with respect, but then Allah is referred to in the same passage in the third person as "He" as if the "We" were an unidentified group separate from Allah. For example, in Al-Hijr 15:23 – 28 we read

*And indeed it is **We** who give life and cause death,*
*and **We** are the Inheritors*
*And verily **We** know the preceding (generations) among you,*
*and verily **We** know the later generations*
*And indeed, **your Lord** will gather them.*
*Indeed, **He** is All-Wise, All-Knowing*
*And verily, **We** created man out of clay from altered black mud*
*And **We** created jinn before from scorching fire*
*And indeed when **your Lord** said to the Angels,*
*"Indeed, **I** will create a human being out*
of clay from altered black mud."

(emphasis mine)

However, I also realised that the Koran was a book of divine origin. Maybe the way I wanted the text to be written was according to my limited earthly view of literature. Allah was the Almighty and His thoughts were greater than mine so He no doubt had a reason for what to me looked like a disorganised composition. And further, all these oddities added mystery to the text and further confirmed to me its divine nature.

Chapter 10

And so a new phase had begun in my life. It was time for a complete change in my entire environment. My results had come back for my 'A' Level Exams and now I was able to pursue university studies in chemical engineering. I had been accepted a place at the University of Vokyalesh, a relatively new and prestigious university at a place south west of Lahore, near Faisalabad, in the small town of Vokyalesh after which the university had been named.

This meant leaving the comfort and familiarity of my home in Alekh-Jahan in Karachi, out of my home environment with my parents and grandparents, and also away from the still raw and horrid memories of the destruction to the Shiite mosque not far from where I lived.

It was also the end of my religious tuition from my Mulvi. Although there had been times when I disagreed with my Mulvi, my Mulvi had after all been in a way my lifeline to the hereafter because it was my Mulvi to whom I addressed any questions about the faith I didn't quite understand and when I needed guidance. My Mulvi gave me a few words of comfort and made me feel as if I had earned my independence. But he also gave me the contact details on a sheet of paper of his eldest son, Muhammad, who often travelled up to Lahore and in the nearby areas for his work, and who also sometimes gave religious instruction, the slip of paper on which he had written his contact details I somehow unfortunately lost.

My parents and grandparents accompanied me on the day of my departure to the central bus station where, laden with a collection of clothes and other necessities, I boarded the first of a series of buses which eventually took me to my final destination.

The University of Vokyalesh appeared from first impressions to have been a university built by the British aristocracy or perhaps the Royal Family. Although modern, the main buildings were styled according to the Victorian era as if this were a Cambridge or Oxford University in a Pakistani setting. The gardens and lawn areas were manicured in the very typical fashion of an English garden. My main lecture rooms were in the south and east wings of the university in large impressive lecture halls.

To the north of the Victorian-styled buildings were more modern looking buildings in tune with twenty-first century Pakistani architecture. These buildings housed the less refined and more earthy aspects of university life, a series of shops, and at the northern most point, the dormitories for those studying engineering and science. My dormitory was Building Z, however, although being named after the last letter of the English alphabet, the dormitories weren't arranged or collated in alphabetical order.

I shared a dorm room with a guy called Maaz from Lemuhamvar. Maaz was somewhat taller than me, thinnish to athletic build, of a very dark complexion, with an abundance of body hair which was evident on his arms and through the V in his shirt, and a neatly kept moustache. Right from the beginning, Maaz and I got on very well. Maaz was one of those people with whom I immediately clicked on first meeting as if we had always known each other, like two gears in a piece of machinery brought together and the cogs just meshed seamlessly into place.

Maaz was studying civil engineering and so there were a few subjects we shared in the first year of our studies, one of them being physics. This class holds a particular memory in my mind because of our lecturer, Mrs Talkhii. Mrs Talkhii wore a veil and this only further accentuated her ruthlessness. While there was strict discipline in school where our behaviour was constrained within the classroom, I had heard that at university the lecture rooms were supposed to be more relaxed because we were, after all, entering our adult years and hence it was expected that we would be treated with a lot less strictness. Mrs Talkhii did not tolerate tardiness in her lectures, especially as we lived on campus and it wasn't a long distance from the dormitories to the lecture room. If ever Maaz or I were late to get up or to complete breakfast which could ultimately cause a delay in getting to the lecture on time, there was immediate panic while biological alarm bells sounded off inside as we dashed to the lecture hall. Mrs Talkhii also didn't appreciate talking in her lecture theatre unless someone was asked a question, and when asked, the person had to stand and provide the answer. And she did not tolerate students who gave wrong answers either. Her approach towards learning was not much different to my first Mulvi, where any mistakes were repaid with violence, although in Mrs Talkhii's case the violence was fortunately merely verbal. Her philosophy was "Mistakes are inexcusable" and I always felt butterflies in my belly whenever she called my name to answer a question. However, if there was one positive that came out of her class it was that I learnt to be exacting with my reading and never allow myself to simply gloss over a chapter in the textbook for the following class but to ensure that I understood everything. In fact, having Maaz as a roommate who was also a fellow classmate in Mrs Talkhii's class was a blessing because we could sound off each other before we went to sleep questions about the topic in the textbook and make sure we could find a quote in the chapter which supported the answers that we provided.

The other classes remain a bit of a blur as the other lecturers were a lot more lax in their discipline. But it was amazing how Mrs Talkhii's rigid teaching style flowed over into the other subjects because Maaz and I were just as studious in our other subjects as we were in physics because of the fear instilled into us by Mrs Talkhii.

As it was at school, every Friday we finished classes early in order for us to go to Friday prayers. Sunni Muslims would gather together in Sunni prayer places and Shiites in their prospective places of prayer. Because of my devotion to the faith, I made it a practice to observe Friday prayers regularly. Maaz, however, wasn't so diligent and he often skipped these prayers especially when there were assignments due the following week and he needed the head start to get the assignments done. Having been familiar with my school friends who weren't as rigid in the faith as I had been at school, I didn't question Maaz on this but totally understood that this was what some Muslims were like.

Mealtimes were held in various canteens around the campus. The closest one to our dormitory was the one I went to the most often for the last meal of the day. Here we ate with other students we had met and befriended in our various classes. This was an opportunity to get to know Pakistanis from other regions around the country with their locally-specific backgrounds.

During our meal breaks, the normal conversations that I was familiar with at school became once again the topic of conversation at university although the slint on the topics had become more sophisticated. There were also much meatier conversations that came out as well as we had all begun to grow into adulthood.

One topic of conversation that remained completely absent was the discussion of religion. We eventually determined who belonged to what religion through non-verbal communication, observing what people wore, where people went, and what people did on certain days or at certain times during the day, but in general religion was a topic that was at best avoided.

But not always.

One evening the topic of Shariah Law was raised. One of my classmates, Zeeshan, was particularly vocal about Shariah Law. He was all for it. This began a discussion with everyone in my group. The reason why Pakistan was in the state it was in was because it had not adopted Shariah Law entirely like Saudi Arabia and to an extent Egypt. If Pakistan could adopt Shariah Law, Pakistan would be a great country in which to live.

While they discussed this point and raised certain points of Shariah Law that they particularly wanted to adopt, I listened in silence. However, eventually I couldn't take it any longer as they continued to further mention aspects of Shariah Law which seemed so outdated and so irrelevant.

"I don't agree," I finally stated abruptly. "The problem is not the adoption of Shariah Law but the lack of democracy. That's why Western countries are so far advanced and we're so far behind them."

This stopped everyone in their tracks. It was like in a movie when the scene is frozen while everyone was sitting there motionless in the act of whatever they were in the process of doing, putting a morsel of food in their mouths, tearing a piece of bread, putting a cup of tea to their lips. The frozen scene remained for some seconds until Zeeshan unfroze the moment.

"You mean to say that if Pakistan adopted an un-Islamic form of government, Pakistan would develop as a country?"

I could feel the terror in everyone at that table when Zeeshan asked the question because there were only two possible answers with one answer being a crime against the state. It was therefore imperative to navigate these troubled waters delicately. All eyes were poised on me but it was difficult to interpret whether out of hostility for my brazen statement in support of the West or fear of the possible entrapment that I would find myself in which would lead to my imprisonment or death.

My mouth had suddenly gone dry and it felt as if the back of my tongue had swollen. But I needed to provide an answer.

"Let me put it this way," I struggled as a start to say but then began to feel confident about the correctness of my point of view. "Historically we know that Shariah Law was not established by the Prophet. Muhammad did not receive Shariah Law through the angel Gabriel. It might have had its time in history in the development of the Arabian Empire but it's not directly a part of Islam."

"How can you say such a thing?" Zeeshan stated quite angrily. "I mean, don't you call yourself a Muslim? That type of comment is anti-Islamic. You sound very liberal in your ways. People who have that type of thinking are nothing but stooges of the West!"

That was a cutting remark but it was one generally thought in Pakistan by anyone who commented against Shariah Law. However, I couldn't let Zeeshan criticize me so easily with that statement.

"Shariah Law is supposed to be a system of law that covers all aspects of life in a community," I argued back. "But it only relates to aspects that were relevant and part of the system of things almost 1,400 years ago. How can Shariah Law be used in the twenty-first century to handle modern aspects of society such as the distribution of electricity, a form of power which was totally unknown back then, or the distribution of water at a time when the bearers of the religion relied on finding water holes and not on modern irrigation systems, to the allocation of funds to the different provinces such as those we have in Pakistan, to computer systems, internet, roads and rail systems, maritime and aviation systems and so on which are part and parcel of the modern world we live in? Shariah Law is a system of law relevant to a place and time in the past and remains in the past."

At this point, I turned and looked across at the next table. It was obvious that our conversation had caught the attention from others in the canteen. But of all those at the next table who caught my particular attention was one young man with a full moustache and a long, thick bushy beard. Our eyes met and for what seemed an eternity we stared at each other eye to eye. It was mesmerising and chilling at the same time. This guy had all the hallmarks of a straight down the line Sunni Muslim because of his facial appearance and because of the clothes he was wearing, totally non-western style of clothing. The only thing missing was the traditional Muslim topi and with that he would have been the whole picture. My accusation of Shariah Law, although this was not considered blasphemous under Pakistani law, to many devout Muslims it was almost considered as such. But this guy's mesmerising glance, as chilling as it was, was not conveying evil or hate. In fact, it lacked any emotion whatsoever. Rather, it was simply a cold emotionless stare.

The muezzin could be heard for prayer and so we got up to go to the prayer room. Zeeshan grumbled a comment that he was surprised that I even considered going to prayer seeing I didn't believe in Shariah Law but I no longer wanted to continue down this fruitless and at the same time dangerous topic of conversation. I was Muslim and I was just as sure and adamant that I was a Muslim despite my rejection of Shariah Law especially as history quite clearly showed that Shariah Law was an invention of men after Muhammad and therefore to me it was a later innovation and even blasphemous to consider it as a part of Islam.

This was another strange aspect of Islam that I came to notice. Even those who belonged to the same sect could enter the prayer room or a mosque to carry out the same prayers in the same way as each other yet there could be stark enmity between them. Because of our argument, I chose to stand as far away in the room from Zeeshan as possible while we both made our confessions and carried out the exact same rite facing the same direction to what was supposedly the exact same Allah, but there was an air of dissent while we did so.

Later that evening, back in my dormitory and doing some late evening reading in preparation for the following day's lectures, Maaz suddenly entered the room noisily, disrupting the tranquillity of the moment and caused me to jump as if I had been stung by a bee or as if someone had stuck a pin in my back.

"Hey, there, Mustafa," Maaz greeted me as he flung his towel on his mattress and began removing his running shoes. As soon as the first shoe was off, the acrid odour of sweat socks intruded my nose.

Maaz read the expression on my face and laughed.

"Don't worry. I'll wash them. I'm just going to have a shower now."

Maaz removed his sweaty shirt to display his thin yet athletic dark hairy chest and stomach. This was the first time I had seen Maaz bare-chested. This simple view of him dragged out forcibly feelings that obviously I had been trying to conceal inside and it was fortunate I was seated at a desk concealing the lower part of my body because otherwise with the little I was wearing my lower abdomen would have revealed to Maaz in no uncertain terms what this spectacle was doing to my body.

Maaz then grabbed a clean shirt and a pair of shorts, and with his towel wrapped about his upper torso disappeared to the common bathroom down the hall. But that view of him shirtless lingered on in my head. And so I was once again caught in this never-ending whirlpool. What on earth was wrong with me? Why did I have these feelings for Maaz, feelings that were obviously the lust that Allah found so perplexing in men? And why did I have these feelings when I really loved Allah and His Messenger, Muhammad? What made it all the more complicated was that I knew Maaz was a nice guy and a friend. Unlike the men of Sodom and Gomorrah, I did not want to violently force my feelings of lust blindly onto Maaz but rather I preferred that they were mutual. Which is what even further complicated the situation. As it was with Reza, my feelings of physical desire for Maaz were intricately entwined with the deep bond of friendship that appeared to be forming between us, which to me felt like love. And while Allah was troubled by this attraction, in what way did it affect Him?

A quick glance at my physics textbook brought to mind Mrs Talkhii. This had a greater effect than a cold shower would ever have to dampen my original feelings of sexual arousal.

However, again, this was not long lived. Eventually I heard a noise and Maaz entered the room. The transformation from his sweaty smelly self to the refreshing, clean look was striking. Maaz was wearing a fresh clean pair of shorts and clean T-shirt with his towel slung over one shoulder and his wet running shoes held out in his right hand which he laid at the dormitory entrance door. He eventually was at his desk with his physics book open.

"So, where are you up to?" he asked me.

I told him up to which page in the chapter I had been reading. Maaz turned around to his textbook and began flicking the pages and then there was a momentary silence.

"Hey, Mustafa," Maaz then said. My mind was now in readiness as the imaginary chapter of the textbook I had just read appeared within my mind's eye, waiting for the question about the chapter Maaz was about to pose.

"Yes, go ahead," I replied to welcome his first question.

"You know, what you were saying at meal time tonight about Shariah Law, I totally agree with you," Maaz said in somewhat of a subdued tone. "I…I wanted to agree with you tonight in the canteen but I was too scared what the others would say, especially Zeeshan."

That wasn't too much of a surprise to me. Maaz was somewhat of a lax Muslim. I considered him to actually be a non-practising Muslim.

"I should've supported you in the discussion," Maaz further said by way of a partial apology. "I just don't have the same amount of courage you have to stand up for our beliefs."

"Yeah, it's not easy to stand up for what we believe," I replied. "What's worse is that Zeeshan and probably everyone else in the canteen just assumed that because I don't believe in Shariah Law, I'm not a Muslim. But I have never considered Shariah Law as a part of Islam. I mean, like I said, go and read the history of Shariah Law and you'll find that it is something that came after Muhammad. I can't understand how anyone can consider Shariah Law a part of Islam. Shariah Law came after Muhammad, it was not written by Muhammad, it wasn't even endorsed by Muhammad, it's not even mentioned by Muhammad. To me, it's purely *bida*, total innovation. As far as I'm concerned, it's the other way around. Those who consider Shariah Law from Allah are not Muslims because they are mixing into the pure religion an impure set of beliefs. Shariah Law is falsehood, and as it says in the Koran in Al-Baqarah 2:42 'Do not mix the truth with falsehood.'"

Maaz gave me a commending nod of the head with raised eyebrows. "Wow! You really are a serious Muslim! You can even quote from the Koran and know exactly where it says it!"

I smiled back at Maaz and enjoyed the compliment. However, the thought went through my mind: shouldn't all Muslims be able to quote from the Koran at will? Don't we all agree that the Koran is Allah's Holy Book, the mother of all books?

"Then...er...," Maaz cautiously continued, "what... er...about the Hadiths? Do...er...you think the...er... Hadiths are also...er...innovation?"

Maaz's hesitation in asking this question was not unfounded. Denying the Hadiths is considered blasphemy in Pakistan, and for both Sunnis and Shiites, those who deny the Hadiths are considered non-Muslim. I felt a flush in my face and my mouth go dry. I had to share the dormitory with Maaz so I couldn't confess something that would cause Maaz to want to kill me.

There was a moment of silent hesitation on both sides. However, fortunately, Maaz was the one to finally break the silence.

"I mean,…er…if…er…I said…er…I…er…didn't believe in the Hadiths either, what…er…would you…er… think?"

It was as if the pressure valve on a pressure cooker had been pressed as I felt the tension disappear. But I still needed confirmation.

"Does that mean," I then asked, "that you don't believe in the Hadiths?"

I could see that Maaz was uncomfortable with the question and his face looked as if colour were drawing out from his skin. This seemed to answer my question without words but I had to be sure.

"Look, if you said you didn't believe in the Hadiths, really, to me I would still think of you as a Muslim because it's the Koran that's the most important. The Hadiths rely on the Koran but I can see how we can be Muslims without the Hadiths."

Once these words were out of my mouth, I realised what I had said sounded like a confession. I was about to add to this that I wasn't actually saying that I don't believe in the Hadiths but Maaz got in before me.

"So, you're a Koranist Muslim, too?" Maaz said with delight spread over his face like stars spread over the night canopy. "This is just too coincidental! You and I, two Koranist Muslims in the same dormitory! What are the chances! This must be from Allah!"

237

Maaz got up, came over to me and kissed me on the forehead. He then danced around as if he'd found gold bullion under his pillow. However, I couldn't express my delight as much as he had. I hadn't actually considered myself as belonging to a separate sect of Islam. True, I had heard of the concept but it had only occurred to me that I no longer believed in the Hadiths but I hadn't quite allowed the concept to gel until Maaz made a point of it. But now that I was sharing a dormitory with someone who claimed to be a Koranist Muslim and he was now claiming that I was one, for the first time I felt like a member of a completely new and different branch of Islam. This therefore should have meant that I could no longer consider myself as a Sunni Muslim because I no longer believed in the Hadiths which contained all the actions of Muhammad, and hence I could no longer determine what was sunna as a result. However, in a way, I continued to consider myself as a Sunni Muslim, but one who did not take the Hadiths seriously.

Maaz and I suddenly were involved in a conversation about the Hadiths and why we had now rejected them and felt that our Islam should be founded on the Koran and on the Koran only.

Once the relief of being able to express openly to each other our rejection of the Hadiths, I suggested to Maaz that we really should get back into revising our physics work in readiness for the following day. And so we did. We spent a couple of hours testing each other's knowledge of what was in the chapter we had just read and, when we both felt comfortable that we knew the chapter well, we closed our books and then went to bed.

But while lying in bed, I stared at the ceiling in the semidarkness and thought about it. There was a certain feeling of guilt and fear as I contemplated the idea that maybe by considering the Hadiths as merely the writings of men and not the inspiration from the Almighty Allah that perhaps I was putting myself in eternal danger. While

238

it had merely been a hypothetical thought earlier on, my discussion with Maaz only confirmed and concreted the concept in my mind to the point that once I had begun down this path, there was no going back. By rejecting the Hadiths, I was rejecting about 1,200 years of Muslim tradition and practice, traditions and practices which had been interwoven into the very fabric of my Muslim being. I then thought of my Mulvi and then my father. Would my Mulvi be disappointed in me after all these years of his training? Would my father violently disown me because I had turned away from what really was only a secondary part of the Islamic faith?

And what about all the other religious scholars who had devoted their entire lives to the study of the Hadiths? Had they dedicated their entire lives to these texts entirely in vain?

While pondering on this, a verse from the Koran came to mind but I couldn't remember exactly how it went. I climbed out of bed and turned on my desk lamp. Maaz did not stir at all but was well deep in sleep. I grabbed my Koran and flicked through the pages to the place where I was sure I had only recently read it and there it was. It was the verse from Surah Al-Imran 3:146 which I read as

And how many a prophet fought with many religious scholars.
But they never lost heart for what befell
them in the way of Allah, nor
did they weaken or give in. And Allah
loves those who are patient.

This verse appeared to be Allah speaking to me. Although the verse talked of many prophets who had fought religious scholars, it appeared to be saying that in the same way as earlier prophets, Muhammad also had strong debates with the religious leaders of the time, no doubt Jewish and Christian scholars, and hence this was a lesson to us. Muhammad showed with his knowledge and his excellent debating skills that Jews and Christians upheld long-held traditions which were in fact unfounded, and Muhammad was able to show how and why these traditions were baseless and really not from Allah. Even though Muhammad was a simple merchant, he stood up to scholars who had spent their lives studying the ancient religious texts. In the end Muhammad came out on top because Allah was with him.

And so this was the message Allah was relaying to me. Even if all the religious scholars of the Sunni and Shiite sects fought ferociously to support erroneous ideas, a lowly university student could still stand up to them when he knew Allah was on his side.

A glowing feeling of warmth filled my heart and removed the guilt and fear for denying the Hadiths. Allah in His majesty had spoken to me at this time of need. Okay, I admitted that I was not a prophet nor was I anywhere near as wonderful as the Prophet Muhammad. But the Prophet was my example and like him I might also one day have to fight for the truth against people like Zeeshan.

I climbed into bed and slumped under the blankets. I made myself comfortable and then closed my eyes. While I contemplated once more that verse from Al-Imran 3:146, a picture formed in my mind of a Sunni and Shiite scholar dressed impeccably in their religious best, completely red faced and frothing at the mouth, violently defending the veracity of Shariah Law and the Hadiths, while the Prophet Muhammad, though simply dressed in everyday merchant clothes and not so impressive-looking, confidently argued back that neither Shariah Law nor the Hadiths had any support from Allah whatsoever.

But while the ship of dreams disembarked from the world of reality and began the smooth sailing into the waters of the dreamworld, the thought then came to me. With all I had learnt about Muhammad and his life history, I had never read or heard about him having any arguments with any religious authorities whatsoever. So how could this verse from Al-Imran 3:146 be an inference to Muhammad?

Chapter 11

When I got up the following day, that question was still hanging over my head. When did Muhammad ever have disputes with religious authorities? And which ones? They could not have been Sunni or Shiite religious scholars because they hadn't existed at that time. The only religious authorities would have been Jewish and Christian scholars. And pagan scholars if such scholars existed. With no reference to this verse, I asked Maaz if he was aware of any fights or disputes Muhammad ever had with religious authorities of his time, and Maaz, like me, confessed that he was not aware of this himself. Maaz then asked me why I had asked him the question. I told Maaz the verse in question. Maaz just screwed up his face and shrugged his shoulders. With that, we both started getting ready for the day.

But before dashing off to breakfast, I decided to have another quick look at the verse in my Arabic-English interlinear. What struck me was the word translated as "religious scholars". It was the Arabic word *ribiyoona*. This word written in Arabic looked very much like both the Arabic and the Urdu word for "rabbis", the religious authorities of the Jewish faith, so although it was true that this was referring to religious scholars in general, in the context of the time, this verse could be talking about disputes that Muhammad had specifically with Jewish religious authorities, especially as it was well-known that the Jews rejected Muhammad and his teaching as it is clearly indicated in the Koran and elaborated elsewhere in other stories about the Prophet.

There wasn't anything particularly controversial about this verse. However, for some reason, because of what we had been taught about the life of the Prophet, there was something unresolved about this verse which sat uncomfortably in the back of my head, like leaning back against the wall while there is a small lump interrupting the otherwise smooth surface.

While chemistry had been a subject I had mastered at high school, at university this subject had taken a step up in complexity and so it was difficult to keep apace. Unfortunately, Maaz wasn't in my chemistry class so I couldn't bounce off ideas from him later in the evening in the dormitory. At school, we had always done our experiments in pairs or in groups so there was always someone else in the group who could assist me in setting up the experiment and interpreting the data. Here at university, we were required to carry out our experiments individually.

We didn't actually start conducting full on experiments till about the fourth week into the course. The first number of weeks were spent learning about how to do titrations using different types of acids and bases, and different types of indicators. Doing titrations required quite a bit of eye-hand co-ordination and there was something about my physical makeup that made this laboratory task difficult.

The person who stood at the bench next to me was the bearded young man who had stared at me fixedly from across the table the day I had spoken against Shariah Law. He was such a beacon of pure Sunni Islam that I wasn't sure if I admired him or feared him. I definitely feared him because of the way he looked at me when I spoke negatively about Shariah Law but since then he had done nothing to make me feel uncomfortable or to show that he completely disapproved of my negative outlook on Shariah Law.

The bearded man was very adept at titrations and he determined the molarity of every acid and base we were supposed to measure with an accuracy and nimbleness that was beyond description. I remember watching him with complete awe.

What I also discovered was that from the angle at which I was standing, I could see when he wrote down in his exercise book the answers to his titrations. Out of fear of not being able to do the titrations correctly and therefore failing the subject, I did something I knew I shouldn't do – I cheated.

Out the front on the trolley was a collection of acids labelled A, B, C, and so on. All these acids were at unknown concentrations and we had to determine the concentration through the titration. It wasn't necessary to do them in order, just as long as we wrote the results in our exercise books against the correct letter. However, out of fear of getting my titrations wrong, I watched the bearded man go out the front, take an acid sample and then I took a mental note of which one he chose. I then went out and got the same one, returned to the bench and performed the titration. However, I fiddled around as if I were trying to adjust the clamp or the bosshead and then stole a glance at the bearded man with his skilful titration. When he wrote down his answer, because I could see the result from the distance I was at, I also wrote down the same answer. And then I performed the titration and tried to get the same result.

The bearded man, however, wasn't only adept at doing titrations. While doing his fourth titration, he manipulated the valve on the burette to allow liquid to flow out and watched the colour change in the conical flask. However, suddenly he stopped, closed the valve and turned to look at me. Once again he stared fixedly into my eyes and that same shudder went up through my spine as it had when he stared at me in the meal room. But then, totally unexpectedly, he winked at me and smiled.

244

"You're having difficulties with titrations, aren't you?" he asked so friendly and so in contrast with the image I had created of him. I couldn't speak so I just replied with a nod.

"Okay, let me just finish this titration and I'll see if I can help you," he concluded. He completed the titration with ease and wrote down the result. He then turned to face me completely.

"Why didn't you ask our lecturer to help you?" he then asked.

"I…I don't really need help. I…I just wanted to confirm that I was doing it right when I watched you," I stammered.

"Titrations are not easy. You're not the only one in the classroom who's having difficulties," the bearded man then said.

I looked around the room and could see the lecturer assisting another student who looked as clumsy as I felt in trying to co-ordinate all this.

"Here, I'll show you what you're doing wrong," the young bearded man finally said.

Not only was the bearded man skilful in doing titrations, his explanation was also skilful. Even though the lecturer had demonstrated the process at the beginning of the class, I realised the way to hold the tap on the burette was counterintuitive. However, although it felt strange at first to hold it the way the bearded man showed me to and which in fact was the way he had been manipulating the tap himself, by my third titration I was starting to get the hang of it. I compared my results for the three titrations I had done and both the bearded man's and my results were equivalent within measurable uncertainty.

At the end of the class, I thanked the bearded man.

"Thank you so much for your help," I emphatically said to him.

"That's fine," the bearded man replied. He then paused and added, "And, so, do you have a name?"

"Oh, yes, sorry," I replied with a laugh. "My name's Mustafa Faakhtaa."

"Hi," he replied and shook my hand. "My name's Yusuf. Yusuf ibn Musa."

Yusuf paused a moment and then added, "So, do you want to have lunch together?"

The canteen near the chemistry lab was in a different wing of the university to where I had my evening meal. At this time I had not made any close friends with anyone in my chemistry class and seeing Yusuf had invited me to lunch with him, I couldn't see any reason not to accompany him.

We grabbed our food on the food trays and made our way amongst the tables and chairs for a place to sit. The canteen was only half full, and this was something that remained a constant whenever we went to the canteen after the chemistry practical, seeing the chemistry prac finished a little earlier than other classes close to this canteen. Yusuf guided me to an isolated table over on the far end of the cafeteria where there weren't any other people in close proximity.

While eating lunch, we chatted. We started telling each other about our backgrounds. I discovered that Yusuf was from Peshawar, a city in the west of Pakistan and close to the border with Afghanistan. Yusuf's father owned a truck driving business which operated within the country and with neighbouring countries such as Afghanistan, Iran and India. Yusuf most probably was going to follow in his father's footsteps, eventually taking over the business when his father was too old to continue but Yusuf's father still wanted his sons to get a university education.

Once we had introduced ourselves and had completed eating, after Yusuf had swallowed his last morsel of food, he took a furtive glance around the room and then in a low voice said to me, "What you were saying the other day about Shariah Law, yes, I agree with you. Shariah Law is un-Islamic."

Yusuf then sat back, took another glance around the room to ensure that no-one was close enough to hear what he had just said. He then turned back and leant close to me.

"There are a lot of things that our government says are a part of Islam when they are not. But it's dangerous to say this out loud because then it is considered blasphemy."

I felt a cold chill run through my backbone, up through my shoulders and to the tips of my fingers. I wasn't sure at first what to say to that. Yusuf stared at me again with those wide round brown eyes as if he were staring into my soul, a stare which was haunting but at the same time hypnotic.

"Look, can I tell you something? And, please, keep this between you and me."

Yusuf had been such a good guy to show me how to do the titrations quickly and efficiently in the chemistry prac class that I felt that I owed him something. So I nodded in consent.

"I'm Muslim," Yusuf continued, "but I don't believe in Shariah Law. And neither do I believe in the Hadiths."

When Yusuf mentioned the word 'Hadiths', his voice had become so inaudible that this word was merely a whisper and the only reason I recognised it was from the harsh aspirated consonants that made up the word, in particular the initial h and the final consonant cluster ths.

"So, you're a Koranist Muslim?" I whispered back and then sat up. Yusuf didn't affirm or deny my question. However, I had to be one hundred percent sure that this wasn't a trap so I leant forward and asked in almost a whisper, "Can I ask why you don't believe in the Hadiths?"

Yusuf took another furtive glance around the room to ensure no-one was in earshot to hear what he had to say.

"It's not safe to talk about these things out loud and here in a public place like this meal room. You can come to my dorm room one night and we can discuss it." Yusuf then smiled and added in a much more comfortable and audible tone, "and we can help you with your chemistry."

I was too eager to wait for another night and so I asked him if I could come over that afternoon after our final class to which Yusuf was more than happy to do.

Yusuf's dormitory was in D block which was east of my dormitory in Z block. To get to his dormitory I had to pass by a small featured lake, which at certain angles looked as if this were a bay to the open sea.

I finally found Yusuf's dormitory, which, like ours, was an imposing building with two storeys, with a long shared balcony which ran the length of the building. Once I had arrived at his door, I spotted what looked like a wooden cutout that had been adhered to the dormitory lintel, what looked like a small white strip of wood and on it in gold writing was what looked like the letters p p p. I knocked on the door and, while I waited for Yusuf to open, I examined the plaque in greater detail and realised that the letters were not in English but in Arabic script, and the three letters were three meems, the Arabic equivalent of the English letter m.

Yusuf finally opened the door and greeted me warmly. But before entering, I pointed at the plaque and asked, "What's that?"

"The three meems: Musa, Massikh and Muhammad. These three bless those who enter within."

Yusuf let me in while this odd statement that he had made about this plaque began to ruminate within. I knew about the prophet Musa, or Moses, the prophet Massikh, or Messiah, and the prophet Muhammad. While these were three important messengers in our faith, this was the first time I had seen them paraded in parallel and on equal terms as they were displayed here. The thought that went through my mind was that this was really strange. Never in my reading of the Koran had I heard of such a thing or practice.

Once inside the dormitory, Yusuf offered me one of the two wooden chairs inside his room. I asked Yusuf about the person he shared his dormitory with and if he also didn't believe in the Hadiths. Yusuf replied that he didn't and in fact the guy he was sharing the room with was his cousin who was studying civil engineering and was currently in class. Yusuf offered me a cup of tea and while he prepared the tea, I glanced around the room. I spotted on the bookshelf another plaque with the three meems and below it was what appeared to be a special enclave reserved for two special books. I recognized one as being the Koran. The other I couldn't quite make out from where I was sitting but it appeared to share equal reverence with the Holy Koran. What kind of Sunni-cum-Koranist Muslim was this Yusuf if he venerated more than just the Koran, and considered another book just as holy?

Yusuf and I worked on our chemistry practical, writing up the report together. I sat at Yusuf's cousin's desk seeing it was free this time of the day. Having Yusuf to help me was very beneficial and we both had our prac reports written up in short time. Once finished, Yusuf offered me more tea. While preparing the tea, I stood up to stretch my legs and stared out of his dormitory window. The view from his dormitory was majestic, with a view over the central lake with a decorative rock motif in the centre. Birds were on this rocky decoration. A gentle breeze seemed to be blowing across the lake causing the surface of the pond to become striated with ripples as if the hand of Allah were gently brushing across the surface of the pond. With Yusuf, a fellow student and a fellow Muslim who held similar ideas as I did about Islam, I felt as if the presence of Allah were here and had guided me to this moment of time.

Once Yusuf had made the tea, he made himself comfortable in his chair.

"Thanks again for your help in chemistry," I said, after taking a sip. Yusuf lifted his teacup and gave a dismissive shrug to indicate that there was no need for such a statement.

"Yusuf, yes, like we discussed earlier, I simply can't believe in the Hadiths," I began and then explained in detail what it was about the Hadiths that made me come to the conclusion, that the Hadiths simply should not be part of the Islamic belief. I explained that what finally made me come to this conclusion was my shock in reading about Muhammad's commandment to drink camel urine as a health measure and also in this same Hadith, Muhammad, who we had been brought up to believe was the perfect human, did what I considered a very despicable thing by brutally killing these perpetrators and to me this could not be a story about the prophet I so loved and idolized.

This opened the dialogue. Knowing the sensitivity of the topic, we spoke in low tones to ensure that anyone outside could not hear what we were saying as what we were talking about would be considered a crime against the state, despite the fact that what we were saying was actually the truth. Because I had expressed my views about the Hadiths, this opened Yusuf up about his understanding of how the Hadiths fit within the world of Islam.

"No doubt you are also aware what it says in the Koran itself about Hadiths and how Allah warned about future generations inventing hadiths after Muhammad had died," Yusuf stated although it was really more of a question. My answer was actually in the negative and with a little embarrassment I shook my head.

"How's your Arabic?" Yusuf then asked.

I smiled embarrassedly. "It's not the best. It's so-so, I guess. I actually started reading the Koran from an English translation but I'm still working on trying to read the Koran in the original Arabic."

"And that's why you probably have missed the warning, because the translators of the Koran from the Arabic into other languages often change the meaning of the word so that the original word is masked. In particular, often when the original Arabic uses the word *hadith*, the translation is often 'narration' or 'statement' or a word of similar meaning, but never 'hadith', because then it becomes obvious that those who believe in the Hadiths are following the corrupt way."

The expression on my face must have said it all. Yusuf then walked over to the small bookshelf which contained the two holy books. He removed the thinner one and, while returning to his seat, he began flicking through the pages. Once he had sat down, he flicked further noisily until he had reached what he was looking for and then passed the Koran over to me.

"Read verse twenty-three."

I took the Koran from his hand. When I looked down, I noticed that this was the same Arabic-English interlinear Koran that I had in my possession. I looked up at Yusuf completely intrigued by the coincidence. But then, why would that be particularly intriguing when surely there were many Pakistanis who possessed such a copy to assist with both reading and understanding the holiest of literature in our religion.

I took a quick glance at the bottom of the page to see which surah I was reading. It was surah thirty-nine, Surah Az-Zumar.

"Read it out loud," Yusuf invited me.

I looked back at verse twenty-three and then read, "'Allah has revealed the best statement – a Book, its parts resembling each other and oft-repeated. The skins of those who fear their Lord shiver from it, then their skins and their hearts relax at the remembrance of Allah.'"

When I had finished, I looked up at Yusuf. Yusuf then smiled.

"Have a look at the Arabic. Look for the word 'statement'. What is the Arabic word above it?"

I glanced through the English translation below the Arabic text until I found the word 'statement' and then looked at the Arabic word above it. Sure enough, the word in Arabic was *hadith*, so this verse actually reads, "Allah has revealed the best *hadith* – a Book, its parts resembling each other (and) oft-repeated. The skins of those who fear their Lord shiver from it, then their skins and their hearts relax at the remembrance of Allah."

As the verse stated, my skin also shivered in awe. The Koran, so the Koran itself said, was the best Hadith. What was implied from this was that, if the Koran is the best Hadith, why would anyone want to refer to a second-best Hadith for information about the divine? It was also clear that the *hadith* in question was the very Koran I was holding, as I was familiar that one of the characteristics of the Koran was that it repeated itself often from one surah to another.

Yusuf must have read my mind because he then asked, "So, the Koran is the best *hadith*. Although it says the Koran is the best *hadith*, does this mean that there are other *hadiths* we can follow as well as the Koran? What about the Hadiths that most Muslims consider as part of the religion?"

Yusuf looked at me again with that stare which penetrated into my very soul. Then after a pause he continued.

"Have a look at Surah Al-Jathiya 45:6 and read what it says. And again, use the Arabic word for the English word 'statement' when you read the verse out loud."

I did what Yusuf said and found the verse. I read it out loud to him as requested, "These are the verses of Allah which we recite to you in truth. Then in what *hadith* after Allah and His verses will they believe?"

This sent an even greater shiver through me. It didn't say it explicitly but the rhetorical question at the end of the verse put it into perspective. If Allah has revealed His verses in the Koran to Muhammad and then to us, what other hadiths did we need? None of the Hadiths admitted that they were the very verses of Allah. The sayings in the Hadiths were simply sayings people said they had heard Muhammad say at some point in time. But none of these sayings were statements that Muhammad said had been revealed to him from Allah through the angel Gabriel.

I took a deep breath. The way Yusuf reacted, it was as if he were reading my mind and recognising the thrill that I was experiencing in finding support from the Koran for something that I had surmised about the Hadiths from my own reasoning. That the Koran backed up this surmisation to me was further evidence of the divine nature of the Koran.

"Yes," he said in a tone which confirmed what I was feeling, "what other Hadiths do they believe beyond the best *hadith*, the verses of Allah? However, keep reading."

Yusuf directed me to Surah Luqman 31:6 where it was written, "And of mankind is he who purchases idle tales to mislead people from the path of Allah without knowledge and takes it in ridicule. Those will have a humiliating punishment". However, the word for "idle tales" in the Arabic was idle *hadiths*, so that this verse actually reads as "And of mankind is he who purchases idle *hadiths* to mislead people from the path of Allah, etc." Yusuf gave me a smile through his beard and pointed out the obvious. The earlier verses I had read confirmed that the Koran was the best *hadith* and the implication was that we didn't need any others. Hence all the Hadiths that came after the Koran had been invented, so the Koran itself testifies, to mislead people. And those who followed these idle Hadiths, as the end of this verse clearly stated, "will have a humiliating punishment".

Yusuf then directed me to Surah Al-Araf 7:185, again requesting from me to use the word *hadith* in the place of the translated 'statement' in the English. I read it out loud as I had done the previous verses, "Do they not look in the dominion of the heavens and the earth and everything that

253

Allah has created and that perhaps their term has come near? So in what *hadith* after this will they believe?"

Once again, here was a verse which ended with a rhetorical question, asking believers which hadith believers will believe in beyond Allah's *hadith*. However, this time, the *hadith* that was being referred to was the universe we saw around us, the "dominion of the heavens and the earth". Again, this verse was calling into question any consideration of any other Hadith apart from the *hadith* created by Allah. In fact, these rhetorical questions made it sound as if the Prophet Muhammad knew in advance that in future generations people were going to create Hadiths, the Hadiths we had come to know so well, as alternate Hadiths to the true *hadith* of Allah. In other words, these rhetorical questions were almost definitively telling us that it is actually wrong to believe in any Hadith apart from what we observed in nature and from the Koran itself, and as it said in the previous verse, that those who follow these Hadiths will end up in hell fire.

A wonderful feeling surged within me because I had earlier come to this conclusion and now I had conclusive proof from the very Koran.

"Yes, not only do these verses question which *hadith* apart from the verses sent down by Allah people will believe in, and therefore shouldn't believe in, Allah also explains something even more emphatic."

Yusuf then invited me to turn to Surah Al-Anaam 6:38 which reads, "And there is no animal on the earth or a bird that flies with its wings, but they are communities like you. We have not neglected in the Book anything."

After I had read this out loud, Yusuf then commented, "It says here that Allah has not neglected anything in the Book, that is, in the verses He has revealed to us. So if nothing has been neglected, why do we need lengthy volumes of Hadiths to add to this everything if everything

254

has been written that has needed to be written? Anything beyond the verses of Allah are therefore not from Allah."

This all sounded wonderful. But why was it that Yusuf and I, two young first year university students, could immediately understand and appreciate that the Koran quite definitely was saying that the Hadiths which came after the revelation of the Koran should not be consulted?

"Turn to Surah Bani-Israil 17:46 to find the answer," Yusuf replied.

I found the verse and read it out loud, "And We have placed on their hearts coverings, lest they understand it, and in their ears deafness. And when you mention your Lord in the Koran alone, they turn their backs in aversion."

This verse in particular almost blew my mind. There was strong emphasis on using the Koran only when talking about Allah. Allah obviously knew after the revelation of the Koran there would be those in the future who would mention Allah in other literature beyond the Koran and when Koranist Muslims talk about Allah in the Koran only, these unbelievers will hate the Koranist Muslims. According to this verse, therefore, it was clear that those who recited from the Koran alone were the true Muslims. It had to have been pure inspiration of Allah which led me to this understanding before I saw the evidence in Allah's Holy Book.

However, the problem was that to say this out loud in Pakistan was a crime. This made the whole Pakistani state in a state of contradiction. On the one hand it had blasphemy laws against those who criticised Islam, but if someone spoke up against the Hadiths which according to the Koran were not Islamic, that person would be prosecuted for his or her support for the Islam as portrayed in the Koran against the false Islam that ran the state.

But Yusuf hadn't finished. He asked me to read the verse from Surah Yusuf 12:111 and use the word "hadith" in place of the word "narration" in the English translation.

The verse read as this: "Verily in their stories is a lesson for men of understanding. It is not an invented *hadith* but a confirmation of that which was before and a detailed explanation of all things and a guidance and a mercy for a people who believe."

While the mention of *hadith* was intriguing, this time my attention was directed to something else mentioned in this verse, the "confirmation of that which was before".

I looked up at Yusuf and asked him what was before it that this *hadith*, the Koran, was confirming. Yusuf smiled that cheeky smile he had smiled at me in the laboratory and winked. He then jumped off his chair, walked over to the bookcase where he had taken the Koran and reached into the shelf to grab the other book which had originally been accompanying it. He then returned to me and handed me the book.

"It's this that the Koran is confirming, the book that came before it," Yusuf replied.

I took the book from his hand and turned to the front cover to examine the title. Instinctively, I turned the book to read the cover as if I were reading the book from right to left as I had done with the Koran which is written in Arabic, but there was nothing on this side of the cover. I therefore turned the book to the other side but there was nothing there either. While turning it from one side to the other, I had seen that there was writing on the spine and so I returned to examine what was written on the spine of the book. It read: Holy Bible, and beneath it, New International Version. I felt the blood rush to my head. The Holy Bible was the Christian Holy Book. What was Yusuf, a Muslim, doing, blaspheming like this, putting the Holy Bible on an equal footing with the Koran? This was totally un-Islamic. The Jews and the Christians had distorted the Torah and the Injeel, so we had been told, and so we were left with only one Holy Book, the Koran. The Koran was the best book, the book of books, the mother of all books. How could the

Koran have an equal as Yusuf seemed to indicate by the way he had placed the two books together in his bookshelf? When I made my protestation, Yusuf simply replied, "Could you read that last verse from the Koran again?" But I didn't have to. Yusuf's request to reread the verse answered the question. The Koran confirms what came before it, and what came before the Koran was the Torah and the Injeel, or what Christians call the Old Testament and the New Testament, or collectively, the Holy Bible. Even though we had been taught that the Holy Bible had been corrupted, we still acknowledged as Muslims that the Koran confirmed an uncorrupted version of the Holy Bible, assuming that such a thing existed. I then looked back down at the Holy Bible and back up at Yusuf.

"But, how can you say you're a Koranist Muslim if you also believe in the Holy Bible?" I gasped.

Yusuf took the Bible away from me as if I were holding something offensive or dangerous and he wanted to remove the danger.

"I didn't say I was a Koranist Muslim," Yusuf replied. "In fact, we don't call ourselves Koranist Muslims, we call ourselves Ibrahimi Muslims. Ibrahimi Muslims are the true Muslims because we follow in the footsteps of Ibrahim, the *hanifa*, that is, the righteous."

"Ibrahimi Muslims? I've never heard of such a thing!" I retorted.

Yusuf simply smiled at what really was a condescending statement.

"No, we are not a big group of Muslims. But we are growing. Because more people are becoming convinced of the light of the truth."

"But how can you be a Muslim and believe in the Holy Bible?" I asked perplexed. It seemed as if Yusuf were saying that he was Muslim and Christian at exactly the same time which to me was totally impossible. Islam and Christianity were very different belief systems.

"Because the Holy Koran says it is," Yusuf replied back softly.

I looked down at the Koran now held in my left hand as if to find the evidence immediately upon the cover of the book.

"Turn to Surah Al-Ma'idah 5:68 and read it out to me," Yusuf then quietly said.

I did as Yusuf instructed and found the verse. The verse reads as follows: "You are not on anything until you stand firmly by the Taurat and the Injeel, and what has been revealed to you from your Lord. And that which has been revealed to you from your Lord will surely increase many of them in rebellion and disbelief. So do not grieve over the disbelieving."

This verse caused an electric shock to flow right through me. The Koran itself stated so clearly that Muslims were to "stand firmly by the Taurat and the Injeel", that is, by the Holy Bible as well as with "what has been revealed to you from your Lord", that is, the Koran. If the Koran was true, Yusuf was right in holding the two books in veneration on his bookshelf. But what troubled me was that, if this is what the Koran says, why hasn't there been a long tradition of Muslims honouring the Holy Bible equally with the Koran? Why had Muslims in general disregarded the Holy Bible in contradiction to what the Holy Koran says about the Bible?

Yusuf was ready with answers. It was clear in many verses in the Koran that the Torah and the Injeel were the words of Allah. Many Muslims state that there was once a pure version of the Holy Bible but the Jews and Christians later made alterations to the texts and now what we have is a corrupted and unreliable version of this. But to Yusuf, this didn't make sense. He told me to think of it this way. Would I, as a devout Muslim, even dare make alterations to Allah's Holy Book, the Koran? If Muslims venerate the Koran so much that they hold it in such awe that they just wouldn't dare make any changes to it, wouldn't Jews and

Christians hold the same awe towards the Holy Bible and hence would not make changes to this book either but do everything in their power to protect it from alterations and preserve it for future generations intact? Further, even Allah said on several occasions, at least twice in Surah Al-Anaam 6, in verses 34 and 115, that no-one can change the Words of Allah. He also says in Yunus 10:64 that "There can be no change in the Words of Allah" and again in Surah Al-Kahf 18:27 "none can change His Words". The Koran acknowledges that the Bible is the Book of Allah, so the Bible is also the Word of Allah, and so, if the Koran is true, no-one has been able to corrupt the Bible. Otherwise, the Koran is lying. But the Koran doesn't lie. Further, if Muslims say that the Bible has been corrupted, what would have been the motivation for the Jews and Christians to corrupt it, seeing one of the concepts of being a Jew and a Christian was to believe that the Holy Bible was the unalterable, inerrant Word of God? If Jews and Christians had felt at liberty to make changes, this was evidence that they actually didn't believe in the God of their holy book.

"And, again, who do you believe? The imams and the mulvis, or the Prophet Muhammad and the Holy Koran? Read what it says in Surah Al-Bayyinah 98:2 and 3."

I flicked the Koran to the page and then read it out loud.

"'A Messenger from Allah, reciting purified pages, Wherein are correct writings.'"

I looked up at Yusuf.

"Have a look at the word above the English word 'writings' in the Arabic."

I looked at it. It said *kootooboon*.

"Yes, *kootooboon*, that is, 'books'. Why do you think they translated this as 'writings'? Because whoever translated this did not want to acknowledge that the Torah and the Injeel, two books revealed before the Koran, are 'purified pages' and that these books are *qayimatoon*, that is, 'correct', and if correct, they cannot have been changed. But even though they translated it as 'writings', it doesn't get away from the fact that the Prophet was reciting from the Bible. He wasn't reciting the Koran when it says here that he was reciting from purified pages which contained correct writings because the Koran was revealed to Muhammad verbally through the angel Gabriel who recited portions of the Koran to him, and then Muhammad memorised these portions. The Koran was not revealed to Muhammad written on pages. The Koran did not come in written form till after Muhammad had died. And look at the name of the surah we find this verse in, Al-Bayyinah, the Clear Evidence. Allah has made it clear evidence how we are to view the Bible."

I have no words to describe the feelings going on inside me at that time. It felt like a fire had passed through my soul. It was as if everything I had learnt about my religion had been a lie and now the truth had been revealed before me from the very book those in authority, my Mulvi, my father, the Pakistani government, claimed to be the Word of God. But while they claimed it was the Word of God, what these same people in authority also claimed was contrary to what was written within it.

Again, Yusuf must have read my mind because he smiled through his beard, nodded, and then said, "Yes. Be careful that you don't get carried away by their deception. Turn to Al-Baqarah 2:159 and read what will happen to us if we don't follow Allah explicitly."

I turned the pages gingerly till I found the verse and read it out loud as Yusuf had requested.

"'Indeed, those who conceal the clear proofs We revealed, and the Guidance, after We made it clear for the People of the Book – they are cursed by Allah'."

Again, another wave of fire passed through my body.

"Allah," Yusuf continued, "has provided us with clear proofs that the Torah and the Injeel are from Allah and that all these volumes of Hadiths are not. The only true *hadith* is the Bible and the Holy Koran. Those who are concealing these clear proofs are cursed by Allah. Later in verse 174 it says that these people will eat fire in their bellies."

I looked up at Yusuf full of terror. In my current situation, I was cursed by Allah and would eat fire in my belly. The shock was paralysing so much so that I couldn't speak. But I didn't have to as Yusuf still had more to say.

"Further," Yusuf continued, "listen to what it says in Surah Al-Baqarah 2:285, 'The Messenger has believed in what was revealed to him from his Lord and so have the believers. All of them have believed in Allah and His angels and His Books'. The Messenger, Muhammad, believed in 'His Books', Allah's *kootoob,* not Allah's book, His *kitaab*. If Muhammad believed in Allah's books, the Holy Bible being one of these books, shouldn't we follow his example and believe in the Bible as well? Isn't this sunna?"

For some moments I was too stunned for words. My mind was now on a see-saw, moving back and forward. On the one hand were the thoughts about how the Bible was now corrupted and no longer formed a part of Islam, and on the other was all the evidence that Yusuf had presented to me from the Koran to contradict all this. Yusuf was extremely patient and allowed a long deathly silence fall upon us while my mind continued in long contemplation.

Eventually after much cogitation I realised the next step. I told Yusuf that I wanted to read the Bible. Yusuf had another copy of the Bible handy, a small pocket-sized version which was no bigger than my outstretched hand. The writing inside was very small but fortunately I wore glasses so it wasn't a strain to read. I thanked Yusuf profusely.

"I'll try and read it quickly so I can get it back to you soon," I said.

"That's yours," Yusuf replied. "It's a gift from me. As Allah says in the Bible, Freely you have received, so freely give."

At this point, there was a sudden noise at the door and in came Yusuf's cousin, Amin. Amin was somewhat taller and thinner than his cousin, with a fairer complexion and unusually lighter coloured hair. He was welcoming and polite as his cousin and he sat and joined me for a brief cup of tea.

Pretty soon I realised it was time to go back to my dormitory and start preparing for physics, and also because I knew Maaz would soon be back and we would go and have dinner at the meal room.

When I returned to my dormitory, Maaz was already there. This was strange because he always came late after a run. He recognised that there was an unusual object amongst the things I was holding and so he asked me, "What's this?"

I handed it to him to have a look. Maaz looked down at it and then back at me in surprise.

"The Holy Bible?" he said with a big grin on his face. "Are you going to read that?"

"Yes, of course," I replied, and threw my exercise books on my desk.

"Can I read it?" Maaz then asked.

I looked at him with surprise.

"Yes," I replied. "If you wish. But please don't take it out of the room."

Then as an afterthought I added, "And when you've finished, we can compare notes!"

My new appreciation of the Christian Bible and my association with Yusuf had a great influence over me as it caused a great paradigm shift in my understanding of Islam, and my initial feelings about how to view the Judaeo-Christian Scriptures had been changed completely. Yusuf had given me a Bible to read and so I set myself a time to read it. As Friday was the day we went to prayers, I made it a habit to dedicate the entire time after the midday prayers to sit and read the Bible.

There were times I could not find my Bible on my shelf and often found it amongst Maaz's things or under his pillow which meant that he had also taken a fascination to reading it. I appreciated that he respected my wishes not to remove it from the dormitory. I only told him not to do so because I didn't want him to lose it.

After what I had discovered about the relationship between the Bible and the Koran as Yusuf had demonstrated to me with complete support from the Koran, I was confronted with yet another form of hypocrisy about the general view of Islam in our country. The Koran is quite clear in its veneration for the Bible. Yet there was no way I could read the Bible in the prayer room like I could read the Koran. While I could have stood my ground and shown from the Koran that in fact the Bible requires equal reverence which means I should be able to read the Bible in this holy place, I thought it wasn't worth the fight and so I decided to search for a remote out-of-the-way place on the campus to go on a Friday afternoon to read it. I discovered a place near the lake where nobody seemed to go at this time of the week. This became my new holy place in which I would read and gain new information about my religion.

The first thing that struck me about the Bible was the way it was written. The Koran is written as a collection of sayings randomly put together. There is no flow. By contrast, the Bible read somewhat like a novel. There was a connected flow from the beginning of Genesis all the way to the Book of Revelation. In fact, the Bible read like the Hadiths in that important sayings and precepts were given a context which explained why something was said, who had said it, where it was said and what it meant within that context. And then from this context how it was relevant to us. What was even more profound was that while there were stories I had been familiar with from the Koran, for the first time I understood the time frame and sequence of events in which these stories took place.

I first read about the Creation, how Allah created the world in six days and then on the seventh day He rested. I read about the creation of humans. It finally became clear where this paradise was that Allah created for the first humans. It was the Garden of Eden. Unlike the vague mention in the Koran, the Bible provided a precise geographical location of where the Garden of Eden was situated, on a river which then branched off into four, the Pishon, Gihon, Tigris and Euphrates. I knew that the Tigris and Euphrates Rivers were the two main rivers that flowed through Iraq which meant that Adam and his wife first resided in the south of this country. This meant that the paradise that they later came down out of was from a place on earth. I simply understood this to mean that the Garden of Eden was located on an elevated piece of land. Also, the tree that they were not allowed to touch was clearly identified in the Bible as the Tree of the Knowledge of Good and Evil. The Bible also explained clearly in what way Satan made Adam and Eve slip, and the punishment they received accordingly.

I then read about Adam and Eve's first sons, Cain and Abel, and how Cain killed Abel. For the first time, a riddle was finally answered in the Bible about where the rest of humanity came from. After Cain killed Abel, Adam and Eve had a third son, Seth, and then Adam and Eve simply had an indeterminate number of sons and daughters.

The story unfolded until I reached the story of Nuh, or Noah. Again, what intrigued me was that there was a genealogical connection between Adam and Noah. Whereas the Koran mentions the different prophets, the Bible actually explained the connection between them both in genealogy and chronology. Although the story of Noah and the Flood is fleshed out much more than it is in the Koran, the moral of the story remained the same, that the unbelievers would eventually be destroyed by Allah.

But after the destruction of all humanity by the Flood, recounted in the Bible was a story I had never heard of before, about how a large group of people who went to a plain called Shinar and built a large tower. They didn't finish completing it because Allah didn't want them to. To stop them completing the building, Allah changed the people from being monolingual to speaking all the languages of the world. This was a story I had never read in the Koran nor heard at Friday sermon but this story gave the origin of all the languages of the world.

The story continued following the genealogy from Noah until the calling of one of Noah's direct descendants, Ibrahim, or as it was in the Bible, Abraham. What was new to me was how that Abraham's name originally was Abram and his wife Sarah was originally called Sarai. They left a place called Ur of the Chaldeans to go to a place Allah would show them. I didn't know where Ur of the Chaldeans was but I guessed that the place they were eventually going to go was Israel as this place even according to the Koran was the Holy Land. The story of Ibrahim in the Bible was quite long and detailed, filling in details I had never known before.

I read about Ibrahim's son, Isaac. I knew nothing of Isaac's life story as it is not recounted in the Koran, except that his mother, Sarah, was old when she gave birth to him. The Bible continued the story of Isaac, relating a strange story of intrigue between Isaac and his wife, Rebekah, and their twin sons, Esau and Jacob. In fact, this story was foreign to me as I had not heard of Esau. However, I could understand why I knew nothing of him because in the end he was of no consequence to the development of the story.

I then read about Jacob and how his name was changed to Israel which also made it plain to me why the modern state of Israel carries the same name. I read how Jacob eventually had twelve sons who eventually became separate tribes, once again, hinted at in the Koran but explicitly told in detail in the Bible. This gave greater meaning to what I had read in the story of Moses where water gushed out of a rock into twelve springs and how each group knew which spring to drink from. The twelve groups obviously were the Twelve Tribes of Israel.

What particularly intrigued me was the story of Joseph. This story is recounted in the Koran but there is no connection to where in time this story took place. However, the Bible gave it a context. In fact, this story helped me to understand the connection between Jacob earlier in the story living in Canaan and then later why Moses brought the Children of Israel out of Egypt. It was because of Jacob's sons selling Joseph as a slave to traders that Joseph ended up in Egypt and then later caused the rest of Jacob's family to go to Egypt. And then, when the descendants had multiplied greatly, Moses brought them out again to take them back to the Holy Land.

I was familiar with the story of Moses from what I had read in the Koran but now there was a connection between the events and their sequence in the narrative. Moses seeing the burning bush, Moses going to Pharaoh to tell him to let the Children of Israel go, the miracles Moses performed before Pharaoh, the plagues he brought on Egypt, the eventual flight from Egypt through the parting of the Red Sea, the feeding of the Children of Israel with quails and manna – the exact nature of manna being described in the Torah – and the hitting of the rock with Moses' staff so that water gushed out finally had a time sequence to the story and made the obscure in the Koran much clearer.

And then I reached the part in the Book of Exodus when Allah gave Moses the Law. What intrigued me was that the Law of Moses was written on stone tablets. The English word used in the Bible was the same as the word in the English translation of the Koran which talks about the Koran having been written on tablets. This struck me as rather strange. I then recalled the movie *The Ten Commandments* I

266

had seen years previous. There is a part in the movie when Allah writes on two large tablets of stone the Laws of Allah. Strangely, it was only now while reading the Bible that this began to puzzle me. Why it puzzled me was that if these laws had been written on stone tablets, how could they have been so easily corrupted like I had been told earlier in my upbringing? But also, why was it that both the Torah and the Koran were both written on tablets, yet we were taught that this was only the case with the Koran?

I read through all the laws all the way to the end of Deuteronomy. Some laws looked similar to laws in Islam such as stoning people for committing adultery and for fornication, but there were many that were very unfamiliar. But there were so many that I could not retain them all in memory on my first reading.

The Book of Joshua was clearly a novel story I had never heard about before. Moses died before reaching the Holy Land and so it was left to Joshua to lead the people into the new country, kill all the former inhabitants and then set up the different regions into twelve areas according to the twelve tribes.

And like the Book of Joshua, the plotline of The Book of Judges was also completely new. As the book relates, once the Israelites had settled in the Holy Land, they stopped following Allah. Allah brought on a foreign nation to suppress them, the people repented and came back to Allah and then Allah removed the yoke of the oppressor, only to have the people forget Allah all over again. This did make me wonder why Allah persisted with these people. However, I knew that in the end, Allah knew best.

The books of I and II Samuel, I and II Kings, and I and II Chronicles to me were simply books of history in the same vein as Joshua and Judges, and in particular the history of the kings and queens of Israel, and then when Israel split into two nations, the kingdoms of Israel and Judah. These stories were both fascinating and also new as none of the events were mentioned in the Koran. What intrigued me about this part of the Bible was the establishment of the Davidic dynasty. Both King David and King Solomon are mentioned in the Koran yet only that they were both kings and prophets. These historic books made the claim that Allah had established a Davidic dynasty which He claimed would continue forever.

This dynasty, however, did not last forever as these books claim Allah said it would. First a great empire called the Assyrians came and conquered Israel. All the inhabitants of Israel were then scattered throughout the empire and the Israelites were never heard of again. Then later another big empire called the Babylonian Empire came down and conquered Judah, and removed the king from the throne.

The original inhabitants of Judah, now called Jews, eventually were allowed to return to Israel to build the Temple in Jerusalem. This occurred because another empire, the Persian Empire, conquered the Babylonian Empire, and the emperors of the Persian Empire allowed the Jews to return to Jerusalem and rebuild the Temple. This was recounted in the books called Ezra and Nehemiah.

I had difficulty reading the books of prophecy which form the latter part of the Old Testament. Although I didn't fully understand everything I read, Allah seemed to be prophesying a new king out of the Davidic dynasty to rule once again in a future time in Israel and that the Torah would once again be the Rule of Law.

Then I read the Gospels. In the Koran the Gospels are called the Injeel. However, I'm still not sure exactly what the Injeel in the Koran is actually referring to. The Arabic word is singular but there are four gospels so I'm still not sure whether "Injeel" refers to all four gospels or to all twenty-seven books of the New Testament.

I found the Gospels particularly fascinating. It is very hard to read the Gospels and not fall in love with the prophet Issa, or Jesus, and his beautiful teachings. In a way, I could understand why Christians could be misled into thinking that Jesus was equal with Allah but to me it still remained clear that even he considered himself merely as Allah's Messenger. True, he referred to Allah as his Father but as the Gospels say in other parts, so were all the believers of Allah encouraged to do so. There was something beautiful in Jesus calling Allah his Father and even inviting us to call Allah our Father that I found quite captivating.

What intrigued me also was how much Jesus quoted extensively from the Torah and the Prophets. Jesus' intricate knowledge of the Old Testament writings stunned those around him especially as he had been brought up as a carpenter. In those days, a simple carpenter did not get a formal education and so was illiterate. So the fact that Jesus could read and further that he could quote from the Old Testament at will to prove a point was absolutely amazing which should have shown to those at the time that Jesus was miraculous and therefore a messenger of Allah. What really further impressed me and made me love Jesus even more was how he healed people from diseases and forgave them for their sins, all this briefly mentioned in the Koran but greatly detailed in the New Testament. But also Jesus had command over natural phenomena, at one time commanding a storm to be quiet and at another how he walked on water. The crucifixion was extremely moving but also understandable as many of the prophets suffered at the hands of the disobedient. However the resurrection showed that in the end, Allah always comes out triumphant.

It was when I got to the letters of Paul that I was even more intrigued. We don't hear of Paul in the Koran. However, there were things in the Koran which I could see came from Paul's letters. For example, in Surah Al-Imran 3:59 a comparison is made between Adam and Jesus where it says that "Indeed the likeness of Issa with Allah is like that of Adam" which sounded similar to Paul's lengthy comparison between Adam and Jesus in I Corinthians 15.

Also, Paul writes in I Corinthians 10:13 that Allah "will not let you be tempted beyond what you can bear" which finds its echo in Al-Anaam 6:152 which says "We do not burden any soul except to its capacity."

What Paul wrote was rather deep and he goes into quite complex argument about things I didn't quite understand. But I decided that on a second reading that maybe I would gain a better grasp of what he was trying to say.

The last book of the Bible, the Revelation, was quite frightening. However, there were many things written in the Revelation that I had heard about in Friday prayers if they weren't directly mentioned in the Koran. Many of the prophecies that we had been taught about the coming of the end of the world had parallels in this last book of the Bible, except that instead of it being Jesus who would return, it would be the Mehdi, with Jesus following behind.

Once I had finished reading the Bible and once again opened the Koran, I couldn't help but see like I had never seen before how much the Koran is more like an appendage or an extension of the Bible and not a separate book. It was the Bible that helped me to understand better the Koran and a lot of the background to the personalities mentioned in it, providing greater depth and understanding as to what occurred in these events and when these events took place.

But what affected me greatly was the fact that the Bible had been written in different languages, and not one of them was Arabic. I first read this in the preface to the Bible Yusuf had given me that this New International Version of the Bible had been translated from Hebrew, Aramaic and Greek.

My Mulvi had spent much of my growing up years trying to get me to recite the Koran in Arabic, trying to get the pronunciation perfect and correct, and paying little attention to the meaning, as if it were the language itself, Arabic, that was important, not the message the Koran was trying to convey. It came to such a point that it was believed that Allah only spoke Arabic, as if Arabic were the pure language of Allah. If this were the case, why then hadn't Allah revealed the Bible in Arabic, especially as the Bible preceded the Koran?

That Allah was not limited to one language came out in the Bible itself. Paul himself said in the Acts of the Apostles chapter 26 verse fourteen that he explicitly heard Allah speak to him in Aramaic – or in Hebrew, as the footnote indicated as an alternate translation of the Greek word. And in Revelation 1:8 Allah says that He is "the Alpha and Omega...who is, and who was and who is to come" where Allah uses the Greek letters, alpha and omega, to symbolise His eternal existence, alpha being the first letter of the Greek alphabet and omega the last. This explicitly demonstrated that Allah was not confined to one language. This then made me question why I had to read the Koran in the original Arabic when Allah Himself operates on a multilingual level. The Bible could easily be read in English and the message was clear enough to understand, so why not the Koran?

This was yet another teaching from the Islamic faith I had come to question and then finally rejected, the necessity to do everything in my religion purely in the Arabic language. Allah was not confined to one language. So why should we be? It was true that the Koran had been revealed in Arabic and the Koran confirms this on several occasions. But the Koran does not say that as a result of this it is imperative to learn Arabic. This was a manmade rule. And to me it was un-Islamic.

For the first time I didn't feel as if I were cheating or offending Allah for using the English translation to assist in understanding what I read. Seeing it was clear that Allah Himself was multilingual, I no longer felt under the compulsion to read the Koran in the original Arabic.

Nonetheless, I had put so much effort into learning the Arabic that I decided to continue all the same. After all,

271

I didn't see any harm in doing so. I simply continued to use my Arabic-English interlinear to help me understand the Arabic but I felt free to read the Koran in the English translation as I was now sure that Allah did not mind. It was the message He was trying to convey that was important, not the medium or language used to deliver it.

But then, the translation became an issue. While it was easier to read the holy books in a language I felt comfortable in, I had learnt a vast amount of Arabic and as a result I could compare the English translation with the Arabic original. And it was the way certain words were translated that troubled me.

Because the Koran was revealed in Arabic, many Arabic words and expressions have become common in Islamic vocabulary irrespective of the primary language spoken by Muslims on a daily basis. This is reflected in the English translation of the Koran where the Arabic word is transliterated when there is already an English equivalent. In the translation, we still read *Allah* for God, *Taurat* for Torah or the Old Testament, *Injeel* for Gospel, *Shaitaan* or *Iblis* for Satan, *Jahannam* for hell and *Qibla* for direction of prayer. Even the names of certain prophets keep their Arabic name in the English translation, such as *Ibrahim* for Abraham, *Musa* for Moses and *Issa* for Jesus. The problem was, I began to notice an inconsistency in the English translation. Sometimes the Arabic word was simply transliterated but on other occasions the word was translated completely. I felt that this led non-Arabic speakers to incorrect or misleading understandings of what the Koran was actually saying.

The translation of the word *hadith* was a point in hand. As Yusuf had pointed out, in the Koran in the original Arabic, we read the word *hadith*, but this word is invariably translated into English as "narration", "statement" or "tale". While this translation is correct, translating the word obscured the meaning of the verses. But I could understand the motive behind translating the word *hadith* in the Koran because by transliterating it as *hadith* it blatantly showed that the Hadiths that were to come were not from Allah.

Yusuf explained to me that the original *hadith* was the Koran and he proved this from the Koran itself. Yusuf also made a statement that the real *hadith* was both the Bible and the Koran together but he did not prove this from the Koran. But on further reading of the Koran, I discovered the justification for this view of the true *hadith* of Allah.

This first came to me when I read the verse from Surah Ta Ha 20:9, where it says "And has the *hadith* of Musa reached you?" The word *hadith* in the English is translated as "story" but in the Arabic clearly it is the word "hadith". And where else do we read the story of Moses except in the *Taurat,* the Old Testament? This became more pronounced when coupled with the verse from Surah Adh-Dhariyat 51:24 which says, "Has there reached you the *hadith* of the honoured guests of Ibrahim?" and then the verses which follow talk about Ibrahim when Allah told him that his wife would have a son even while she was old and barren. Again, this narration came from the Old Testament, which again implied that the Old Testament was the *hadith.*

It was the verses from Surah Al-Waqia 56:77, 78 and 81, which spelled out clearly the identity of the true *hadith* of Allah, where it says, "Indeed, it is a noble Koran, in a Book well-guarded...then is it to this *hadith* that you are indifferent?" The "this *hadith*" in verse 81 refers back to the "noble Koran" in verse 77. However, verse 78 says that the noble Koran is not itself a book well-guarded, but is *in* a Book well-guarded, that is, part of a collection. Putting all this together, the Bible and the Koran together were the Book well-guarded and were the true *hadith* of Allah. By going back to the original language, this concept becomes clear. This further confirmed Yusuf's and now my total rejection of later Hadiths, and further it made me realize that according to the Koran, it was not only the Koran that was the *hadith,* it was also the Bible.

Like the Arabic word *hadith*, there were other words that were sometimes transliterated and sometimes translated in the English translation, and as a result the message was obscured for the non-Arabic reader.

One of these was the word *qibla*. The word *qibla* is an Arabic word and means "direction" and is the word used to describe the direction of prayer, that is, the direction in which all Muslims should pray when they pray to Allah. This *qibla* appears in the Koran in Al-Baqarah 2:142 where it says, "The fools among the people will say, 'What has turned them from the Qibla to which they were used?'" and then the following verses explain the change of the *qibla*. We had been told all our lives that what this passage of the Koran was talking about was the direction of prayer towards Mecca, that when we prayed five times a day, it was not only the prayers but also the direction in which we prayed that was of paramount importance. What we had also been told and what this verse was implying was that there had been two *qiblas*, the first one was towards Jerusalem and in particular towards Al-Masjid Al-Aqsa, that is, the Al-Aqsa Mosque, but then this was changed by Muhammad when he received the revelation to change the *qibla* to Mecca which is now the *qibla* of today. The same word, however, is used elsewhere, but instead of simply being transliterated, it is completely translated. This is found in Surah Yunus 10:87 where Allah spoke to Moses and Aaron by saying "Settle your people in Egypt in houses and make your houses places of worship". This verse related to the time recorded in the Torah when the descendants of Israel were in Egypt and were being persecuted by Pharaoh when Moses and Aaron were about to take the Children of Israel out. The point was that the English expression "places of worship" in the original Arabic is *qibla* so that this verse should read "Settle your people in Egypt in houses and make your houses a *qibla*". I could understand why the translators did not want to use the word *qibla* in the translation because then

274

this would raise the question as to why there was a *qibla* in Egypt, in particular, the very houses in which the Children of Israel lived, when according to Muslim understanding there had only ever been two: one towards Jerusalem and one towards Mecca. This certainly raised the question in my mind as to why Allah kept changing the *qibla*. But then Allah was All-Wise and All-Knowing and He knew what He was doing.

Another was the word in Arabic *khalifa* which in its transliterated form has become a standard English word in the form of "caliph". The original meaning of the Arabic word is "representative" and the general understanding of a *khalifa* is that he or she is a representative of Allah on earth. We had been told as Sunni Muslims of the four rightly guided Caliphs, Abubaker, Omar, Uthman and Ali, who were the four successive leaders of the Islamic religion after the death of Muhammad. Also, Muslims today are in expectation of a global caliphate ruled by a world-leading caliph and hence the general understanding of *caliph* is one human being among all of us especially chosen by Allah to represent Him on earth. However, the word *khalifa* in the Koran is often translated as "viceregent" or "successor" and thus hides what a caliph is according to the Koran. For example, in Surah Sad 38:26, Allah says, "O David! We have made you viceregent on earth". Here Allah was speaking about King David, the first king of the tribe of Judah who established a dynasty in about 1,000 BC, the dynasty of which we read about in the biblical books of I & II Samuel, I & II Kings and I & II Chronicles. However, the word "viceregent" in the original Arabic is *khalifa* and hence this verse should read "O David! We have made you *caliph* on earth". I really didn't have a problem with recognising David as a caliph but I guessed that this put in question why we talked of the "rightly guided caliphs", Abubaker, Omar, Uthman and Ali, when King David of the Jews was also a caliph. Was he not also rightly guided? This then

275

gave greater weight on Muslims to seriously consider the Psalms, called *Zaboors* in the Koran, because if David was a rightly-guided caliph, and as it says in Bani-Israil 17:55 that Allah "gave David Zaboor", then the Psalms of the Old Testament are from Allah.

But then the Koran says that all humanity, men and women, boys and girls, all of us humans who populate the earth are in fact the real caliphs. When transliterating and not translating the word *khalifa*, this is seen first in Al-Baqarah 2:30 when Allah is about to create the first man and woman, and Allah says to the angels "I will create *caliphs* on earth". The implication as we read on in the later verses is that Allah did not specifically mean that Adam and Eve only were the caliphs but all humans in general. This comes out later when reading about Noah and his family being the sole survivors of the Great Flood and Allah saying in Yunus 10:73 "We saved him and those who were with him in the ship and We made them *caliphs*". Again, the implication was that it was not only Noah and his family who were made caliphs, they were the only humans on earth at the time and hence they were the forbears of all humanity, all caliphs, that were to later come. And then there was the verse in Surah Al-Fatir 35:39 which says, "He is the One who made you *caliphs*" where Allah is speaking to all of us, all humanity. Using the English word "caliph" in all these verses showed that the idea of having a one-world caliphate ruled by an international caliph in some ways was absurd and further un-koranic because the real caliphs according to the Koran were all of us humans.

But what really troubled me was how some words were actually translated incorrectly. I saw this particularly with the translation of the Arabic word *noor*. *Noor* simply means "light" and is translated as such in verses such as in Surah Al-Ahzab 33:43 where Allah says that He has brought "you out from the depths of darkness into light (*noor*)" and from Surah az-Zumar 39:69 which says that "the earth will shine with the light (*noor*) of the Lord." In fact, there is an entire surah called An-Noor, The Light, the 24th surah, and one of its verses illustrates why it is so named when we read verse 35 "Allah is the light (*noor*) of the heavens and the earth". But I was surprised to see in my Arabic-English interlinear, when referring to the moon, the translation was "reflected light". For example, in Yunus 10:5 this verse reads "He is the One Who made the sun a shining light and the moon a reflected light (*noor*)". What stunned me was that not only did the translation of the word *noor* become unjustifiably "reflected light", in the actual interlinear, underneath the Arabic word *noor* was the English "reflected light". Oddly, there was an inconsistency with this. In Surah Nuh 71:16 in the same Arabic-Interlinear we read in the English that Allah "made the moon therein a light (*noor*)" where the word "reflected" does not appear. I could understand why the translators wanted to change the meaning of *noor* in reference to the moon as "reflected light" because we now know that the moon has no inherent light of its own but what we see is simply the reflection of the light from the sun. But shouldn't we as Muslims simply accept the word for what it says and not tamper with Allah's chosen words, making alterations to the translation to mislead the non-Arabic reader into believing that what is written on the original Koran in heaven is something different? This made it appear as if the translators were embarrassed by the use of *noor* in reference to the moon and so they wanted the word to say something that it didn't, to reflect our current understanding of the true nature of the moon. This tampering with the translation I found very unnerving and thought that the translators should have been honest, for there was a good reason why Allah had used this very word in the first place and one day it would be revealed to be the right one.

This was the same with the word *ayaam*, which in English is "days", being the plural of the Arabic word *yom,* "day". For example, in Al-Baqarah 2:184, it says that fasting is for a "limited number of days (*ayaam*)" and later in verse 196 when talking about Hajj it is prescribed that they should "fast for three days (*ayaam*) during Hajj and seven days (*ayaam*) after returning." Then later in Al-Imran 3:41, the sign that Zakariya's wife would have a child was that Zakariya "will not speak with people for three days (*ayaam*)". However, verses which refer to the creation of the heaven and the earth translated the Arabic *ayaam* as "epochs", that is, as long, unspecified lengths of time. For example, in Surah As-Sajdah 32:4 it says that "Allah is the One Who created the heavens and the earth and whatever is between them in six epochs (*ayaam*)". This same declaration is made also in Surah Qaf 50:38 where it says "We created the heavens and the earth and whatever is between them in six periods (*ayaam*)" and again in Surah Al-Hadid 57:4 "He is the One Who created the heavens and the earth in six periods (*ayaam*)". I saw no justification for translating the word *ayaam* as "epochs" except to reflect what has resulted from scientific research that the universe took millions upon millions of years to come into its formation. That we were to understand that the universe was created in literally six days seemed even more evident when I looked up the English translation of the Koran made by Abdullah Yusuf Ali where in these same verses the word *ayaam* was translated consistently as "days". And this idea that the universe was created in literally six days was simply a reflection of what it said in the Torah in the very first chapter, that the universe was created in literally six days.

But what particularly bothered me the most was the copious insertions of the name of the prophet Muhammad, written as "Muhammad SAWS" in brackets in the translation in my Arabic-English interlinear when Muhammad's name did not even appear at all in the original text. My translation of the Koran by Abdullah Yusuf Ali did a similar thing but used the word "prophet" in brackets instead of putting the name. When reading the original Arabic, however, there was no clear indication that these verses were actually directed at Muhammad or said by Muhammad, or to any of the prophets or to anyone in particular.

For example, in Surah Al-Imran 3:68, it says that "the most worthy people to claim relationship to Ibrahim are those who follow him and this Prophet". My Arabic-English interlinear added "Muhammad SAWS" after the word "Prophet" but there was nothing in the original Arabic which clearly indicated that this was the particular prophet the Koran was talking about. As the Koran points out in other places, Muhammad is not the only prophet, he is simply one among many. Also, in Surah Abasa 80, the surah starts off by saying, "He frowned and turned away." Again, there was the insertion in brackets in the English translation of the words "Muhammad SAWS". But once again, there was nothing in the original Arabic text which indicated that the one frowning and turning away was the prophet Muhammad. In fact, what struck me as odd was how that there was an abundance of insertions of "Muhammad SAWS" in the English when in contrast the actual name "Muhammad" is rather scarce in the original text. But what particularly troubled me was that the non-Arabic reader was being made to believe that the identity of "this Prophet" and the one who frowned was definitively Muhammad when the Koran in the original Arabic did not indicate this at all and hence there was a possibility that it could be referring to someone else.

These mistranslations and interpolations of words into the English translation bothered me immensely. Although the translators had not tampered with the original Arabic of the koranic text, by interpreting these words differently to what the words actually meant in the Koran, and adding words to the English translation which did not appear in the original text to me meant that the translators wanted the text to say something that it didn't actually say, especially when they were embarrassed by what the text actually did say. Therefore the translators made the English translation say what they wanted it to say although it didn't say this in the original Arabic. While they may not have tampered with the original words, the manipulation of the translation was still tampering with the text. Instead of sitting back and accepting with awe and being totally afraid to make any changes to what was written, the translators had actually taken the liberty to make changes to the text that they saw fit. This struck me so powerfully. How could these translators sincerely believe that the Koran was the unalterable Word of Allah and hold such reverence and awe towards this book yet at the same time feel the liberty to make changes in the meaning and insert additional words when creating the English translation so that the translated version said things that were not in the original text?

This caused the question to return to me that Taheer had once asked me and which was suggested by the Hadiths. Taheer had asked the poignant question: how can we be sure that the Koran had not been manipulated before we received the final version? According to the Hadiths, variant copies of the earliest versions of the Koran were completely burnt. Why? Were there other versions of the Koran which said things that the rightly guided caliphs didn't want the Koran to say and hence the evidence of what was originally written destroyed? If the copiers of the Koran were in awe of the text coming directly from Allah, even with the variations, how did they have the courage, indeed, the audacity to burn any of the variants if they had all come from Allah? And so it was with the English translation. How was it that the translators felt comfortable enough to add words, translate the same word in different ways and alter the meanings of words to make the English version hold a meaning that wasn't apparent in the original Arabic?

After months of the friendship that was developing between Yusuf and me, Yusuf must have felt that he had won my trust and so he invited me to attend a mosque dedicated to Ibrahimi Islam. There was a tacit understanding that where we were going and the reason for going there was not something to be declared publicly. I could totally understand this because any forms of Islam which deviate from the standard Sunni or Shiite beliefs are considered heretical in Pakistan, and groups of people who follow these divergent forms of Islam are often threatened verbally and often physically attacked by merciless mobs.

The Ibrahimi Muslim day of prayer is Saturday, beginning at sunset Friday afternoon and ending at sunset Saturday afternoon. The reason for this is because this is the Sabbath. The day which Allah sanctified according to the Torah was Saturday, the Sabbath, or as it is in Arabic, *yom assabt*, and as Allah says in An-Nisaa 4:154, "Do not transgress in the Sabbath". In fact, this struck me very powerfully, and further raised the question as to when Friday became the Muslim holy day for prayer because there is nothing in the Koran which gives Friday its sanction.

We went to pray one Saturday morning. It was important, so Yusuf explained, to dress soberly, as if we were attending a birthday party or some similar formal affair.

We arrived at a rather imposing building. It looked simply like the residence of a wealthy person and I soon discovered that for much of the week, that was what it was. The owner of the house had converted to Ibrahimi Islam and had decided to make his house a house of prayer for those in true devotion to the correct form of Islam.

The house was a large two storey building. We first went around to the back courtyard, a large yard surrounded with imposing fences and hedges which prevented prying eyes from looking inside. There were two large water fountains and taps for us to do our ablutions before going to pray but what surprised me was that these people did not wash themselves in any particular order as I had been taught. What was further surprising was that both women and men came to the same place to wash, although not at the same fountain.

I was taken inside through the back door which led to a large downstairs room, an open space which could house the 200-odd people who had come to pray there. What was further amazing was that both men and women occupied the room inside, although women and men sat on opposite sides of the room.

We all sat on the floor. Prayer mats had been laid out over the otherwise marbled floor more for the comfort of those present, not as a requirement on which to pray. I noticed over on the women's side there were a few older women and they were seated in chairs. This indicated to me that either these women had converted to Ibrahimi Islam only recently or this was evidence that this version of Islam had been around for a while. When I turned around to look at those congregated with me on the men's side, I also noticed a few older men in the same condition.

What intrigued me was that we all sat around in an arc towards a centre. This was strange because in the mosque, all devotees were arranged in parallel lines, all facing in the direction of the mithrab which in turn faced towards Mecca. And further, when I thought about the orientation of this house and where we were, this semi-circle faced towards a direction which from a quick glance outside to see where the sun was, was actually facing in a direction roughly east, which was in direct opposition to the direction we should be facing, as Mecca is west of Pakistan.

While we were settling in and taking a place on the floor, there was a man at the centre, where all our faces pointed towards, who had his back to us and who was rocking back and forth and chanting, holding what appeared to be an open scroll. However, from the sound of the chanting, I did not understand a word of it. It wasn't in English, nor in Urdu, nor was it Arabic.

Eventually, the man toned off in what sounded like a last sentence, ended with "Amen" and then turned around to look at all of us. He placed the scroll on a special stand to his right and then returned to the centre, smiled and gesticulated for all of us to stand up. We did so and the man at the centre then turned again with his back to us. He then spoke out loud and said in English

Glory be to You, O Allah!

and this was repeated by everyone gathered together. He then repeated this in Urdu and then in a language I didn't recognize.

This leader then turned around to face us and then quoted the verse from Al-Baqarah 2:136

We believe in Allah and what is revealed to us and what was revealed to Ibrahim and Ishmael and Isaac and Jacob and the descendants, and what was given to Moses and Jesus and what was given to the prophets from their Lord. We make no distinction between any of them. And to Him we are submissive.

and everyone then repeated it as a prayer, again, first in English, then in Urdu and then in a third language which I wasn't familiar with but I just listened when Yusuf recited it.

The leader then prayed another prayer in all three languages, the first part I was unfamiliar with but recognized that it came from the Injeel, the second part being the Al-Fatiha, the first surah of the Koran:

Oh, Allah, holy is your name.
Your kingdom is coming.
Your Will be done.
Give us this day our daily bread
And forgive us our sins

As we forgive those who are indebted to us
And lead us not into temptation.

In the name of Allah,
the Most Gracious, the Most Merciful.
Praise be to Allah,
the Lord of the universe.
The Most Gracious, the Most Merciful.
The Master of the Day of Judgement
You alone we worship and
you alone we ask for help.
Guide us on the right path.
The path of those on whom you
have bestowed your favours,
not the path of those who earned your wrath,
and not of those who go astray.

Amen

The man then opened his eyes and signalled for us to sit back on the floor. He then stretched out his hands to all of us sitting there and said "Peace" and suddenly the congregation was abuzz with the sound of "peace" being said by all those around us, sometimes in English, sometimes in Urdu, accompanied by handshakes and broad welcoming smiles. Once silence had returned, everyone looked back to the leader and the leader walked over to what looked like a lectern and began his talk. It was obvious that he read from a variety of texts, and I recognized all of them as being either from the Torah, the Injeel or the Koran. What struck me the most was that all these readings were carried out in English, not in Arabic. I guessed that this part of the service was the sermon as the leader then went on to explain how the passages he had read were relevant to our daily lives.

What intrigued me so much about the ceremony was that it was conducted in a language we all understood, women and men were assembled equally together, and the only movement when praying was clasping hands and closing eyes. And of course, prayers were not directed towards Mecca.

A number of other rituals were carried out but I have long since forgotten the details. However, I can still remember that the ceremony closed with the leader saying

All the praise be to Allah, the Lord of the worlds

Amen

which like all the other prayers was said in English, Urdu and this mysterious third non-Arabic language.

What pricked up my attention with the last prayer was that I realised that this had come from the verse in Yunus 10:10 which says, "Their prayer therein will be, 'Glory be to you, O Allah! And their greetings therein will be 'Peace.' And the last of their call will be 'All the praise be to Allah, the Lord of the worlds'."

When the ceremony was over, the people slowly dispersed and this left me with Yusuf and a few other people. Yusuf introduced me to the leader of the ceremony. His name was Amani. He looked like he was in his late 30s to early 40s, with a bushy beard but it was obvious that it had been trimmed. I thanked Amani for being able to spend time at his place and to observe the ceremony. Amani in turn told me that I was welcome to come and talk to him at any time if I wanted more information about this version of Islam.

Eventually Yusuf and I left and went back to the university campus. But instead of going back to our dormitories, we sat at the lake near his dormitory in an area away from everyone, where we could talk openly and freely without people hearing what we had to say.

What had struck me about the ceremony was just how different it was to what happened in the mosque, to the point that one couldn't really call it Islam. But Yusuf's religion was based on the same Koran as the one I believed in. So what accounted for the differences?

The name they gave themselves, that is, Ibrahimi Muslims, comes from what it says in the Koran in Al-Imran 3:95 that we should "follow the religion of Ibrahim" and in verse 67 that Ibrahim "was a true Muslim". Further, it says in Al-Baqarah 2:135 that "We follow the religion of Ibrahim." In fact, Ibrahim holds an extremely important position for all humanity as it says in Al-Baqarah 2:124 that Allah made Ibrahim "a leader for mankind". Further, Ibrahim played a significant role in the development of Islam as it was Ibrahim who laid the foundations of the House, the Kaaba in Mecca, or Bakkah, as it says in Al-Baqarah 2:127 and Al-Imran 3:95, 96.

Their confession of faith was based on the verse in Al-Baqarah 2:136. But also, even with their adoration of Ibrahim, they acknowledged that even Ibrahim begged of Allah to send Messengers after him as Ibrahim said to Allah in Al-Baqarah 2:129 which explained that even though they gave Ibrahim immense credence, they also acknowledged the other Messengers, including Massikh and Muhammad. Their whole belief made me question the Shahada, our declaration of faith, that "There is no God but Allah and Muhammad is His Messenger", as this declaration was totally absent from the Koran. Not only so, the koranic statement, the statement that had come directly from Allah through Gabriel to Muhammad stated quite emphatically that Muslims were not to make any distinctions between the prophets whatsoever which in a way made the Shahada contradictory to the Koran, and somewhat blasphemous. Yusuf was therefore right. The Koran does not say that we are to believe in only one prophet and to adore him and ignore all the rest. The Koran emphatically declares that the true believers acknowledge all the prophets equally. Further, the Koran is very clear in stating that Allah gave Moses the Torah and Issa the Injeel, and although not stated, it was understood that Allah also gave Muhammad the Koran.

"But what is your qibla?" I asked. "I noticed that we weren't facing towards Mecca as we are supposed to do in the mosque."

"The true qibla," Yusuf replied, "is towards what it says in the original Arabic, the *Al-Masjid Al-Haraam*, the Forbidden Mosque. This cannot be the Kaaba in Mecca because this mosque is not forbidden because we can go there at any time on Hajj. What *masjid* is forbidden to us humans? It is the holy house of Allah, His throne and His palace in the heavens. We are forbidden to go there because of what happened in the beginning when Adam and Eve sinned and were cast out of paradise and how they were made flesh and forced to live in this physical world as fleshly beings. Only in our purified state after we have died will we be able to re-enter this Holy House of Allah, *Al-Masjid Al-Haraam*. And where is this Holy House? It is not in a place in our space-time dimension. It is in the space-time realm of the Almighty. As Allah says in Al-Baqarah 2:115, "And to Allah belongs the east and the west, so wherever you turn, there is the face of Allah." When we pray, we are to pray towards Allah, not to some object. And it doesn't matter which direction we pray in, in whatever direction we pray, we are praying towards the face of Allah. Those Muslims, falsely so-called, who insist that we should pray in the direction of Mecca are in essence telling us to pray to the black rock. This is idolatrous. They do this to follow their own wicked desires. But as for the true believers of Allah, as it says in Luqman 31:22, "Whoever submits his face to Allah...has grasped the most trustworthy handhold". Allah's face is everywhere so those who pray in all directions have grasped the most trustworthy handhold.

Further, there is a story in the Gospels when the prophet Issa went to Samaria and met a Samaritan woman. There was a dispute about the qibla, whether it was towards

Jerusalem as the Jews believed, or towards the mountain near Sychar in the north of Israel as believed the Samaritans. Issa then tells the Samaritan woman, 'Believe me, woman, the time is coming when you will worship Allah neither on this mountain nor in Jerusalem. The time has come when the true worshippers will worship Allah in spirit and in truth, for they are the kind of worshippers Allah seeks. Allah is spirit, and His worshippers must worship in spirit and in truth'. The qibla originally was towards Jerusalem, but it was revealed to Issa that the qibla had been changed towards the spiritual world, the world of the unseen. Later Muslims corrupted the understanding of the verses in Al-Baqarah to make it sound as if they were to pray to a particular place on the earth. But that doesn't make sense. If Allah is everywhere, does it make sense to pray towards a particular point on the planet? To do this means that this point has become our central focus and is more important than Allah, to whom we should be praying. And seeing it doesn't matter which way we turn our face there will we see the face of Allah, it doesn't matter which direction we are facing when we pray. The true Al-Masjid Al-Haraam is the true seat of Allah in the spiritual world of the unseen."

What Yusuf had to say made sense. I was absolutely stunned by his analysis. But further, it made me feel extremely uncomfortable that I had been praying towards the black rock in Mecca for all these years. What was I supposed to do now when I prayed?

"The Koran," Yusuf continued, "does not say in vain in Al-Imran 3:71, 'O People of the Book! Why do you mix truth with falsehood and conceal the truth knowingly?' and later in verse 78 'And indeed, among them is a group who distort the Book with their tongues so that you may think it is from the Book but it is not from the Book. And they say, 'This is from Allah', but it is not from Allah. And they tell a lie about Allah while they know.' There are a lot of practices that have crept in over the years introduced into Islam and which have polluted Islam. We need to bring the believers back to the true Islam of Ibrahim the *hanifa.*"

What Yusuf had to say to me absolutely stunned me and it actually supported something I had initially thought. Praying to Mecca can't be from Allah because we are praying to the black rock. Yusuf's explanation of what the true qibla was made so much more sense. Allah's face was everywhere and so it was not imperative to pray in one particular direction, for by doing so we make this object more important than Allah. And this is blatantly idolatrous.

However, I realised for my own safety, I needed at least in public to pray towards Mecca together with other Muslims in the prayer room or at the mosque. After all, it did say that "wherever you turn, there is the face of Allah" so even when I prayed in the direction of Mecca, that was one direction in which I could turn and still be praying towards the face of Allah.

I asked Yusuf about the different languages that were used in the ceremony. I recognized English and Urdu but not the third.

"The third language we spoke was Pashto," Yusuf replied. "Many of us who are here from the university who are Ibrahimi Muslims are Pashtoon by background and hence that's our mother tongue. So when we gather here in Vokyalesh, we recognize that the two main languages of Pakistan are English and Urdu, and some of us Pashtoons like to pray in our mother tongue, Pashto. Back in Peshawar, we often only pray in Pashto when the congregation is made up of only Pashtoons."

"And not in Arabic?" I asked impressed.

"No," Yusuf replied. "Allah is not limited to one language. He is the Almighty. He is beyond language. This is why His Holy Books were sent down in different languages, the Old Testament in Hebrew and Aramaic, the New Testament in Greek, and the Koran in Arabic. There is no monopoly on the language used in worship. We are to worship Allah in spirit and in truth in the language that we speak. This idea that Allah only speaks in Arabic and only understands us in Arabic is blasphemous because it limits Allah. I mean, I speak three languages, English, Urdu and Pashto. If I, a mere mortal, can speak three languages, can't Allah the Almighty?"

I was absolutely impressed by Yusuf's explanations. I was also impressed overall with the Ibrahimi Muslims and their ceremony in general. Their religion was more egalitarian between the sexes and throughout the ceremony they used the languages of the people.

And what really was admirable was that they upheld, in the same way as the Koran upholds, that the Torah and the Injeel with the Koran are the Words of Allah. Everything about the Ibrahimi Muslims really spoke to my heart.

The verse from Al-Baqarah 2:130 then came to mind: "And who will turn away from the religion of Ibrahim except the one who fools himself?" From what I had learnt from Yusuf and the Ibrahimi Muslims, I had been fooling myself. And I no longer wanted to remain a fool.

Chapter 12

My association with Yusuf affected me greatly. Because the Koran was so anchored to the Judaeo-Christian Scriptures, I failed to see how the Holy Bible had not continued as a significant part of the Islamic religion. I couldn't help but notice like I never had before how connected to the Holy Books of the Jews and Christians the Koran was, and the history of Muslims disregarding the Bible saying that it had been corrupted made less sense. When we read the Koran, it is quite clear that the Old and New Testaments were books sent by Allah to His former prophets, Moses and Jesus, as the Koran says on many occasions. It was difficult to read through any of the surahs of the Koran without coming across a reference to a famous personage from the Bible or the mention of the Torah and the Injeel themselves as revealed Scripture from Allah.

This first becomes evident on reading the second and largest surah of the Koran, Al-Baqarah. In fact, after reading the first, short, seven-versed surah, Al-Fatiha, as soon as I began reading the introductory verses of Al-Baqarah, I felt I was now able to answer Taheer's question about the opening passage of this surah where it says in the very second verse, "*dhalika alkitabu*", that is, "*that is the book*". After reading the Bible, this statement appeared to be Allah stating to His readers that "that" book, the Bible, that I had just been reading "is the Book" and "there is no doubt in it, a guidance for the God-conscious" as the rest of the verse points out. Because, after reading the Bible, the Koran continues on from where the Bible leaves off, not introducing a new narrative and new ideas, but rather confirming those that had been established a long time beforehand in the biblical texts.

Reading on into this second surah further reinforced the concept that the Koran was not an independent, isolated book but simply an extension of the previous books sent down by Allah to His Messengers. For example, it says in Al-Baqarah 2:89, that "there came to them a Book from Allah confirming what was with them" and then in a few verses later in verse 97 it is written, "Whoever is an enemy to Jibreel – for indeed he has brought it down upon your heart by the permission of Allah, confirming what came before it", these verses clearly stated that the Koran came, not as some independent revelation totally in isolation and in a vacuum, but as a confirmation and in complete dependence on what had preceded it, that is, the Bible.

What intrigued me was that the English translation of "before it" was in Arabic *baina yadahi,* which literally translates as "between his hands" and the picture that formed in my mind when I read these verses in the original Arabic was Muhammad sitting in the cave holding the Bible between his hands as if he had been in meditation after reading from it. Then suddenly the angel Gabriel appeared to him, revealing to him the Koran, holding the Koran in one hand and pointing with the other to the Bible between Muhammad's hands, an absolute glow coming from both books to confirm their connection and equal holiness. This same expression *baina yadahi* is found again in the beginning of the third surah, Al-Imran, in the third verse where it says, "He revealed to you the Book in truth which confirms that which was before it (*baina yadahi*)." Again, the image of Muhammad holding the Bible between his hands while the angel Gabriel revealed to Muhammad the Koran was the picture that formed in my mind as I read this in the original language. This is repeated again in the Koran in Surah Al-Ma'idah 5:48, Surah Al-Anaam 6:92, Surah Yunus 10:37 and Surah Yusuf 12:111, and I was aware that when ideas were repeated in the Koran, they were there for emphasis and hence it was so clear to me that Allah had been emphasising this point all along, that Muhammad held the Torah and the Injeel between his hands when the Koran was revealed, and to me, this then had to be sunna, that Muslims should also be holding the Bible between their hands and reading it in the same way as they read the Koran.

The identity of what it was that the Koran was confirming is made clear beyond a doubt in Al-Baqarah 2:53 where the Koran says that "We gave Moses the Book". The Book that Allah gave Moses without question was the Torah. The thing was that the Koran says this time and time again throughout the entire Koran either in exactly these words or using similar expressions, in Al-Baqarah 2:87, in Al-Anaam 6:91, in Al-Anaam 6:154, in Hud 11:110, in Bani-Israil 17:2, in Al-Qasas 28:43, in As-Sajada 32:23, in As-Saffat 37:117, in Ghaffir 40:53, in Fussilat 41:45, in Al-Jathiya 45:16, in Al-Ahqaf 46:12 and An-Najm 53:36. Such abundant repetition therefore meant extreme emphasis. The Torah emphatically and unequivocally is the Book of Allah.

That this book given to Moses was the Torah and is named as such eventually comes out in verses such as in Surah Al-Ma'idah 5:44 where it says that "We revealed the Torah wherein is Guidance and Light. The Prophets who submitted judged by it for the Jews, as did the Rabbis and the scholars as they were entrusted with the Book of Allah." Not only does this verse confirm that the Torah is a book from Allah, this verse from the Koran actually states that this very Torah is *the* Book from Allah.

In fact, after reading the Koran from beginning to end, it became so clear to me that the Torah is given great appeal as the original book and comes across as the real Mother of the Books, the foundation book upon which all other subsequent books are built.

Not only did Allah confirm categorically that the Torah is His Book, Allah is angry at those who deny this established fact. For example, in Al-Baqarah 2:101 Allah speaks quite gravely about the people of Muhammad's time where it says, "And when a Messenger of Allah came to them confirming that which was with them, a party of those who were given the Book threw away the Book of Allah behind their backs". The Book of Allah as it says in Surah Al-Ma'idah 5:44 is the Torah, and these people were throwing the Torah, "the Book of Allah", behind their backs. I mean, it was beyond a doubt that this was the book which was being referred to because it had already been established in other verses that the Torah was the Book of Allah. Also, it definitely could not have been the Koran because we knew that Muhammad did not bring the Koran as a book but as a recitation. The Koran was not put together into a physical book until well after Muhammad had died, traditionally under the auspices of Caliph Uthman who according to the Hadiths was the first person to command the Koran to be written down and put together in book form.

What was striking about this verse was that there was a warning to those who treated the Book of Allah with contempt, that is, they threw the Book of Allah behind their backs. It became so clear to me that Allah was saying the exact same thing to our current religious authorities, especially those who had told us that the Torah and the Injeel had been corrupted and therefore should not be taken seriously. This total disregard for the Torah was in a way our religious authorities' contempt towards the Torah, the modern version of the Torah being thrown behind their backs, and hence I could feel the same warning was towards us who treated the Torah in this way.

The Injeel, or the Gospels, is also given reverence in the Koran, although not referred to as strongly as the Torah. However, it is not treated insignificantly. We read that the Injeel is also the Book of Allah in verses such as Surah Maryam 19:30 where Issa says of Allah that "He gave me the Book", that is, the Injeel. However, the Injeel is more often than not referred to as "what was given to Issa", and this expression is repeated several times throughout the Koran such as in Al-Baqarah 2:136, Al-Imran 3:84, Al-Ma'idah 5:46 and Al-Hadid 57:27, once again the repetition of this expression was obviously for emphasis and to show undeniably that the New Testament was as much the Book of Allah as the Torah was.

In fact, that both the Torah and the Injeel were established Books of Allah comes out quite emphatically and unequivocally in the third surah, Al-Imran, right at the beginning of the surah in verse three where it states that Allah "revealed the Torah and the Injeel". In fact, Muslims are required to consult the Bible as it says in Surah Yunus 10:94, "So if you are in doubt concerning what We have revealed to you, then ask those who have been reading the Book before you."

And like the Torah and the Injeel before it, so the Koran was revealed by Allah, once again, not as an isolated book but as an extension and confirmation of that which had preceded it. This in itself meant that the Koran acknowledged the pre-existence of the Torah which meant that the Koran could not have been eternal as we had so often been told, because if the Koran were eternal, then most definitely the Torah would also have had to have been eternal. In fact, the Koran is so intricately bound to "the Book", that is, The Torah, that Allah states in Surah Saba 34:31 "And those who disbelieve say, 'We will never believe in this Koran and that which was before it'" where the believers are actually required to believe in, not only the Koran, but also in the Holy Bible, the Torah and the Injeel. What was particularly striking about this last verse was that it clearly stated that the unbelievers, the *kaffeers*, were those who refused to believe in what came before the Koran, the Holy Bible.

And to really show the connection between all these Holy Books, it says in Al-Baqarah 2:285, "The Messenger has believed in what was revealed to him from his Lord, and the believers. All of them have believed in Allah and His Angels and His books" where the believers, and even Muhammad himself, believe in Allah's books, *kootoobihi*, not His Book, *kitaabihi*. The requirement of the believers to believe not in one book singular but in the Holy Books plural is also stated clearly in Surah An-Nisaa 4:136, Surah Al-Taubah 9:111 and Surah An-Nahl 16:44.

This meant that according to the Koran itself, a true Muslim has to believe in the Bible to be considered a Muslim. To me, this meant that Yusuf and all these Ibrahimi Muslims were the true Muslims.

So why did Allah give Muhammad the Koran, then, if there already was the Book on earth as a guide for humankind? I felt the answer came from the verses in Yusuf 12:2, Ta Ha 20:113, Az-Zumar 39:28, Fussilat 41:3, Ash-Shura 42:7 and Az-Zukhruf 43:3 where it says that it is an Arabic Koran or "A Koran in Arabic". So the Koran alone is not the Book of Allah or at least not the sole Book of Allah. The Koran was a book sent down from Allah in Arabic to an Arabic speaking prophet to an Arabic speaking audience, and hence this implied that the Koran was specifically aimed at the Arabs, not for all humankind.

This to me was a great revelation. In fact, it was a great revitalisation of my faith. This new appreciation of the Koran and its connection to the Holy Bible brought new life into the faith that I had been having doubts about.

This was all a great paradigm shift but I accepted it willingly because I believed in Allah and His Books, and I certainly didn't want to go to Jahannam in the next life for holding to erroneous beliefs. In fact, I had no difficulty altering my view of the Koran and its connection to the Judaeo-Christian Scriptures because this was what the Koran had told me to do. The idea that the Koran had existed as an eternal document in isolation was something that people had told me but was completely contradicted by the Koran itself, the Book which to me was the bedrock of my faith. People could say what they liked but in the end I had to believe in what Allah said through His Books. Hence I was willing to reject the idea that the Koran is eternal, that there was only one Holy Book to believe in, and that there is only one language Allah communicates in because all these ideas were clearly unkoranic and hence un-Islamic.

The greatest irony of all was that I was totally aware that the way I understood what the Koran was telling me could be viewed as blasphemy. It was a doublethink situation where I had to agree with what the religious authorities told us, that the Bible had been corrupted and could not be trusted and therefore we were required to believe in the Koran alone, yet the Koran itself told me the complete opposite. Insisting vocally that the Bible being treated with equal reverence to the Koran was Islamic could lead me to serving jail time because it could be considered blasphemous. That is, declaring publicly that I supported what was written in the Koran would be considered as blasphemy against the Islamic religion purported by the State.

This also put me in somewhat of a difficult situation. Allah says to us in the Koran in Al-Baqarah 2:174 "Those who conceal what Allah has revealed of the Book, and purchase a small gain therewith, they eat nothing except fire in their bellies…and they will have a painful punishment". This verse seemed to be indicating that I actually was required to openly confess my belief in what the Koran says about the Holy Bible. But if I kept this quiet and hid this discovery "to purchase a small gain", that is, to avoid a prison sentence and even death, I could end up in serious punishment in the Hereafter.

Because this was all new information, I decided to keep this to myself for the time being until I could be sure of what I believed. In any case, this holistic, complete view of the Koran as an extension of the Holy Bible, although a reawakening of my entire religious experience, it was all a very new approach to the faith. Given time, I was sure that my faith in this new outlook of how the Bible fit within the view of my religion would become firm and strong, and that would be the time when I would feel confident enough to speak out boldly in support of the Bible.

Or so I thought.

It's amazing when you read a text for the first time that you overlook certain things that on the second reading become glaringly obvious. This was the case when I read the Bible once again, in particular, the story of Abraham.

I was out in my chosen secluded place in an out-of-the-way area of the campus reading the Bible intently as I had done every Friday afternoon after prayers. I arrived at the biography of Abraham when the smooth, gentle stroll through the pages was suddenly halted abruptly at the full realisation of how the Bible describes Abraham and his entire family relationship, in particular, his relationship with Hagar. We had been told that Hagar was Abraham's second wife. However, according to the Bible, Hagar was Sarah's maidservant. I wasn't sure of the meaning but guessed in some way Hagar was Sarah's slave. Also, the Koran doesn't say where these two women came from. But the Bible does. The Bible says that Sarah came from Ur of the Chaldeans whereas Hagar was from Egypt. How Sarah acquired a slave girl from Egypt was left to the reader to work out. The problem was, on closer scrutiny, there was nothing in the Koran to contradict this relationship as it is described in the Bible.

The reason for Hagar and Ishmael being expelled from Abraham's household was also different to what I had been taught. We were told that Allah told Abraham to send his second wife, Hagar, and her son, Ishmael, into the desert as a test so that Abraham could prove to Allah that he was worthy to be called the Father of the Prophets. But I did not understand the test. There seemed to be no rhyme nor reason for this test and what the outcome should be.

The explanation in the Bible, by contrast, made more sense. Sarah was infertile and was desperate to have a child. To achieve this end, she told Abraham to sire a son through Hagar. I guessed from the story that it must have been a custom at that time for wives to use their slave girls to bear children when the wife was infertile, something that Allah obviously condoned. Hence, Hagar bore Abraham a child, Ishmael. However, eventually, Sarah managed to have her own child, Isaac. The problem for Sarah was that Ishmael, the son of Sarah's slave girl, was still a son of Abraham. This made Ishmael a potential rival to the inheritance. I could totally appreciate Sarah's predicament in the biblical account. Sarah did not want Ishmael, the son of her maidservant, to rival her own son, Isaac. If Hagar had simply been Abraham's second wife as we had been told but which is not mentioned in the Koran, while Sarah may have been jealous that the second wife managed to bear a son to Abraham, Hagar still had equal right to Abraham's attention and Ishmael had total right to inheritance despite how jealous Sarah may have been. It would not matter how jealous Sarah was of Abraham's second wife and her progeny, there was absolutely nothing she could do about it. It therefore made absolutely no sense how Sarah could convince Abraham to send his son Ishmael away together with his mother as Ishmael was legitimately Abraham's son through a legitimate wife. By contrast, the biblical account, as much as I didn't like it, made a hell of a lot more sense.

Further, what struck me about this part of the story in the Bible was that Hagar and Ishmael were cast away from Abraham's family when Isaac was weaned. Now, according to the Koran, in reference to giving birth and the early years of childhood, it says in Al-Ahqaf 46:15 that "the bearing of him and the weaning of him is thirty months", which means that after the nine months of carrying the child in the womb, the remaining 21 months was dedicated to weaning. Now, the Bible says that when Abraham was 99, Ishmael was thirteen. Isaac was born when Abraham was 100, which means that Ishmael was fourteen when Isaac was born. The Bible then says that it was when Isaac was weaned that Abraham sent Hagar and Ishmael away, which meant that Ishmael was no older than sixteen when he and his mother were sent away from Abraham's family. Why this struck me was because it says in Al-Baqarah 2:127 that "Ibrahim was raising the foundations of the House together with Ishmael". I had always assumed that Abrahim built the House with Ishmael and not with Isaac because Isaac had not as yet been born. I had also always assumed that Ishmael was quite a grown up man, at least in his twenties, when he and his father built this House. Going by the biblical reckoning, if Abraham built the House with Ishmael, Ishmael would have had to have been a young, pre-adolescent at the time. It was still possible I surmised, but it just seemed more plausible and realistic that Ishmael would have been a grown man at least in his twenties when he built the House with his father.

What also struck me as odd was the lack of mention of Mecca in the Bible. Nor does the Bible mention the Kaaba or any house built by Abraham and Ishmael as it is stated quite emphatically in the Koran. According to the Bible, Abraham lived and roamed about in a region called the Land of Canaan, a place I had never heard of before, but I guessed that it had to be somewhere in modern day Palestine because in Genesis 15:18 Allah promised to give Abraham land extending from the Nile River in Egypt to the River Euphrates in modern day Iraq, and three verses later we read that the Canaanites lived in this land. Also, Abraham journeyed to Hebron, and I had heard of Hebron in the news and that it was a city in the modern state of Israel. The only things that Abraham tended to build, according to the Bible, were altars of stones.

There was, however, mention of the cave of Machpelah where Abraham buried his wife, Sarah, where Abraham himself was later buried by both Ishmael and Isaac, and I wondered if the name Machpelah was a variation of the word Mecca. I thought Machpelah could possibly be a candidate. I surmised this because Mecca is also called Bakkah in the Koran and I knew that Bakkah meant "weeping", so Machpelah could be a place of weeping because it was the place where Abraham wept for the death of his wife, Sarah, and then Abraham's sons wept for Abraham when the great patriarch died. However, it was also clear from the description in the Bible that Machpelah was in, or at least near, Hebron, a city in Israel, extremely far from current day Mecca.

I wondered, then, if this was the real place to which the original qibla had been. We had been taught, and the Koran talks about, the change of qibla. The Koran does not say specifically that the original qibla was in the direction of Jerusalem but simply says that the qibla had been changed to face the Forbidden Mosque. Although traditionally it was considered that the first qibla was towards Jerusalem, I surmised that perhaps it could have been Machpelah, and possibly Machpelah was a variant of Mecca, and simply the old "Mecca" had been replaced with the new.

Even so, when I looked up all the cities that Abraham had travelled through as it said in the Bible, Bethel, Hebron, Beersheba, and even travelling down to Egypt, there was not one mention or even suggestion that Abraham travelled as far south as the current day holy city of Islam. Yet we had been taught that Mecca in Saudi Arabia was the Holy House that had been built by Abraham and Ishmael.

The story became even more intriguing when I read about the relationship between Abraham and Isaac. All through my growing up it had been clearly stated that Ishmael was one of the sons of Abraham and indeed he was the firstborn, and Ishmael played an extremely significant role as it was through Ishmael that the great prophet, Muhammad, was born. But the Bible clearly stated that Isaac was the favoured son. While it was true that Ishmael was, in fact, the firstborn of Abraham, Ishmael, according to the Bible, was the son of a maidservant. Isaac, by contrast, was the son of Abraham's wife. What was striking, and came across as blasphemous, was that the Bible says it was Isaac who Allah told Abraham to sacrifice, not Ishmael. However, on reading the Koran to show up the contradiction, I was amazed to discover that the Koran does not say which son was sacrificed. So where did this idea come from that Ishmael was the son Allah told Abraham to offer up as a sacrifice, an event which we celebrated every year during Eid-ul-Adha?

What gave greater significance to Isaac was his miraculous birth. While Ishmael was born from a woman like any child is born, Isaac was born from a miracle, the miraculous birth from a woman who was extremely old and well past her child-bearing years which even the Koran acknowledges in Hud 11:72. This made Isaac special in contrast to Ishmael. It becomes even clearer later in the Bible that Isaac was the chosen son when in Genesis 25, after the death of Sarah, Abraham marries another woman called Keturah and has children through her but it is made very clear that although Abraham had many children, Isaac was the sole heir of everything Abraham had owned, and as it says in verse 11 that Allah blessed Isaac, and Isaac alone.

While at first this came across as blasphemous, on further consideration of the Koran, I couldn't help but see that the Koran actually supported the biblical portrayal of Isaac. We hear of Abraham and Ishmael in the Koran, but nothing of Ishmael's descendants. By contrast, we hear of Abraham, Isaac, Jacob and Jacob's descendants, exactly as it is presented in the Bible. Further, the Old Testament continues the history through the descendants of Isaac and Jacob, for all the great prophets who came later, Moses,

Aaron, David, Solomon and Issa, all of these prophets came directly through the line of Isaac. This entire support for the descendants of Abraham through Isaac both from the Bible and the Koran led to strong evidence that in the end Isaac was, after all, the favoured son, just as the Bible said and which the Koran actually confirmed.

What was further amazing was that the descendants of Ishmael are mentioned in the Bible but they are not mentioned in the Koran. However, what we were taught as Muslims about Ishmael's descendants was exactly in accordance with what was written in the Bible, which therefore implied that Muslims did believe the Bible was the Word of Allah if they believed this piece of information. But this lack of mention of the descendants of Ishmael in the Koran seemed to me a tacit acceptance that in the same way that the Bible favoured the descendants through Isaac, the Koran in its mention of Isaac's descendants but not of Ishmael's subtly implied the same favouritism.

The koranic support for the descendants of Abraham through Isaac came out even more pronounced in verses like Al-Baqarah 2:122 where Allah says, "O Children of Israel! Remember my favour which I bestowed upon you and I preferred you over the worlds". Israel was just another name for Jacob. And Jacob was the son of Isaac. So Allah is quite emphatic that He preferred the children of Israel, that is, the children of Jacob, who was the son of Isaac, as the preferred descendants over the descendants of Ishmael. This is further strengthened by the verse in Yusuf 12:6 where Allah says to Joseph "And thus your Lord will... complete His favour on you and on the family of Jacob as He completed it on your two forefathers before, Ibrahim and Isaac". This total focus on the descendants of Abraham through Isaac and not through Ishmael struck me as very pronounced. In fact, the Koran shows in several places that it was through Isaac and Jacob and not through Ishmael that Allah bestowed His favour. For example, in Surah Maryam

303

19:49 Allah says that "We bestowed upon Isaac and Jacob", in Al-Anbiya 21:72 Allah says, "And we bestowed upon Isaac and Jacob" and in Surah As-Saffat 37:112 and 113 it says that "We gave glad tidings about Isaac, a Prophet from among the righteous. We blessed him (that is, Abraham) and Isaac". But the verse that sent shivers up my spine was the verse from Surah Al-Ankaboot 29:27 which says, "And we granted him Isaac and Jacob and We placed in his offspring prophethood and the Book." It is not clear who the "his" is referring back to in this verse, Isaac or Jacob, but it doesn't matter. Prophethood and the Book according to this verse were both granted on Abraham's descendants via Isaac and Jacob. There is nothing in the Koran which says that prophethood nor a book were granted to the descendants of Ishmael.

But the thing that troubled me the most was the relationship between Abraham and Sarah according to the Bible. Sarah was not only Abraham's wife, she was also his half-sister. This struck me completely off balance because this type of relationship is haram in the Koran, and also in the Bible. Allah tells Moses in Leviticus 18:9 "Do not have sexual relations with your sister, either your father's daughter or your mother's daughter, whether she was born in the same house or elsewhere". However, when Abraham and Sarah arrived at a place called Gerar, Abraham told everyone that Sarah was his sister because he was afraid that those in Gerar would kill him if he had said Sarah was his wife. Having told everyone that Sarah was his sister, the king of this place, Abimelech, took Sarah from Abraham to marry her. As a result, Allah appeared to Abimelech in a dream and told Abimelech that Sarah was in fact Abraham's wife and if Abimelech touched her, Allah would kill him. Abimelech then restored Sarah to Abraham and asked Abraham why Abraham had lied to him. Abraham replied that he was afraid the people of Gerar didn't fear Allah and therefore would kill him because of his wife and so he told everyone that Sarah was his sister. But then, as it says in Genesis 20:12, Abraham further adds, "Besides, she really is my sister, the daughter of my father though not of my mother". This shocked me how that the great prophet of Allah, Abraham, could do something which is haram and yet Allah blessed him.

But Abraham, the Father of the Prophets, was not alone in having a haram relationship. Abraham's nephew, Lot, according to what is written in Genesis 19, had a haram relationship with his two daughters, and instead of being punished severely in some way as others who have haram relationships are condemned with lashings and stoning, Lot becomes the father of two nations, Ammon and Moab. This same Lot to whom Allah, as He states in Al-Anbiya 21:74, gave "judgement and knowledge" not only had sex with his daughters, something great came out of these haram sexual liaisons.

Lot was not the only prophet to have a haram relationship which brought forth great nations. Jacob, or Israel, is also considered a prophet in Islam yet according to the Bible, Jacob like his grandfather Abraham had a haram relationship. In Leviticus 18:18 Allah commands "Do not take your wife's sister as a rival wife and have sexual relations with her while your wife is living." Marrying your wife's sister is also stated as a haram relationship in the Koran in An-Nisaa 4:23. Yet Jacob, according to the Bible, contravened this law and took Leah and Rachel, two sisters, as his wives. What was even further troubling was that it was through Jacob that the whole nation of Israel gets its identity, and it was this nation that Allah chose over all the worlds, yet the Children of Israel are descendants of a man who had a relationship that was haram.

Further, Jacob's fourth son, Judah, from whence the religion of Judaism comes, also had a haram relationship according to the Bible. However, the entire story as to how Judah ended up having a haram relationship was just awful and I couldn't understand why the Jews would want to preserve this story in the Torah when it sounded as ghastly as something that came out of the Hadiths. Judah had a son called Er. Judah arranged a marriage between Er and a woman called Tamar. However, Er was wicked. What it was that Er did that was so wicked was not mentioned in the Bible but as a result Allah killed him. So Er's brother, Onan, was required to marry Tamar. This later was revealed to be a precept from the Torah in Deuteronomy 25 that if a man dies and his wife does not have children from him, then his brother marries his older brother's widow but the children are considered the children of the dead brother. Onan refused to have children with Tamar because as it states in this precept, Onan's children would not be considered his children but the children of his wicked older brother, Er. So, in contempt towards this precept, whenever Onan had sex with Tamar, before he climaxed, he withdrew and all his sperm went on the ground. This to Allah was a very wicked deed so Allah killed him. Judah had a third son, Shelah, but he was too young to marry. Judah told Tamar that she was to return to her father's house until Shelah was old enough to marry. However, when Shelah had reached marriageable age, Judah forgot this arrangement. But Tamar didn't. However, instead of simply going to Judah personally or sending a messenger to Judah saying, "Excuse me, but I see your son is old enough to marry so let's do what needs to be done", Tamar decided to sit by the roadside and make out that she was a prostitute. That she knew this would work means that Tamar was aware that her father-in-law made the regular practice of frequenting prostitutes, something we were told that holy men would never do. According to plan, Judah saw Tamar, thought she was a prostitute, and then paid her for the deed. Some months later, someone told Judah "your daughter-in-law Tamar is guilty of prostitution, and as a result she is now pregnant." Judah then replied "Bring her out and have her burned to death!" I couldn't help but feel for every woman who is the victim of men's hypocrisy and double standards. Judah, an unmarried widower, had sex with a prostitute and he considered this to be okay especially as he derived pleasure from it. That Judah's daughter-in-law, an unmarried widow, had sex to derive her own pleasure from a sexual encounter was not equally okay but rather this fired Judah into a killing rage. As it occurs in Pakistan, Judah didn't say something like, "let her and the man with whom she had prostituted be burnt to death", rather, it was only Tamar who was to be burnt and the man who had got her pregnant somehow let off. The double standards in the story are further highlighted when considering Judah's attitude towards Tamar when Judah thought she was an unknown prostitute. Judah obviously didn't care that he didn't know the true identity of the prostitute even though he had to have known that this prostitute had to be somebody's daughter or daughter-in-law. All that concerned Judah was what he could get out of her.

The twist to the story is that in the end, Tamar is actually exonerated for orchestrating a sexual encounter with her father-in-law despite the fact that it is a haram relationship, both according to the Torah and the Koran. Further, Tamar's orchestration of this haram liaison led Judah to admit at the end of this story that Tamar "is more righteous than I", calling this haram sexual relationship a righteous act.

But the verse in this chapter which troubled me the most was Genesis 38:15. When Judah was walking along the roadside and saw Tamar sitting there, this verse says that Judah "thought she was a prostitute for she had covered her face". This was one of those moments when I sat up, looked around, looked back down at the verse to reread it, and then in shock closed the Bible and went for a walk. According to the Torah, the Book of Allah, when a woman covers her face, this means she is a prostitute. I thought of all those men who make their wives cover their faces, or

307

worse, those women who willingly choose to cover their faces thinking that they are doing Allah's will, yet according to Allah's holy Torah, these same women are proclaiming that they are prostitutes.

I walked around the campus in a daze. By tradition we believed that the biblical texts had been corrupted. This would enable me to dispense with these stories as being corruptions made by later Jews to an originally pure text. But the Koran unequivocally and without mistake declared the Torah to be the Book of Allah. Further, there is absolutely nothing in the Koran to support the belief in the corruption of the biblical texts. Even further, the Koran stated quite emphatically that "none can change His Words", and because the Torah was clearly and unequivocally Allah's Words, then when I read the Bible I was reading the unchanging Words of Allah.

But even so, I tried to imagine Jews in the past deciding to corrupt the Torah by inventing this story. Why would anyone invent this story in all its ghastliness as their means of tampering with the text? It would have made more sense to me that this story had originally been in the text and, out of embarrassment, the Jews had taken it out.

The only resolution I had was to think that the story did not mean what it appeared to mean and there was something else to the story that I was missing.

On this thought, I went back to reading the Torah. But again, I was shocked to see yet more haram relationships in connection with the prophets.

When I reached Exodus and the story of Moses and Aaron, I was once again struck by a haram relationship which instead of being punished was made a blessing. According to Exodus 6:20, a man called Amram, who is called Imran in the Koran, "married his father's sister Jochebed, who bore him Aaron and Moses". In opposition to what both the Bible and the Koran said about marrying one's father's sister, not only did Amram commit this sin, from this sin was born the most influential of all prophets in both the Bible and the Koran, the prophet Moses.

Again, relationships that went against what was taught in Islam came out further with King David. According to II Samuel 3:2-5, the Prophet David had six wives, and then later he took on his seventh wife, Bath-Sheba. How Bath-Sheba became his seventh wife was just shocking. Originally, Bath-Sheba was the wife of someone else, namely, a man called Uriah the Hittite. The Prophet-King David saw Bath-Sheba washing herself one afternoon and because she was so beautiful, David organised for her to come to the palace so that he could be intimate with her. Now, the Torah says quite explicitly in Leviticus 20:10 that "If a man commits adultery with another man's wife...both the adulterer and the adulteress must be put to death", the same ruling which applied under Islam. Yet King David and Bath-Sheba managed to be spared this punishment, even when their adulterous relationship was made known. Further, when the Prophet David found out that Bath-Sheba was pregnant, he tried to cover up the crime by getting Uriah the Hittite to back out of the battle that he was currently fighting on behalf of David and his kingdom, and have a few days repose with his wife. However, because Uriah was in total devotion to King David, he refused to return home in favour of doing his duty for God and king, and continued to fight in battle. So the Prophet David orchestrated Uriah's death and tried to make it look like an accident.

It wasn't only that King David got off lightly for committing adultery. Although King David had seven wives, it was through Bath-Sheba, with whom he had had the adulterous affair, that the next Prophet-King was born, King Solomon. This made absolutely no sense to me. David had six legitimate wives through whom the Prophet-King Solomon could have been born, but Allah chose to bring forth the Prophet Solomon through a relationship that had started out as an adulterous affair.

It wasn't only that King David got away with adultery and unlawful murder. King David had seven wives, and the Koran only permits a maximum of four. Yet in II Samuel 12:8 it says that Allah gave David his first six wives. So why did Allah give David six wives yet command in the Koran that a man can only have a maximum of four?

But there was even more about King David. Prophet-King David had an unusual relationship with Jonathan, the son of King Saul. In I Samuel 18:1, it says that Jonathan loved David intensely, "as himself". For someone like me who knew what it was like to have intense feelings for another man, I couldn't help but see that there was something more in this relationship than just *jigari dosts*, that is, close buddies. As the story unfolds, the relationship between Jonathan and David becomes quite intense and reaches a climax when Jonathan is killed on Mount Gilboa. At his death, David laments Jonathan by saying in II Samuel 1:26 "I grieve for you, Jonathan my brother, you were very dear to me. Your love for me was wonderful, more wonderful than that of women". When a man loves a woman, so it was universally established, physical intimacy was a part of that love. So if Jonathan's love for David was more wonderful than the love of women, what else could be inferred from this than the obvious? This made the Prophet David at least bisexual. Did this mean that David was excused for his relationship with a man because it was tempered with his relationship with women?

Once again, another prophet who had a haram relationship was King Solomon, as he had, as it says in I Kings 11:3 "seven hundred wives". This far surpassed the maximum allowance of four wives as it states in the Koran. Yet Allah allowed Solomon, both King and Prophet, to exceed the limit exceedingly.

In a way, I could get away with dispensing with the stories about David and Solomon because these stories were recounted in the biblical books of I & II Samuel, I & II Kings and I & II Chronicles. The Koran says that the Torah, the Zaboor and the prophetic books are from Allah. The books of Samuel, Kings and Chronicles are not considered books of prophecy but rather historical accounts and hence were subject to error and it was possible that these accounts about David and Solomon were not quite true.

But I couldn't do this so easily with Issa in the Injeel. The prophet Issa strangely has no spouse, even in his 30s. This came across as particularly odd to me. I knew the social pressures on us to get married and have children, social pressures that yet awaited me but which Issa managed to avoid. In the Injeel and the Koran, Issa's celibacy eludes any explanation. However, there is an oblique explanation for this which comes out in the fourth Gospel where we read about "the disciple whom Jesus loved". The thought that went through my mind was that whoever wrote this couldn't spell it out explicitly exactly what this love between the Prophet Issa and this unnamed disciple really entailed. Seeing the Prophet Issa through his actions and miracles showed that he loved everyone, including his twelve disciples, what special and distinct love would Jesus have expressed to one of his disciples over any of the others? And if Issa had such a relationship with another man, once again, why was Issa allowed this haram relationship which is forbidden to the rest of the believers?

And as it was with the Torah and the Injeel, so it was with the Koran. Our great Prophet Muhammad also had haram relationships. While I could dispense with the accounts of David and Solomon having more than four wives because these stories were not recorded in revealed texts, I could not do the same thing with the Muhammad. As it says in An-Nisaa 4:3, a man can only have a maximum of four wives and yet the last and greatest Prophet exceeded this,

311

in some accounts having eleven wives at the one time, in others fourteen. But not only did Muhammad have all these wives, Muhammad married a woman which according to the same Koran was a haram relationship. In Surah An-Nisaa 4:23 it says that it is haram to marry your son's wives, yet according to what we had been told and which comes out implicitly in Surah 33:37, Muhammad married the wife of his son, Zaid bin Harithah.

This was all absolutely overwhelming, that all the great prophets named in the Bible and the Koran blatantly contravened the relationship laws yet were elevated in status to the height of prophets and therefore direct communicators with Allah. And the texts which talk about these haram relationships were preserved and copied through the millennia and no-one else seemed to have had an issue with this. So I reasoned that the problem was with me. I had to be missing something. The problem was, who could I ask? It was not like back in Karachi where I could ask my father or my Mulvi.

Although Maaz was not the most religious person I knew, seeing it was safe to ask him controversial questions about Islam, I thought I'd put the question to him.

We had both settled into bed. While staring into the darkness, pondering on this thought, I put the question to him.

"Hey, Maaz?" I asked.

I heard a sound from Maaz's direction which meant that he probably had moved.

"Yes, Mustafa," he replied sleepily.

"Why did Muhammad have more than four wives when the Koran states in Surah An-Nisaa 4:3 that a man can only have a maximum of four?"

There was a moment of silence before Maaz's voice could be heard again.

"What on earth possessed you to ask that question now, this late at night?" Maaz asked.

I didn't have an answer to this question. The real reason was that I couldn't sleep because this question was sitting on my mind without resolution. I heard movement in Maaz's bed and then a sigh.

"I guess," Maaz said somewhat frustratingly, "that there is a reason. With Allah, there is always a reason. It's not up to us to question Allah. So, roll over and go to sleep."

I wasn't satisfied with this answer and so remained quiet. Maaz must have appreciated the vagueness in his answer because he then let out a deep sigh which meant he was now wide awake and so he continued.

"You really pick the times to ask!" Maaz grumbled.

I didn't know what to say to that and remained silent. Because of his comment, I was going to tell him not to worry about it but that maybe we could talk about it the following day but Maaz continued.

"Okay," Maaz then grunted. "I'm awake now and I can tell you won't sleep till you have an answer!"

I felt embarrassed. But before I had the chance to say anything, Maaz spoke.

"Okay, now, remember," Maaz begin through a yawn, "that Muhammad was special. He was the Prophet of Allah. If Allah allowed Muhammad to have more than the prescribed four wives, there was a reason for it. Muhammad didn't marry to fulfil his sexual desires as unbelievers accuse him of. My Mulvi once told me that Muhammad used some of his marriages as a means of creating bonds between groups of people. Muhammad was a leader and so marriage was a way to create relationships with warring factions because then they would be related. For example, Muhammad married the daughter of a Jew to create a bond with the Jewish tribes in his region and create peace between the Muslims and the Jews there."

I looked up into the darkness.

"But aren't we supposed to follow the sunna of Muhammad?" I asked.

313

"Well, yes," Maaz replied. "But remember that Muhammad was a prophet, He was *the* Prophet. Just because he had more than four wives contrary to what the Koran instructs, and the Koran even states that Allah allowed this special dispensation to him in Surah Al-Ahzab 33:50, this doesn't give us permission to go against what the Koran says. Yes, we must follow the sunna of Muhammad but of ultimate importance is to follow what we have been instructed by Allah through the Koran. Does that make sense?"

I lay looking at the ceiling trying to digest Maaz's words which were the same words I had heard elsewhere about the justification for Muhammad marrying more than four wives. No, this didn't make sense. But I was trying hard for it to do so. My utter silence to his explanation told Maaz loud and clear that his explanation had not answered my question. I heard a further sigh from Maaz.

"Well, okay," Maaz continued, answering the question I did not pose, "remember that not only did Muhammad gain special privileges because he was a prophet, he also had certain obligations that we are not under. For example, in Surah Bani-Israil 17:79 Allah tells the Prophet and the Prophet alone 'And from a part of the night, arise from sleep to pray the Tahajood prayer as an additional prayer for you'. This prayer was incumbent on the Prophet Muhammad as an obligation of his prophethood but is not incumbent on us. Our obligation is to follow what is written in the Koran, even if what the Koran tells us is different to what Muhammad did."

I lay in the darkness reflecting on what Maaz had told me but there seemed to be two standards: the Koran and the Prophet. While Maaz tried to find a solution to my question, what he was saying made less and less sense.

"But, Maaz," I replied, "it says in Surah Al-Ahzab 33:21, 'Certainly, in the Messenger of Allah you have an excellent example for anyone whose hope is in Allah'. Doesn't that mean that following the sunna of Muhammad actually means doing what Allah wants of us? I mean, the whole idea of sunna is that Allah created Muhammed as an example for us to follow. The assumption is that Muhammad lived his life in accordance with what is written in the Koran. So what Muhammad did in his life we should do in ours. Hence what the Koran commands us to do and how Muhammad lived his life should both be the same, such as the number of wives a man is allowed to have. But if Muhammad married eleven women and the Koran says we should not marry more than four, do we follow Muhammad's example or the Koran?"

There was a long moment of silence until Maaz's exasperated voice was heard.

"I don't know!" Maaz replied frustratingly. "Can't you just accept what the Koran says without having to raise all these questions? Just do what it says in the Koran and everything will be okay. Okay? If you keep questioning the Koran like this, you're going to end up in serious trouble!"

So that was the end of question time. Maaz didn't clarify my question, he made it all the more confusing. And I had to be fair to him and allow him to sleep. The problem with the contradiction of following the sunna of Muhammad and following the Koran was my issue for the moment and it was selfish of me to keep Maaz awake as well when the issue didn't bother him. It was therefore comforting when I heard Maaz snoring and so I knew he had fallen into deep sleep.

But I kept thinking of the verse from Al-Ahzab 33:21, where Allah had set the Messenger of Allah as an example for us to follow. This should mean that the Prophet followed the Koran implicitly and to the letter, and did not deviate to the left nor to the right, following the right way. And as Muhammad, so should we, as it says in Surah Bani-Israil 17:77 that "you will not find any alteration in our Way" and in An-Nisaa 4:68 that "We have guided them to the straight way". However, other verses such as Surah An-Nisaa 4:26 say that "Allah wishes to make clear to you and to guide you to the ways of those before you" hinting that there is more than one way. So, how many ways were there for us to follow?

I was finding that this way, this *assiraat amoostakeem* or "straight path" as we prayed in the Al-Fatiha was splintering into different branches. These branches then led off in all sorts of directions, turning into an extremely complicated maze from which I was unsure that I would ever come out of.

Chapter 13

I really didn't know how to sort all this out. Our religious authorities had told us that the Torah and the Injeel had been corrupted and it was for this reason that we as Muslims didn't have to consider them or take them seriously. From what I had discovered about the haram relationships by the great prophets, I could understand why they said this and I wanted to agree. However, what was strange about this was that many Muslims sometimes used the Christian Bible to prove a point and to give evidence to the veracity of the Koran. This therefore had to mean that these Muslims were sure that these parts of the Bible they used had not been corrupted. But what was their criterion on deciding which parts of the Bible were corrupted and which parts weren't? How were we to know whether or not those parts of the Bible which were used to support the Koran were parts of the Bible that had been corrupted leading the Koran to be corrupted? And if the religious authorities were so sure which parts they knew were corrupted and which ones weren't, why didn't they simply publish a new Bible containing only those parts they were sure had not been corrupted and allow these uncorrupted parts to be read in the mosque seeing these religious scholars acknowledged that the Torah and the Injeel had once been the pure words of Allah?

And then there was the other side. The Ibrahami Muslims believed that the Torah and the Injeel had not been corrupted. Their belief was actually well-founded in the Koran itself. Further, their claim made more sense. If Allah is All-Powerful and as He says in Al-Imran 3:3 that He sent down the Torah, the Injeel and the Koran, then if

317

Allah protects His Holy Books from corruption, the Torah and the Injeel had not been corrupted. For otherwise if we said the Torah and the Injeel had been corrupted, by logic this means that it was possible that the Koran could also have been corrupted. All the verses which say that "none can change His words" weren't helpful in this case because if this only applied to the Koran then we'd have to say that the Torah and the Injeel were not the Words of Allah. But the Koran said that they were.

Further, Issa said in Matthew 5:18, "I tell you the truth, until heaven and earth disappear, not the smallest letter, not the least stroke of a pen, will by any means disappear from the Torah until everything is accomplished". Was this a corrupted verse in the Gospel? Both an affirmative and negative answer had their problems. If I said no, then why did most of our Muslim scholars preach that Allah gave Moses the Torah and then allow the Torah to be corrupted? And if I said yes, then were these words from the Koran, "none can change His words", a similar corruption as those of Matthew 5:18?

Which led to the next problem. We believed that the prophets were sinless, sinless meaning that they followed all the laws of Allah. But if Allah had clearly given laws about who one could marry and how many wives one could have, and the major prophets contravened these laws, then in what way were these prophets sinless? How many laws from the Bible and the Koran could the prophets break and still be viewed as sinless?

Hence, I realized I was in the same predicament as mainstream Muslims. I wanted the Bible to be perfect and uncorrupted because the Koran equates itself with the Bible and hence by logic the Koran rises or falls with our view of the Bible. On the other hand, I wanted the Bible to be corrupted so that I didn't have to face the issues in the Bible which troubled me.

I wondered if there was a middle road, where we could believe that the Bible is corrupted and uncorrupted at the same time. In fact, when I thought about it, this middle road I was so desirous to exist was the road that religious scholars of our faith had been walking down for centuries.

I wondered if Yusuf had an answer. He and all the Ibrahimi Muslims were confident that the Judaeo-Christian Scriptures were the perfect Word of Allah. Hence I guessed they had explanations to find a resolution to this problem. Desirous for an answer, I longed for an opportunity to speak to Yusuf about this and was surprised how quickly such a moment arose.

The following morning, we arrived at our chemistry class to discover that our lecturer had taken ill and because of the short notice a replacement teacher could not be found in time. So the class was cancelled. As a result, Yusuf suggested that we go into the town and spend the morning there.

We went to an area close to the bank of the Ravi River. It was an area away from the main part of the township, away from the hecticness and pandemonium of the central market, away from the maddening throngs of people and the constant intrepid sounds of motor vehicles.

"I've always wanted to walk along the bank of this river," Yusuf commented with a sigh of pleasure in his voice, "but as you know, one cannot walk around here on one's own without being mugged or assaulted in some way."

This was the strange reality of Pakistan. It was amazing that this was a country which was governed on the principles of the Koran, Allah's perfect book, and yet being hassled on the street and mugged by fellow Muslims was just part of everyday life in this country. Just because the Koran said that thieves should have their hands cut off meant nothing considering the amount of theft that occurred, especially as being mugged was expected as a part of everyday life.

Along this section of the Ravi River was a long walkway laid parallel to the river along which people could stroll, and there were quite a few people coming and going along this pathway. Yusuf, however, said that he had the desire to walk along on the bare ground itself and feel the very earth beneath his feet. So we removed our shoes and socks, and began our journey walking along on the grassy and muddy patches close to the water.

We chatted for some time as we walked along. Yusuf began to tell me more about his background and his past. He was born in Peshawar and spent all of his growing up there. And being from this area, he was a Pashtoon, born into the most common tribe in this part of the country.

Yusuf told me a very intriguing story about the Pashtoon identity. Pashtoons, so it was believed, were actually one of the tribes descended from one of the sons of Jacob, the grandson of Abraham. The story I had read in the Bible about the Assyrians coming and taking the Israelites away from the northern kingdom came to mind and it was thought that those Israelites simply became absorbed into this great empire, never to continue in their identity as Israelites. However, there were Pashtoons who claimed that their Israelite identity was never completely lost. There were certain traditions which they still observed which supported this. For example, when a man marries, if he dies, especially while young and his wife has not yet had any children, his younger brother is required to marry his brother's wife and sire children in his brother's name. This is not a part of Islam but I was now familiar that this was a part of the Law of Moses. Yusuf made a sordid joke about this by saying that he hoped that his brother would marry a beautiful woman for Yusuf to inherit, but not too beautiful that Yusuf would be tempted to force the issue and speed up this tradition.

The Pashtoons, however, were often discriminated against in Pakistan. As cricket is a favourite sport amongst

Pakistanis, during his younger years, Yusuf often played cricket in a team made up of Pashtoons against another team of Pakistanis of a different ethnicity. In one of these matches, after Yusuf had taken a good swing at the ball and gone for a run, one of the cricket players of the opposite team deliberately tripped him up to ensure that he was run out, and after falling, this opponent called him a Pashtoon dog. He had been told by his parents and everyone in the Pashtoon community to not let this worry him as the Pashtoons were considered by all those around them as lesser human beings, but this was because they were jealous of the Pashtoons' direct association with Jacob to whom Allah had said in the Koran that He preferred him and his descendants over all the worlds.

The Ibrahimi version of Islam, so Yusuf explained, arose out of this acknowledged tradition that Pashtoons were related to the Jews as the Pashtoons were descended from one or several of Judah's brothers and hence in the same way that the Jews venerated the Torah, so did the Ibrahimi Muslims. The Ibrahimi Muslims, in reality, were right to have this view of the Torah as this view was well attested to in the Koran itself.

When Yusuf reached this part of the conversation, I realized why Ibrahimi Muslims accepted the Torah and the Injeel so reverently. Unlike Muslims who had no ancestral connection with the Torah, Ibrahimi Muslims, in particular, Pashtoon Ibrahimi Muslims, most certainly did. It was no doubt because of this that they could not simply dismiss the Torah so readily. Although the Prophet Muhammad was indirectly related to the Jews, Muslims of non-Pashtoon nationality had an easier job of discrediting the Torah because the Torah was not written by an ancestor of Muhammad or by anyone in Muhammad's direct family line. But for the Pashtoons, discrediting the Torah was almost identical to discrediting their own identity as Pashtoons and discrediting their direct descendancy from their ancestors who had lived with and were eye-witnesses to the great prophet, Moses.

"It's mainly the Sunni Muslims we have the most difficulty with," Yusuf continued. "We suffer the most persecution and violence from them than any other group. Even in Peshawar, Sunni Muslims often insult us or attack us, saying that we are not Muslims because we still follow the Torah and the Injeel, and that we don't pray or follow Islamic rites like they do, even though we follow the Koran, especially verses which say quite clearly that Allah has given different rites to different people, and that the Torah and the Injeel were sent down to us just like the Koran."

When Yusuf said this, I felt sorry for the persecution he had suffered for his beliefs. It was when he had said this that I felt I had received a revelation. This unfortunate persecution that the Pashtoons suffered perhaps was the evidence to show that Allah disapproved of the Ibrahimi Muslims' continued veneration for the Bible when they should now dispense with it and follow only the Koran. This was possibly Allah's way of trying to get the Ibrahimi Muslims to actually acknowledge that they need to move on from the Torah and the Injeel and follow the Koran uniquely and in its entirety. I made a comment to this effect which made Yusuf stop in his tracks.

"But the Torah and the Injeel *are* the Words of Allah," Yusuf stated emphatically. "They were sent down in the same way as the Koran was sent down from Allah. The Koran itself acknowledges this. You cannot be a true Muslim if you don't acknowledge this."

"Yes, we Muslims do acknowledge this," I said by way of reply. "But later Jews and Christians distorted the Torah and the Injeel so now what we have in our possession is not the pure original Torah and Injeel. They are corrupted versions of the original Torah and Injeel."

Despite the questioning in my mind and what I knew what the Koran said about the Torah and the Injeel, I realized I kept going back to this default position about the Torah and Injeel having been corrupted.

"But the Koran doesn't say that," Yusuf objected. "That's what the Sunnis and other mainstream Muslims say because they want to follow their own personal desires and totally discredit the Torah and Injeel that Allah originally sent down to us. Both you and I as Muslims, if we believe in the Koran, we have to acknowledge that Allah also sent down the Torah and the Injeel and they remain unchanged whether we like it or not. The Koran does not say that the Torah and the Injeel have been distorted!"

When Yusuf said this, suddenly, like a great awakening, the verses in the Koran which talked about those who refuse to believe have their hearts and minds covered with a veil came to mind. Maybe this was the real problem with Yusuf and the Ibrahimi Muslims in their continued insistence in the belief of the uncorruptness of the Bible. And then, verses which talked about distortions suddenly became lucid in my thinking and I felt the presence of Allah speaking to me to help Yusuf open his heart to the truth. Yes, yes, I thought, there were verses which claimed the Bible had been distorted and Allah was showing me these verses right at this time when I needed them.

"But, Yusuf," I replied, "if the Torah and the Injeel have not been distorted, what does the verse in An-Nisaa 4:46 mean where it says, 'Among the Jews are those who distort the words from their places'? This is quite clearly saying that the Jews distorted the Torah, making changes to the verses so that what we now have is a corrupted version of the original perfect Torah."

Yusuf gave out a frustrated sigh. "Mustafa, the Koran does not say that the actual text was corrupted. Muslims who say that the Koran says that the actual text of the Torah and the Injeel has been distorted are themselves distorting these verses. As it says in Surah Al-Ma'idah 5:41 'They distort the words from their context'. That is, the distortion being talked about here is not the actual changing or altering of words in the text but merely changing the meaning of the words out of their context. This is made clearer in Al-Imran 3:78 where it says, 'And indeed, among them is a group who distort the Book with their tongues so that you may think it is from the Book, but it is not from the Book. And they say 'This is from Allah,' but it is not from Allah'. This clearly shows that what is being distorted is their tongues, not the manuscript. In fact, when you read the other verses which talk about distortions, it is quite clear that the issue was that people were claiming that the texts said something but what they were saying was not in the text. This is further evident in verses such as in Al-Baqarah 2:75 where it says, 'Do you hope that they would believe you while indeed a party of them used to hear the words of Allah and then distort it after they had understood it, knowingly?' Notice that these people distort what they hear, not the words in the text as they are copying it. Show me a verse in the Koran which says that the Torah and the Injeel had been distorted in the past which is why the Koran was brought down from heaven to completely replace them."

I tried to think of a verse in the Koran which supported this. I was so anxious for there to be one but no verse was forthcoming. If Allah had been present earlier when these verses I quoted to Yusuf came to mind, it seemed that Allah had now gone and left me to continue this discussion on my own.

However Yusuf continued. "It also says in Al-Baqarah 2:121 that 'Those to whom We have given the Book recite it as it should be recited.' It doesn't matter which Book is being referred to here, the Torah, the Injeel or the Koran, whoever was given the Book recite it how it should be recited. Those who distort it distort it with their tongues."

Once again, I didn't like what Yusuf was implying when he quoted this verse. I looked around at the view, at the Ravi River, the trees lining the river and the other people who had come to take a stroll. And then something that I thought was helpful to my argument came to mind.

"But, Yusuf, there are contradictions between the Koran and the Bible, and this shows that the Bible has been corrupted. I mean, sometimes you read something in the Bible and then you read the opposite in the Koran, like the Injeel says that Issa was crucified but the Koran says that he wasn't. This just goes to show that they cannot both be from Allah, and that one of them has been corrupted."

"No, the Torah and the Injeel were not corrupted," Yusuf contradicted me. "And they don't contradict the Koran. If there appear to be contradictions, they are only apparent contradictions. It is simply our lack of understanding that makes us believe that there are contradictions."

Yusuf sighed and then continued. "I mean, do you serious believe this? Do you seriously believe that Allah sent down the Torah and while the Jews distorted the text Allah just stood there helpless or indifferent, allowing the Jews to continue to follow a distorted version of His Word until the Injeel was sent down? And then, after He sent the Injeel, He allowed once again the people to distort His Word but still live with this distorted text for six hundred years until Allah sent down the Koran? If that's what you believe, then your Allah is not Almighty nor All-Powerful. And if that's the case, who's to say that the Koran has not been distorted and Allah needs to once again in the future bring down yet another book to replace the last three that have been distorted?"

Yusuf humphed, put his hands on his waist and continued. "I mean, what do you understand by what it says in Al-Ma'idah 5:43 when Allah said to Muhammad, 'But how can they appoint you a judge while they have with them the Torah, wherein is the Command of Allah?' Allah was speaking to Muhammad and Allah acknowledged that the Torah contained the Command of Allah, the Torah that existed at the time of this revelation. And the next verse states, 'Indeed, We revealed the Torah wherein is Guidance and light.' There is absolutely no hint nor suggestion that the Torah was now in a corrupted form and no longer to be considered at this time when Allah was speaking to Muhammad. Rather, Muhammad acknowledged the Torah and so should we."

I didn't know what to say to that. But Yusuf continued. He repeated the verses that I was familiar with that "None can change His Words". If the Torah and the Injeel had been corrupted then these verses about Allah not changing His words were wrong. He once again showed up the flaw in my argumentation, that if the Bible had been corrupted, this meant that Allah sent down the Torah which was subsequently distorted but Allah did nothing to oppose the corruption, then Allah sent down the Injeel and again allowed the Injeel to be corrupted, and then Allah sent down the Koran and then He finally said, "Okay, I won't allow *this* book to be corrupted."

At that point, we heard someone calling Yusuf's name. Yusuf and I turned around and saw Yusuf's cousin, Amin, waving to get us to come over. Amin was accompanied by a group of other university students, and among this group was Maaz.

Yusuf and I first walked down to the water to wash off the mud from our feet, then carefully strolled up a small stretch of grass onto the concrete pathway where we put our socks and shoes back on before finally wandering over to the crowd. The people amongst the group were students from the university campus. Except for one man who I had never met before. This guy was the cousin of Haseeb, one of our classmates within this group. But it was Maaz who introduced me to him simply because this man like me came from Karachi. His name was Muhammad. In our short discussion, I discovered that he came from the same area as I had come from in Alekh-Jahan and he was familiar with my suburb. Although I had never met him, there was something familiar in his features that made me think that I had seen him somewhere before. What was really curious about his features was that he had unusually bushy eyebrows that actually joined together like an arrow head pointing up at a freckle amazingly located exactly in the centre of his forehead.

Muhammad soon excused himself and said he had to go. He said farewell to Maaz and Haseeb, then to everyone else in our group, and then left.

I then heard Yusuf ask why they were all in town and not in lectures.

"Didn't you hear?" Arsalan asked. "There was some celebration among the lecturers last night. There was some sort of feast. The food, however, can't have been terribly good. Quite a number of the lecturers got food poisoning."

"Oh my goodness! Are they okay?" Yusuf asked.

"Not today, at least. They were taken to hospital. It's quite the scandal! We'll have to wait and see tomorrow if classes have resumed! So at least for today, we're free, so we thought we'd come into town."

We spent the rest of the afternoon at a chai hotel in the centre of town just generally chatting and having a good time before heading back to the university to grab something to eat at the university cafeteria. While we relaxed and chatted, Maaz was obviously not his generally cheerful self. Physically he was with us but because I knew Maaz, I could tell that mentally he was somewhere else.

Later that evening, we were back in our dormitory. Maaz and I were working on our respective university course work. Maaz seemed unusually quiet and morose. I simply thought that he was worried about an upcoming exam he had to study for which explained his rather depressive behaviour. Eventually Maaz broke the silence of the moment.

"So, who was that guy you were walking around with?" Maaz asked me.

327

It was a question that hit me out of the blue. I looked up at him and paused before answering.

"He's the guy in my chemistry class, Yusuf, the guy from the Ibrahimi Muslim religion who gave me the Bible."

"So, what were you talking to Yusuf about?"

This seemed like a strange question. I really didn't know why Maaz suddenly had a strong interest in my conversation with Yusuf. But because he asked, I needed to give him an answer.

"Yusuf is an Ibrahimi Muslim," I replied. "You know, these Muslims I've told you about who believe that the Torah and the Injeel are as much the holy words of Allah as the Koran is."

Maaz gave me a strange look.

"But all Muslims believe the Torah and the Injeel are of Allah."

"Yes, they believe that the Torah and the Injeel *originally* were the pure holy words of Allah. However, Muslims in general, at least Sunni Muslims believe that the Torah and the Injeel we now have are corrupt versions of the original Torah and Injeel that were sent down by Allah. So we don't have to take the Torah and the Injeel as seriously as we do the Koran. But the Ibrahimi Muslims say that the Torah and the Injeel are not corrupted. The Torah and the Injeel that we have today are the same Torah and Injeel that were revealed respectively to Moses and Issa. As a result, we should be honouring the Torah and the Injeel in the same way we honour the Koran."

Maaz stood up and looked rather shifty as he walked around the room. He then stopped.

"Would you like some tea?" he then asked.

I replied in the affirmative. Maaz then began preparing tea. I could tell there was something troubling him so I came over to him and touched his back between the shoulder blades.

"Are you okay?" I asked.

Maaz set the water to boil and then turned around.

"And does Yusuf believe in Muhammad?" Maaz then asked. "Is that part of the Ibrahimi Muslim belief?"

I looked into Maaz's face bewildered by his strange comment.

"Well, yes, of course," I replied. "Their belief in Muhammad is not called into question. They still continue to believe in the Koran. It's just that they accompany this with the belief that the Torah and the Injeel are also true and so they conduct the rites of their religion in accordance with all these holy books, not just the Koran."

Maaz turned back around and continued preparing the tea. I took this as a signal to return to my chair. Once seated, I looked back up at Maaz who still had his back towards me. Maaz finally finished preparing the tea and brought my mug over to the table at which I was seated, and then sat down on his chair.

Maaz stared into his mug of tea.

"Is everything alright?" I asked rather concerned.

"Have you ever wondered," Maaz finally opened his mouth, "what the true identity of the Muhammad in the Koran really is?"

This was a question that struck me as completely bizarre. It was an extremely silly question on first hearing. What a question to pose? Of course we all knew the identity of the Muhammad in the Koran. It was the Muhammad we all knew from history, the Arabic prophet to whom the angel Gabriel revealed the Koran, the final revelation from Allah. To his question, I answered that it was universally acknowledged the world over that we all knew the true identity of Muhammad.

"Are you so sure about that?" Maaz questioned, this time rather menacingly.

Again I answered affirmatively. It was like being questioned whether or not I acknowledged that two plus two is four. Who would even begin to question this?

"You've read the Torah and the Injeel," Maaz continued.

"Yes," I replied measuredly.

"Whose name features prominently in the Torah?"

I took a moment to think. When I considered all five books of the Pentateuch, if I excluded Genesis and considered the other four books, Exodus, Leviticus, Numbers and Deuteronomy, the name which featured regularly was quite evident.

"Moses," I replied.

"Moses," Maaz echoed. "Allah gave Moses the book, as it says in the Koran."

"In several places," I added emphatically.

"And in the book Allah gave Moses, Moses's name features the most."

"Well, yes," I replied.

Maaz took a sip of tea.

"And in the Injeel," Maaz continued, "whose name features the most?"

This was easier to answer than the first question.

"It is Issa," I replied emphatically.

"Yes, Issa," Maaz once again echoed. "What was given to Issa was the Injeel and as a result the Injeel mentions Issa's name more than anyone else as it was the book given to Issa."

Yes, I thought to myself. Why does this strike you so odd?

Maaz took another sip of tea, looked down at his mug and then up at me.

"What about the Koran?" Maaz then asked. "To whom was the Koran given?"

"To Muhammad," I replied, almost in frustration. "We all know that."

"And how many times is Muhammad mentioned in the Koran?" Maaz then asked. "That is, by name?"

I looked up at the ceiling and tried to think about all the mentions of Muhammad in the Koran. While I agonized over the number I guessed there must have been, Maaz answered his own question.

"Four!" Maaz stated emphatically. "Four times. Five times if you include the name 'Ahmad'."

I began to ponder on what Maaz had said and realized he was right. Muhammad is named very sparingly in the Koran. As I allowed the verses of the Holy Koran to run through my mind, I realized that other named prophets, including those mentioned in the Torah and the Injeel, in particular, Ibrahim, Moses and Issa, are mentioned by name much more frequently and prominently throughout the Koran than the great prophet of our religion, Muhammad, the very prophet who features in the Shahada. The name Ahmad was considered by Sunni Muslims to simply be a variant of the name of Muhammad. Ahmadiyyah Muslims, by contrast, claim that it is in reference to their later prophet, Mirza Ghulam Ahmad.

I hadn't had a chance to digest this information when Maaz continued.

"Not to mention, not only is Muhammad's name mentioned only four times, very little else is known about Muhammad in the Koran."

I frowned and shrugged my shoulders as the non-verbal way to say, "So what?"

"Again, going back to the Torah," Maaz then continued, "tell me about the Prophet Moses. What do we learn about Moses in the Torah?"

I wasn't sure what Maaz was actually asking me so I didn't respond. So Maaz answered his own question.

"We learn *everything* about Moses. We read about his birth, we read about his adult life, we read about how Allah spoke to him and how Allah gave him the Torah and when Moses died. Moses's whole biography is present in the Torah."

I looked on at Maaz not sure what he was trying to say.

"And the Injeel," Maaz continued. "What do we learn about the life of Issa? Everything! We learn everything! Just as it is with Moses, we read about Issa's birth, his adult life, what Allah taught him to say, all the way to his death and resurrection."

This time I knew where this was leading. Maaz asked me the question and I already knew the answer but I still allowed him to give it.

"And in the Koran? What do we learn about the life of Muhammad? Absolutely nothing! Don't you find that a little strange?"

This had already gone through my mind. Everything we had learnt about the life of Muhammad, his birth, his calling to be a prophet, the angel Gabriel appearing to him with the recitations of the Koran, his subsequent life, and his final death, none of this featured in the Koran. This information came from elsewhere. But not from the Koran.

"Have you ever pondered on the Shahada?" Maaz continued. "'There is no God but Allah and Muhammad is His prophet'?" Maaz quoted this in the original Arabic. "But," Maaz then continued, "what does the Koran say? Yes, the Koran does say that there is no God but Allah. But nowhere in the Koran does it make that end statement that we make in the Shahada. But our constant repetition of the Shahada makes it sound as if we are quoting from the Koran. But what does the Koran say about the prophets?"

Maaz looked down at his tea and then looked back at me. I stared at Maaz not knowing what to say. Maaz then reached over to his bookshelf and grabbed his Koran. He then passed it over to me.

"Read out aloud what it says in Al-Baqarah 2:136."

I took the Koran from Maaz's hand, opened it, flicked through the pages till I found the verse and then read it out aloud as requested.

"'We believe in Allah and what is revealed to us and what was revealed to Abraham and Ishmael and Isaac and

332

Jacob and the descendants, and what was given to Moses and Jesus and what was given to the prophets from their Lord. We make no distinction between any of them."'

I was expecting Maaz to say something immediately after I had read the verse but he just looked at me for a moment as if he were expecting me to make a comment. He then broke the silence.

"So did you notice any prophets missing from that list?"

"Well, no," I replied. "I guess it wasn't important to name all of the prophets. I guess just the most important ones."

"And would there be any of the important ones that may have been omitted?"

I read the verse again. Was there something that Maaz was trying to get at?

"No," Maaz continued. "This verse doesn't mention Noah or Lot or Shuaib, probably because what they had to say is probably not relevant to us modern Muslims."

"Yes," I replied hesitantly.

Then suddenly the realization hit me and I read the verse again: "We believe in Allah and what is revealed to us and what was revealed to Abraham and Ishmael and Isaac and Jacob and the descendants, and what was given to Moses and Jesus and what was given to the prophets from their Lord." For the first time I realized what Maaz was trying to say. Of all the great prophets that Muslims believe in, the greatest of them all and the one who is revered above all of them by every Muslim of every sect, the name of Muhammad was missing.

I gasped and looked at Maaz. Maaz looked back at me. The look on his face was as horrifying as the feeling I felt within. How was it that I had read this verse many times and not seen it? If there were any prophet that should have been mentioned on this list, it should have been Muhammad. Yet, Muhammad is mysteriously absent. Not only so, included in this list of names is the statement "what

333

was given to Moses and Jesus" that is, the Torah and the Injeel. So why didn't the verse say something like, "and what was given to Moses and Jesus and Muhammad"? Both the name Muhammad and a comment about what was given to Muhammad were distinctly absent from this verse.

Two other verses suddenly came to mind and I hastily turned to them to confirm what they had to say, the one from Surah Al-Imran 3:84 which says, "Say, 'We believe in Allah and what is revealed to us and what was revealed to Ibrahim and Ishmael, and Isaac and Jacob and the descendants and what was given to Musa and Issa and the Prophets from their Lord. We do not make any distinction between them'" and the one from Surah Ash-Shurah 42:13 which says, "He has enjoined for you that religion which He enjoined upon Noah…and what We enjoined on Ibrahim, and Musa, and Issa". In all these verses, what was glaringly absent was Muhammad's name and what was given to Muhammad. And later when I once again reread the Koran in its entirety, I would discover that there is nothing in the Koran which talks about anything being given to Muhammad.

I was beginning to lose my breath. This was extremely disturbing. But Maaz hadn't finished. He took a gulp of tea this time, placed his mug on the table and continued.

"Muhammad's name is mentioned only four times in the Koran. But what is the real identity of the Muhammad mentioned in the Koran?"

Once again, the question sounded ludicrous. Okay, Muhammad's name was only mentioned four times but we all knew who our great prophet was. Or so we thought.

"Have you ever pondered on the verse from Az-Zumar 39:23, 'Allah has revealed the best *hadith* – a Book its parts resembling each other and oft-repeated'?"

I didn't actually understand what Maaz was getting at when he quoted this verse. It seemed as if he had completely changed subject. I was trying to find meaning to this sudden change of subject, but the way Maaz looked at me, I felt I needed to answer the question.

"Not really," I replied. "I mean, I have always been aware that the Koran repeats itself often but I felt that this was purely for emphasis. It is a poetic technique of the Koran."

"So, for example," Maaz then said, "in the story about Lut, Allah saved everyone in Lut's family except Lut's wife as it says in Al-Hijr 15:60 as she lingered behind. However, in Ash-Shuara 26:171 it says an old woman was condemned to the same fate as the Sodomites because she lingered behind. Because these accounts are repeated, we can safely infer that the unidentified old woman in Surah Ash-Shuara is simply Lut's wife in Al-Hijr 15:60?"

"Ah, well, yes," I replied cautiously.

"Then, read out the verse from Al-Imran 3:144."

I turned the pages to the passage and then read it out aloud. "'Muhammad is only a Messenger. Verily, all Messengers have passed away before him'," I quoted.

"This has a parallel passage," Maaz then said. "And like the relationship between Lot's wife and the old woman, they are both talking about the same person."

Maaz was looking at me intently. I grabbed my cheeks and allowed my fingers to slide over my lips in thought.

"Look up Surah Al-Ma'idah 5:75," Maaz then said, "and read it to me."

I turned the pages gingerly to the passage Maaz had told me to and then read it out loud.

"'The Messiah, son of Maryam, was only a Messenger. Surely Messengers have indeed passed away before him'," I quoted but this time it felt as if all my blood suddenly drained out of my head and I was going to faint. I had already reached the conclusion, but Maaz stated it out aloud for the two of us for good measure.

"These parallel passages show the true identity of Muhammad in the Koran. As it says in Az-Zumar that

335

passages are oft repeated, the repetition reveals the true identity of Muhammad. The Muhammad of the Koran is none other than Issa."

"No, it can't be," I gasped, almost losing my breath. "Issa was one prophet, Muhammad was another. How on earth can you say that Issa and Muhammad are the same person? Just because these two verses sound the same, it doesn't mean that they are both referring to the same person."

As much as I made the statement, what Maaz had originally started to tell me was making more and more sense. The lack of the mention of Muhammad, his birth, his life, his revelations from Allah, his book and his death, all this was so lacking in the Koran. And there was an explanation for this, that the Muhammad in the Koran was not who we had been told that he was. But I refused to accept this and had to come up with a counterargument.

"But," I said by way of objection, "Issa was never called Muhammad. He is not called Muhammad in the Injeel. So how can he be the Muhammad in the Koran?"

Maaz got up and poured himself some more tea. He then asked me if I wanted some more. I definitely needed it. Maaz poured me more tea, placed the pot down and then continued.

"We think of Muhammad as a name now. And, yes, it is a name. But it is a name with a source. The word 'muhammad' simply comes from the Arabic word *hmd*. As you know, many Arabic words are made up from a root of three consonants, which we call a triliteral root. *hmd* has the meaning of 'to praise', 'to glorify' such as in the expression, *al-hamd-ulillah*, that is, 'praise God', or in Surah Bani Israel 17:79 where it talks about the *Makaam-e-Mahmood*, 'the praised place'. As you also know, when we put an m before a triliteral root, we make this a noun. For example, we know that a 'masjid' or as it is in English, a mosque, is a place to 'sajada', from the triliteral root *sjd*, to prostrate. We see this in other words in the Koran. A 'muhsina' is someone who does good, coming from the triliteral root *hsn* meaning 'good'. Therefore, 'muhammad' is a person who is *hmd*, that is, someone who praises, or someone who is praised, a praised one."

"And Muhammad is to be praised," I stated emphatically. "This is why he was given the name Muhammad, 'the praised one'!"

Maaz leant back in his chair.

"Yes, I can see that when I think of our religion in general. But once we remove the Hadiths and we are left with the Koran together with the Torah and the Injeel, the identity starts to take on Issa."

Maaz took another sip of tea and then returned his mug to the table.

"What other passages in the Koran mention Muhammad?" he continued. "What about what it says in Al-Ahzab 33:40, 'Muhammad is not the father of anyone of your men, but he is the Messenger of Allah and the Seal of the Prophets'? Can you see how this fits the identity of Issa better than Muhammad? In the Injeel, we read how Issa never married and so he never had any children. By contrast, the prophet Muhammad we are taught about in our religion was the father of two baby boys. Granted that these boys died in infancy. But Muhammad was also the father of the man, Zaid ibn Harithah. So the Muhammad mentioned in this verse cannot be talking about this Muhammad we have been led to believe it is. In fact, the idea that Muhammad had descendants who came after him comes out in the expression the *Ahlul-Bayt*, the House of the Family of Muhammad, who the Shiites particularly acknowledge."

I gasped in horror. Once Maaz mentioned it, it was almost impossible to see it in any other way than that the Muhammad in Al-Ahzab was talking about Issa. Further, the last part of the verse, that Muhammad was "the Seal of

337

the Prophets" also matched up with Issa. According to the Injeel, Issa was the last and greatest of all the prophets that were to come according to what was prophesied in the Old Testament Prophets. In fact, this verse reminded me of what I had read in the New Testament in Hebrews 1:1, 2 where it says that "In the past God spoke to our forefathers through the prophets at many times and in various ways but in these last days he has spoken to us by his Son." Even though I acknowledged that Issa was not Allah's son in a biological sense, this verse from Hebrews and other passages in the Injeel indicated that Allah had sent prophets in the past and Issa was the last and greatest prophet which is why he was honoured with the epithet of "son". So, this verse from Al-Ahzab could actually be a reference to Issa. But it could still refer to the Islamic Muhammad if we took other things into consideration.

"But Zaid ibn Harithah was Muhammad's *adopted* son," I gasped, almost choking on my tongue. "So, Muhammad, the Muhammad that we were brought up to believe in, he still fulfils what is written in this verse."

Maaz looked at me with a wry smile.

"I will grant you that," Maaz replied. "However, to make this verse fit the Muhammad of the general Muslim perspective is at best ambiguous and it requires some lengthy argument to make the Muhammad of the Islamic tradition fit the Muhammad of Al-Ahzab. But not Issa. Issa fits the identity of the Muhammad in Al-Ahzab as effortlessly as Cinderella's foot into the glass slipper. The Injeel reveals unequivocally that Issa never married and therefore never had any children, neither sons nor daughters, nor adopted sons or daughters, nor did he leave a family in his posterity, an *Ahlul-Bayt*, and therefore he is unequivocally fatherless in all senses of the word."

My mind digested this statement a moment before I continued.

"But what about the other verses in the Koran which speak of Muhammad?" I gasped.

"There is the verse in the surah named after Muhammad," Maaz replied, "in Muhammad 47:2, which simply states, 'And those who believe and do righteous deeds and believe in what is revealed to Muhammad'. This verse applies equally to Issa if he is the true Muhammad, or to the Muhammad of Muslim tradition. This would be the only verse that tells Muslims to believe in what was revealed to Muhammad, that is, the Koran, if this is what this verse is referring to. But it could equally be referring to the Injeel which was revealed to Issa.

The other verse that mentions Muhammad is from Surah Al-Fath 48:29 and simply states, 'Muhammad is the Messenger of Allah, and those with him are firm against the unbelievers'. Again, this verse could equally apply to the Muhammad of Islamic tradition as it could to Issa."

I thought I was going to faint. This was just too mind-blowing. The Issa of the Injeel could not by any means be the Muhammad of the Koran.

"No, no, no" I gasped, "it's not possible. The Muhammad of the Koran cannot be the Issa of the Injeel because Muhammad is greater than Issa."

"You think so?" Maaz questioned. "Well, then, why did Allah say to Issa in Al-Imran 3:55, 'O Jesus! Indeed, I will take you and raise you towards Myself, and purify you from those who disbelieve and I will make those who follow you superior to those who disbelieve on the Day of Resurrection'? Why did Allah say this to Issa? Why do we find absolutely nothing in the Koran that says this or anything remotely like this about Muhammad? This verse unequivocally and categorically states that those who will be superior over everyone else on the Day of Judgement are those who believe, not in Muhammad, but in Issa, if Muhammad is the 7th Century Arabic Prophet. According to this passage in Al-Imran, it is not the belief in Muhammad that makes us superior but the belief in Issa. Unless, of course, Muhammad is Issa."

Again, a shiver went up my spine up into my head which almost made my head spin and made me want to pass out. But like a drowning man grabbing at straws, an explanation came to mind.

"Okay, he's not mentioned by name. But there are many references to the Prophet without his name, simply as the Prophet. And there are many verses which say that."

"But which prophet are these referring to?" Maaz then asked. "If we are to believe in all the prophets equally, the Koran itself requires us not to choose one prophet over another. So how do we know for sure which prophet these verses are talking about when we are required to make no distinctions between the prophets?"

Again, I could see that Maaz had a point.

"But further," Maaz continued, "many of these verses which Muslims claim refer to Muhammad do not refer to Muhammad when we see these verses in the light of the Bible."

"Such as?" I gasped.

"Turn to Al-Araf 7:157 and read it out to me."

I did as Maaz told me. I flicked through the pages and then read the passage out loud: "'Those who follow the Messenger, the unlettered prophet, whom they find written in what they have – the Torah and the Injeel'."

"Muhammad," Maaz then said after I had finished reading, "of Islamic tradition is not mentioned in the Torah nor in the Injeel. Muhammad of Islamic tradition is not mentioned in the Bible at all. So, this verse is not talking about Muhammad. It's talking about someone else, an unlettered prophet named in the Holy Bible."

I felt my muscles tense up. I already knew where this was leading before Maaz pronounced it out aloud.

"And which unlettered prophet is that? It's Issa, Jesus," Maaz stated. "Issa was the unlettered prophet. Don't you remember reading in the Gospels that Jesus was the son of a carpenter? And it says in the Gospels how people were shocked to hear Jesus because he was someone who had never learnt and yet he was proficient in the Scriptures. As it says in John 7:14, Issa went to the Temple and began to teach, and the Jews were astounded and asked him how he had all this knowledge when he had never studied. He had never studied and therefore he was illiterate because in those days, unlike today, carpenters and all lowly tradespeople never got an education, this education including the ability to read and write."

Maaz paused for a moment and then continued.

"They say that Muhammad was illiterate. But there's a problem with this idea. We are also told that Muhammad was a merchant. To be a merchant, you need to have some form of literacy. So really these verses in the Koran which talk of the 'unlettered prophet' cannot be talking about Muhammad. The Muhammad of Islamic tradition does not fit this description of an unlettered prophet unless we discount any stories that make him a merchant."

My mind was going into a tail spin. But I had to counterclaim this or go mad.

"Muhammad was a merchant," I argued back, "but this doesn't mean he was literate. Maybe he was good at maths, at least adding, subtracting, multiplying and dividing, but this doesn't mean that he necessarily had the ability to read and write."

But the more I thought of it, while I tried to make this square peg fit inside a round hole, I had to be honest with myself and see that while there was some plausibility in what I had said, it was stretching the idea quite a bit, like one of Cinderella's step sisters trying to force into the glass slipper her oversized foot.

"But this unlettered prophet as it says in this verse," Maaz continued, "was mentioned in the Torah and the Injeel. Given this information, this verse overwhelmingly

341

refers to Issa. So when it says in Al-Araf 7:158 'So believe in Allah and His Messenger, the unlettered Prophet', it's talking about Issa."

Maaz took a sip of tea.

"To further confirm the true identity of this prophet, it says in Al-Jumuah 62:2 'He is the One Who sent among the unlettered a Messenger from themselves reciting to them His Verses and purifying them and teaching them the Book'. Although there is a story where an angel came down and purified Muhammad, there is nothing in Muhammad's biography where he purified anyone. However, again, when we read the Injeel, Issa purified many people. We read in the Injeel that Issa healed people from their sicknesses and forgave them of their sins. In fact, it says on a number of occasions in the English translation that he cleaned them. 'Clean', 'purify', these words are similar. And according to the Injeel, Issa did a lot of 'cleaning' of people, purifying them. And like the repetition we find in the Koran, we find other verses which repeat this such as in Al-Imran 3:164 where it says, 'Certainly Allah bestowed His favour on the believers when He raised among them a Messenger from among themselves, reciting to them His Verses and purifying them'."

The evidence just kept stacking up higher and higher that the Prophet being overwhelmingly talked about in the Koran was Issa. Yes, Jesus, the unlettered prophet, he was mentioned in the Torah and the Gospels. In the Old Testament he was not mentioned by name but the prophecies in the Old Testament testified of his coming, which was made certain throughout the Gospels when so many passages from the Old Testament turned out to be prophecies fulfilled in Issa. And Issa was the one who went around and purified people, cleansing them of their diseases and forgiving them of their sins.

"Also," Maaz continued, "there is a verse in Surah Al-Bayyinah 98:2 and 3 which states, 'A Messenger from Allah, reciting purified Scriptures, wherein are books right and straight'. Which Scriptures in books right and straight was this Messenger reciting from? This can't be talking about Muhammad because he recited what the angel Gabriel recited to him from only one book. But again, remember how in the Gospels we read about Jesus quoting from the books of the Old Testament, not simply one book, but many."

Again, this information just overwhelmed me. When Maaz quoted these verses, it was like looking through a microscope, and adjusting the lens until the image had become completely in focus. The Jesus we read about in the Gospels fit this image of the Messenger reciting from books, exactly how it was mentioned in this verse.

"Oh," Maaz then stated. "I can now answer the question you asked some weeks ago about the verse from Al-Imran 3:146. The verse actually reads as, 'And how many a Prophet fought; with him fought many religious scholars'. What this verse implies is that the Prophet fought *with* religious scholars, that is, both the Prophet and the religious scholars fought against a common enemy. However, I think your misinterpretation of this verse might actually be the right way to understand it. For a start, with which religious scholars could Muhammad have fought alongside? They could not have been Muslim religious scholars because, I mean, it is impossible that there were Muslim scholars at the time of Muhammad because Islam hadn't as yet become a religion, especially as the Koran had not been entirely revealed. And scholarly work written about the Koran came out many years after Muhammad had died. This leaves Jewish and Christian scholars. And pagan scholars, if such things existed, although I don't think pagans did much writing. But Muhammad as far as I know never fought *with* Jews and Christians, scholars or otherwise. He spent his time in campaigns *against* Jews and Christians, including their scholars. The way you misinterpreted this

343

verse, I think your understanding is actually correct, that the Prophet fought *against* religious scholars. But further, the word translated as 'religious scholars' in the original Arabic is *ribiyoona* and looks amazingly like the plural word of the English 'rabbi', that is, 'rabbis', that is, the Jewish scholars. Now recall the stories in the Gospels about Jesus. In the second chapter of Luke, when Issa was twelve years old, he was found in Jerusalem discussing with the Jewish teachers of the Torah, the rabbis. And through much of the Gospels, Issa argues vehemently with the religious scholars of his day, the Pharisees, the Sadducees, and the scribes, all of them rabbis, which is what led him to being crucified."

I wanted Maaz to stop. I didn't want to hear any more of this. But Maaz went on relentlessly.

"But think of it further, Mustafa," Maaz continued. "We read about the birth of Issa in the Koran, how it was miraculous, how he was born of a virgin, he could speak as a baby, he could perform miracles such as changing clay images of birds into real ones. But the Muhammad of Islamic tradition, he was born in the ordinary way. There was nothing miraculous about his birth. And further, the birth of the Muhammad of Islamic tradition is not even mentioned in the Koran. The Koran, therefore, seems to be admitting overwhelmingly that Issa is the special messenger of Allah, that Issa is the real Muhammad."

Maaz paused for a moment. All this information was like blows from a boxing opponent. In a metaphorical sense I was now on the floor. But there was no repose. The blows kept coming.

"Another thing," Maaz continued, "is the verse from Al-Hujurat 49:7 which says, 'And know that among you is the Messenger of Allah'. Now, this verse has been translated incorrectly from the Arabic into English. And for good reason. The original Arabic uses the word *feekom*, that is, 'in you', not *bainakoom*, that is, 'among you', so this verse really reads as, 'And know that in you is the Messenger of

344

Allah'. Muhammad cannot be among us anyway seeing he is dead. However, the verse in the original Arabic says that this Messenger is *in* us. Which Messenger, then, is in us? The thing is that this verse from Al-Hujurat sounds almost exactly the same as what St Paul wrote in II Corinthians 13:5 about Issa where he writes, 'Do you not realise that Christ is in you?' which therefore reveals the true identity of the Messenger who is in us."

I was now starting to lose my breath. I felt as if I were asphyxiating. What Maaz was saying made so much sense. The awful thing was that once my eyes were opened and I could see what Maaz was saying, I could no longer view the Koran in the old way I had been viewing it.

Maaz kept on whether or not I wanted him to.

"And remember," Maaz continued, "the other night when you asked about the verse from Surah Al-Ahzab 33:21, which says, 'Certainly, in the Messenger of Allah you have an excellent example for anyone whose hope is in Allah'? Why is it that this verse is in the Koran and yet there is nothing in the Koran which talks about the life of Muhammad, the 7th Century Arabian Prophet? But if the true identity of the Messenger in this verse is Issa, we don't need the Hadiths, because we just have to turn to the Injeel, also the Book of Allah as even the Koran itself confesses, to read about the exemplary life that Allah's Messenger led, in which we find an excellent example."

There was a long moment of silence after Maaz had made this last statement. I looked at Maaz and he stared back at me, the expression on his face was dead and frightening. It took a moment before I could catch my breath to enable myself to say anything.

"Are you implying that Muhammad, that is, the Muhammad of Islamic tradition, doesn't exist in the Koran?"

Maaz looked at me with a strange smile and shrugged his shoulders.

"But there are other verses in the Koran," I suggested, "which talk about the Messenger and the Prophet without exactly identifying who this Messenger or Prophet is. So some of these could be referring to Muhammad from what we know of history."

Maaz slowly picked up his mug of tea, took a sip and then placed it down again.

"Yes, that's true. If you go through all the verses in the Koran which use the word 'messenger' or 'prophet', sometimes this messenger or prophet is clearly identified as Issa, or as Moses, or any of the other named prophets in the Torah and Injeel. Sometimes the messengers are angels. But as you say, there are times in the Koran when we are left to guess the identity of the messenger or prophet. Take for example Al-Anfal 8:1, where it says 'They ask you concerning the spoils of war. Say, 'The spoils of war are for Allah and his Messenger'.' And again in Al-Anfal 8:41 'And know that anything you obtain as spoils of war, then indeed, one fifth is for Allah, and for His Messenger'. The identity of this messenger is not made clear in the Koran. However, we are told without any particular justification that it is Muhammad. But it could be any unknown person all the way up to the changing of the qibla."

"Then it has to be Muhammad in these verses," I retorted emphatically, "if it is the Messenger at the time of the changing of the qibla."

"So we've been told," Maaz replied measuredly.

Again, a terrible feeling passed over me when Maaz said this. Maaz remained silent for a moment. In fact, he remained silent for a good while. I guessed it was deliberate because I had to initiate the conversation to continue.

"So what have we been told that is not the reality?" I asked impatiently.

Maaz leant back and gave out a sinister laugh.

"'Indeed,'" Maaz then said, "'the worst of living creatures in the sight of Allah are…those who do not use their intellect' as it says in Al-Anfal 8:22. One of the many contradictions of the Islamic faith, don't you think?"

During the entire conversation up to this point, I had assumed that Maaz still considered himself a Muslim. This last statement indicated to me for the first time in this entire conversation that what he had been presenting to me was more than a simple reevaluation of how we approached the religion. This last statement indicated that Maaz was beginning to lose his faith. But as he spoke on, I could understand why.

"Tell me, why was the qibla changed?" Maaz asked me.

"Because Allah wanted it changed from Jerusalem to Mecca," I replied.

"And why? Why was it originally towards Jerusalem?"

I tried to think long and hard about it. We had always been told that the first qibla, or as we knew it in Arabic, the *Qibla Awal*, had first been towards Jerusalem. This made sense because Jerusalem was originally the Holy City. From reading the Old Testament, I had learnt the full significance of this city, that it was in Jerusalem that the first House of Allah, the Jewish Temple, had been built. It had remained an important city right up to the Prophet Issa who did most of his preaching there. Even the Muhammad of Islamic tradition ascended to heaven from this city and not from Mecca which gave Jerusalem its great importance. I gave Maaz this explanation.

"And why," Maaz then asked, "was it changed from Jerusalem to Mecca?"

I thought this was a strange question. I thought it was pretty obvious as to why. Mecca was the centre of the new emerging religion of Islam. Allah wanted to show that He had changed his favour from the Jews and the Christians to the followers of His last prophet, Muhammad, who spent much of his life in Mecca. So it made sense to change the qibla accordingly from Jerusalem to Mecca.

"And is this supported by the Koran?" Maaz asked.

347

"Well, yes, of course," I stated emphatically. "It's quite clearly stated in Al-Baqarah."

"Yes, it's stated quite clearly in Al-Baqarah," Maaz echoed my statement. "And what does it say? Does it say that the qibla was changed from Jerusalem to Mecca?"

"I don't know the wording exactly," I replied.

"Well, turn to Al-Baqarah 2:144 and read it out loud."

I did what Maaz told me, turned to the passage and read it out.

"'Indeed, We see the turning of your face towards the heaven. Surely we will turn you to a direction of prayer that pleases you. So turn your face towards the direction of Al-Masjid Al-Haraam'."

When I had finished reading from the passage, I looked up at Maaz.

"The Koran does not say that the original qibla was towards Jerusalem," Maaz said, "or to any place on earth. Rather, it says that Allah saw this unidentified 'you' facing towards the heaven when Allah changed the qibla. So the qibla direction according to the Koran was from heaven to Al-Masjid Al-Haraam."

I was stunned when Maaz said this and speechless. But Maaz continued.

"But, yes, we have been told that traditionally there had been a qibla direction, not towards the heaven, but to another destination, to the Al-Aqsa Mosque in Jerusalem. It also says this in Sahih Bukhari that the original qibla was towards Jerusalem. That makes sense because this was the original holy city of the major prophets in the Torah and the Injeel. But then, don't you think it's strange how that it says in Al-Baqarah 2:125 that Allah says to 'remember when We made the House a place of return...for those who circumambulate' and later in verse 127 it says that 'Ibrahim was raising the foundation of the House'? The identity of this House is brought out in the next surah, in Al-Imran 3:96, where it says, 'the first House set up for mankind is at Bakkah', that is, Mecca. If Abraham laid the foundations of the House in Mecca, and this was the 'first House set up for mankind', doesn't that mean that the qibla had been towards Mecca ever since ancient times? So this would mean that the qibla was originally towards Mecca, then it was changed to Jerusalem later, and then back to Mecca."

I was further stunned. What Maaz was saying was right. We had been told that there had been the *Qibla Awal,* the first qibla, and this was changed. We had simply been told that this was changed from the Al-Aqsa Mosque to the current direction to Mecca. But the Koran told us that Abraham and Ishmael built the House, which we had always understood was the Kaaba in Mecca. If this was so, the earlier descendants of Abraham should have been praying the qibla towards Mecca from the beginning, and this should have been the *Qibla Awal.* This means that if there had been a qibla towards Al-Aqsa Mosque, then this could not have been the *Qibla Awal* but a later change from the original qibla and then the change in qibla from Al-Aqsa Mosque back to Mecca would rightfully have been a restoration of the original qibla. And this would be mentioned somewhere, at least in the Holy Books. But there was nothing. As I had read in the Torah, there was no mention of Abraham building the House with Ishmael. In fact, there was nothing about Abraham going that far down south in Arabia. And further, the Koran acknowledges a change in qibla, but says in Al-Baqarah 2:144 that the change in qibla was from the sky to Mecca. This to me sounded like a change of qibla from what Issa had said in the Gospel of John chapter four when he told the woman of Samaria that the qibla was originally towards Jerusalem but then Issa said that praying would no longer be to any place, which implies that people then prayed to the sky, the heavens, where Allah resides. So the mention in the Koran sounded as if the qibla change was from the direction hinted at in the Injeel.

I looked up at Maaz and didn't know what to say. However, Maaz seemed to have followed my thought process when he took up the conversation even further.

"Oh, yes, the story gets even more interesting!" Maaz said and the tone in his voice sounded defeatist. "Muhammad's biographer, ibn Hisham, who wrote in the 8th Century, well over a hundred years after the death of Muhammad, claims that Allah is the Lord of Becca, or Mecca, and that Allah created Mecca at the time He created the heavens and the earth. Why then didn't Abraham, the Jews and the Christians pray towards Mecca prior to the arrival of Muhammad if Allah had created Mecca before He had created everything else in the universe? After all, it says later in the verse from Al-Baqarah that when the qibla was changed to face Mecca that 'those who were given the Book know well that it is the truth from their Lord'. And again, why is it that in Al-Baqarah we read that Allah told this unidentified 'you' that He would change the qibla from the heaven to Al-Masjid Al-Haraam, clearly indicating that this was a new qibla and a qibla 'that pleases you', if Mecca had been created at the same time as the creation of the universe? If what ibn Hisham wrote, that Allah created Mecca at the creation of heaven and earth, then this implies that Mecca was important to Allah and He wanted the qibla to be in this direction because it pleased Him. However, the qibla change according to Al-Baqarah was made to please an unidentified 'you', whom we have always been told was Muhammad. But hadn't the qibla towards Mecca always pleased Allah seeing He had created it at the time of the creation of the universe? And the Koran states that Ibrahim laid the foundations of the House at Bakkah and we would assume from this that Ibrahim and his descendants had been using this House at Bakkah as their qibla. Which would then be assumed that all the later prophets, Moses, David, Solomon and Issa, should have been praying to Mecca and that it would be so clearly spelled out in the Bible. But this changing of the qibla in Al-Baqarah clearly shows that the changing of the qibla was something new, not a restoration of the qibla to its original direction."

Again, I didn't have an answer. This was all becoming terribly confusing. But Maaz kept on like an incoming tide.

"But let's get back to Al-Aqsa Mosque," Maaz continued. "Let's say that the original qibla had been towards Al-Aqsa Mosque. Why was the first qibla towards Al-Aqsa Mosque? When was Al-Aqsa Mosque built?"

I began trying to go through everything that I had learnt about the change in qibla. I guessed that the mosque was originally there during the time of Muhammad. I had heard something about this mosque being restored during the time of Caliph Umar.

"It was built in the 700s," Maaz said gruffly.

Once Maaz had said this, there was a silence in the room like an oppressive blanket had been thrown over us. I don't know where Maaz got this information but the confidence in his statement indicated to me that he was sure of its certainty. Immediately my head began doing the calculation. Muhammad traditionally died in 632 AD. This meant that the Al-Aqsa Mosque was built at least 68 years after the Prophet had died. So if the qibla was changed from Al-Aqsa Mosque to Mecca, then it had to have occurred at least 68 years after Muhammad's death.

"Okay, then," I replied. "If there was no building there at the time, that just means that the qibla was not changed from Al-Aqsa Mosque but from Jerusalem in general, where the Temple of the Jews originally stood."

"I like your optimism," Maaz replied. "But even so, when you look at the history of all the mosques, mosques originally were facing Jerusalem up until the early 700s. So, if the qibla did not change till the early 700s, what does this tell us about the origin and the dating of the verses in Al-Baqarah 2:142 and onwards about the changing of the qibla

351

if this change did not take place until the 700s, one hundred years after Muhammad had died?"

"No, you're wrong! You're lying!" I snapped.

Maaz looked at me with empty eyes as if he had not registered what I had said.

"Further," Maaz continued, "if the Al-Masjid Al-Aqsa was not built until the 700s, what do you understand of this verse from Bani Israel 17:1 which says, 'Exalted is the one who took His servant by night from Al-Masjid Al-Haram to Al-Masjid Al-Aqsa whose surroundings we have blessed'?"

I thought I was going to pass out.

"Which makes you wonder," Maaz added, "what the identity of the servant in this verse is."

My first impulse was to get up, walk over to Maaz and simply beat him to death. How dare he say all these things he was saying and completely bring into question everything we had learnt about Muhammad, the qibla and Mecca. At one point I felt nauseated and thought I was going to be sick. A good mouthful of tea helped to assuage this feeling.

I then went back over the verse in my mind. Maaz was right. If the Al-Aqsa Mosque was not built until the 700s, then the servant mentioned in this verse from Bani-Israel 17:1 could not be Muhammad. But who was it? This then made me understand what Maaz had been trying to tell me earlier about the identity of the Muhammad in the Koran and the uses of "messenger" and "prophet" throughout the Koran that we had naturally assumed were talking about the traditional Muhammad of the Shahada. If the scant mention of the name Muhammad in the Koran could readily be identified as an alternative name for Issa, then all the other verses which simply use "messenger" or "prophet", unless the context specified who this messenger or prophet was, although they could refer to the Muhammad of the Shahada, like the servant in Bani-Israel 17:1, they could just as well be talking about any other messenger or prophet who now remains unidentified. And further, they could be an unidentified messenger or prophet who came after the Muhammad of Islamic tradition, possibly the same person as the servant in Bani-Israel 17:1.

The other thing that went through my mind was, if what Maaz had said was true, that the qibla did not change until the early 700s and if the verse from Bani-Israel mentioned Al-Aqsa Mosque which was first built in the 700s, this meant that the Koran could not have been completed under the rule of Caliph Uthman. This then made me ask Maaz.

"Then if the Koran mentions the Al-Aqsa Mosque, then there are things in the Koran which could not have been revealed to Muhammad."

"Again, the Koran seems to indicate that originally the Koran itself was something else other than what we have been told that it is," Maaz replied dryly. "This Surah, Surah 17, Surah Bani-Israel, suggests that the Koran itself was originally not the Koran, the one you're holding in your hand," and when Maaz said this, he nodded in my direction at what I was holding, "but in fact was something else, another book, the original Book of Allah."

I felt a cold chill pass up between my shoulders and through my hands which were holding this book.

"In Bani-Israel 17:104 to 106," Maaz continued, "we read that Allah 'said after him to the Children of Israel, 'Dwell in the land, then when the promise of the Hereafter comes, We will bring you as a mixed crowd. And with the truth We sent it down, and with the truth it descended. And We have not sent you, except a bearer of glad tidings and a warner. And we have divided the Koran so that you might recite it to the people at intervals'.' Notice how Allah in verse 104 is talking to the Children of Israel. He tells the Children of Israel that 'We sent it down' and then reveals the identity of what He sent down in verse 106, that is, the Koran. What was given to the Children of Israel was the Torah. This implies that the Koran in this verse is synonymous with the Torah."

I was absolutely shocked when Maaz had said this.

"No, it can't be," I objected.

"Other verses also suggest this," Maaz further replied as if he hadn't heard what I had just said. "In the same Surah, Bani-Israel 17:60, it says, 'And We did not make the vision which We showed you except as a trial for mankind, as was the cursed tree mentioned in the Koran'. This verse is saying that there is a cursed tree mentioned in the Koran, a different and distinct book to the book in which this verse is written, which indeed it must be. Because the cursed tree is mentioned in the Torah."

"No, no, stop," I gasped.

But Maaz didn't stop.

"Also," Maaz continued, again not paying any attention to my protests, "it says in Surah An-Naml 27:76 'Indeed, this Koran relates to the Children of Israel'. We are told that the Koran, this Koran," and again, Maaz pointed at the Koran in my hand to emphasize the point, "is for everyone in the world, whereas the Torah was given to the Children of Israel. So, the Koran in this verse must simply be a synonym for the Torah."

When Maaz said all this, this took me back to the strange reference to the Torah being written on tablets of stone and how the same thing was said about the Koran. This then made the connection. The word "Koran" must have originally been a synonym for "Torah".

"But also," Maaz continued, "when you read through the Koran, the Koran itself talks about the Koran already complete as a book. For example, in Yunus 10:61 we are told to 'recite from the Koran'. This cannot be referring to the traditional Koran because the entire Koran had not been completely revealed to Muhammad till close to his death. And this surah, Surah Yunus, was not the last surah revealed to Muhammad, which means that the Koran

354

you're holding in your hand had not been completely sent down until some time after this verse had been revealed to Muhammad. And, of course, we have been told that the Koran was not made into a book until after Muhammad's death, during the reign of Caliph Uthman. Now, this verse says to 'recite from the Koran', and in order to recite from the Koran, the Koran has to be a book to recite from. And have a look at the other verses in the Koran which speak of the Koran. In the mind of the writer of these verses which talk of the Koran, this Koran was a complete book. If this was a complete book, then it can't be the traditional Koran of Islamic belief. It has to be another holy book. And the Bible, or at least the Torah, fits this description."

"No, no, no," I whispered and shook my head vigorously. "I don't believe you! What you are saying is totally wrong!"

So many thoughts went through my mind. I had to take a grip on myself. I first wanted to throw my mug at Maaz and break his skull. Then I thought of getting up and strangling him to death for his blasphemy. It took all my willpower to get a grip on myself and not let myself be overcome by my emotions.

"Don't take my word for it," Maaz then broke through my thoughts. "Prove me wrong, if you can. In fact, I want you to prove me wrong. I want someone to come with conclusive evidence to show that all that I've just told you is preposterous and that everything we have been taught about Islam is substantiated by what is written in the Koran."

Maaz then looked at me. He then stood up, turned and looked out the window as if there were something in the darkness worth looking at.

"I wish," Maaz then said. "I wish that guy had not told me all this. I wish I hadn't listened. But that's the problem. Once your eyes are open, you can't close them again. Like they say, once an arrow leaves the bow, it never returns."

This last statement bewildered me and I wondered who it was he was talking about. But while thinking on this, Maaz then looked at his watch.

"It's late," he concluded. "And I've had enough of this conversation. I'm going to bed."

Chapter 14

For days after these conversations, the first with Yusuf and then the other with Maaz, my mind was in constant motion trying to resolve all these issues. What was I to make of Yusuf's critique about Allah's perfection? We had been told that the great Creator, Allah, gave the Book to Moses but then some unknown Jews corrupted Allah's Words and forced generations of believers to live under a corrupted version of His Book, to be followed by Allah giving Issa the Injeel and again, allowing His Book to be once again corrupted by unknown people, presumably Christians, and as a result generations of believers were forced to follow a corrupted version of His Word, only to finally have Allah send down the Koran and this time Allah decided to ensure that this Book would be protected. As blasphemous as the thought was, this made out that the Almighty Allah was somewhat clumsy, that He could not ensure the first two books He sent down remained free of corruption.

Unless I followed what Yusuf said, that the Koran clearly says that "None can change His Words", and seeing the Torah, the Injeel and the Koran were evidently the Words of Allah as it says so in the Koran, none of these could have been distorted as we had been traditionally told. But then, if the Torah and the Injeel had not been corrupted, then all the haram relationships of the great prophets or the prophets who were born from a haram relationship, all these had to be explained.

And then I thought about what Maaz had said about the identity of Muhammad. I tried to contradict his line of argumentation and reject everything he had said as utter unfounded rubbish and the words of an infidel, a kaffeer, a non-Muslim. It just couldn't be possible. As sound as his argumentation was and well-founded with copious backups from the Koran, I just couldn't believe it, no-one would believe it. If what Maaz had told me were true, this meant that our entire religion was based on a lie. How could people spend their entire lives over the centuries dedicated to a fantasy? All we had learnt about the traditional Muhammad had to be true because it had been told for centuries over a large area of the globe without contestation. But when I tried to use this as an argument, a saying I had once heard kept coming to mind: "Tell a lie a thousand times and eventually everyone will believe it". And I had heard about the Concorde Effect, where people start out exerting all their effort on a project, spending large sums of money and an equivalent amount of time, and the further they get into the project, the less likely they are to abandon it even when it's obvious that the project in the end will reap no rewards and all this expenditure of time and effort will lead to nothing. I could see the same with my religion. It had been said for many centuries that Islam was the true religion founded on a 7th Century Arab called Muhammad and because it had been said over and over again for centuries, it was accepted as the truth. Further, millions of people had lived their lives in accordance with this belief, much of it to their inconvenience, that even if they were shown unequivocal evidence that their entire belief was simply not true, they were unlikely to abandon the religion because they had placed upon themselves great restrictions and spent an immense amount of time and energy following the precepts of the religion that it would be absolutely unthinkable to admit that in the end the paradise they hoped to obtain as a result of living this austere life might actually not exist.

The problem was that despite the fact that I didn't want to believe what Maaz had said, the evidence was just so overwhelmingly strong in his favour. Further, this

Muhammad-Jesus identity made me see things about my religion that I hadn't noticed before. We criticized the Christians for associating Issa with Allah when he was only a prophet. But one of the offshoots of what Maaz had shown me about the Muhammad-Issa identity was that for the first time it showed me just how similar our adoration for Muhammad was and that it was no different to the Christian adoration of Jesus. I saw Islam as a parallel religion to Christianity in this respect. The only difference was that we did not say that Muhammad was Allah or equal to Allah. However, just about everything else we said about Muhammad was the same as what the Christians said about Issa. Muhammad will intercede on our behalf on the Day of Judgement, and that's what it said in the Bible about Issa in verses like Matthew 10:32, 33. The Koran tells us to believe in Allah and His Messenger in several places such as in Al-Imran 3:32 & 132 and An-Nisaa 4:14 & 59, that is, we were not simply to believe in Allah but in Allah and His Messenger as if these two were in total unity, in the same way that the Bible says that believers should believe in Allah and Issa as it says throughout the Gospels. And like it says in the Bible, there are many prophets, yet Jesus eclipses them all and becomes the central prophet of adoration so that all the other prophets while acknowledged as prophets fade into the background. This singling out of Issa made sense if, like the Christians claim, Issa were Allah. As Muslims, we did the same thing with Muhammad, yet the Koran said quite specifically that all the prophets are equal and "we make no distinction between them" so it made even less sense to set Muhammad in the unique position that he holds in the minds of most Muslims. Even the Shahada in this light came across to me as quite blasphemous in its singling out of Muhammad as the only prophet of Allah in contradiction to what it says in the Koran.

This was yet another difficulty I was having with my religion. Words and definitions were changed but the actuality remained the same. Just because we didn't say that Muhammad was Allah, our total adoration for Muhammad above all the other prophets, that we had to believe not only in Allah but in Allah and His Messenger together, and what we had been told about how Allah Himself has singled out Muhammad as the best and highest human where he will be assigned a place in the highest heaven and will intercede on our behalf, all these aspects of him gave him godlike qualities. Everything we said and believed about Muhammad made him out to be a deity. Yet to say that Muhammad was a god or equal to Allah would be considered blasphemous. This meant that we could believe, understand, venerate and adore Muhammad as a deity, but we just couldn't use the actual words to say that he was one.

I had noticed this before with our denotation of angels. We criticized polytheistic religions such as Hinduism because of their illogical belief in many gods. But while we said we didn't believe in any other gods apart from Allah, our understanding of angels was no different to what polytheists understood of the lesser gods in their pantheons. We could appreciate and understand that the angels in so many respects had godlike qualities, being extremely powerful and being immortal, but we simply couldn't use the actual words to define them as gods.

It was the same with the worship of the black rock in Mecca, and in particular the kissing of it. In every aspect, this total devotion for the black rock, to which we had to face five times a day in prayer, was blatantly obvious an act of idolatry seeing it had all the hallmarks of idolatrous worship. Yet, although it was so clear that the reverence and adoration of the black rock in Mecca was idolatry, we simply couldn't use the word to describe it as such.

This change in the meaning of words also came out when I considered the Arabic word Al-Masjid Al-Aqsa. I knew that the word *masjid* came from the Arabic *sajada* meaning "to prostrate" and hence a *masjid*, or as it is in English, a mosque, was simply a place to prostrate. Although the word "masjid" itself doesn't specifically denote a building, all masjids that I knew of were buildings. I mean, whenever Muslims go to new places in the world, one of the first things they do is build a masjid and it was universally understood that a masjid was a building inside which Muslims could pray. Even the Koran itself acknowledges that masjids, or mosques, are buildings in verses such as Al-Hajj 22:40 where it is written, "And if Allah does not check the people...surely, the monasteries, churches, synagogues and masjids in which the name of Allah is mentioned would have been demolished". To be demolished, a mosque has to be a building or a construction of some kind, and because it was clear that synagogues, monasteries and churches were buildings, equating masjids with these other buildings meant that the writers of the Koran clearly acknowledged that masjids also were buildings. What conclusively shows that masjids are all buildings is what it says in Al-Taubah 9:18, that "the mosques of Allah are only to be maintained by those who believe in Allah." If all the masjids of Allah are to be maintained, they have to be a structure of some kind to receive regular maintenance.

This understanding of what a masjid is, then, becomes problematic when considering the Al-Masjid Al-Aqsa, the Al-Aqsa Mosque. I totally refused to believe Maaz when he told me that the Al-Masjid Al-Aqsa was built in the 700s, about a hundred years after Muhammad had died. We all knew that the Al-Masjid Al-Aqsa was built on the precinct where the Temple of the Jews once stood. Although not all Muslims were aware of this, I knew that the well-known Dome of the Rock was built right over the central area where the Jewish Temple had once stood and was actually a separate building to the Al-Masjid Al-Aqsa, although the Al-Masjid Al-Aqsa stands not too far from the Dome of the Rock on an area that had once been part of the Temple precinct. However, what I discovered from the internet was that it was universally acknowledged that at the time of Muhammad, there were actually no buildings on the Temple precinct at all and in fact this area was ignominiously used as a dumping ground. Some said that the Al-Masjid Al-Aqsa was actually built during the reign of the Caliph Omar but this appeared to be a building of little real significance and that the actual Al-Masjid Al-Aqsa we are familiar with today was a building constructed in the 700s, at the time Maaz had said that this great mosque came into existence. Because it is universally acknowledged that there was absolutely no building there at the time of Muhammad, the verse from Bani Israel 17:1 that says that "Exalted is the One Who took His servant by night from Al-Masjid Al-Haraam to Al-Masjid Al-Aqsa whose surroundings We have blessed" is interpreted as meaning that the entire area of the Jewish Temple precinct, although completely barren and devoid of buildings, was considered Al-Masjid Al-Aqsa. Like those who gave this definition, I also so desperately wanted this to be true. However, as it seems to be in other verses in the Koran about masjids, even this verse seems to indicate that masjids are buildings, because Al-Masjid Al-Haram, which we understood to be the Kaaba, is a building, the House that Ibrahim built, which infers that seeing Al-Masjid Al-Haraam is being equated with Al-Masjid Al-Aqsa, then Al-Masjid Al-Aqsa is also a building. Further, the verse states that Allah has not only blessed Al-Masjid Al-Aqsa but the area which surrounds Al-Masjid Al-Aqsa which further implies the existence of a building around which an area was blessed.

Which therefore created a problem. Who was this servant in Bani Israel 17:1? We had always acknowledged that it was Muhammad and this verse was referring to the night Muhammad rode the buraq into heaven and met all the earlier prophets. If the writer of this verse had the actual building of Al-Masjid Al-Aqsa in mind then the servant in this verse could not have been Muhammad. So who was it? I also realized that this verse said absolutely nothing about who this servant was and what happened after the servant reached Al-Masjid Al-Aqsa. All the verse says is that "Exalted is the One Who took His servant by night from Al-Masjid Al-Haraam to Al-Masjid Al-Aqsa". And that's it. Everything else is inferred. And if Al-Masjid Al-Haraam was built in the 700s, this verse was revealed at a time after Muhammad had died. So did the angel Gabriel reveal this to a later prophet after Muhammad? If so, his identity evades us.

As always, one way to try to at least appease the confusion in my head was to put the question to my uni friends and see if they could assist in finding a resolution to the inconsistencies in our belief and once again help me to feel assured of my faith. One evening at the cafeteria while we congregated to eat the evening meal, I asked those at the table with me about the Al-Masjid Al-Aqsa.

My uni friends all stared at me speechless for a moment.

"How do you come up with these bizarre questions?" Arsalan asked me.

I shrugged my shoulders and screwed up my face.

"I'm just curious," I replied. "And I thought one of you might know something about it."

Everyone looked at each other before Arsalan gave his tuppence worth.

"Al-Masjid Al-Aqsa was built by Prophet Adam, I think," Arsalan replied.

"How do you know that?" I asked.

Arsalan looked around at the other uni students and then back at me.

"I don't know," he replied. "I think I heard it at Friday prayers."

"Wasn't Al-Masjid Al-Aqsa built by Prophet Ibrahim?" Haseeb, another uni student at the table put forward.

"Well, it can't have been by Prophet Ibrahim," I replied, "because it says in the Koran that Ibrahim built the House of Allah in Bakkah, that is, in Mecca. And further, Jerusalem only became the Holy City when King David took this city from a people called the Jebusites and it was his son, King Solomon, who finally built the Temple."

"Then it was King Solomon who built Al-Masjid Al-Aqsa," Haseeb stated confidently.

"Mmmmmmmmmm. Well, not exactly," I replied. "The ritual inside the Temple did not include circumambulation like that at Mecca. Not to mention, the ritual inside the Temple involved mainly the offering of animal sacrifices, and we don't sacrifice animals in mosques. In fact, there was no prostrating in the Temple like in the way we prostrate inside a mosque. So that means that Solomon's Temple could not have been Al-Masjid Al-Aqsa."

"That's because," Arsalan piped up, "Jerusalem isn't the holiest place on earth. I remember hearing a story that when Allah created the earth, before Him, between His hands appeared a beautiful blue pearl, and while Allah was looking at it, under His strong gaze, it became bigger and bigger until it turned into planet earth. The entire ball was blue because the entire surface of the earth was covered with water. And then the areas of brown began to appear, this being the formation of land. The very first piece of land to form was the area of land on which we find the Kaaba today. This is the evidence that the Kaaba and the area around the Kaaba is the holiest place on earth."

This caused an animated conversation of confirmation and disputation. What particularly intrigued me about Arsalan's anecdote was that this description of the earth sounded like the images that we saw on television of the manned missions to the moon and the amazing photos of the earth from outer space. This story obviously had to have been a recent innovation, especially as for many centuries, the Hadiths and other commentaries of the Koran supported the koranic idea that the earth was flat.

What had started out as a question about Al-Masjid Al-Haraam in particular and the nature of a masjid in general evolved into a question about the holiest place on earth. Two parallel ideas evolved from this discussion, each contradicting the other. One was that Mecca, also known as Bakkah, had always been the holiest place in the eyes of Allah. It had been so since the beginning of time, at least according to ibn Hisham, or it had become so from the time of Ibrahim, as it states in Al-Baqarah 2:125 and Al-Imran 3:96, although this could simply mean that Mecca was always holy but no Holy House had been built on it until Ibrahim built it. But if Ibrahim had established a House at Mecca towards which all the believers should pray, which descendant of Ibrahim changed this direction of prayer from Mecca to Jerusalem – Isaac? Jacob? David? Solomon? Issa? – from which it would once again be returned to Mecca? And if it had been changed from Mecca to Jerusalem, why did Allah allow this if the first holy place Allah created right at the beginning of Creation together with heaven and earth was Mecca?

Then there was the other idea. Jerusalem was originally the holy place and the first holy house was built there. As Arsalan first stated, this was apparently built by Prophet Adam, although I don't know where he got this information apart from hearing it at Friday prayers, although I had also heard something similar in my earlier years. If we went by the Holy Books, the first mention of Jerusalem being the holy place is in Genesis 14. After Ibrahim had rescued Lot from a king called Kedorlaomer, a man called Melchizedek who, as it says in verse eighteen, was "the priest of the Most High God" and also identified as the King of Salem, or King of Jerusalem, blessed Ibrahim. Although it isn't spelled out plainly in this passage from the Torah, it is understood that if this great priest of the Most High God had the power and authority over Ibrahim whom Allah had appointed as the leader of humankind as it says in Al-Baqarah 2:124, this implied the city Melchizedek presided over as priest and king must have been extremely significant. Then later we read how Jacob fled from his brother Esau and arrived at a desolate piece of land on which he slept and dreamed about a stairway fixed to the earth and which led up into heaven to the throne of Allah, a stairway upon which the angels ascended and descended. When Jacob woke up the following morning, he was afraid and said in Genesis 28:17 "This is none other than the house of God" and so he called the place Bethel which is Hebrew for "house of God". The true location of Bethel is not universally agreed upon as, from what I discovered on internet, some say it is Jerusalem while others say that it is an area north of Jerusalem. In any case, Bethel is within the vicinity of Jerusalem if it is not Jerusalem proper. Later, King David took this city from the Jebusites, the assumption being that at some time the Israelites had not had control of this city, and King Solomon built there the first House of God, the Jewish Temple. Later, Jesus recognised Jerusalem as the Holy City as it clearly comes out in the Gospels. And although Jerusalem is not named in the Koran, Jerusalem is still recognised by Muslims as being a holy city because in Arabic, Jerusalem is called *Al-Quds*, "The Holy", as the name comes from the Arabic triliteral root *qds* meaning "holy". Although the Koran itself does not say that Jerusalem is the holy city, the Koran does recognise Israel as the Holy Land as it says in Al-Ma'idah 5:21, supporting what it says in the Bible about Israel, such as in Zechariah 2:12, thus at least acknowledging the land to which Jerusalem was the chief city was holy.

And then the holy place was moved from Jerusalem to Mecca in order to please the unidentified "you" in Al-Baqarah 2:144.

And, of course, there was yet another anomaly about holy places. In Exodus 3, Moses was on Mount Horeb where he saw the burning bush and Allah told Moses to remove his sandals because where he was standing was holy ground. This is echoed in the Koran in Ta Ha 20:12 although in this koranic verse the area is called "the sacred valley of Tuwa". If Mecca was the most holy place established in the beginning of time, why did Allah appear to the great prophet Moses in this locality and not in Mecca?

Which raised yet a further question in my mind. What makes a piece of land holy? Allah created the entire world, so didn't that mean every strip of land Allah created is holy because Allah created it?

The discussion about Al-Masjid Al-Aqsa and holy places became a very long discussion. But it was never resolved unanimously what these were as different people had different ideas about their true identity. What struck me the most was how that each of us had different opinions about these different issues, and these issues remained completely contradictory and irreconcilable.

And it wasn't only these issues. It was the same for many issues. And it wasn't only between Sunnis and Shiites. Even fellow Sunni Muslims – which in a way I still considered myself to be even though I no longer took the Hadiths seriously – had different interpretations of what they read in the Koran. I found it really odd how that the one book that Allah sent down, instead of being a cause of unity, actually ended up being the source of division. We often got into really heated debates over what certain verses in the Koran actually meant. Many of these issues never got resolved. Fortunately, what was admirable about my uni friends is that after a heated argument, which sometimes almost came to blows, within a day or two a peace was once again restored as if it was understood that we were not rabbles of the lower caste but educated gentlemen of higher education. But despite the return to peace, the conflict continued within me as I thought about how the Koran caused the fights in the first place. Why couldn't Allah make His Book clear and easy for everyone to understand so that we could agree on every principle? Already it was difficult to know what it said in His Book because we had been told that we had to read it in the original Arabic which was not the first language of anyone of us at university, to further make what is written obscure and ambiguous, and as a result cause the many faceted factions among the believers.

But while opinions were divided on other topics, there was one on which everyone seemed to be united, and that was the subject of homosexuality. Sex and sexuality was not a subject talked about openly because sex outside of wedlock was a grave sin, irrespective of whether it was with a woman or a man. And it just wasn't something that married people talked about in open society. Although it could safely be assumed that married couples engaged in sex, what they did exactly when they were naked together was something that was considered too personal to share with the general public.

However, whenever a small circle of us young men congregated somewhere, there were times when the topic of sex got raised and, despite the fact that they couldn't be talking about sex with their wives as none of my uni friends were married, they were explicit about their sexual lives. Some of the guys talked of girls they had had during their times at school and others about how they had met up with prostitutes. In fact, there were a few times when some of my uni friends admitted to going off campus from time to time to frequent brothels and use a bit of the money their parents had given them for their education on an hour or so in the pleasures of the flesh. There was a lot of boasting about their masculine triumphs and what they had done. On a few occasions, my uni friends noticed that I didn't contribute to the conversation. When I remained silent on the subject, my uni friends began to question why I was quiet and whether or not I was still a virgin. It was during these times that I expressed my objections to their loose behaviour because of what our religion expected of us. But what was strange was that these uni friends of mine actually mocked me by

368

saying that I certainly had sexual urges like they all had and if I didn't, then I probably didn't have a penis. These uni friends mocked me and made me a laughing stock because of my lack of enthusiasm to engage in these discussions about their sexual conquests, even though I objected because we knew that in our religion, sexual intercourse outside of marriage, *zinna*, was punishable by stoning.

If there was ever a moment that I really appreciated my religion, it was at this time, because my religion gave me the excuse as to why I didn't talk about having sex with a woman. There was simply no way that I could do so without gagging at the thought.

The other thing that saved me was that I had begun to take up exercise. It was at this stage that I began working out at the gym and going swimming. It must have begun to show because my uni friends often commented that I must be getting into shape because I wanted to impress the girls.

These two aspects took the heat off me being considered a heejrah. Gay men were heejrahs. And heejrahs were simply men who looked like men on the outside but acted like girls, were thin and feminine like girls and who spoke like girls. But I didn't act like a girl, and now I was working out and exercising contrary to what is expected of a girl, so my uni friends did not suspect my homosexuality at all because I didn't fit the stereotype. Anyone else, however, who did was often mercilessly made fun of. And when the topic of homosexuality was raised, it was always condemned vehemently and the story of Sodom and Gomorrah used as support for the hatred and intolerance of this variant form of sexuality.

Another horrible word used to describe homosexuals was the Urdu word *gandu*. This was not a word to be used in polite society. I found this word to describe homosexuals debasing but also hypocritical. The word *gandu* comes from the Urdu word, *gand*, which refers to one's behind, and hence a *gandu* is someone who likes to give his behind in pleasure.

I found this debasing and hypocritical because this word exposed the intimate nature of what occurs between two men when they have sex. But why was it okay in this case to declare to all what two men did together naked in private away from the public eye? What I found hypocritical about it was, if I were to meet one of my uni friends when he was married and say to his wife, "Oh, so you're the woman who takes my friend's penis up the vagina?", this would be a scandalous comment – not to mention I would probably be beaten to death. What was further hypocritical about this was that some of my uni friends who frequented prostitutes sometimes boasted how they had penetrated the woman through her behind. If I met one of these guys later in life and he was married, how would he like it if I said in general public that his wife was a *gandu*, assuming that if he had this type of sex with the prostitute, he probably did the same with his wife. What a man and his wife do naked in private remains their private business. So why was there not the same respect given to what two men or what two women did together in private?

This only caused more confusion inside me. As it was at school, my uni friends justified *zinna*, or as it roughly translates into English, fornication. Sex was a natural urge. Even though our religion condemned sex before marriage and, once married, outside the marital state, my uni friends justified this by saying that sex is after all a fundamental natural urge and a strong one, and Allah no doubt would forgive any of our friends for giving in to it. I remember also on other occasions my uni friends explaining to me that some men had such strong sexual urges and that's why Allah allowed a man to have more than one wife so that he doesn't commit adultery. I found this justification for the satisfaction of heterosexual men's sexual urges one-sided. A lot of leeway was given to counter for the male heterosexual sexual urge.

But this was not granted to women at all who could only have one man, and in some cases she had to share a man with other women. The justification for this was that women were not as sexual as men and didn't have the same urges.

And homosexual men were simply not allowed to have sex. The justification for this was that men just shouldn't have sexual feelings for other men, and like Allah Himself questions in His holy Book, my uni friends simply could not comprehend why a man would want to have sex with another man and hence such men should be rightfully punished. Further, it was often said that it was unnatural and a distortion of Allah's creation.

But while my uni friends lacked any understanding of what it was like for a man to be physically attracted to another man, I knew what it was like. It wasn't that I was not attracted to women, worse, I was sexually repulsed by them. Having to marry one woman was bad enough but this awful situation would be quadrupled if I had to marry four. Even worse if in heaven I would be granted 72. But as for my uni friends claiming that my sexual attraction towards men was unnatural, I didn't understand what they meant. I could feel my sexuality was very much a part of me, a part of my nature, so to me it had to be natural. So what did they mean it was unnatural? As for a distortion of Allah's creation, even if it were, who was it that distorted the sexual attraction? It occurred in me spontaneously, which meant that the distortion was done by something or someone beyond my power, and the two most powerful beings more powerful than humans were Allah and Satan. The trouble was, the Koran does not say that homosexuality is a distortion, let alone offer an explanation as to what is the source of this supposed distortion. And a distortion implies an originally undistorted form, but from as early as I could remember, I was always sexually attracted to men and my sexuality had never been changed and therefore distorted as the word "distortion" implies.

Maaz, however, was always noticeably absent from these conversations. In fact, this was something that I began to realize about Maaz, that he never discussed sex with anyone, at least when I was around.

Maaz for a while remained an enigma in some ways. He was somewhat of a loner. The fact that he chose running as a sport in a way showed that he really wasn't the greatest socialite. This didn't mean he kept to himself completely. He was a very friendly guy, and when in the company of our friends, particularly at dinner after lectures, he was a good joker and joked around a lot. He was witty and he had an amazing ability to play with words. But he reminded me of a cat. He slipped in and out of our social circles quietly and indistinctly. He would appear at one moment and no-one would have noticed where he had come from but simply we would suddenly realize that he was there. And just as mysteriously he would again disappear and no-one would have noticed the time he left, only that suddenly we realized he was no longer there. And he seemed to be always running. He often ran around the running track on the university campus. But he also every now and again, often on a Friday when I had gone to pray, would run off somewhere and I wouldn't see him again till just before sunset.

Because I shared a dormitory with him, it was difficult for the two of us not to get personal with each other so there were things that I knew of him that my other uni friends probably didn't know. After all, it was like living with a family member. We often discussed uni work but we also talked about our past lives. As for belief, after Maaz had shown me about what it said in the Koran about the prophet Issa and his conclusion of the Issa-Muhammad identity, it appeared that Maaz had completely lost his religion. I wanted to ask him about it and if this were the case to try to bring him back to the true religion of Islam. But each time I thought about it, I realized that before I could even start, all the arguments that supported the Issa-Muhammad argument stacked up as high as Mount Everest and there was nothing I could think of as a suitable counterargument. And when I thought on this topic, it made me further question my faith. So I preferred not to think about it, which then made me not want to raise the topic with Maaz.

Inexplicably, after that long night's discussion, whereas Maaz had come across as completely depressed about this rude discovery in the Koran, it was not long after that that his whole persona changed and he seemed a lot happier and relaxed, as if a weight had been bearing down on his shoulders and someone had come along and removed this weight. He had become friendlier, more helpful and much nicer. And a lot more tactile.

From the moment I met Maaz, I knew I admired him physically. The first time he removed his shirt and I saw him bare-chested, I couldn't believe that I would be sharing a room for the duration of my university studies with a guy who looked so physically good. Maaz more than anyone inspired me to get into shape, and so while Maaz ran, I worked out some days and swam others. The offshoot was that the exercise made me feel mentally and emotionally better, and often when I felt down or tired before I exercised, I realized how better I felt after an hour of physical exertion. But that Maaz also noticed the change in my physique was a double plus although I didn't realize to what extent he appreciated it.

Once while we were studying, when it was Maaz's turn to ask me questions, he got off from his chair, came over to me and then he proceeded to massage me to check that I wasn't cheating by looking for the answers in the textbook but rather telling him the answer from all the memorization I had done. When it was my turn to question him, I then reciprocated the gesture. Eventually, this became a ritual.

Maaz would massage my shoulders while asking questions and then I would massage his in return when I asked questions back.

While my physique changed, Maaz commented on the improvement. He said he could feel it each time he massaged me. And Maaz knew how to massage. I asked him if he had ever officially studied how to do massages but he replied that he had simply picked it up from his older brother who was an athlete and who had shown him how to do it, as his brother had learnt this from his trainer.

It was an evening on the last day of the weekend. It was close to bedtime, and Maaz and I had worked hard physically during the day and mentally that evening. When we had reached a point when we could no longer study anymore, Maaz asked me if I wanted a cup of tea. After he had prepared the tea, before pouring it, he noticed me stretching and moving my shoulder in a circle.

"Are you okay?" he asked me.

"Yeah," I replied. "It's just that my left shoulder, my back and my left leg feel somewhat sore."

"How about you get on the bed and I'll give you a massage," Maaz said.

I dutifully obeyed.

"Take off your shirt and your shorts," Maaz then said.

I sat up, removed my shirt, then my shorts, and dressed only in my underpants I lay back on the bed.

"Okay," Maaz said. "Where exactly does it hurt?"

"My left shoulder, my spine and my left calf muscle."

Maaz removed his T-shirt and then went to work with his wonderful manual magic. It was absolutely delightful. I just groaned with pleasure as he made every muscle from the back of my neck to my feet feel loose and relaxed. Maaz continued to my right shoulder, then down my back. He skipped my midriff and then continued down one leg and then the other.

Maaz then told me to roll over on my back. And there was Maaz, on his knees on the bed, bare-chested. Already the massage he had given me helped the blood circulate through my body, but on seeing his beautiful physique, the blood channelled to the one member of my body which responded appropriately to this vision. Immediately I felt embarrassed but hoped that Maaz wouldn't notice. I moved to make myself comfortable and spoke to Maaz so that he would look me in the face and not look at the rest of my body. However, once settled, Maaz adjusted his position on the bed and in so doing looked down and saw a part of me standing to attention.

Maaz remained motionless for a moment, staring at this protrusion. Oddly, the sudden terror that I felt only made the protruding implement even firmer. Now I was completely horrified. What was Maaz going to do in this situation? Surely there were other biological explanations for this natural phenomenon than the one that seemed so obvious in this situation. I had no way out. I shared this dormitory with Maaz and if Maaz interpreted my body language in the way that seemed evident, I wondered if I would ever get out of this room alive.

Maaz himself froze for a moment. He kept his eyes transfixed on the lower part of my abdomen for some time with his hands up in the air ready to continue the procedure. But finally he was able to gain some composure. He turned back to look at me in the face. But I couldn't understand the expression on his face. It was blank, with nothing to indicate in which direction the events were going to proceed. Eventually Maaz moved, but instead of continuing the massage, he came and lay next to me, reached his right arm over me and brought me close to himself. He then slipped his left hand under the pillow next to my right ear and held my left ear with his right hand. And then he kissed my forehead. He then looked at me through his dark brown eyes as if he were looking right into my soul.

375

"I love you, Mustafa," he whispered, with a tremolo in his voice. It felt as if time had completely frozen. Maaz once again kissed my forehead and then added, "I love you, and I think you love me, too."

And what a night it was. During the entire event, all inhibitions were blocked out of my mind. Maaz may have been great at massaging but this obviously was only one of his many physical talents.

But the next morning was awkward. Both of us barely spoke a word as we got ready for lectures. Our interaction with each other was polite but aloof, both of us unsure of what we could say to each other about the events of the previous evening.

During lectures that day, I couldn't stop thinking about it. There was total confusion about what Maaz and I had done and how it was perceived in the Koran. The only mention in the Koran about men having sex with men was the Sodom and Gomorrah story but the men in that story simply wanted to gang rape the angels simply to fulfil their lusts. What the Koran said about these men and what had occurred the night before between Maaz and me simply were not talking about the same thing. What Maaz and I had done was an expression of love, both physical and emotional, the physical aspect deepening the emotional. For the first time, I realized what a married relationship was supposed to be about, the uniting of two people who loved each other and who could express this love in all its forms. But now it had become so clear to me that I would never be able to do this with a woman. True, I could love a woman. But any expression of love I had for a woman would only be as deep as that which I had for my sister, my mother and my grandmother. With a man, however, and in particular, with Maaz, this physical expression of love had greater depth. In fact, what I felt throughout the entire moment was so intense and so beautiful that I felt that this could only have come from Allah because something so beautiful and magic could only come from the highest good in the universe.

This therefore created cognitive dissonance between what I felt about Maaz and what I understood about my religion. This sexual expression, the intense, beautiful, physical expression of love between two men and two women in Pakistan was so despised and looked on so much as an ugly detestable thing, and this view by our society and by what was written in the Book of Allah further made absolutely no sense.

Maaz and I got over the first difficulty in this, accepting what had happened between the two of us. Once over the awkwardness, we allowed the event to occur again. And again, And again. Of course, we had to be so delicately careful not to express or show our feelings for each other outside our dormitory. Our dormitory itself became a solace from the rest of our oppressive society, almost a holy place to continue these intense beautiful expressions of love which I interpreted as a gift from Allah. As much as our society and our religion seemed to claim that this expression of love was wrong, my very being simply could not accept this understanding of it.

Was it possible, then, that the words used in the Koran to condemn this form of love actually had a different meaning to what we had been traditionally told? Was it possible that we could alter the meaning of the words in the Koran which condemned the sexual attraction between men in the same way as it was with other words, such as the altered meaning of the word "masjid"?

Chapter 15

If there wasn't enough going on in my head trying to resolve all this information and at the same time maintain the integrity of the Koran, what now had begun between Maaz and me was only more material to throw into the chaos. I still wonder to this day why I continued to believe in Allah and the Koran when all the evidence was screaming at me that the Koran was not to be taken seriously. Maaz finally admitted at one stage that he no longer believed any of it. He chose to keep this between him and me, which was quite understandable because confessing this to the general public was a death sentence. But he didn't try to convince me that I should come to the same conclusion. Rather, he only said in one comment that he no longer considered himself a Muslim and then remained quiet on the subject. He didn't even say anything to the effect that he couldn't understand why I continued to believe in the faith. Rather, he made this confession to me so I knew where he stood. But to everyone else, he was a Muslim, paying lip service where it was necessary but in the privacy of his own little world, he began to live his own life. And while I continued to maintain that the faith was true, I could still understand why he had come to this conclusion. As it was, I knew if I wanted to get him back to the faith, I had to come up with convincing arguments to demonstrate that the Issa-Muhammad relationship in the Koran was a mirage and that the traditional understanding that Issa was one prophet and Muhammad was another was the true understanding. But I had nothing to support this.

Maaz therefore could continue this relationship that had formed between us with a clear conscious because all the obstacles that had been put in the way by the religion to say that it was wrong for him had been removed. But I hadn't reached this stage yet. If there ever was a moment in which I found myself in the throes of doublethink, it was at this time. According to my religion and the mores of our society, what was happening between Maaz and me was wrong and evil, and I believed that. Yet everything about it, especially the intense love that was exchanged between us and the positive feelings it engendered in us told me that this was in fact right and good, and I believed that, too. When I think about it now, I can understand why people develop split personalities, especially people who are entrenched in a religion like Islam where they want to believe in the veracity of their religion on the one hand while at the same time are confronted with reality which shows the contrary.

But that wasn't the only thing that was pouring confusion into the pot. Another event was occurring in parallel which added yet more questions to my mind. It all began prior to what had started between Maaz and me, at the time earlier in the story when I had decided to get into shape.

There was a small gym in the south western wing of the university which had next to it an indoor swimming pool. It took some courage for me to actually front up to the place but eventually I made my way there wearing what I felt was appropriate garb for a workout. A feeling of anxiety crept over me as I approached the building in which the gym was housed because my awareness of my physical shape would only be heightened when I entered and saw all these beefy guys going hell for leather while I, with a thin, emaciated and somewhat shapeless body, struggled at my first attempts to do any exercise.

The first thing that struck me as I entered the gymnasium was the silence, and on a quick glance around it was obvious that there was nobody there. That in itself was a relief as I didn't have to then be shown up for my lack of physical ability.

I began to walk around the room, looking at the different workout equipment but I had no idea with which to begin or how any of the gym equipment was used. I was about to touch one of the pieces of gym equipment when I heard someone enter and call out to me, "Are you okay there?"

I turned around to see a man in his late 20s early 30s dressed in obvious gym gear which conveyed beyond a doubt that he was a regular gym fanatic. He also had obvious musculature that was evident in those parts of his body which were not hidden under cloth. My hormones instantly went into overdrive just at the sight of him, and then my reasoning side looked at him perplexed, wondering how many centuries it would take me at the gym to get my body into similar shape.

This man's name was Rameez, and because I was a student, I called him Rameez Bhai. He was a gym instructor employed by the university and on campus for students who wanted to avail themselves of the gym equipment and the swimming pool. Rameez Bhai was obviously very observant and could tell with a simple glance that this was my first time at a gym. However, before long, he sat me down and asked me a series of questions about my health, my diet, and what I wanted to achieve from a regular exercise regime. To this last question I was going to say that I wanted a body like his but the double meaning in the answer took a grasp on my tongue causing me to stutter, and seeing the perplexed look on Rameez Bhai's face, I thought of an alternative answer to the question and simply said that I wanted to look and feel a lot healthier.

Rameez Bhai wrote up a program and then it was time to begin. And he was a wonderful and considerate gym instructor. Before getting into the instruction of the program, he explained to me that physical exercise was helpful not only for building the body but also for stimulating the brain. When he introduced me to certain weight-bearing exercises and handed me what looked like ridiculously light weights which to him would feel as light as a pencil, he made me feel reassured of myself that I was starting from the beginning and there was no shame in this. He explained that this was the same with our religion, that when we started out on our journey in Islam, we had to start with the basics until we further studied and developed into our religion. I didn't see the relevance of this at first. Further, it gave me flashbacks to all that I had learned up to that time about my religion and how the deeper I delved, the more questions it raised.

The whole time I was there, I was the only person exercising. I asked Rameez Bhai if anyone else actually used the equipment and he replied that they usually came later in the afternoon or much earlier in the morning and that it was unusual for anyone to come at this time. As a result of this, I made sure that I came at this time to the gym as much as I could so that I could work out without the embarrassment of seeing the much better looking guys in all their fitted out glory. Unfortunately this was not always achievable and there were times I had to share equipment with guys who were in much better shape than I was.

At the end of my first workout, Rameez Bhai then suggested that I learn to swim. I looked at him blankly not really knowing what to say.

"It's good exercise," Rameez Bhai continued. "It's aerobic and it exercises the whole body."

There was a slight pause and then Rameez Bhai added as an afterthought, "Even the Prophet told us that there were three essential things that all men should know how to do and one of them is to swim. And which definitely makes sense in Pakistan. You never know. One day you might get caught in a flash flood and this skill might save your life."

I was mystified by the comment about the Prophet. I had never heard of such a thing. And it made even less sense when describing someone who had spent most of his time in the deserts of Arabia. Rameez Bhai's religious description of the benefits of swimming in particular and for exercise in general however had its practical side. Allah created our bodies and we show our respect to Allah by looking after and maintaining our bodies in good working order. After all, how can we continue to do good works for Allah if our bodies aren't fully functional? I could see this as a wonderful piece of advice and it made sense. But then I wondered why such a logical, full sensical piece of advice hadn't made its way into the Koran?

So, I signed up for swimming as well. Rameez Bhai encouraged me to come to the gym every day and alternate my exercise regime, one day weights, the next day swimming. And it was important to have one day off. The choice of day off was easy as I set aside Friday as a day for devotion.

The aftermath of the first workout was definitely felt the following morning and for the first time I realized muscles in my body that I thought I didn't have. At that time, Maaz joked about it and got a good laugh out of my discomfort. But he was also very encouraging and told me not to give up like a lot of guys do after their first couple of tries at the gym.

It was partly Maaz's encouragement but probably moreso what Rameez Bhai told me about what the Prophet had said about exercise that kept me going. If the Prophet said it, this was indirectly from Allah and for someone who was still strongly bound to religious principles, this spurred me along against all odds.

The weight-lifting regime was relatively easy as I only needed to concentrate on one part of my body at a time. Learning to swim, however, was a lot more complicated. Rameez Bhai taught me to swim breaststroke and freestyle. It wasn't too long before I grasped how to swim breaststroke and this was my preferred swimming stroke but Rameez

Bhai encouraged me to master swimming freestyle as well. Breaststroke, however, remained the swimming style I most often adopted when I swam laps at the pool.

With mere persistence, especially over the summer break when there weren't many people on the university premises so I could spend a large swab of the day in the pool, eventually I went from feeling as if I were going to die of exhaustion struggling from one end of the pool to the other to being able to swim several laps in one go without having to stop for a break. After a year of this, I was able to swim an entire kilometre nonstop. And it was at this time that my uni friends started to comment about how much my physique had improved. And it was especially complimentary when Maaz said it. And of course it became even further worth it when Maaz finally took an interest in me physically.

That there were certain days through the week when I was the only person at the gym meant that Rameez Bhai had my total attention. Rameez Bhai, so it turned out, was quite religious, or at least, religion appeared to occupy his mind a lot. This was so incongruous. Exercise and religion didn't seem to occupy the same fields of thought and yet Rameez Bhai wove the two together like a carpet weaver. It was true that religion permeated much of our lives but I didn't expect it to be a topic of conversation in between grunts and groans. It began with Rameez Bhai asking me questions which I considered quite simple and superficial. But then his questions became delving, and that's when I realized that he, like many of my Muslim friends and acquaintances, had very limited knowledge of what was written in the Koran, and further, he could not distinguish between what did and didn't constitute the religion in general. I didn't say it as bluntly as this but I explained to Rameez Bhai that the true religion of Islam had its source in the Koran and the Koran alone, and all other information, particularly from the Hadiths, was questionable and not to be taken seriously. Each gym visit when we were alone together became an opportunity for Rameez Bhai to give me knowledge about physical education and for me in return to give him knowledge about the Koran. Every time he asked me a question, I had an answer from the Koran, and this once again revitalized my faith and, combined with the excretion of endorphins, this made me feel good about myself as a person and helped me to disregard those aspects of the religion that I thought I was having troubles with.

Rameez Bhai became quite keen in our conversations about religion. It became quite intense when one day after I had completed my hour, Rameez Bhai asked me, "Do you like camping?" and then after a slight pause he added, "And fishing?"

"I guess," I replied hesitantly.

"Would you like to go camping with me next Saturday afternoon? We can do some fishing and while there this would give me the opportunity to talk with you more."

This made me nervous and it took me a moment to reply. Being together only with Rameez Bhai in all his beautiful manhood would be awkward for me. However, Rameez Bhai insisted vehemently as he needed someone he could trust and with whom he could talk about religion. He wasn't comfortable speaking with religious leaders, so he said, as often the questions he asked troubled them and often had them telling him to simply believe what he was told without question to avoid going to Jahannam in the next life.

That following Saturday, Rameez Bhai took me in his car and we went to a place not too far from the university but far enough to be away from any human habitation. It was barely a ten minute drive away from the main buildings of the university, but was still considered part of the university compound. Entrance was through a security gate. It resembled a VIP camping ground dedicated to special officials but it was simply an area dedicated to the lecturers of the university and the students who studied there. The place Rameez Bhai took me was a tributary of the Ravi River which was joined to a lake, with a backdrop of trees to one side. Once parked, Rameez Bhai removed the tent from the back of his car and I helped him to set it up. Although a large spacious tent, it became obvious that we would be sleeping quite close together.

We then set up a cooking area. As is required in Pakistan, the cooking area was set up in such a way to prevent the fire from spreading as loose embers had the potential to float on the wind and then cause raging bushfires. Rameez Bhai set up our fishing rods. We then cast our lines, sat by the lake and waited. Rameez Bhai was obviously much more adept at fishing than I had ever been and before long he had caught three large fish which eventually constituted part of our evening meal.

Later that afternoon, Rameez Bhai got a fire going over which he proceeded to cook the catch of the day. The fire was small and well-guarded, but this didn't completely stop its danger. In one moment there was a sudden gust of wind out of nowhere which blew the fire in such a way that a fog of embers suddenly enveloped us like a cloud of fire. I could feel the burning embers against my skin and I guess Rameez Bhai felt the same because we both acted reflexively and simply jumped into the lake. Soon we were once again standing up, completely sopping wet, looking down at our clothes. I looked at Rameez Bhai whose fantastic body had become even more evident through the clinging wet clothes around his body. I looked back at my clothes and could see pinpricks of holes where the embers had burnt through the cloth. Once we realized we were both okay, we sloshed back out of the water and returned back to the fire. Rameez Bhai checked the fish and after being satisfied that the fish was thoroughly cooked, he returned to the lake with a bucket of water and then poured it over the fire to completely extinguish it. There was an ebullient energy in his desire to ensure that all the fire had been thoroughly extinguished which intrigued me.

Eventually, when I thought about what had happened, there was something comic in it that caused me to laugh and comment on the ridiculousness of the situation. But Rameez Bhai looked on intently at the remnant of the fire which was now a damp, black mess. Then Rameez Bhai's face took on a terrible contortion and he began to sob uncontrollably. I was first at a loss what to do. Rameez Bhai was a grown man, and a man in an authoritative position at my university. Through his spasms he dropped the bucket and then tried to wipe his eyes with one hand while holding his other arm across his stomach.

"Sir?" I asked nervously and hesitantly. "Sir? It's okay. The fire's out."

Rameez Bhai was still spasming from his outbreak. Eventually, I just did what I thought I should do. I came over to him and put my arm over his shoulder.

"Sir," I said quietly, feeling strange that I, in my position as a student and an inferior was acting like the carer. "Sir, it's okay. The fire didn't spread anywhere. And we're okay. We're not burnt. And the fish is okay too. It was only an accident."

Rameez Bhai then just turned to face me, wrapped his two muscular arms around my shoulders and cried into my not-so-muscular chest. It was a very awkward and embarrassing situation to be in but I simply responded by rubbing his back.

Eventually Rameez Bhai was able to get a grip on himself.

"I'm so sorry," he finally spoke up when he pulled himself away from me. "I'm so sorry, Mustafa. Look at me crying like a baby."

I said everything was okay, although extremely puzzled by his sudden emotional outburst. We then began getting dinner ready. The sun had just kissed the horizon at this stage. Rameez Bhai suggested that we make another fire over the black, wet mass of charcoal. Despite the moisture, eventually another fire was burning and it looked so peaceful and serene in the backdrop of the darkness of the evening. Rameez Bhai said nothing to explain his strange emotional outburst but simply engaged in small talk while it appeared that he was trying to get his emotions back under his control.

Once we had eaten and completed our last prayers for the evening, we sat down next to the fire. Rameez Bhai had gone quiet for a moment and then he looked at me with a troubling expression on his face.

"Mustafa, do you believe in Jahannam like they say so in the Koran?" he asked.

I nodded in affirmation. The Koran speaks often and explicitly about Jahannam. This caused me to have flashbacks of the very first Mulvi who gave me religious instruction as a young child and this Mulvi ensured me again and again that such a horrible place existed.

"So," Rameez Bhai then continued, "I guess we had a taste of Jahannam earlier when that gust of wind blew embers onto our clothes. Did you feel the embers burning your body when they got onto your skin?"

I wasn't sure whether he meant this as a joke or that he was serious, so I simply nodded and then told him that I also felt the pinpricks of pain which made me spontaneously jump into the lake.

"Have you ever wondered," Rameez Bhai continued, "that you may not actually make it into paradise? Do you think you are good enough to make it? Don't you ever worry that you may slip in your faith and this result in you not making it into paradise after all?"

I had to agree with Rameez Bhai about this. In fact, this was the first time after such a long time that Jahannam had become once again a part of my consciousness and once again filled me with the fear of the possibility of ending up in this horrible place if I didn't follow the religion explicitly.

"Doesn't Jahannam make you question how compassionate Allah is?" Rameez Bhai then asked.

This sent a shiver down my spine because the very idea of even questioning Allah could anger Allah so much that He would force us into Jahannam, even though the question itself was valid.

"But also," Rameez Bhai continued, "when I die, what will happen to me? Is there really a paradise and a Jahannam like it says in the Koran? I know on the whole I'm not a bad person. But if I were to die tonight, would Allah think I was good enough to make it into paradise?"

I looked out into the distance and then back at Rameez Bhai.

"If you sincerely believe in Allah, in His Prophet Muhammad, and follow the five pillars of our faith, Muhammad will no doubt intercede on your behalf and you will then be granted passage into paradise."

Rameez Bhai remained quiet for a moment but eventually asked, "We only need to follow the five pillars of the Islamic faith to make it into paradise?"

I replied that this was so.

"So, does this mean all Sunnis and Shiites, Salafis and Ahmadiyyahs, all of these Muslims, despite their differences, will make it into paradise?"

"Yes," I replied in all confidence.

"And what about Christians and Jews," Rameez Bhai then asked. "Will they make it into paradise?"

"Well," I replied after a slight pause of thought, "it does say in Al-Baqarah 2:62, 'Indeed, those who believed and those who became Jews, and the Christians, and the Sabeans – who believed in Allah and the Last Day and did righteous deeds, will have their reward with the Lord'. So, yes, they will make it into paradise, too."

There was a moment of silence.

"Then," Rameez Bhai resumed, "if it requires believing in Allah and doing good deeds and following the five pillars of Islam, what happens when young children or babies die? Where do they go?"

The question stunned me. My thoughts ran through the imaginary Koran in my head to find an answer to this question but I realized the Koran does not address this issue. My Mulvi had once told me his take on this but this was written in the Hadiths and I had already dismissed the Hadiths as unreliable so I could not be sure if what he had told me was valid. While trying to find an answer, Rameez Bhai began to sob.

This stopped the conversation for a moment and I could see that Rameez Bhai was trying to fight his emotions, as it was generally believed that grown men shouldn't cry. The distraught look on his face and his bloodshot eyes with tears welling in them like pools was a distressing view to behold. Eventually Rameez Bhai was able to compose himself and apologized for his repeated sudden emotional outburst. He paused for a moment and then spoke again.

"My wife and our one year old daughter died in a car accident last year –" Rameez Bhai began but did not finish the sentence, although what was not said was understood. Out of sympathy, I simply put my arm around his shoulder until he was able to compose himself again. Now I realized all the questioning. Eventually Rameez Bhai could hold himself together.

"It's okay," he then said. "I'm sorry. I know it's not very manly to weep like a baby."

I removed my arm from his shoulder and we both stared at the fire.

"Mustafa," Rameez Bhai then said and looked at me, "I'm really glad to have met you. And I'm really glad to talk to you because you are one of the few Muslims I know who really knows the Koran well and the depths of the religion.

And you listen to me and don't judge me for questioning. I'd really like to talk to you more."

What Rameez Bhai said touched me to the very heart and once again removed all the doubts and contentions I had about my religion. I was further touched that someone much older than me looked up to me when it came to questions about religion.

But I also realized that I really didn't have an answer to Rameez Bhai's question. What happens to babies and young children who die too young to know who Allah is and who have never practised any of the five pillars of Islam?

That evening under the canopy of stars and the sounds of the night serenading us, Rameez Bhai and I engaged in conversation totally unrelated to religion. Rameez opened up to me about his life. He told me where he had grown up, why he had become a gym instructor and how he ended up at our university doing the work he did. He shared stories of his childhood, amusing stories about awkward moments in his teen years and of proud moments in his later life. I listened intently as he opened up his entire life to me.

Soon it was time for us to go to bed. That night we slept together in the tent. It was somewhat awkward sleeping so close to an adult who was also an authoritative figure but eventually I was able to fall asleep.

Back at the university after our camping trip, one evening in the cafeteria, while sitting with all my classmates, I put the question to all of them completely out of the blue.

"Where do babies and young children go when they die when they are too young to know who Allah is?" I asked.

"What on earth made you ask that?" one of those sitting at the table asked me in such a way that it sounded as if it were a question that was too irrelevant to ask.

"I found out that a friend of mine," I continued, not revealing who this friend was, "had a wife and a young child of one year who died in an accident. He asked me where his young daughter is now, in paradise or somewhere else."

This caused a flurry of conversation. Some of my university friends just made comments like, what did it matter? Why should we worry about such a thing? We are all now grown up. Allah will deal with the children who die too young to know who Allah was. One of them said that Allah knew what their future would be anyway and would decide their fate based on that. This was met with a violent rebuttal that it would not be fair of Allah to decide the fate of a young child on what he or she might have done with their lives. It isn't fair to judge people on things that they might have done, they should be judged on what they actually did. Otherwise, why didn't Allah just end the world right now and start Judgement Day and simply send all those people yet to be born to paradise or Jahannam based on what Allah surmised they would have done had they been given a chance to live?

Another said that if the parents were Muslims, the child would automatically go to paradise whereas children of non-Muslims would go to Jahannam. This was counterclaimed by another who said that this would not be fair because children can't be blamed for what their parents did. As it was, some people grow up in Jewish or Christian homes and in later life convert to the true religion of Islam so it would be totally unfair to just assume that the children of parents of a different faith by default end up burning forever in the fires of Jahannam.

Yet another said that he had heard that all children below the age of reason go to paradise but to the lowest part of paradise where they will enjoy a limited form of paradisiacal pleasures. This occurred irrespective of the religion of the parents. Again, this was counterclaimed, someone arguing that it was unfair that young children who died before the age of reason went to a lesser paradise simply because they never had the opportunity to prove that they were worthy to make it into a higher level of heaven.

What impressed me the most was that while my uni friends made propositions of what they thought would happen to babies and young children when they die too young to know enough about Allah and the Islamic faith, none of them quoted from the Koran to support their answers. And in fact, what they said found absolutely no support from the Koran at all. What they were saying was what they would like the situation to be rather than providing evidence from the Koran as to what the situation actually was.

From this discussion, yet another issue puzzled me. If what was required to get into paradise was a conscious effort to actually follow the five pillars of Islam, why would Allah even allow babies and young children to die in the first place? If this life we lived in were a test that the Almighty Creator of the universe had set for all humans to determine whether or not they were worthy of paradise, it made absolutely no sense why Allah did not give each and every human being an exact amount of life time to be able to carry out the five pillars. Further, because we earned reward points for the number of times we observed the different pillars, this meant that the longer the lifespan a person had, the greater number of reward points that person could earn to be used in the blissful life in paradise. If, for example, good Muslims who said all their prayers regularly and fasted every single Ramadan and Eid-ul-Adha and then died in their early twenties, they could never gain the same number of reward points as good Muslims who had said all their prayers and did all the fasts and then died at, say, seventy. Would the diligent, fully observant Muslims who died in old age be rewarded much greater than the diligent, fully observant Muslims who died at young ages? And what would have been the reasoning for Allah allowing one person to live to seventy and gain a much greater number of reward points while another was forced to die at a much earlier age and gain so much less when that same person who had died young would probably have gained the overabundance of reward points had they been given enough lifetime to do so?

And then what about Jews, Christians and Sabeans? The Koran says that these people also will receive their reward, yet these people do not follow the five pillars of Islam but follow a different set of rites and rules. And if Jews and Christians will go to paradise, why did Allah need to send Muhammad as a new prophet to establish a new religion if there were already religions Allah had established on earth through which people could make it into paradise? Suddenly I had a fresh, new lot of questions which were poured like a carbonate salt into the bubbling pot of my acid solution of confusion.

The conversations that Rameez Bhai and I engaged in obviously led to Rameez Bhai's increased religious fervour. Prior to meeting him, I had never seen him once in the prayer room for Friday prayer. However, now he came every Friday at exactly the same time as I went there and we prayed together. After prayers, we often sat together and discussed aspects of our religion with readings from the Koran. Some of my university friends who only made a sporadic appearance for prayer would often later make derogatory comments about me and how I came across as excessive in my religion. However, others were a lot more sympathetic and praised me for my devotion, commenting that they wished they had my determination in the faith. Some of them even asked why I was bothering to study a science at university and rather not doing religious studies so that I could become a Mulvi or other religious scholar. While I could understand what they were saying, at the same time I thought of Muhammad, the founder of our religion. Muhammad, so we had been told, was a merchant and he managed to hold down an occupation while being a religious leader, although I guessed when I really thought about it, Muhammad eventually had to give up his occupation as a merchant to lead the people the way he did. Even so, I didn't feel the calling to become a religious scholar but felt that I could still carry out my duties as a humble servant of Allah while working in an occupation of a secular kind.

The Jahannam issue obviously troubled Rameez Bhai immensely as he often came back to this subject. He himself raised the question as to how Allah could be compassionate and yet He created the unimaginably torturous hell as it is described in the Koran. This idea about Allah sounded so incongruent. Further, the idea was raised as to what would happen if his wife and baby daughter hadn't made it into paradise but Rameez Bhai had, and so he was forced to watch helplessly from the sidelines while his wife and baby daughter suffered in agony. It says in Ibrahim 14:49, 50 about those living in paradise that they "will see the sinners that day bound together in fetters their garments of liquid pitch, and their faces covered with fire". While standing on the outside of Jahannam looking in at his wife and baby daughter suffering unimaginable torture, was Rameez Bhai supposed to turn to Allah and say to Him, "Yes, Allah, You are the most Compassionate and the most Merciful. You are the greatest!" and then turn back and watch on while his wife and baby daughter yelled and screamed in pain, their bodies being contorted by the flames and in place of their heads was what looked like the top end of a burning torch? I didn't have answers to these questions either and the thought was sickening, causing me to raise questions and doubts about my faith. But I knew there had to be logical answers to explain all this and eventually I would be able to explain this to Rameez Bhai.

Suddenly, without warning, one Friday, Rameez Bhai didn't turn up for prayers. He had been so meticulous, almost like clockwork, coming to pray every Friday, especially as the idea of Jahannam drove him to dedicate himself entirely to the religion.

It wasn't until the next time I went to the gym to do a workout that I saw him and was able to question him about it. I noticed this time during this workout that there was a sudden lack of discussion about religion and Rameez Bhai was completely focused on my exercise program and how I was progressing. When I had completed my hour, I questioned Rameez Bhai.

"I noticed you didn't come for prayer last Friday," I stated.

"No, I didn't," Rameez Bhai replied rather evasively. "I went on Saturday."

The expression on my face must have said everything because of what Rameez Bhai then asked me.

"Mustafa, would you like to go camping with me again?"

Again, I didn't say anything, bewildered by this sudden change in behaviour.

"I have something to tell you," he then added. "But not here. I need to tell you in private."

The following Saturday afternoon, Rameez Bhai and I went back to the camping ground we had gone to earlier. Contrary to his character in the past, Rameez Bhai talked about everything and anything that was not related to religion. However, I could feel that Rameez Bhai was avoiding the issue, or more to the point that he was building up enough courage to say what he needed to tell me.

We eventually finished eating and Rameez Bhai boiled water over the fire to make tea. While the tea brewed, it was like Rameez Bhai was also brewing in his mind what he wanted to say to me. Once he felt ready, he first looked at the fire and then turned to me.

"Mustafa, I've become a Lashkari Muslim."

I looked at Rameez Bhai bewildered.

"You've become a, what is it?" I asked perplexed.

"A Lashkari Muslim. There is a new prophet who has appeared in Pakistan, Ahmad. He has come as a Messenger and a Holy Prophet to the Urdu speakers of Pakistan, bringing a new holy book."

"An Urdu-speaking prophet? A Messenger and a Holy Prophet? Of what religion?"

Rameez Bhai looked at me a little perplexed.

"Of Islam," he replied as if this were obvious.

"An Urdu-speaking prophet of Islam?" I asked. "But how can there be a Prophet in our modern times? It is quite clear in Al-Ahzab 33:40 that Muhammad is the last of the prophets."

Rameez Bhai poured tea into our mugs, handed me mine and then placed his on the ground beside him.

"Yes, it says in that verse that Muhammad is the *Seal* of the prophets. But that doesn't mean that He is the last. And in any case, the Koran says that there will be future prophets after Muhammad."

"Future prophets after Muhammad? How can that be?" I asked perplexed.

Rameez Bhai got up, went to the tent and returned with his Koran. He then sat back down, flicked through the pages until he reached the page of his choosing. He looked at me and then back down at the Koran.

"Listen to what it says here in Yunus 10:47: 'And for every nation is a Messenger'. If Muhammad was the last Prophet, then who is the prophet to Pakistan? Pakistan became a nation in 1947 and Allah promised in His holy book that 'for every nation is a Messenger.' Allah says this again in An-Nahl 16:36, 'And certainly We sent to every nation a Messenger.' If Allah sent a Messenger to every nation, then once Pakistan had become a nation, then Allah had to send a Messenger to uphold the integrity of the Koran, His Holy Book."

Rameez Bhai spoke with such eagerness and enthusiasm but this troubled me. This went against all I had learnt about my religion, because we had been told over and over that Muhammad was the last and greatest prophet, so great that Allah no longer needed to send any more messengers. The verse that had been used to support this was the verse from Al-Ahzab 33:40. This verse says that Muhammad is the Seal of the Prophets. We had always assumed that this meant that Muhammad was the last of the prophets. But on reflection, and from what Rameez Bhai himself said, "seal" doesn't necessarily mean "last". And when I really thought about it, I realized that I could not see a direct connection between the words "seal" and "last". But I knew that there had to be one because my Mulvi and all our religious leaders had told us that this was so. However, in the light of the verse from Yunus 10:47 which states that "for every nation is a Messenger", and seeing new nations came into being after Muhammad had died, and no doubt Allah knew that there would be new future nations after Muhammad, this led to the obvious conclusion, that when it says that Muhammad is the Seal of the Prophets, this had to have a different meaning to what we had traditionally been told. Otherwise this would be a contradiction in the Koran, where on the one hand it is understood that Muhammad was the last messenger and there would be no more messengers after him, and yet on the other hand it is understood that there would be later messengers after Muhammad sent to the new, emerging nations that would arise in the future times after Muhammad's death.

But that wasn't the only challenge to what we had been traditionally told about Muhammad and the Koran. Why did we need a new Koran and one in Urdu?

"Because," Rameez Bhai continued in full enthusiasm, "as it says in Surah Ibrahim 14:4, 'And We did not send any Messenger except in the language of his people so that he might make the Message clear to them.' We are not Arabs and our first language is not Arabic. We are Pakistani and we speak English and Urdu. English is spoken in many countries but Urdu is specifically the language of Pakistan. Allah has finally fulfilled His promise and sent us a

Messenger speaking in the Urdu language and bringing us a Koran in this tongue."

No, I thought, as we had been told, Muhammad was the great prophet, the last prophet. I could feel myself getting all worked up.

"No, this is not true. These verses don't mean what you say they mean," I stated indignantly and also in nervousness.

"Well, if they don't mean this," Rameez Bhai replied softly, "then what do these verses mean?"

"I don't know but they don't mean what you say they mean," I stated militantly.

"But that's not an answer," Rameez Bhai replied softly and confidently. "You can't say these verses mean something other than what they say and then not explain how."

I couldn't resist the peacefulness in Rameez Bhai's composure, as if suddenly all the chaos that had been tormenting him had finally come to rest. This only made me all the more confused and anxious.

"I don't know. I will eventually find out," I cried out in despair.

"Mustafa, please be calm," Rameez Bhai then said to pacify me.

This was a jolt back to reality. I took a few deep breaths.

"So, what does this Ahmad teach?"

Rameez Bhai sat back and adjusted himself.

"You know all those verses in the Koran which talk about Jahannam? Well, Ahmad says that these verses have now been abrogated. As it says in An-Nahl 16:101, 'We substitute one verse for another verse, and Allah is most knowing of what He sent down' and in Al-Baqarah 2:106 'Whatever we abrogate of a verse…We bring a better one'. Ahmad said that it had been revealed to him by Allah that these verses about Jahannam and the terrors of this place are abrogated – replaced – with better verses which talk of better punishments and more in line with Allah's compassion and mercy."

"Better punishments?" I gasped.

"Yes, better punishments. Punishments that are commensurate with the crime. But also punishments that take into consideration those who are related or connected to those being punished. You see, what Ahmad said was that we are not isolated individuals. While we are on earth, we make connections with family and friends, and we also make enemies. Sometimes we make enemies because we purposefully do bad things to people, and sometimes we make enemies because other people want to use and control us and we won't allow this. On Judgement Day, when it comes to deciding our fate, we can call to witness those we have loved and done good deeds to to testify of our good works. Our enemies can also testify against us. But Allah will know whether our enemies intended bad to us simply because of their own evil character or they will lay testimony to Allah of the bad things we truly have done to these people and that we deserve to be punished accordingly. Allah will take all this into consideration. So I can testify on behalf of my wife that she was not a bad person and had been a good wife, and that she should be spared punishment even if she appeared to be not a very good Muslim."

All this was confusing and upsetting. It was one thing to hear him say that there was a new prophet in our time and further a new prophet who spoke our language. It was another to hear about a Koran that had verses changed where older ones were substituted with better verses. Can a perfect Allah bring better verses into His already perfect book? But while this was logically impossible, Rameez Bhai supported this claim with verses from this very Koran.

But what really struck me deep within my soul were the punishments we received on Judgement Day. We had always been told that Allah was the Compassionate and the

Merciful and yet those who did not follow Him and His Book explicitly would suffer unimaginable punishment for the rest of eternity. And that was the cold reality. But now I was hearing about another Allah, one who was much more compassionate and much more merciful than the one I had known. Instead of depending on the clemency of the Prophet, someone we had never met, to intercede on our behalf, we could call on the clemency of family members and friends, people we have loved and been good to. In fact, I saw the deeper repercussions of such a theology. Anyone who believed in what Ahmad claimed about Judgement Day would ensure that during this lifetime they did good to as many people as they could because they relied on these people on Judgement Day to plead for them. But as much as this sounded like a better theology, it was not from the Koran, not from Muhammad.

"No, sir," I stated. "This is all wrong. Don't be led by Shaitaan. You know how Shaitaan can mislead us into believing in the wrong God and then Allah will send us to –" but I couldn't end the statement because it simply showed up how sadistic the Allah of the Koran really was.

I stood up. I was trembling from anger and confusion. I wanted to run away from this place but I was trapped as we were in a remote place and it was now dark.

"Mustafa! Mustafa! Please, settle down," Rameez Bhai commanded. "You're being irrational!"

Because he was an authority figure, I instinctively obeyed.

"Mustafa," he then said softly. "Come and sit down."

I sat back down next to him and stared into the fire.

"Mustafa," he then continued. "Don't make conclusions straight away. I know this sounds new and different, and I felt the same way when I heard about this. But let Allah and His truth shine through. If Ahmad is wrong, let it be proved."

He then paused before continuing. "When you have a chance, read from Ahmad's Koran. As it says in the Koran, in Surah Az-Zumar 39:23 that 'Allah has revealed from time to time the most beautiful message in the form of a Book. The skins of those who fear their Lord tremble thereat'. See how Allah reveals beautiful messages in books from time to time? He has revealed the new Koran in Urdu. And I have read it. And I can tell you that my skin trembled when I read it. This already to me is the evidence that this new Koran is from Allah."

Rameez Bhai paused for a moment, and then turned to me and stared straight into my eyes.

"It may be," Rameez Bhai concluded, "that it is Shaitaan who is trying to stop you reading it and seeing the light of Allah through it."

The look in Rameez Bhai's eyes and what he said were mesmerizing. It took a moment for me to say something in return.

"Do you have a copy of his Koran here?" I asked.

"No," Rameez Bhai replied and then sat back. "As you probably can appreciate, Ahmad's Koran cannot freely circulate here at this time. What he is saying will no doubt stir up a lot of resistance. But remember. That's what happened to all the prophets before Ahmad. It happened when Muhammad came. It happened when Issa came. However, I can give you a pdf copy of it. Read it for yourself and then make a judgement."

Rameez Bhai then placed his arm over my shoulder and squeezed me into his chest as punctuation for the end of this statement.

"Believe me, you'll have a completely new outlook on our religion once you have read Ahmad's Koran. It will change your life."

Rameez Bhai then removed his arm and stood up.

"Anyway, it's late, now," he concluded. "I think we should go to bed. We can continue this discussion at another time. Once you've read Ahmad's revelation from Allah, I'd like to discuss this further."

Chapter 16

That Rameez Bhai had begun to follow a supposedly Muslim religion which centred on a prophet who came after Muhammad meant that Rameez Bhai was endangering his entire eternal life. If he continued in this belief, eventually he would reach a point of no return which meant he would become swept up into a belief system so far removed from the pure version of Islam we were all familiar with and this would inevitably result in him experiencing the horrors of hell for eternity as a result.

I needed professional help. I also wanted anonymous help. People who held to heretical ideas in Pakistan were often met with brutal attacks. Already there was an underlying cold war between the Sunnis and the Shiites in Pakistan which sometimes erupted like a dormant volcano into conflagrations from time to time. Sects considered further outside the conventionally accepted and tolerated Sunni and Shiite sects were treated a lot worse. In particular, adherents to the Ahmadiyyah movement, started by Mirza Ghulam Ahmad in the late 1800s, were often met with violence and were totally refused to be accepted as Muslims by the Sunni-Shiite pact. This was something at least that the Sunnis and Shiites could agree on, even though much of what members of the Ahmadiyyah movement believed about Islam was the same as what the Sunnis and Shiites believed, in particular, that Muhammad was the prophet from Allah, the Koran was the holy book of Allah and that there were five pillars of Islam. The principal belief held by the Ahmadiyyah movement that Sunnis and Shiites could not tolerate was that Ahmadiyyahs believed in a prophet who came after Muhammad. Worse, this prophet claimed to establish a genealogical line of prophets descendant from Mirza Ghulam Ahmad, a sort of dynasty where each successive prophet or caliph was replaced after he had died by someone of the successive generation.

I'm not sure what worried me more about Rameez Bhai, the potential violence that would be inflicted on him in this life, or the surety of the violence inflicted on him in the next.

I eventually went to one of the Sunni mosques in the centre of the town and organised an audience with the local imam. Accompanying the imam was a madrassa boy of about thirteen years of age who the imam spoke to as if this young boy were his valet. At one time, the imam told the madrassa boy to bring tea for him and me. I then gave the imam the background about this new prophet and what Rameez Bhai had told me about him without revealing Rameez Bhai's name. Once I had completed the background, the madrassa boy returned with a silver tray, and well balanced on it were two mugs of tea. He then offered one to the imam and the other to me. I thanked him for the tea and then turned back to the imam.

"What am I to do?" I asked him.

"The Ahmadiyyahs believe that they have a new prophet. They follow his teachings and interpretations of the Koran. I'm sure everything written in their literature and their interpretations of the Koran are all wrong."

"The Ahmadiyyahs believe in a new prophet after Muhammad, peace be upon him," the madrassa boy commented. I was quite surprised that he felt he had the right to express his opinion. But what was really creepy was that I could see elements of me in this madrassa boy when I was his age, young, idealistic and totally unaware of the problems in my religion that I would later be exposed to.

"That's evidence enough," he continued in full assuredness. "We don't need any more prophets after Muhammad to teach us the right path to Allah. We already have the Koran and the Hadiths which tell us the correct message. And, anyway, if he wants to be swept along by this new heretical faith just to follow his own desires and then go to Jahannam, that's up to him. He'll find out on Judgement Day what a big mistake he made!"

The imam with a hand gesture dismissed the madrassa boy, and the madrassa boy turned and left. However, I was horrified by this comment. I couldn't cope with the callousness of it. Rameez Bhai was no-one of consequence in his life so it was so easy for him to simply condemn Rameez Bhai to eternal torture.

"He's actually not following the Ahmadiyyah religion," I corrected. "It's a religion called Lashkari Islam. But like the Ahmadiyyahs, their prophet's name is Ahmad."

"Another self-proclaimed prophet," the imam then said. "May this false prophet and those who blindly follow him be condemned to an eternity of torture!"

Now it was the imam's comment I was horrified to hear. But I also knew this was the general default comment. As soon as anyone proposed ideas contrary to the status quo belief, it was an instant "send them to eternal torture". There was no thought of, "Mmmmm. So let's investigate this. What are these people actually saying? Could there be any truth to any of it? Is it possible that this is actually from Allah?"

The imam knew nothing about Lashkari Islam and this new prophet, and in the end could not help me any further except to tell me that it was clear in the Koran that Muhammad was the Seal of the Prophets, which he interpreted as we had always done that Muhammad was the last of the prophets, so for anyone to claim that there were any prophets after Muhammad and any holy books apart from the Koran, this was evidence enough that this new prophet was not from Allah.

I went away from this imam no more enlightened than I had been when I went to see him. But what kept going through my mind when this imam made this accusation against those who claim that there were prophets after Muhammad was that it sounded extremely similar to the religions prior to Islam.

In particular, I thought of Christianity. I remember reading in the New Testament what was claimed about Issa. In the Gospels, Issa recounts a parable about a man who owns an extensive vineyard and then hires workers to maintain it. Every now and again, the owner of the vineyard sends messengers to get fruit from the workers. But each time a messenger is sent, the maintainers of the vineyard beat the messenger or kill him. In the end, the owner of the vineyard sends his beloved son thinking that the workers in the vineyard will reverence him. Of course, they don't, but rather kill him, and so the owner of the vineyard finally comes and destroys them. The point of the story was that Issa, like the son of the vineyard owner, was the last messenger sent to preach to the people on earth, represented by the workers of the vineyard. In fact, the New Testament is clear in showing that Issa was the last and greatest prophet. And I had heard Christians claim that Jesus was the last messenger, the understanding being that any messengers after Issa could only be false prophets. I could imagine that those in Christian majority countries would make the same claim about Muslims, that it was obvious Muslims were going to hell because it was clear that there was no prophet after Issa and no book was sent by Allah after Allah sent down the New Testament. So when Muhammad came, it was quite understandable why the Christians totally rejected Muhammad. I imagined being a Christian in the early 7th Century and being told that there was someone claiming to be a new prophet, Muhammad, with a new book, the Koran, when as a Christian we already had a Messenger, Issa, and the Book from Allah, the Torah and the Injeel. Without further investigation, it would have been quite easy to have simply dismissed Muhammad simply because he was the new prophet on the street.

There was therefore a danger in being dismissive. It could be history repeating itself. The Jews rejected Issa because they believed that Moses was the great prophet and there was no need for a new book after the Torah. The Christians rejected Muhammad because they believed that Issa was the last and greatest prophet and there was no need for a new book after the Injeel. Was it possible that Muslims could be making the same mistake, rejecting Ahmad simply because they believe we no longer need another prophet after Muhammad and another book after the Koran?

The difficulty in Pakistan was getting information. Information outside what was allowed by the Islamic government and anything that was considered un-Islamic, even if this information was backed by what was written in the Koran, was difficult to come by. Knowledge was best acquired via the internet and even then that was in some ways policed. I eventually was able to find out information about the Lashkari Islam movement through an anonymous blogger.

From this blog I discovered the origins of Lashkari Islam. It all started in the 1900s when India was still part of the British Empire and Pakistan had not as yet become a nation. In the north west of British India, south west of the Kashmir region, there had been a great forest fire. Many villages in the area were affected and many people were killed. A few managed to escape. In particular a woman who was heavily pregnant managed to escape on the water on a make-shift raft which floated her out of the smoke and came to rest further down the river where the raft settled on the bank. There she was discovered by a local farmer of the township who had observed the smoke from the distant mountains. The local farmer took her back to his place where his wife looked after her. The woman from the raft told the farmer and his wife about the fire, the great smoke, and why she had fled on the raft, all of which the farmer, his wife and all those in this small township had witnessed from a distance in any case. The woman then told the farmer and his wife that she knew she was going to die that night and so she wanted them to raise the child. She also told the farmer's wife that Allah had heard her prayer because the farmer's wife was barren and she would never be able to sire her own children, but now the son she had prayed for would be born. Later that night, the woman went into labour. At one moment during her labour, she suddenly went into deep reverie and said that she could see in a vision from the same place she had fled a brilliant light shining over the mountain. Suddenly there was a great earthquake and the mountain split into two, forming two peaks, and the great light continued to shine over both peaks. Then she gave out a great cry and her son was born. Later that night, the woman herself died.

The news of the arrival of the woman on the raft spread through the small township and eventually reached the local religious authorities. The religious authorities saw something significant in this child because of what it said in Surah Ad-Dukhan 44:10 – 13, that they were to "Watch for the day when the sky will bring a visible smoke…when, verily there had come to them a reminder."

The farmer and his wife raised the child. They decided to dedicate the child to Allah and give him proper religious instruction on top of a standard school education. The farmer and his wife decided to call this new child Ahmad, a variant of the name Muhammad, in honour of Allah and the prophet who had answered their prayer to bring this couple a child. Little did they realize at the time that the choice of name was prophetic, for in Surah As-Saff 61:6, Issa prophesied that a Messenger would come after him "whose name will be Ahmad."

Ahmad grew up in the turmoil that followed the establishment of Pakistan as an independent country. He was sent to the madrassa to learn about his religion and to be able to read the Koran. But what troubled him the most was the constant conflict between the Sunnis and the Shiites. Although his father, the farmer who had found his mother on the raft, was a Shiite, Ahmad could understand the Sunni approach to Islam, especially as he felt that the Shiite veneration of Ali was sheerk. But Allah had directed his biological mother to be discovered by Shiite Muslims and ensured his survival through them. This made him unsure as to which was the correct version to follow. But what completely struck him was that according to either religion, it wasn't only those who didn't believe in Allah and his Messenger that were going to Jahannam, those who followed the wrong sect of Islam would also be going to Jahannam. So what if the Sunnis were right? Ahmad recognized that his parents were poor and illiterate. As a result, they simply did not have access to learning. Further, they couldn't read and secondly they did not speak a word of Arabic and hence would not have been able to read the Koran even if they had been literate. As a result, they were completely reliant on the religious authorities of their sect. And because they were not very well educated, they naturally believed everything their Shiite religious scholars told them. So, if Shiites were going to Jahannam, this meant that Ahmad's parents were going to Jahannam. This came to Ahmad as an injustice on Allah's part.

As Ahmad grew, he helped his father with farm work and on many nights he read the Koran to his parents, first reading it in Arabic and then translating it into Urdu. What puzzled Ahmad was that it didn't matter which language one spoke, there was one message. His parents did not speak Arabic, but from Ahmad's translation, his parents eventually got the message in Urdu. Hence, this need to do everything in Arabic greatly troubled him.

It was when Ahmad read the verse from Yunus 10:47 which says that "for every nation is a Messenger" and the verse from Surah Ibrahim 14:4 which says, "And We did not send any Messenger except in the language of his people so that he might make the Message clear to them" that Ahmad realized the truth. Because Allah does not lie, this meant that because Pakistan had become a new nation and that the local language was Urdu, Allah would soon send a message through a Pakistani prophet in the Urdu language. As a result, Ahmad prayed earnestly every night for this messenger to come. Little did he realize at the time that he was that chosen Messenger.

Ahmad grew and while he learnt the occupation of his father, there were times when he would retreat into an isolated place away from the township to meditate. It was on the night of the spring equinox when Ahmad had gone to meditate that Ahmad suddenly saw a shining light descend, more brilliant than the sun. It was the angel Gabriel. Gabriel spoke to Ahmad, confirming that the smoke from which his mother had fled was a fulfilment of the prophecy in Ad-Dukhan, that Ahmad had been chosen to be the reminder to the nascent Pakistani nation, to bring the message in a new book, the *Kitab-e-Hidayat*, or as it is in English, *The Enlightened Book*, as Allah had promised in the Koran. Gabriel then presented a book to Ahmad in the form of a scroll.

"Eat it," Gabriel said. "It will be bitter to the mouth but sweet to the belly. Once you have eaten it, the words will become part of you. Write the words down. But keep the book hidden in the east until I come again to you." And then Gabriel left him.

Ahmad did as he was told. As Gabriel had said, the taste of the scroll was bitter to the mouth but once eaten it felt sweet inside his belly.

He returned home and told his parents about the vision. His parents were not sure what to make of it. Their only comment was that it was possible that Allah had revealed to him a vision but they did not know what else to tell him.

That night Ahmad went to his room. While his parents slept, he couldn't sleep. He felt the impulse to write. So he got out of bed, took out one of his exercise books from school and began writing. And he wrote. And he kept writing until late into the night. Once completed, he looked for a place to hide the exercise book in which he had been writing. Gabriel had said to hide it "in the east", so Ahmad hid it in a secure place in the east of his room. He then got into bed and went to sleep. Three months later, on the day of the summer solstice, Ahmad once again went out to the isolated place to meditate. Once again, Gabriel appeared to him. This time he told Ahmad to make a copy of the Kitab-e-Hidayat but this time he was to keep it hidden in the north. Once back home, after his parents had gone to bed, he did what the angel Gabriel had told him, wrote another copy of the Kitab-e-Hidayat and when he had finished it, he hid what he had written in the north of his room. This was repeated at the autumn equinox and the winter solstice. After having written the book four times and having hidden each copy, one in the east of his room, one in the north, one in the west and one in the south, in a dream, Gabriel appeared to him once again but this time in a strange form because Gabriel had four arms. And in each hand he held a scroll, and each arm pointed in the direction of one of the cardinal points: east, north, west and south. Ahmad knew what the message Gabriel was giving him. He had written four copies of the Kitab-e-Hidayat. And it was now time to go out and spread the message.

Ahmad first read the Kitab-e-Hidayat to his parents. His parents marvelled at the wonder of the text. They immediately understood that this book was just too beautiful to be the creation of humans and so it had to have come from Allah. They further realised that Ahmad not only was the promised child they had prayed for. Ahmad was also called to be a prophet of Allah.

Ahmad tried to spread the message but it was received with contempt. He first spoke with the local imam of the Shiite community. The imam simply said, "You have just invented it. You are just a clever poet. Bring us a sign like the former Messengers brought if you speak truly." Ahmad spoke of his origins and of the visitation by the angel Gabriel. But the imam simply wouldn't listen and told Ahmad that he was merely a mischievous boy. If he truly were a messenger, so the imam claimed, he would be able perform a miracle, a sign, to confirm his calling as a prophet. Ahmad then told this imam, "Yes, I will bring you a sign. Come the next spring equinox, before the monsoon season while it is still dry, behold, there will be a terrible storm and this mosque will be struck severely by lightning." The imam simply laughed and mocked him, together with all those congregated at the mosque, and Ahmad was sent away.

Ahmad then spoke with the local imam of the Sunni community. This imam said, "You have just invented it. You are just a clever poet. Bring us a sign like the former Messengers brought if you speak truly. Are we to leave the Koran and follow a mad poet, a young boy like you? Are you telling us to abandon the religion that our forefathers believed in?" Once again, Ahmad spoke of his origins and of the visitation of the angel Gabriel. But the imam would not listen and once again Ahmad was told that if he could perform a miracle, this would convince the imam of his calling. Ahmad then told this imam, "Yes, I will bring a sign. At the next spring equinox, before the monsoon season has yet started and it is still dry, behold, there will be a terrible storm, and this mosque will be badly damaged by a great gust of wind." The imam simply laughed together with those congregated at the mosque and Ahmad was sent away.

The following spring equinox, there developed a great thunderstorm. The people of the township found this extremely strange and frightening that a great storm developed too early in the year because the monsoon season always started later in the summer. It was quite a violent storm, bringing down heavy rain with a majestic yet terrifying display of lightning accompanied by strong gusts of winds. The two buildings, however, that suffered the most from the storm were the Shiite mosque, which was struck by a large bolt of lightning, and the Sunni mosque which was greatly damaged by a strong gust of wind.

But even these clear miraculous signs did not convince the imams of the Shiite and Sunni mosques that Ahmad was a messenger of Allah. These imams obstinately refused to believe in Ahmad's message. However, many who had heard Ahmad prophesy the sign of the storm at the spring equinox now believed and became convinced that Ahmad was a messenger, and so a serious following developed. But pretty soon Ahmad was met with terrible reprisals and death threats which meant that he had to escape. He and his closest disciples escaped to India, to Gujarat. His disciples quickly made the decision to make copies of the Kitab-e-Hidayat. One of his disciples, Rumainsa, who later became Ahmad's wife, took the manuscript and wrote it up in beautiful calligraphy and created the beautiful artistic copy that the final form would be replicated in.

Ahmad married when he was thirty-three and had two daughters. He was captured by fanatics at the age of 40 and brutally murdered. However, his disciples continue the work of spreading his message from India, trying to win the hearts of the Pakistanis to the message of Allah in the language of the people.

Rameez Bhai, as promised, brought to me a pdf copy of the Kitab-e-Hidayat on a USB that I then loaded onto my laptop. There was also a sound recording of someone reading, or probably better said, chanting the text so that I could both listen and read along at the same time. I listened to the chanting with earphones on. I certainly couldn't have this sacrilegious text being read out aloud in our dormitory.

The first thing that struck me about the Kitab-e-Hidayat was that I could understand it on first listening to it. Whereas Arabic is a foreign tongue and as a child I could only appreciate the beauty of the recitation of the Koran on first hearing it because of the mysteriousness of the sound, the recitation of the Kitab-e-Hidayat was both beautiful to listen to and further I understood every word the reciter was saying as it was in my own language. Just as the Koran states that when we listen to the Koran, it causes us to shiver, the Kitab-e-Hidayat caused a shiver to pass through my spine and out to my extremities as I listened to the reciter chant the verses of this new Koran in the Urdu language. In fact, just on the first listening, it was absolutely mesmerising. And as it was with the result of eating the book as the angel Gabriel had commanded Ahmad, my first reaction was resistance because it was foreign and new, but once I had begun to read it and allowed it to enter my consciousness, the message was sweet within me.

But what really struck me completely was the layout. The Koran is arranged into surahs. Each surah has a different number of verses, and, starting with the second surah, Al-Baqarah, as we proceed through the Koran, the surahs become shorter and shorter until we reach the final surah, Surah An-Nas. In the Kitab-e-Hidayat, by contrast, the very first and the very last chapter are both called *ibadats*, that is, prayers, made up of seven verses. Between these two ibadats are the 98 *sabaks*, or lessons. Each sabak is made up of exactly 49 verses. There is a total of 100 parts, two short ibadats and 98 sabaks, 98 being twice 49, 49 being seven times seven, and hence the number seven featured prominently in the entire structure. The symmetry of it was amazing. Just looking at the structure of the Kitab-e-Hidayat, it was difficult, almost impossible, to view it as simply the work of a mad poet. Rather, by contrast, it was the work of a genius.

But also the message it conveyed was beautifully arranged. Many of the sabaks talked about one of the prophets of the past and from this prophet a lesson and a point of instruction was made.

What intrigued me was that Muhammad, the Arabic prophet, was only mentioned in one sabak, one prophet amongst the others. While much of the content was familiar, it was the part about how Muhammad was an Arabic prophet sent to the Arabs that intrigued me. But it became more intriguing when it said in Kitab-e-Hidayat why the horrors of Jahannam were so explicit. As it says in Al-Taubah 9:97, "Arabs are stronger in disbelief and hypocrisy and more likely not to know the limits of what Allah has revealed to His Messenger", and it was because of this strong inclination to disbelief and hypocrisy that the Arabs required a strong description of the horrors of the afterlife to get them to act righteously. I was absolutely stunned by this comment about the Arabs in the Koran and when I looked it up in my Arabic-English interlinear, I was amazed to see that this was so. What troubled me was that the English translation of the Arabic word in this verse, *al-a'raabu*, that is "Arabs", was "Bedouins". Or possibly it was the Arabic translator who was troubled and chose to translate the word as "Bedouins". As awful as this portrayal of the Arabs comes across in the Arabic holy Book, this actually gave greater credence to the idea that the descriptions of Jahannam were not to be taken as horrific as they came across in the Koran. It also created a plausible explanation as to how the reality of Jahannam was not the ghastly place as it is described in the Arabic Koran and hence more in line with Allah's compassion.

The last sabak was dedicated to Ahmad, the author of the book, or as it would be supposed, the one who had received the Kitab-e-Hidayat to deliver to the new nation of Pakistan. Ahmad must have pre-empted what I was later to discover from Maaz about the Koran and the lack of the mention of Muhammad because this last sabak talked about Ahmad's birth, his life, his preaching, and even of his death. I found this quite unusual because if Ahmad had written this, he knew of the details of his death before it occurred.

Some sabaks fascinated me. There was one sabak dedicated to Zoroaster, the prophet of the Persian religion which was established thousands of years ago. What intrigued me was that Ahmad acknowledged Zoroaster as an ancient prophet of Allah, someone who is not named in the Koran. He also acknowledged that it was Zoroaster who initiated the need to pray five times a day and that the devotees must wash themselves before praying. Prayers were then to be said towards a source of light, the sun during the day, a candle or a burning fire at night. It was obvious from reading this where Islam received these concepts. As for praying towards a light, the sabak makes reference to the verse in An-Noor 24:35 that "Allah is the light" and it is therefore to this light that the believers should still be praying.

Another sabak which fascinated me was the sabak dedicated to the Sabeans. There is mention of the Sabeans in the Koran but who these Sabeans were had always been a mystery to me. In the Kitab-e-Hidayat, the Sabeans were also called *sophians*, followers of *sophia*, the Greek word for "wisdom". I was later to find out that there was a group of mystics during the Roman Empire called the Gnostics who believed in having special *gnosis* or "knowledge" through which they attained eternal life. However, these people did not call themselves Gnostics but rather followers of *sophia*. The identity of the Sabeans as the Gnostics made sense to me when I discovered the writings that the Gnostics venerated and how there were similarities between the Gnostic texts and verses in the Koran, such as the miracle of Jesus when he turned clay birds into real ones, and the belief that Jesus was not really crucified but was only made to appear so. The message that this sabak was telling readers was that believers should always look for knowledge and wisdom, increase learning, not just in the holy books but in all areas of life, including from our observation of nature as we did in the sciences as it was implied in the verse from Surah Al-

Araf 7:185 where it asks the reader, "Do they not look in the dominion of the heavens and the earth and everything that Allah has created?" as it is not only knowledge from books but knowledge from the universe we observe that helps in this life and in the life of the Hereafter. But because it was not clearly spelled out exactly who these sophians really were, I eventually realised that the identity of the Sabeans could also have been the Greek philosophers, the lovers of *sophia*, in particular Socrates, who was also a believer in only one God. But it didn't really matter the real identity of the Sabeans, the Gnostics or the Greek philosophers, the moral in this sabak remained the same.

Yet another sabak which fascinated me was the sabak of the Way. As it says in the Koran about following the way, or the straight way as it says in the Al-Fatiha, this sabak went on to show that following the right way was a common message in other belief systems. In the New Testament Issa said he was the Way in John 14:6, and in Acts 9:2 the believers were given the epithet of the People of the Way. This was reflected in a belief system in China called Taoism, so named because it requires people to follow the Tao, the Chinese word for "Way". I was reminded of the number of times I had read in the Koran about following the straight way or the straight path and this sabak hinted that these concepts in the Koran had come from both of these two earlier sources. This sabak then continued to talk about the significance of the Way and that we need to follow our own personal Way to Allah. This touched me quite profoundly because I could actually see the unity in the Koran which talked on the one hand about one way but then in others about many ways. What the Kitab-e-Hidayat actually indicated was that we had to find our straight way back to Allah, each way back to Allah being personal and individual, which brought out the overall unity in the Koran where it talks about one way on the one hand and then many ways on the other.

Sabaks that did not focus on a particular prophet spoke of rituals and practices that were to be established. Practices that were addressed in the Kitab-e-Hidayat that differed dramatically from Koranic Islam were fasting and the qibla.

Fasting for Lashkari Muslims, so the Kitab-e-Hidayat said, was to be established four times a year, at the spring equinox, the summer solstice, the autumn equinox, and the winter solstice, and each of these times for three days, that is, the two days preceding then on the day itself. This was called the "Ramadan" fast. The explanation for this was that the word "Ramadan" was made up of the four letters, r, m, d, and n, and each letter was connected to one of the solstices and equinoxes, although I've forgotten exactly how now. Where it says in the Koran in Al-Baqarah 2:185 that fasting had been established on the month of Ramadan because this was the month in which the Koran was revealed, this sabak explained that because the Islamic calendar is lunar, the month of Ramadan continually shifts throughout the year and so that over a 36 year period, Ramadan occurs at every time of the year making this an empty statement seeing Ramadan occurs at all times throughout the solar year. Seeing Allah created the solar year as a definite cycle, the fasting should occur at fixed times. This sabak further explained that the word "month" in this verse should be understood as "fixed time", and as Ahmad was first revealed the Kitab-e-Hidayat on the night of the spring equinox, then he was later told on the summer solstice, the autumn equinox and finally the winter solstice to make a copy of the book, this then explained why these four specific days of the year were holy. As for why Lashkari Muslims needed to fast for the two days prior to the equinoxes and the solstices, there was a justification for this but I have since forgotten what it was.

What was also amazing was that this fasting was a total abstinence of food for three days, day and night. And unlike the fast of Ramadan, Lashkari Muslims were not only recommended but they were actually required to drink water during this fast, but only water, pure, unadulterated water. The justification for this was because water was given for purification, for as it says in Al-Anfal 8:11, Allah "sent down upon you water from the sky to purify you with it and remove from you the evil of Shaitaan". The Kitab-e-Hidayat stated that total abstinence from food was for purification, and Allah created water for purification, and hence both an abstinence from food coupled with the drinking of pure water during the fast was for double purification.

As for the qibla, there was an allusion to what Issa said in the Gospel of John to the woman at the well that Allah is a spirit and He requires believers to worship Him in spirit and in truth. That there was no particular point on earth towards which the devotees were to pray had its justification from the Koran. What it said in the Kitab-e-Hidayat was similar to the verse that Yusuf had quoted me in Al-Baqarah 2:115 that "to Allah belongs the east and the west, so wherever you turn, there is the face of Allah", the Kitab-e-Hidayat adding north and south so that all four cardinal points were mentioned. This was coupled with the sabak about Zoroaster and praying towards the light of Allah. Allah is everywhere and so the qibla was towards Allah, the light, who is everywhere, not to one point on the planet. This struck me very powerfully and further accentuated how idolatrous the qibla towards Mecca truly appeared.

Ahmad also addressed other issues. The Kitab-e-Hidayat had a detailed explanation in one of its sabaks about where people go after they die. Children under the age of reason and unborn foetuses that die before they have the time to live out their lives and prove themselves worthy of paradise are reborn in another world or in another location on this earth where they can live out their lifespan. This idea of other worlds that exist is supported by what it says in many places in the Koran about Allah being the

Lord of the worlds, or in Arabic, *rabi al-ghalameena*, the first mention being in the Al Fatiha, the prayer we said several times a day. Also, the Koran states in Surah At-Talaq 65:12 that there are seven earths. From this, the Kitab-e-Hidayat goes on to explain that if someone dies in infancy, this means that this world or the specific location on this world is not a suitable place for the young child to be able to carry out the test and so the child is then sent to another world or another location on this world in which it can continue in a more hospitable environment where it has a better chance to grow and prove itself ready for paradise.

It also addressed the issue of hell. As it said in the sabak about Muhammad, the horrific descriptions in the Koran were made for a people in which the Koran itself states are the strongest in disbelief and hypocrisy. The Kitab-e-Hidayat by contrast explains that the reality is that people will suffer a commensurate punishment in line with the crime they committed, just as Rameez Bhai had explained to me. And as Rameez Bhai had explained, it spoke of how one could call on loved ones and those one had done good to to intercede on one's behalf to convince Allah to allow one into paradise. The actual punishment that people would receive for their crimes was that they would be forced to feel what it was like to have been the recipient of the crime. This meant, for example, that a mass murderer would have to feel the terror and pain of each and every person he murdered, not only the physical pain that he inflicted on them but also the emotional trauma that the victims and those associated with the victims felt during and after the ordeal. Further, with the concept of worlds, it came across as apparent in the Kitab-e-Hidayat that Ahmad believed in reincarnation, as a rebirth either again in this world or into other worlds as a way to be punished for sins. For example, a husband who treated his wife cruelly in this life would be forced as punishment to be reborn as a woman in another world and be treated cruelly by a cruel husband until the person had learnt the lesson. He would then be further forced to be born again in another world as a man and be given the test again to treat his wife correctly. This would keep going until he had finally learned to be fully righteous and acceptable to enter paradise.

And unlike in the Koran where the unbelievers will have to suffer the pain and torment of hell forever, what happens to the unbelievers, or as it says in the Kitab-e-Hidayat, the evildoers is that they will first pass through a place of fire, but this place is not eternal. They enter this fiery place and remain there until all their evil deeds are burnt off and they have returned to their original, undeveloped soul-form. Once outside this fiery place, they will see far off those who were enjoying the pleasures of paradise, while they watch on, hungry, thirsty and in remorse. They will then be forced to be reborn to once again make themselves better people and worthy of the paradise Allah had created for all humankind. Ahmad found justification for this view of the afterlife in the Koran in verses such as Al-Baqarah 2:28 where it says, "How can you disbelieve in Allah? When you were dead, and He gave you life. Then He will cause you to die, then He will bring you back to life, and then to Him you will be returned" and in Yunus 10:4 where it says that Allah "originates the creation, then He repeats it, so that He may reward those who believe and do good deeds". The idea that in the end we will be returned to Allah implied that in the beginning we came out from Allah in some initial, original, undeveloped form and that to develop our souls Allah required of us that we experience life on earth. Somehow this life was a purifier of the soul and the earlier we understood this and learnt from it, the sooner we would achieve full purification and could finally return to Allah in full form, a completely developed soul ready for paradise.

Further in this description was something very similar to what it says in An-Nisaa 4:1 that Allah created souls to have a mate, so that we were actually only half of our entire

421

selves. We would know when we met the other half of our soul when we met someone with whom we fell completely in love with and we wanted to remain with that person all the time being together as a pair. What was intriguing about the Kitab-e-Hidayat was that this remained ambiguous. It did not state that the other half of our souls ended up in the body of a person of the opposite sex. Hence I could see that this could be interpreted as any type of pairing, between a man and a woman, but also between two men and two women. And like the brief mention in the Koran, the Kitab-e-Hidayat left a lot of questions unanswered, such as whether or not we were destined to meet up with the other half of our soul in this life or whether we were supposed to be reunited with the other half of our soul before we entered paradise, or what the fundamental reason was as to why Allah created our souls and then split them in two in the first place before placing each half inside a fleshly body.

However, as intriguing as it was, I didn't fully understand why Allah created initial-form souls to then experience the life-death-life-death-life cycle in order to purify them and didn't simply make pure forms of us right at the beginning. Further, I didn't like the idea about being punished in one life to experience bad times for wrongdoings in a previous life because I felt this would lead to the idea that when we saw people experiencing a cruel life, they themselves were to blame for it because of their misdeeds in a life previous to this one. Even so, there was also a warning in this sabak about those who looked on at the suffering of others and did nothing to help, that they would also be punished in a future life by suffering a similar fate as those neglected. This sabak was rather brief in its description of this idea of reincarnation, I guess in an attempt to confine the idea to 49 verses, that to me it wasn't totally clear what Ahmad's overall grand scheme of the development and purification of souls was meant to look like and how all these rewards and punishments worked over the entire scheme of things.

And I wasn't really sure how Ahmad finally resolved this complex issue about reincarnation but then I didn't research this aspect in much detail or look up any of the tashrees to find out.

But it wasn't only the content of the Kitab-e-Hidayat which intrigued me. What was further amazing was the language. It was written in poetic form and in such a way that there were often times more than one way to understand a passage, yet both understandings sounded valid and complementary.

While the Kitab-e-Hidayat was considered the divine message, one of the books from the Enlightened Book in heaven, like it was with the Koran, there were passages that were unclear and it was difficult to know what they were talking about. Now that Ahmad the prophet was dead, devotees had written books to elaborate on the verses in the Kitab-e-Hidayat in the same way as the Hadiths were supposed to elaborate on the Koran. There was a link on the pdf to where I could find these *tashrees*, the Urdu word for "translations". I scrolled through each of them quickly without actually reading the contents just to see how long they were and I was amazed at the volumes of works written just to explain the meaning of this book. I was further amazed at how quickly the amount of literature to support Lashkari Islam was produced in such short time.

But while the Kitab-e-Hidayat came across as beautiful and complete and as a new Word of Allah, it simply sounded like an elaborate fabrication. The only sure evidence that I had that it was more likely an invention than a reality was the fact that the Kitab-e-Hidayat describes Ahmad's later life and ultimate death and yet Ahmad had received the Book while he was still young and alive. If the Kitab-e-Hidayat were truly a revelation from Allah, this would lend further weight to the miracle of the Kitab-e-Hidayat that Ahmad's future life and ultimate death had been predicted and Ahmad became aware of it before it happened. But

423

logic kept telling me that this was the key to realising that in the end this was all a complete fabrication by someone else, perhaps this Rumainsa who took on the task to decorate the Kitab-e-Hidayat. I particularly felt that the entire Book could have been invented by a woman because it had a feminine touch. And if Rumainsa had been the real author of the Kitab-e-Hidayat, it would make sense for her to attribute the book to her husband, Ahmad, or to totally invent Ahmad, because in general, women were considered inadequate to be prophets of Allah according to many Muslims and hence the chances of anyone listening to her and believeing her message would have been extremely small.

In any case, I just knew that just because someone can create an amazing piece of literary artwork did not mean that the artwork came from beyond the world in which we lived nor had its sanction from the Almighty. I still could see that there was actually no truth in this religion at all and I was ready to argue against it.

Chapter 17

"Good evening," Rameez Bhai welcomed me at the door of his sleeping quarters, and seeing he was a teacher, his dormitory was a lot more spacious than the students' dormitories. His quarters contained both a central living room from where I saw two other doors lead off to other rooms in the residence. Accompanying Rameez Bhai was another very muscular and fit looking guy called Tasneem, a man of fair complexion and light coloured hair which made me wonder if he had some European mixing in his bloodline. Both welcomed me as their special guest into the central room onto one of the armchairs.

On the coffee table in the centre of the room was an assortment of drinks but what struck me was that among the tea, water and soft drink there was also beer. Lashkari Muslims, so I found out later, allow for the consumption of alcohol for it says in An-Nahl 16:67 "And from the fruit of the datepalm and the vine, you get strong drink". 'Strong drink', so it was explained later, in the original Arabic is *sakaran* and simply means "alcoholic drink". Unlike mainstream Muslims who believe any drinking of alcohol is haram, Lashkari Muslims claim the Koran teaches that it isn't alcoholic drinks themselves that are the problem but the overindulgence in them, which is why it is written in An-Nisaa 4:43, "Do not approach prayer while you are intoxicated until you know what you are saying". This verse clearly shows that people can drink alcohol but they shouldn't pray when they've had too much to drink. Also, the Koran talks about the drinking of wine in paradise, as it says in Surah Muhammad 47:15, "A Parable of paradise, which is promised to the righteous, therein are rivers of unpolluted water, and rivers of milk whose taste does not change, and rivers of wine delicious for those who drink". The Lashkari Muslim explanation of what appears to be a stark contradiction to what it says in Al-Baqarah 2:219 that, "They ask you concerning wine and gambling. Say, 'In them is a great sin, and some profit for men; but the sin is greater than the profit'" and Al-Ma'idah 5:90 that "intoxicants…are an abomination from the work of Shaitaan" is that Allah quite clearly explains that there is a profit in drinking wine but the sin is the excess drinking, that is, drunkenness. In these verses from Surah Al-Baqarah, Surah Al-Ma'idah and Surah Muhammad, the word for wine is *khmr* and this word comes from the Arabic root meaning "cover". So where it says in Al-Baqarah 2:219 that there is benefit and sin in wine, the benefit is the health benefits wine brings to the body when drunk in small doses and in moderation, and the sin is when people overindulge and hence their minds become befuddled and "covered" so they cannot think straight and don't know what they're saying or doing. Otherwise it would be extremely odd if wine, an intoxicant, is an abomination from Satan and yet people will be drinking wine in paradise which was supposed to be a place free of Satan's abominations.

I was one of those mainstream Muslims who believed that the drinking of alcohol was haram so I chose to do the right thing and avoid the alcohol and so I chose to drink tea.

We all sat down in this central room in Rameez Bhai's dormitory and though our conversation started off on topics of a general nature, my heart was troubled over Rameez Bhai's total acceptance of this modern Islamic sect. However, I couldn't help noticing Rameez Bhai's new persona, how he came across as greatly relaxed and assured of himself which came in contrast to our earlier conversations when he seemed very troubled and in constant mental anguish. In fact, the peaceful aura that seemed to surround both men was unmistakable. It was as if it emanated out of their inner souls and filled the room like the light from a large candle, both warm and enchanting.

But it was a false peace, I thought to myself, one brought on by Shaitaan. As it said in the Koran, Shaitaan will mislead people and further, that Allah allows people to continue to follow their evil desires but in the end He will punish them in Jahannam being tortured with boiling water and raging fires. But I didn't want Rameez Bhai to suffer eternal torment in Jahannam, and it was only in this life that it was possible for me to prevent him from going there. If Rameez Bhai had been caught in a blazing bushfire, I would definitely have done anything I could to rush in to save him. He was on the course to enter a blazing eternity and this was the only opportunity for me to pull him out. This was my duty as a Muslim. But it was Tasneem who brought the topic of conversation to its proper focus.

"So, did you read the Kitab-e-Hidayat?" Tasneem asked. "And how did you find it?"

"Yes," I replied, "I did read the Kitab-e-Hidayat. And I found it interesting. For a start, the Koran and the Kitab-e-Hidayat don't always agree on certain points."

Tasneem sat back and smiled. "No, it's not that the Koran and the Kitab-e-Hidayat don't agree. It's what we have been told how the original Arabic should be read that doesn't agree with the Kitab-e-Hidayat. The original Koran was perfect but when later Muslims decided to add the diacritical marks, in many places they put the dots and the vowel points in the wrong places and hence this has caused the misunderstandings that have crept in over the centuries over what the Koran really meant to say."

"Then why do we need a new Koran?" I asked. "Why didn't Ahmad simply come with the Koran and rearrange the diacritical marks to reveal what the real message was in the Koran that earlier Muslims overlooked? After all, there is only one Koran. This Koran is for all humanity. Why do we need a new Koran?"

"Mustafa," Tasneem replied, "it is not up to us to question Allah and ask how Allah does things. Whenever Allah tells us to do something, we simply have to obey Him. We cannot tell Allah how we want things to happen. It's the other way around. When Allah does something, it is up to us to simply believe and obey Him. And we could use the same argument with mainstream Islam. If the Torah and the Injeel had been corrupted, why didn't Muhammad just come along and remove all the corruptions in the Holy Books and bring them back to their pure, unadulterated form? Why did he rather come along with an entirely new book?

As for there being only one book from Allah, Allah knew in advance that there would be criticism of a new holy book because this is why Ahmad prophesied in one of his sermons, 'Those who were given the Book will rise up against the prophet and His revelation that is to come, confirming and correcting what is with them. Many of them will say, 'Another holy book? How can he say such a thing? We only need one holy book, the Koran! And it is the Arabic Koran!' Don't they know that there are many nations and that Allah created all nations and languages? So how can there be only one holy book in only one language? Haven't they read in their own Koran where it says 'And for every nation is a Messenger' and that Allah 'did not send any Messenger except in the language of his people so that he might make the Message clear to them'? Do they not have eyes to read and intellects to reason?' Allah is quite clear in saying that Messengers are sent to nations bringing a message in their languages. Allah sent the Torah to the Jews in their language, in Hebrew, He sent the Injeel in Greek at a time when the entire Roman Empire spoke Greek, and then the Koran to the Arabs in the Arabic language."

It appeared that Ahmad was fully aware of the resistance that would arise over his new holy book and so he was ready to defend his position. But Tasneem's explanation also raised, at least in my mind, a further problem.

"Does this mean," I then asked, "that there are Korans in different languages sent to every nation of the world? And every time a new country is formed, Allah sends a Koran in the language of that new country?"

"But isn't that what it says in the Koran?" Tasneem then asked, obviously rhetorically.

"Then where are all these Korans in different languages?" I retorted.

"Have you travelled the world and seen people reading Korans in different languages?" Tasneem asked. "If Allah has said He sent Messengers with messages in their languages, then there obviously have been Korans or other holy books sent down in different languages. I would say that if we can no longer find these holy books, this is because as Allah says, He sends Messengers but the people to whom these Messengers are sent no doubt killed the Messenger and destroyed the book in which the message was written. It says this in the Koran. And as Ahmad said in another of his sermons, 'the Muslims condemn the Jews for killing their prophets. But how are Muslims any different, those who kill the Messengers of Allah?'

But also, as Allah says in Surah Al-Hijr 15:87 'And We have given you seven of the Oft-repeated and Great Koran'. What you have to understand here is that the number seven isn't always to be understood literally as a number. 'Seven' in a way means 'complete'. So in this verse from Al-Hijr, Allah is not saying to us that He has given us literally seven Korans, therefore there are seven holy books sent to seven different nations. It means that He has given us all completely of His Word to all the peoples and nations of the earth. When we put all these books together, then we have a complete set. This is the beauty but also the difficulty of Arabic. Sometimes words have more than one meaning and we have to use our intellect to fully grasp what Allah

429

is saying to us. Which is further reason why we here in Pakistan need a holy book in our language because we don't speak Arabic, we speak English and Urdu."

Every point Tasneem made made sense. The Koran itself said that for every nation Allah sent a Messenger and further that the message was sent in the language of the people. Books seemed to be the popular medium through which messages were delivered and this verse from Al-Hijr, at least the way Tasneem interpreted it, meant that there were Holy Books sent via messengers to all the nations of the world. The Koran did say that Allah sent messengers to different nations and therefore if He sent messengers to countries as far flung from Arabia as New Zealand or Iceland, it would have made no sense in sending a messenger carrying the Koran in only the Arabic language for otherwise the message of the Koran would have been lost. If, for example, the Messenger of Allah had gone to Iceland and spoken in Arabic and presented an Arabic book, the Icelanders would not have understood what the Messenger was saying and would have just stared at him wondering why he was getting all flustered.

As for the interpretation of Al-Hijr, what Tasneem said was also right. As my Mulvi had explained when interpreting the verses in Al-Ma'idah 5:38 and in Al-Taubah 9:29 about the interpretation of the word "hand" in these passages, my Mulvi's justification was because Arabic was this amazing language where words could have several different meanings. Tasneem, I could see, had as much right to interpret the word "seven" in the expression "seven of the Oft-repeated and Great Koran" in a different way to what the word actually means in its normal sense, using the mystery and complexity of the Arabic language as justification. Although I didn't agree with Tasneem's interpretation, I had to admit deep within my heart that the way he moulded and reformulated the meaning of this verse had its validity when we considered the number seven in our understanding of the divine, as the number seven has a recurring theme in our religion, such as Allah creating seven heavens and there being seven days in a week, and this gave support to the idea that the number seven held great importance with Allah, not merely as a number but as an idea, the idea of Allah's completeness.

But I was still convinced that Lashkari Islam was wrong. And I had a sure reason why it was wrong.

"But how can there be," I then asked, "a prophet today in the twenty-first century, or in the twentieth century when Ahmad came, when it quite clearly says in Al-Ahzab 33:40 that 'Muhammad is...the Seal of the Prophets'? If Muhammad is the Seal of the Prophets, how can there be any prophets after Muhammad?"

Although Rameez Bhai had given an explanation of this verse, I still wasn't satisfied as his explanation was not clear and went against the hundreds of years of tradition of understanding this idea that Muhammad being the seal of the prophets simply meant that Muhammad was the last of them.

Tasneem took a sip of his drink, placed his glass on the table and sat back.

"Yes, it says here that Muhammad is the *seal* of the prophets. It does not say that Muhammad is the *last* of the prophets. Ahmad explained in one of his sermons that Muslims have been misled by this interpretation of this verse and to their delusion and destruction. And it was quite plain there in the Koran. Nowhere in the Koran or anywhere does it say that after Muhammad there would be no more Messengers. This verse simply says that Muhammad is the Seal of the prophets, and what this means is that Muhammad brings all the prophets together. Before Muhammad came, people followed different prophets, some Moses, some Issa, some Zoroaster, but they were not united. Muhammad came and became the "seal" that bound these prophets together so that those who said they

431

followed Moses or Zoroaster, for example, could also say that they followed Issa as well, and not consider themselves followers of different prophets with different messages.

Also, aren't we told that the Koran is an eternal book with a message for all eternity? If this is the case, why does Allah say in Al-Ahzab 33:45 'O Prophet! Indeed We have sent you as a witness'. Muhammad is now dead and has been so for about 1,400 years. This would mean that if this verse in the Koran were speaking about Muhammad the Prophet being sent as a witness, the Koran is only relevant to the time of Muhammad because Muhammad is no longer here."

"He might no longer be alive," I retorted, "but his message is still with us in the Koran. Although Muhammad may be dead, the message he sent, the Koran, is still alive and is still a witness to us today."

Tasneem looked up at the ceiling and back at me.

"Yes, I see your point," Tasneem replied, "and this would make sense if this was the only verse which says something like this. But what about what it says in Surah Al-Hujurat 49:2 'O you who believe! Do not raise your voices above the voice of the Prophet'? If the prophet mentioned here is only Muhammad, then this verse is only relevant during the time that Muhammad was alive. I mean, we cannot raise our voices above the voice of the Koran, so this verse implies that the prophet is alive. And if the Koran is eternal, it is expected that there will be prophets alive while the Koran is with us and there are certain ways we should act when we find ourselves in the presence of the Prophet. Again, it says in Surah Al-Mujadila 58:12 'O you who believe! When you privately consult the Messenger, then offer in charity before your private consultation.' If there is no Messenger alive in our day, how can we in our modern times follow this verse and privately consult this Messenger? And we can't privately consult the Koran. So the Koran, being eternal, is clearly telling us that there will be Messengers alive in our time with whom we can consult."

I thought of what Tasneem was saying but didn't have an answer. I was trying to think of a couterargument but none was forthcoming. Rather, Tasneem kept showing yet more verses in the Koran which validated this point of view.

"Again, what about other verses that talk about the Prophet or the Messenger? In Al-Ahzab 33:30-33 it says that the wives of the prophet are instructed about their conduct, that they should not commit adultery or other unseemly conduct but act righteously, they should pray regularly, give zakat, and not show off their beauty in public but only to their husband. If this passage were speaking only about Muhammad, then why is this command in the eternal Koran? Again, in Al-Ahzab 33:53 we are told that whenever we are invited to a meal with the Prophet that we should not linger with the Prophet while the meal is being prepared nor should we hang around afterwards once we have finished because this is burdensome to the Prophet. If this is only addressed to Muhammad, then why is this in the Koran as a message to all Muslims? Again, it says in An-Nisaa 4:59 'Obey Allah, and obey the Messenger, and those charged with authority among you. If you differ in anything among yourselves, refer it to Allah and His Messenger'. If we have a dispute and we are told to refer our dispute to the Messenger, there has to be a messenger, a prophet, alive at the time for us to refer to in times of dispute. Again, in times of war, the Koran clearly states in Al-Anfal 8:41 that 'out of all the booty that you may acquire a fifth share is assigned to Allah and the Messenger'. If this verse is referring only to Muhammad, then what do we do in our time if there are no messengers or prophets if we go to war and then it comes time to distributing the booty? Otherwise this verse makes absolutely no sense or it is aimed at a particular people at a particular time and therefore it is not a Koran for all time.

And if these verses aren't relevant for our time, then what about the rest of the Koran?"

I was absolutely stunned to silence by Tasneem's explanation. Further, for the first time I realised something I had never noticed before, that we had simply assumed that every reference to "Messenger" or "Prophet" in the Koran was talking about Muhammad. But who said that these passages referred to Muhammad? After all, the Koran also acknowledged other characters as prophets, not just Muhammad. That Tasneem said that these references to "Prophet" and "Messenger" were also valid today as evidence that there will always be prophets and messengers among us and these mentions of messenger and prophet could equally be applied to Ahmad, this further showed that the messenger and prophet in these passages in the Koran are simply unidentified.

"I mean," Tasneem continued, "those Muslims who deny that there are prophets today are no different to those living in Joseph's day. As it says in Ghafir 40:34, 'And to you there came Joseph in times gone by, with clear signs, but you ceased not to doubt for which he had come. At length, when he died, you said: 'No messenger will Allah send after him'. Thus does Allah leave to stray such as transgress and live in doubt'.' When Messengers came, they always prophesied of future Messengers to come, and nothing is said of a last Messenger. Ibrahim prayed to Allah to 'raise up in their midst a Messenger' in Al-Baqarah 2:129, a prayer that is continually fulfilled with prophets again and again being raised up in the new nations that form. Even Issa prophesied of a Messenger to come after him in Surah As-Saff 61:6 and actually names him. As it was in the time of Joseph, so it is in our time that many Muslims say that after Muhammad, 'No messenger will Allah send after him', something that is not supported by the Koran and which will cause these people to be punished accordingly."

434

These verses that Tasneem quoted me were so convincing that I simply didn't know what to say. But worse, there was a curse for not believing in modern day prophets. So what if Ahmad actually was a true prophet and I refused to believe in him? Could it be that the Koran itself was telling me that my denial of Ahmad as a prophet to the Pakistanis was a transgression and a doubt towards Allah, and such transgression and doubt would lead me to punishment?

But as convincing as they were, I was desperate for a line of argument that showed up an error in the Lashkari Muslims' outlook on this modern religion. I struggled to come up with something and eventually put forward my next argument.

"But how can there be a new and different holy book in modern times? Allah sent the Koran, and if Allah sent it down, it has to be perfect. If it is perfect, how can there be a new holy book, even if it is in a different language?"

Tasneem took a sip of his drink while Rameez Bhai looked on in expectation.

"Mustafa, you are taking things well out of hand and out of context. Don't you, as a Muslim, believe that Allah first sent the Torah and then the Injeel? If Allah sent these, then the Torah and Injeel also were perfect. We are often told that the sending down of these messages is like teaching children at school. Allah sent the Torah and this is like children going to primary school. Allah then sent the Injeel and this is like going to high school. Then Allah sent the Koran and this is like going to university to complete a degree. Well, now Allah has sent down the Kitab-e-Hidayat in our modern times and this is like completing a postgraduate diploma.

As we increase in knowledge and as we progress, the Holy Books progress with us. It states this quite clearly in the Koran. In An-Nahl 16:101 it says that, 'We substitute one revelation for another, and Allah knows best what

He reveals'. So the Koran as one revelation has now been substituted with the Kitab-e-Hidayat a new revelation, and Allah knows best about what He reveals to us."

I wanted to react in anger at Tasneem. How dare he say that the Koran I had been brought up with was now being replaced by a new Holy Book in the twenty-first century. The Koran as it was revealed to Muhammad was complete. Why did it need changing? But really, who was I arguing this point with? Tasneem or Allah? After all, Tasneem had quoted directly from the Koran and it was the Koran itself that confessed and prophesied that older revelations would be replaced with newer ones.

My mind was in a daze and I could no longer think clearly. I was now seeing even more problems in the Koran that I didn't want to see. So I attacked at the only thing left that I had to attack.

"But how do you know," I stated in a fluster, "that Ahmad is a prophet? How do you know that the Kitab-e-Hidayat is a direct message from Allah and not something that he simply made up? How do you know he's not just a poet who has composed something together, writing things he'd like Allah to have said when it was simply something that he himself invented?"

Tasneem sat back in his chair, closed his eyes, then opened them again, and then once again sat forward.

"Mustafa," he said quite sternly, "this is what they said about Muhammad. In Surah Al-Anbiyaa 21:5 it says when talking about prophets, 'Nay, they say, 'Muddled dreams; nay, he has invented it; nay, he is a poet'.' And again in Surah Adh-Dhariyat 51:52 'No messenger came to those before them, but they said 'a magician or a madman'.' These verses are not talking only about Muhammad because the Koran is eternal. And as it happened in Muhammad's day it's happening now in the days with Ahmad. People think of him as a poet who simply invented out of his own mind the Words of Allah, and others think he was mad. But we know he is a true prophet in our time because Allah in the Koran promised us this. And there was the sign of the smoke when he was born which Allah had prophesied in Ad-Dukhan 44:10, saying, 'Watch for the Day that the sky will bring forth a kind of smoke plainly visible' and how that Allah questions the people in verses 13 and 14, 'How should they have a reminder. Seeing that a Messenger explaining things clearly has come to them. Yet they turn away from him and say, 'Tutored, a man possessed!'' Allah will then punish us for rejecting Ahmad when Allah has given clear signs that Ahmad is a prophet in our time. And like Muhammad, Ahmad brought a sign, the sign of the storm in the spring equinox. And like in the days of Muhammad, the obstinately disobedient refused to believe him. But we know Ahmad is a messenger of Allah because of the prophecy Allah made about sending messengers to every nation, and Ahmad has brought us the Kitab-e-Hidayat."

Tasneem took a sip of his drink, placed his glass back on the table and the added, "And be serious with me, Mustafa. When you read the Kitab-e-Hidayat, weren't you moved by its moving imagery, its rhythmic verse, its enchanting rhetorical devices? It is such a moving piece of writing. How can it simply be the writing of a human? And Ahmad wrote it down all in one night. It's not humanly possible to write down a manuscript in the way Ahmad did, the number of chapters, the exact number of verses in each chapter, and the beauty of his Urdu in a single night. And no-one is able to produce anything like the Kitab-e-Hidayat. As it says in Al-Baqarah 2:23 that 'if you are in doubt about what We have revealed to Our slave then produce a chapter like it.' No-one can produce a chapter like what we find in the Kitab-e-Hidayat in the eloquence of the Urdu and the depths and profundity of its message."

While I agreed with Tasneem that the Kitab-e-Hidayat was written in beautiful and moving Urdu, so was the poetry by Ghalib, one of our national Urdu poets. But no-one claimed that Ghalib's poetry was too beautiful to be a mere human creation. As for writing it down all in one night, how did we know for sure that this is what really happened? How did we know that Ahmad, or any of his supposed followers, hadn't made the entire thing up?

The test, however, to produce a chapter like it caught me in a trap. This test was subjective. If someone did decide to take up the challenge and write a chapter like a sabak from the Kitab-e-Hidayat, what were the criteria to judge that the invented chapter was like a sabak in the Kitab-e-Hidayat? By the number of verses? the choice of vocabulary? the theme of the chapter? For the first time I realised just how subjective this test was and with no clear criteria to say exactly what is meant by a sabak that is like a sabak of the Kitab-e-Hidayat, there was no sure way to use this test to prove conclusively the Kitab-e-Hidayat's real origins.

I further realised that we could say this about any form of literature. Could anyone write a chapter, that is, an Act like an Act from one of Shakespeare's plays? What would be the criteria for deciding how like an Act of one of Shakespeare's plays an invented Act needed to be to pass the test? And if it's impossible to write an Act like the Act of a Shakespearean play, was this evidence of the divine nature of Shakespeare and all his literary works?

Which then made the challenge in the Koran itself just as meaningless. Muslims often boast that the evidence that the Koran is from Allah is because no-one can imitate any of its chapters, but the same could be said of the Kitab-e-Hidayat or any literary work. So, was this evidence that these forms of literature were from Allah? If not, then what about the Koran?

Hence, this affected the way I viewed the Koran. It was often said that the Koran had to have been from Allah because it was written in moving Arabic, and indeed various parts of the Koran when read by a professional

Arabic reader did sound rather moving, even those parts of the Koran which made little sense or were completely nonsensical. And I had never heard of anyone producing a surah like a surah from the Koran. But while I had in the past accepted this as sufficient proof of the Koran's divine nature, I just could not accept this same evidence as evidence that the Kitab-e-Hidayat was from Allah.

By the end of the evening, I was completely mentally exhausted. It was as if my mind had done the workout that my body usually did at Rameez Bhai's gymnasium. But Tasneem showed no signs of fatigue. He looked like the professional gymnast who at the end of his training session was just as refreshed as he was when he first entered the room. But he also had something to tell me.

"Mustafa," he said, "what I admire about you is that you sincerely question your faith and don't just accept things blindly. But I can also see that you are obviously looking for something which you haven't yet found. But let me help you. You will never truly be led by Allah until you let go of everything you've been told and completely submit to the will of Allah and be guided by Him. You're trying to grasp Allah using reason and your intellect but it requires more than this to understand Allah and His ways. Allah has sent His new Messenger to us, to us Pakistanis, to us who speak Urdu, to teach us the straight path and the only way to Allah. Those who refuse to follow Ahmad simply want to continue to follow their own desires. You need to let go of what you *want to be* true and finally accept what *is* true. Until you finally accept Allah and His Messenger Ahmad, you'll always be caught in your mental turmoil."

I didn't know what to say to that. All I wanted to do was get away and go back to my dormitory. Tasneem and Rameez Bhai stood up and accompanied me out of their dormitory and into the night. Tasneem first shook my hand and then it was Rameez Bhai's turn to do so. Rameez Bhai then made a final comment.

"So, will I see you tomorrow at the gym?"

I nodded in reply.

I then left Rameez Bhai's dormitory and wandered back to mine. I looked up in the deep, dark sky and saw the crescent moon embedded against the starry backdrop. It felt as if I were staring into an abyss, and that that abyss was staring back into the emptiness of my inner being.

Chapter 18

I still maintain contact with Rameez through Facebook and through much of the other social media we have at our disposal these days. He is also one of the few people I felt I could trust to disclose about what had happened in my life, no doubt because we are both in a similar situation that we have to continue to hide our controversial ways that we understand and approach the Koran. He is somewhat disappointed by my total rejection of all religions and obviously stunned by my sexuality. But he has continued to be a friend. He told me that I stood by him during a very dark moment in his life and because of this he felt somewhat indebted to me and therefore was happy to maintain the friendship. He is once again married and now has two daughters with the hope of having more children.

Years later I thought about Lashkari Islam from a different and non-religious perspective. I could totally empathise with Ahmad. During his time, he had difficulty in trying to make sense out of all the Muslim sects in Pakistan, and indeed, throughout the Muslim world who all claimed that they had the Word of Allah, the Koran, yet they were all divided. In particular he had difficulty with the division between the Sunnis and the Shiites, and no doubt on further exposure, between other sects of Islam such as the Salafis, the Koranists, the Alhamaddiyyahs, and all who claimed that Muhammad was the Messenger of Allah and the Koran was His Word. But all these sects were separate and rival entities. I was faced with the same problem from my own growing up in the Sunni sect, my exposure to the Shiite sect through Reza, the Ibrahimi Islamic sect through Yusuf and now the Lashkari Islamic sect through Rameez.

But Ahmad, no doubt, had another issue to contend with. Why was it that Muslims believed that Allah's message was sent to all the world but it was only written in one language, Arabic? Was Allah a limited monolingual? If Allah created all the languages, weren't all languages special to Him? And this seemed obvious from the verse which said that Allah sends messages in the language of the people. If Allah loved the Pakistani people so much that He allowed it to form as a separate state from India, then Allah loved the language of the Pakistanis as well especially as Pakistan did not adopt Arabic as the official language. English, it was true, was one of the main languages used in daily communication but this was a language from a different country and a different cultural group. But so was Arabic. Urdu was uniquely Pakistani. And if Allah loved Pakistan enough for it to become a nation devoted to Him, Allah wanted to speak directly to this nation He loved through their unique language.

Among the many problems that the Kitab-e-Hidayat created in me was just how beautiful it was constructed. The seven-versed first ibadat and the seven-versed last ibadat end-to-end with the entire book made up of 98 sabaks each containing 49 verses, and covering many of the topics as it did in an eloquent manner was an amazing feat of poetry. Further, each sabak talked about one unique topic, nothing was repeated. And each sabak contained one complete thread of thought that it made it easy to read a sabak in its entirety following its logical flow.

This contrasted strongly with the Koran. In contrast to the Kitab-e-Hidayat, the Koran looked like an agglomeration of different texts hurriedly put together. And the fact that there were so many repetitions of the same story made it appear as if there originally had been variants of how these stories were related in written form and all these variants were hastily shoved together haphazardly as if the chief editor of the book wanted a final version by a strict and tight deadline.

For a long time after my discussion with Tasneem, I found myself in constant mental turmoil trying to work everything out in my head about Islam, Muhammad and the Koran. I could totally understand this Ahmad and his followers. The Koran speaks a lot about the Torah and the Injeel, and Muslims on the one hand acknowledge that these are from Allah but then on the other claim that these books have been corrupted. But as Yusuf ibn Musa showed, the Torah and the Injeel could not have been corrupted if it is acknowledged that they are the words of Allah as the Koran says quite clearly that "none can change His Words". However, Muslims in general and Sunni Muslims in particular say that the evidence that the Torah and the Injeel had been corrupted is that they contradict the Koran. But now Ahmad was claiming that he was a messenger of Allah and that the Koran had been corrupted which is why he had to bring a new message, and in the fulfilment of one verse in the Koran it was brought in the language of the people, in particular, in Urdu. And in the fulfilment of what it said in the Koran, earlier revelations were substituted with later ones, where some former verses were replaced with those that were new.

Yet, Ahmad still quoted from the Koran to give support to his claim. If the Koran had been corrupted, how was Ahmad so sure that the verses he quoted which justified his new version of Islam weren't from those parts of the Koran that had been corrupted?

But the fundamental question to me was, how did we know that a person was a prophet of Allah? What criteria did someone have to fulfil before we could accept that this person was a prophet? Muhammad claimed to have visitations from the angel Gabriel, and so did Ahmad. Muhammad's birth had miracles associated with it, and so did Ahmad's. It was claimed that Muhammad performed

443

certain miracles such as splitting the moon, and so it was claimed with Ahmad when he supposedly brought the freak storm on the spring equinox. Muhammad brought a book which was claimed to be an extension from earlier holy books and so did Ahmad. Many denied Muhammad's claim to prophethood, and so it happened with Ahmad. Many claimed Muhammad was a poet and that he was mad, and so it was said about Ahmad. Muhammad came with many completely new rites and rituals supposedly to replace the rites and rituals that earlier religions, in particular Jews and Christians, observed, and so did Ahmad. I tried desperately to find something that was different between Muhammad and Ahmad so that I could conclusively state that Muhammad was definitely a prophet and Ahmad was definitely not. Yet I could find nothing. And what was further torturing me was, if I reject Ahmad as being a prophet because there was nothing about him that demonstrated overwhelmingly to me that he was a prophet of Allah then what was the basis for my belief that Muhammad was a prophet of Allah?

What particularly created great anxiety in my thinking was that the story of Ahmad going out to an isolated place and having a visitation from the angel Gabriel just sounded so outlandishly puerile and ludicrously silly and I could readily understand why the imams of the mosques accused Ahmad of being a mischievous boy. If one of our uni friends such as Arsalan, Haseeb or Zeeshan had come to us at the meal room and told us that the night previous they had had a visitation from an angel, I was sure that they would be mocked and laughed at because of how stupid they sounded. And yet the entire religion of Islam rested completely on the belief that Muhammad was visited by an angel, a story I had heard not from Muhammad himself but from other people. Further, the acceptance of the divine nature of the Koran rested entirely upon this story, and it was upon this story that our blasphemy laws were based which ultimately ruled the lives and the fate of the citizens of our country.

And then Maaz showed me that the Muhammad in the Koran was possibly Issa and the qibla change occurred about a hundred years after the traditional Muhammad had died which put in question the very existence of Muhammad. The storm that this created in my brain simply became too overwhelming.

I was sick for days after that. The following day I broke out in a cold sweat and had strange spasms in my left arm and leg, and I broke out in a strange and itchy rash on my neck, around my belt line and around my wrists. When Maaz got up and saw me, he completely freaked out and immediately organised someone to come and take me to the dispensary.

I was placed in the dispensary in one of the beds. A local doctor was called in and it was obvious that everyone was concerned about the state of my health. In fact, they were so concerned that they called my parents. The nurses began extracting blood from my arm and taking urine samples to see if they could find the source of this strange illness.

The following day, one of the nurses came to see me but this time not with needles to prod into my body or to administer any drugs.

"Er, you have some visitors," she said with a smile.

She then turned around and there behind her entered a man and a woman.

"Mother and father," I asked in a feverish groan. "What are you doing here?"

"Oh, son, what's the matter?" my mother asked in anguish as she came over to the bed and immediately held my hand. "The university called us and said that you had been taken gravely ill and they didn't know what it was that was causing you to be so sick!"

My parents then sat on either side of the bed.

"What happened?" my father asked me gravely.

What on earth could I tell them? As usual when it comes to questioning the religion, sometimes you just have to be quiet, and if you can't be quiet, you are forced to lie for self-preservation.

"Are you finding your studies too difficult?" my father asked. "Would you like to take a break for the rest of this semester and resume next semester?"

My father then looked at my mother then back at me.

"No," I replied. "It's okay. I guess I wasn't expecting university study to be so straining." I then went on to talk about how some subjects at university were much more complicated than I had expected. My parents remained somewhat concerned and continued to badger me to come home for the rest of the semester and return when the new semester began when I would be a lot more refreshed.

Soon after, one of the nurses entered the room.

"You have another visitor," the nurse said. It was Maaz.

I introduced Maaz to my parents and told them that he was my roommate. Maaz was a gentleman and with respect greeted my parents in the standard highly respectful way that is carried out in Pakistan by a young person to one's elders. At this stage, the doctor arrived and asked to speak with my parents in private and soon my parents left.

Maaz then sat on the bed next to me.

"How are you?" he asked and the look on his face was somewhat disconcerting. "You won't die on me, will you?"

This last statement was typical of his cheeky nature, but it also spoke volumes of what he really felt about me. Maaz then moved closer to me.

"Can I ask you a personal question?" he asked. The way he was poised towards me, I was nervous what my parents would say if they saw him this close. I nodded in affirmation.

"Do you think you were struck ill like this because you are beginning to realise that our religion Islam is probably not true, and moreso, the Koran is actually not infallible?"

When Maaz asked me this, the blood rushed to my head. I could feel my heartbeat increase rapidly and where the rashes had earlier appeared I began to feel terribly itchy again. The expression on my face must have answered his question so that there was no need to verbalise it.

"I know how you feel," Maaz then stated in a low tone in reinforcement of my silent affirmation and sat up. "I think I've also come to the point where I no longer believe any of it. After listening to all the arguments by our uni friends and how there can never be a general consensus of what is right and wrong in the religion, and finally discovering that Muhammad in the Koran clearly has to be Issa, the religion simply can't be true. I don't believe in any of it anymore. And like you, I went through a time of depression as a result of this."

Maaz making this acclamation about his doubts about the Koran made me extremely nervous. If anyone could hear what he was saying, they could accuse him of apostasy and the punishment was death.

"They tell us," Maaz continued, "to study hard, read, learn, show your devotion. Don't let up. Put your full effort into it. But then many of us see things we don't want to see."

Maaz stopped for a moment and I hoped he would not go on. But he did.

"But they don't realise that when we read and study and really get into it, there are certain unexpected consequences that arise as a result."

While saying that last comment, my parents and the doctor returned to my bed.

"What unexpected consequences?" my father asked.

I didn't know where to look when my father asked this question.

"Excuse me, sir," Maaz replied. "Like suffering a little bit from the strain of studying."

My father looked at the doctor and the doctor's face expressed the non-verbal comment that this was proof of what he had been speaking about to my father earlier. This led my father to further urge me to quit my studies till the end of the semester and then resume them the following semester after a good rest. I said I would only agree to this if I could continue to reside on the university campus during that time.

Maaz, the gentleman that he was, rescued the situation. He suggested to allow me a moment to think about it while he took my parents on a tour and showed them around the university campus. They were gone for quite some time.

When they returned, Maaz hung around only for a short moment and then with deep respect left us. Once gone, my parents then started commenting about Maaz. He had been such a gentleman. He escorted them around the entire campus, had shown them our dormitory, the cafeteria, the tea room, he had even taken them to the gym where Rameez Bhai was my instructor, and shown them at least the chemistry block although he didn't know exactly where my chemistry lectures were held. But being the conversationalist that he was, he no doubt entertained them with ease because my parents' glowing comments about him were greater than positive, as they commented on how he was both a fine Muslim and a fine gentleman. And he must have convinced them that I was in good hands if I took a semester break from my university studies and stayed on the university campus.

While they spoke positively about him, there was an underlying nagging feeling troubling me. My parents thought that Maaz was hospitable, polite, courteous and a gentleman. But they also thought that he was a heterosexual Muslim. But he wasn't. He was my lover. And like me, he was losing his grip on the religion, in particular, the belief that the Koran was perfect and divine. Had my parents suspected or even discovered either of these two aspects of him, their whole concept of him would have turned one hundred and eighty degrees and they would have thought of him as a slimy, evil apostate, a filthy gandu. Everything good about his nature and his disposition would simply have been eclipsed because, although he had sexual attraction like everyone else, that sexual attraction was not directed in the direction my parents and the general society wanted it to be. And despite his gentlemanly nature, his apostasy and his love for me would be the storm cloud that completely obscures the grandeur of the sun.

And this ate at me. I also doubted the Koran and I loved Maaz. Neither of these inner thoughts and feelings could be expressed outwardly because both were crimes against the state, one being a thought crime, as thoughts against the Koran were also crimes against the state, the other a "feeling crime", a crime of feeling deeply for someone, feelings that our society and government did not want to exist.

I had seen enough contradictions, inconsistencies and double standards within the Koran and amongst the different factions which claim that the Koran is perfect. But indoctrination is not an easy thing to escape. I still believed that the moment would come when Allah would finally reveal the veracity of the Koran which would eventually give me the solid basis on which I could finally stand on my faith.

Chapter 19

I don't know what ever happened to Maaz. It was my first relationship with a man and I will never forget him as long as I live. If Pakistan had been like Western countries where gay marriage had been legalised, I guess Maaz and I would have eventually married and lived together quite happily.

After my parents had come to visit me in the dispensary, within a day or two I began to feel much better and my symptoms had almost completely disappeared. The doctor was convinced that my sudden ill health was simply stress related and put it down to a sudden crisis. He assured my parents that these things do happen to some of the students and that I would be fine. It was agreed that I could take a semester break from my studies and remain at the university. I was given strict instructions not to do anything in the form of formal study. My parents then bid me farewell and returned to Karachi.

The break served me well. I used the time at the gym and the swimming pool. And in the evenings the time was spent with Maaz. But it then meant that Maaz would now be finishing his university studies a semester earlier than I would, something I hadn't counted on until we neared that time.

In the last couple of months before Maaz was to complete his last exams and finally complete his degree, he once again changed in composure from his jolly, happy-go-lucky self and fell into a morose and reserved state, very much the same as when he related to me the Issa-Muhammad identity. I left him in peace because I knew that eventually he would speak to me and tell me what was troubling him when the time was right. And that night finally arrived.

We had come back from the cafeteria after eating the evening meal and began settling down for the evening. Maaz, however, had become shifty and listless in a way that troubled me. I knew something was wrong, but it appeared to be more wrong than usual.

"Maaz, is everything okay?" I asked after pausing to look at him. Maaz looked down and away from me at first but then turned to look at his desk. From the angle I was standing I could see he was biting his bottom lip. I could also see that the eye on the side of the face I could see had begun to tear up.

I walked over to Maaz and rubbed his back between his shoulders.

"Hey, Maaz. What's wrong?"

Maaz then turned towards me, wrapped his arms around me and planted his face into my chest. For a good while he wept and the feeling of his tears was felt through my shirt and onto my chest. As troubling as it was, I had to wait till he was in a condition to talk to find out what it was that was troubling him so much. Eventually, he removed his face and looked me directly in the eyes.

"Mustafa," he said, "I hope you understand that I love you. And I will always love you. But this is Pakistan and I have to get married."

The news was unwelcome but not unexpected. As much as I would have liked things to have been otherwise, in the end we lived in Pakistan and a man simply cannot love another man like a man is supposed to love a woman.

Maaz then released himself from my grip and moved away.

"Would you like some tea?" he asked and then began preparing it. I replied that I would have some with him.

"When are you getting married?" I asked him while he went through the preparation ceremony of the tea. He poured tea into our respective mugs and then handed me mine before sitting down at his desk.

"After I finish university," he replied. "Not straight away, of course. My parents assume that it won't be long before I get a job once I've graduated so they have arranged a future wife for me."

Maaz picked up his tea, stared into the contents of the mug and then put the mug back down on the table.

"I mean," he continued, "I've known this girl for a while. My parents were aware that she and I got along as friends so no doubt they have been speaking with this girl's parents to organise our future together."

This was the first time I had heard any association Maaz had with a woman. But what was even further telling was that Maaz never mentioned this girl's name. She remained to me an unknown entity, someone I shouldn't know, someone who he obviously didn't care for in a deep way.

"But we can still see each other after you marry," I more asked than stated.

"Mustafa," Maaz then gruffed frustratingly, "two men cannot love like this, not here in Pakistan. We hear of marriage between two men and two women in the West. But in Pakistani society and in the Islamic world, you know as well as I do that it will never be. The Koran forbids what we're doing. The Koran says that this type of love is reserved between a man and a woman."

Maaz paused for a moment and then added. "And it doesn't even matter if we no longer believe that Islam is true or that the Koran is not perfect. We can't even admit this, let alone that we love each other."

Maaz took a sip of tea. I followed suit and did the same.

"Where did this hate for men who love men and women who love women come from?" Maaz then asked, looking up at the ceiling, despondent anguish in his voice. "If only there was one prophet who loved another man and Allah protected him and allowed those who came after to realise that this is just another form of love."

"But what about Issa?" I asked.

452

"What about Issa?" Maaz asked back, looking into my face.

"In the Injeel, it says that Issa the prophet had a special love for one of his disciples. And Issa never married. And his relationship with this special disciple was rather peculiar."

"Where does it say that?" Maaz then asked and took another sip of tea.

I walked over to my bookshelf, pulled out the Bible Yusuf had given me, came back, sat down and flicked through the pages till I reached the passage.

"In John 13, at the time that Jesus was betrayed, just before Judas betrayed him, while they were having dinner together, Issa prophesied that one of his disciples would betray him. When he said that, it says here that 'the disciple whom Jesus loved was reclining next to him. Simon Peter motioned to this disciple and said, 'Ask him which one he means'. Leaning back against Jesus, he asked him, 'Lord, who is it?'' Notice how it mentions how there was a disciple whom Issa loved. Issa obviously loved all his disciples. But there was one disciple singled out as the disciple whom Issa loved, and this disciple reclined next to and leaned back onto Issa. The way it is written, it sounds like they were lying together like you and I do sometimes here at night alone. This same Gospel in other places talks about this specific disciple being the disciple whom Issa loved, so it can't be the general love that Issa had to everyone that he is talking about but a special love for this disciple."

Maaz stared at the wall then turned back to face me.

"That's in the Injeel," he replied gruffly. "Even if it were true, no-one would accept this because it is in the Injeel, not in the Koran. All Muslims would simply reply that this is a corruption created by later Christians and cannot be trusted or relied on. The only way that Muslims could ever come to at least a thought that the relationship between two men and two women is acceptable is if such a person is mentioned in the Koran."

"But Issa is mentioned in the Koran," I replied.

"Yes, but not this incident you just quoted. And even so, this relationship with this other disciple from what you've read is merely an implication. It is not unequivocal that they were not merely very close friends."

To a point I could agree with Maaz. But at the same time, with my feelings for Maaz and the close relationship that we held together, it was almost impossible to read about the relationship between Issa and this disciple as it is described in the Injeel and see that it was something different to the relationship that Maaz and I held.

"If you could find a prophet in the Koran," Maaz concluded, "who unequivocally could be proven to have had a relationship with another man, maybe there would be a plausible argument, at least a foothold into the possibility of accepting such a relationship."

A quick run through the mental Koran in my head and the significant people inside of it indicated that no such person existed. On the contrary, it seemed clear that such a figure would never exist, especially in light of the story of Lut and the people he was sent to, who were condemned because they exercised their lust on men and not women.

However, what went through my mind was that, as I had read in the Old and New Testaments, and what was known of Muhammad in the Hadiths, all the prophets had haram relationships or were direct descendants of people who had had haram relationships. So, if the prophets could have relationships which went against what was commanded in the Torah and the Koran, why couldn't Maaz and I have a relationship that was haram? As it was with the prophets, the haram relationships in the end did not seem to affect or hurt anyone, so why couldn't this be the same if Maaz and I had a haram relationship?

However, even though I could see this, I was no match against the megalith that was Pakistani society and the Pakistani government. So I was forced to accept that what had started between Maaz and me would soon come to an end. We still had months ahead of us before he finished university. Knowing that the time was short meant that we were intimate a lot together. It was a strange psychology, or perhaps quite expected. Maaz and I knew our time together was limited and fell within the bounds of our time together at the university.

My feelings for Maaz were strong and they overrode any thoughts of us sinning. Those verses in the Koran which spoke against the sin of the people of Lut, as much as their sexual orientation was towards their own sex, it came across that it was the fact that they were only interested in having sex with other men through violence that made it wrong. This seemed to be what the Koran was alluding to. My feelings for Maaz, on the contrary, were nothing like what was described in the Koran. I did not want to rape Maaz and I certainly did not want to hurt him. It was yet another mismatch between what I read in the Koran and how I felt. The Koran was speaking about the lust of nasty, violent men who raped other men. But my feelings for Maaz, were they really lust? Could they really be placed in this same category?

It was making less and less sense to me. Why had Allah created Maaz and me to have these feelings for each other? And why does He ask with great perplexity, "Would you really express your lust towards men and not towards women?" when He is supposed to know all things? And not only should He understand this, even if He didn't appreciate it, why on earth did He create these desires in the first place? If Allah hated the feelings Maaz and I had for each other, Allah was the Almighty and all He had to say was "Be!" and whatever He wanted came to be. This meant that if Allah wanted Maaz's and my feelings for each other to no longer exist, He simply had to say "No longer be!" to our feelings for each other and they would no longer exist. And Allah would no longer have to go on perplexed and disgusted.

Our last night together was a long night. We didn't sleep much. Most of the night was spent in intimacy and simply holding each other closely. There was nothing left to say and what we wanted to express to each other did not require words.

The following morning Maaz had to finally leave. I watched him as he packed his things. We both remained silent. When Maaz had finally prepared all his things together, he just looked at me with a despondent grin on his face but with sadness in his eyes and said, "Ok, let's do it. It's time to go."

I accompanied Maaz to the bus stop where the buses came to pick up students from the university and take them either to the airport or to the main bus station in Lahore from where these graduate students would then continue their journeys back to their home cities.

Just before Maaz got on his bus, he turned to me and we had one last long embrace. It was an embrace I wanted to last forever. We then separated and Maaz looked at me through his deep brown eyes. Maaz had one last thing to say before he mounted onto his bus.

"Mustafa, we could have made it together. Life would have been a wonderful experience with you around. But unfortunately the Koran has won. My family has won. Our society has won."

He shrugged his shoulders and then concluded.

"Who knows? Maybe our children will rise up and remove the burdensome yoke from our shoulders so that they can live in a freer world than we ever experienced."

Maaz then grabbed my shoulders, kissed me on the forehead and finally got on the bus.

I was all cried out to react to this last statement. Like Maaz, at this stage I felt too tired to fight. Islam was like a huge force which did everything to eat up our happiness, a force much stronger than either of us put together.

I watched Maaz take his seat. I dipped my hands into my pockets and suddenly became aware of something papery in my left pocket that hadn't been there before. I pulled it out to find a couple of sheets of paper folded over several times. I unfolded it to see beautiful handwriting, written in elegant Urdu. It was a letter from Maaz. I looked up again at the bus and Maaz looked back at me, smiled and winked. With that the bus pulled away. I stood and watched it as it disappeared into the distance.

Once the bus had disappeared, I stood and read what Maaz had written. It was a long letter. It told of his undying love for me, how I had made his stay at university a beautiful one and he would never forget me as long as he lived. Once I had read it, I folded it up and put it back in my pocket and then walked back to my dormitory.

That would be the last time I had any contact with Maaz. After that, he completely disappeared. I couldn't find him on social media, I couldn't find him anywhwere. He completely vanished out of my life like the vapour emanating from the top of hot cup of tea.

It was now an empty time. The vacuum left by Maaz's departure out of the university and out of my life gasped mightily for something to fill it. This emptiness, this bitter sorrow had to have been for a reason. And there must have been a good reason for it in the long run. Maaz and I had given up on each other for the sake of the Koran and the Islamic religion which permeated our entire society. So this religion had to be right, the Koran still had to be the Word of Allah.

This just showed the strength of the chains that bound us to the belief in the Koran. Even though the evidence had mounted up so much against the Koran to show that in fact the Koran had its faults and after all looked more like the creation of fallible humans and not of an infallible God, my loss of Maaz made me once again clutch tighter to the Koran. The Koran had to be the truth.

My other university friends had all graduated and suddenly I found myself even more alone. But I begged my parents to allow me to stay on campus during the summer break. This gave me an opportunity to avail myself of the gym and the pool, both working out for the sake of my fitness and because the exercise helped me somewhat to get over the pain of my separation from Maaz.

And then Maaz's replacement arrived. His name was Junaid. Junaid arrived a couple of weeks after Maaz had left. He had convinced his parents to allow him to get to the university early and stay there over the summer break before he started lectures. I guessed later as I got to know him that he probably simply just wanted to get away from his parents as soon as he could.

Junaid was a tall, thin, smooth, clean-shaven guy. Like Maaz, he was studying civil engineering, and like Maaz he was a runner. But he also immediately came across as quite the renegade. He was rather messy and disorganised, but at the same time had an agreeable sense of space where he didn't infringe his messiness onto my territory. And he kept rules only as long as they were of benefit to him and broke them when he knew it wouldn't harm anyone else and in particular when he knew he wouldn't get caught. But somehow there was something about him that I liked, and it didn't take me long to be settled with him in the same dorm room.

It also wasn't long before I noticed that his observance of rules was the same with his Islam. If Islam were clothes, on him they would be threadbare. He was a Shiite Muslim and I only discovered this when I noticed he wore a pendant with an image of Muhammad on one side and Ali on the other similar to what Reza used to wear. But it became clear in some of our short evening discussions before going to sleep that his knowledge and understanding of Shiite Islam, or any Islam, was terribly superficial and further he didn't try to get any more knowledge into his head about it than what had already been placed there by his community. But he still believed sincerely in Allah, Muhammad and the Koran. I could never quite work out this seeming contradiction in his person. His belief in the religion was loose, but any suggestion that the religion may actually not be at all true he always dismissed vehemently.

My whole social interaction with him was limited to some evenings before going to sleep so I didn't really know him terribly well at the beginning. But then I really didn't want to either.

One evening I arrived back in the dormitory and Junaid was already there. As soon as I walked in the door, I noticed him jump off his bed and rush over to my small bookshelf. I was quite incensed that he had felt that he could take licence in my private affairs but, before I could say anything and express my disapproval, Junaid beckoned me to allow him to explain his intrusion. He had noticed my Bible amongst my books. The Bible, as far as he was aware, was a forbidden book. When he noticed that I had a copy, he couldn't resist having a read of it. Being forbidden was what gave it its great appeal.

This led him to share a secret with me. He managed to gain access to books, books that were not easily accessible in Pakistan. As it was, the types of books that we had available at our libraries on the university campus were restricted to topics that related to the subjects that we were studying or a limited collection of other books for leisure that were sanctioned by the government. As for local public libraries, there were no such things. If we wanted to read books outside the realm of our religion, we had to buy them or they simply weren't available. At least not openly. Junaid asked me, seeing I had managed to get my hands on a Bible, did I have access to other forbidden books. I explained that I only had this book. I didn't have the opportunity to tell

Junaid how I had acquired this book and its significance to our religion before Junaid asked me, "Would you like to read more forbidden books?"

I had obviously won Junaid's trust, at least in becoming a member of this secret society who had access to forbidden reading material. The nature of these forbidden books had me burning with curiosity to know what it was that made them so controversial. I never got to know Junaid well enough to find out where he gained access to these books and how far reaching this sharing and distribution of forbidden books really was, and really, in the end, for Junaid's safety I really didn't want to know.

It was from this that I discovered that Junaid was an avid reader. What was absolutely bizarre about his lecturous appetite was that he had not read the Koran nor any of the Hadiths. I could only guess that because of his psychology and renegade nature, if society told him to read these, he felt that they were not something worthwhile reading. Forbidden books were much more enticing. And once he realised I was interested in reading these forbidden books, Junaid spent more time in the dormitory in the evening reading these books himself.

There was something deliciously iniquitous about him coming to the dormitory at night with his shoulder bag and then carefully removing the contents, one of which would be books wrapped up in newspapers. I was under strict instructions that I could not remove the book from the dormitory. I could only read it in the dormitory and keep it hidden when I was out. During the summer break, I had plenty of time to read and I read a lot.

I was amazed at the types of books which Junaid seemed to think were forbidden. The first number that he brought back to the dormitory were books in Urdu. It was obvious that these books had passed through many hands as the pages were somewhat stained and tattered, and some pages were dog-eared. They were interesting novels and the storyline allowed me to float away into another world. But I found nothing particularly controversial in the contents. I sometimes wondered if Junaid had done this on purpose to test me.

One book he brought home which to me could be classed as forbidden was George Orwell's *Animal Farm*. The copy I gained access to was withdrawn from a library outside of Pakistan. I asked myself whether or not the books were smuggled into the country from outside or simply friends or family members who lived in foreign countries brought them back into the country and somehow they circulated through this so-called forbidden ring.

The Introduction in *Animal Farm* showed that this was a copy of the book for use in high school when studying English literature. Somewhere in the Introduction, it was explained that the book was written with a view of criticising the emerging Communist Russia back in the early 1900s. The storyline was about animals on a farm that revolted against the ruling humans, eventually chasing them off the farm, and then the animals running the farm themselves. As a result, anything that the humans had done or anything that was considered a human trait was treated as haram.

Although it was supposed to be run as a collective where all the animals were supposed to be treated as equals, eventually the pigs became the rulers. But while reading the book, chills went up my spine when I noticed that the same criticism fit rulership under Islam. What affected me the most was the establishment of the Seven Commandments and then how the ruling animals, the pigs, manipulated the meaning of the words to justify their contravention of these commandments.

The particular commandment that I recognised a chilling similarity was the fourth commandment about beds. Because humans slept in beds, beds were associated with humans and so the fourth commandment stated that "No animal shall sleep in a bed." However, later, the pigs realised how much they themselves enjoyed sleeping in the humans' beds and so they contravened this commandment. But they also justified it. They reinterpreted the meaning of the word "bed" by saying that a bed simply was a place where someone sleeps such as a pile of straw in a shed. However, to the reader, and to the more intelligent animals, it was clearly understood what was meant by a bed when the commandment was made, that it specifically was understood as the place where humans slept, and as everything associated with humans had been made haram, sleeping in the humans' beds was haram. But because this commandment had become troublesome to the ruling authorities who wanted to enjoy sleeping in the humans' beds, the pigs simply reinterpreted the meaning of the word. This reminded me so much of what we did in Islam when we criticised those of other religions. In particular what came to mind was the vehement criticism of idolatrous worship of objects made of rock in other religions and then those in our religion found delight in the idolatrous act of worshipping and kissing the black rock in Mecca and hence found justification for allowing the practice.

But it wasn't only reinterpreting words, it was also the manipulation of the text. This same commandment initially stated that "No animal shall sleep in a bed". But this was then altered to "No animal shall sleep in a bed with sheets". The pigs argued vehemently that this commandment had always been this way, that the additional words "with sheets" were always a part of the commandment. I saw the disturbing similiarity in this and what I had discovered with the English translations of the Koran. On numerous occasions, extra words were written into the English translation that were not a part of the original Arabic text in such a way that it made it appear that this was how the text had always been understood. But it further sent a shiver down my spine when I thought about the hadith Taheer had mentioned about the burning of alternative Korans during Uthman's reign which implied that possibly earlier versions of the Koran were burnt so that the final version of the Koran could be declared as always having been written in this way from the very beginning.

I was further troubled when Junaid got his hands on another of George Orwell's books, *Nineteen Eighty-Four*. In the dystopic world presented in this book, the whole world was ruled by an ultimate leader carrying the epithet Big Brother, and below him a small privileged elite, who not only controlled what everyone did, they also controlled what everyone thought. The storyline follows the protagonist, Winston Smith, who recognises faults in this so-called perfect regime and who is particularly troubled by the manipulation of information. Smith thinks he finds an ally in a man called O'Brien. But this O'Brien ends up being part of the ruling elite and deliberately wins Smith into his trust so that O'Brien can expose Smith's real thoughts about the ruling authorities. Eventually O'Brien tortures Smith thoroughly into submission to follow the party line. What amazed me was that I could readily see the similarities between Big Brother and Muhammad. In the same way that all wisdom and useful knowledge was attributed to Big Brother, who actually ends up being a fantasy figure, in the same way many hadiths attribute every type of useful knowledge to Muhammad. In fact, it wasn't an uncommon thing for people to say that all knowledge in the West, all advances in medicine, all technological advances, all advances of our understanding about the workings of the cosmos, even the technology that the Americans used to get men on the moon, all this was said to have been knowledge gained from Muhammad and which was included in the Koran.

But what further impressed me about the world of *Nineteen Eighty-Four* was the manipulation of the meaning of words. In particular there was an institution called the Ministry of Love. The Ministry of Love was where those who opposed the ruling authorities were tortured with the cruellest of tortures. The comparison with the depiction of Allah was striking. Just about every surah of the Koran starts with the phrase "In the name of Allah, the compassionate, the merciful" and yet this same Allah is the orchestrator of this place called Jahannam where the cruellest of tortures will be inflicted on those who oppose Allah's regime.

What was even more astounding was that Junaid read these same books but did not quite make the connection with what these books said and the society in which we lived. Junaid may have been a renegade in ways but he never questioned the bare bones that Allah was the true God and Muhammad was His prophet.

Strangely, however, it wasn't a book about dystopic societies which had the greatest impact on me. It was a book which had the innocuous title of *The Greek Alexander Romance* by Richard Stoneman. When Junaid presented this book to me, as usual wrapped in a few pages of newspaper, there was an internal sigh of relief that I would be able to read a book that would be relaxing. But as I read through this book, I couldn't help but notice the similarities between the depiction of Alexander the Great in this forbidden book and the character called Dhul Qarnain in Surah Al-Kahf 18:83 – 98. Prior to reading this book, I had not cared about the identity of this character and was simply happy for him to remain incognito, as the true identity of this character had no particular meaning to me. However, now that I noticed the peculiar similarities between Alexander the Great and Dhul-Qarnain, I decided to do an internet search to find out if there was certainly a connection between the two. Some Islamic scholars did favour the idea that Dhul Qarnain was in fact Alexander the Great, whereas others identified Dhul Qarnain with Cyrus the Great of Persia, and then there were those who said that the Koran deliberately does not intend to identify Dhul Qarnain with any historical figure. However, the more I researched it, the more the information

I gleaned pointed strongly and unequivocally to identifying Dhul Qarnain with Alexander the Great, to the point that it was impossible to resist the direct connection between the two.

I didn't have a problem with this identification of Dhul Qarnain with Alexander the Great. In fact, what this showed me was that when someone subjects himself to Allah, Allah grants him the power over all things, for as it says in the surah which speaks of him, in Al-Kahf 18:84, "We established his power on earth". This meant whoever Dhul Qarnain was, the Koran clearly showed that Allah blessed and favoured him to the point of establishing him great power over the earth.

But then again, this troubled me somewhat. Why did Allah make Dhul Qarnain the ultimate power over all the earth at one time in history and yet His greatest prophet, Muhammad, fell well short of world rulership?

I decided to read more about Alexander the Great and find out just how extensive his power was. But by doing so, I discovered more things about Alexander the Great that I was not prepared to discover. Alexander the Great, so all the sources I checked on internet said of him, had three wives, one less than the prescribed maximum of four as the Koran commands. But then I read about Alexander the Great's possible same sex relationship with Hephaestion. There were arguments on internet between those who stated definitively that this great historical figure who had at one time ruled the world, at least, what those in this part of the world believed was the entire world, had a long-term sexual relationship with another man. It was true that Alexander was married to Roxana and then took on two other wives after her. If Alexander also had an affair with Hephaestion, this would make Alexander the Great at least bisexual. But the issue in question was, if Alexander had a sexual and intimate relationship with Hephaestion, why did Allah make Alexander great?

What was even further troubling were the arguments put forward to deny that the relationship between Alexander and Hephaestion was anything more than merely platonic. The society in which Alexander lived, so the argument ran, had no problem with same sex relationships as such relationships were considered part of the social norm. Seeing it was considered normal, it is strange those living at the time of Alexander did not overtly claim that the relationship between these two men was sexual when it would not have been embarrassing or a shame to admit to such a thing. This implied that a sexual relationship actually didn't exist between the two.

But it didn't matter whether it could be conclusively proven that the relationship between Alexander and Hephaestion was sexual or not. The fact still remained that the society in which Alexander lived welcomed same sex relationships and it was out of this society that Allah called Alexander and made him Great. Even if Alexander himself was not homosexual or bisexual, many in the society over which he ruled were and lived openly in same sex relationships. To me, this was like Allah blessing the inhabitants of the cities of Sodom and Gomorrah by making one of their people ruler of the entire world.

This was the final straw which broke the camel's back. Maaz had advanced the proposition and now it had been confirmed. One man in the Koran who Allah blessed, and blessed to an extremely elevated degree to become the ruler of the entire world, this great ruler, Dhul-Qarnain, Alexander the Great of Macedon, at least approved of same sex relationships and could have also been in one himself.

For the first time in my life, instead of making excuses for my religion, I was now filled with complete anger and indignation towards it. For the first time I admitted to myself that the Koran was not a divine revelation from Allah but the compilation made by humans. And what made me further angry was that I had lost Maaz because of it.

But with this anger, I was overwhelmed by fear. The realisation that the Koran is the work of humans and was open to criticism like any other form of literature was not something I could confess openly, not even to Junaid. This realisation that the Koran is not perfect was a thought crime against the state.

Chapter 20

It wasn't an easy transition from believing with all my heart in my religion and in particular believing that the Koran was the infallible Word of Allah, to appreciating that the Koran is a human creation. This last part of the journey where my mind had finally come to this realisation but my heart just didn't want to let go was like a rollercoaster ride of emotions from one day to the next. There were nights when I couldn't sleep, being overwhelmed by a great feeling of fear that I would be cast into Jahannam in the next life for the very thought of the Koran being a humanly written book. I often had nightmares of my first Mulvi metamorphosing into Malik, the angel who presides over Jahannam, grabbing me by the shirt collar and with a grimacing face shaking me vigorously telling me that now it is too late, while behind him I could see the bright orange flames flickering like hungry tongues wanting to consume again and again and again my body forever while I burned for eternity, feeling the horrendous pain of the flames. I would often wake up in the middle of the night in a cold sweat. But when I went back to sleep, the Mulvi would turn into the character of O'Brien in Orwell's *Nineteen Eighty-Four* and I would be doing everything to confess on the outside that I still continued to believe that the Koran was perfect, knowing inwardly that the State simply wanted me to believe this merely to have control over me.

Other dreams had Maaz in them. In these dreams, I was taken back to the time before Maaz had left the university and in my mind I was thankful that we still had time together before he left. It was when I woke from these dreams that I was filled with a feeling of anger towards the religion I was now leaving, and remorse for the loss that I had suffered because of it.

The problem was that I had no-one I could talk to about it. All around me, everyone was Muslim. Even Junaid, as renegade as he was, clung to some essence of Islam, even if only tenuously. I therefore didn't really trust telling him about how my feelings for Islam and the Koran had changed. What was worse, they had changed because of him. Had he not sourced so-called forbidden books for me to enjoy, I can only guess that I would never have ended in this position so quickly. I did think that the way I had been viewing the evidence, I would have eventually arrived at this position sooner or later. My mind was slowly changing to finally reject the Koran anyway, the so-called forbidden books were simply the catalyst which sped up the process.

The awful thing at this time was how alone I felt. All my former uni friends had graduated and gone. All my new uni friends, as far as I was aware, all still believed that the Koran was the infallible Word of Allah. And I lived in a world where I couldn't confess what I'd come to realise, and that I had reached this understanding not out of obstinate disobedience as the Koran indicated, but from careful reading and study of the Koran, from other literature supposedly associated with the Koran, and from my own critical thinking.

Strangely enough, a verse from the Koran itself came to mind and one that Maaz had once quoted, from Surah Al-Anfal 8:22 which says, "Indeed, the worst of the living creatures in the sight of Allah are the deaf and dumb, those who do not use their intellect". What kept going through my mind was the absolute contradiction and moreso the absurdity of this verse. This verse was declaring that we should use our intellect, and critically reason about things and not just accept what we were told. I had used my own intellect and reasoning skills to finally come to the conclusion that the Koran is not the creation of a perfect, almighty divine being but the work of imperfect, fallible humans. This verse also says that Allah hates those who are deaf and dumb, and in this context this means deaf to knowledge and evidence, and dumb in not wanting to speak out against lies and hypocrisy, and declare the truth to all. The absolute irony and therefore absurdity of this verse was that elsewhere in the Koran and our very religious leaders declare the opposite, complete blind submission to the Koran and punishment for those who critically think and voice their criticisms out loud.

This reminded me so much of Orwell's *Nineteen Eighty-Four* and the Ministry of Truth. This ministry churned out literature, such as newspapers and books, that had been manipulated to tell the masses what the ministry wanted the masses to believe, lies declared to be the truth, and how the protagonist, Winston Smith, was brutally tortured for using his intellect and bringing forth evidence that exposed the lies.

I just didn't know what to do. I didn't know what my future held. I felt so alone. My future looked bleak and I felt extremely depressed and despondent. I guessed I would be following the same path as Maaz and getting married to a woman, and then continuing my life, on the outside living as one person, on the inside being a completely different person, totally unhappy and simply existing. It was a terrible prospect of life but I just didn't see any other way to live.

In my last year at university, one of our assignments was to complete a field study. We were taken as a group to a fertiliser factory in the north east of the country. This fertiliser factory was close to the river and in a central location to which lots of farmers came to buy fertiliser for their farms. We were to stay there for a few days and so in the evenings we stayed in a guest lodge near the factory. On the second day of our visit, part of our task was to take a sample of the river water at different points along the bank a couple of hundred metres apart. A couple of my uni friends and I had begun this part of the project. We were at one of the places on the bank obtaining a sample of water. I was crouching down, with one hand on the ground, trying to get my balance so that I could scoop water into one of the plastic containers I had been provided with when suddenly I heard yells behind me. When I looked back up towards the factory, I could see people waving arms furiously and yelling for us to run. My classmates who had accompanied me were already halfway back up the embankment. Before I had a chance to register that this was the beginning of a flash flood, I felt the force of the water push me and the next thing I was underwater. All I could hear was the roaring of water in my ears. I struggled, slashing around, trying hard to get back to the surface, each time taking a large gulp of air before being once again pulled under the surface of the water. I was in complete desperation. My mind also was in turmoil matching the tumult of the water. Events of my past and people who played a significant role flashed before my eyes. I first saw my first Mulvi and him grabbing my shirt collar, telling me that Allah would throw me into hell for eternity. I was suddenly filled with unimaginable fear, thinking that the water pulling me around was this Mulvi's Allah Himself, finally coming to punish me. Strangely, for the first time, instead of calling out to Him for mercy, all I could think of in my mind was, "Go away! Get away from me, Allah!" in terror as if He Himself were this tumultuous water.

I then thought of my grandparents, then my parents. Then I thought of my old friend Reza, Rubasha's brother, the Shiite Muslim.

"Please, Reza's God, the God of the Shiites, please save me," was the thought that went through my mind. The struggle continued under the water and this time I felt as if there were in fact two beings fighting with each other, one trying to drown me, the other trying to save me. I kept fighting and for a moment I managed to surface and take a gulp or two of air. But this didn't last long before I was once again sucked under the tumult.

My mind then conjured up Yusuf ibn Musa. His God, the God of the Bible, especially the God of the New Testament, this God was merciful.

"Please, God of Yusuf ibn Musa, save me," was the thought that went through my mind. Again, I felt as if the titanic struggle in the waters was the struggle between two titanic beings struggling over my body. Once again I had a moment when I resurfaced and could take a gulp of air before being pulled back under the tumult.

Then Rameez Bhai came to mind. "Please, the God of the Lashkari Muslims, help me," was the thought that passed through my mind.

Suddenly the water felt a lot calmer. My head bobbed up above the surface of the water while I began to swim breaststroke. What I could see around me seemed to be one large brown ocean and within that ocean lots of large trees scattered around the place. Where I was, the water was flowing at a much slower and manageable pace which enabled me to manoeuvre towards what looked like a line of trees perpendicular to the flow of the water. There were five, one very large, tall tree sticking up courageously out of the flood waters, and two either side of it, the tops of them bobbing about two metres above the water. I simply swam in the direction of the trees and while doing so, something that Rameez Bhai had said to me came to mind, how that learning to swim might one day save my life. I was amazed at how prophetic these words ended up being.

The current wanted to drift me away from the trees but fortunately I was strong enough to swim against the current and eventually reach out for the outermost tree in the line. No sooner had I grabbed onto one of its branches when I heard someone calling out. I reached out blindly in the direction of the voice. Fortunately when I actually saw him, he was just within reach and our hands joined. While the other man continued forward, I held securely onto the tree while maintaining a firm grip on the man as well. The force of the water although strong was not strong enough to pull us apart and I was able to pull him towards me. At that moment I felt grateful for all the working out I had been doing in the past because I could feel that the workout had given me the strength to hold onto this man and pull him against the current back towards the line of trees.

It was just a matter of moving to the central tree. I told this stranger to hang onto one of the branches of this small outer tree and then manoeuvre himself to the large tree in the centre. But the stranger said he couldn't move. I told him to hold on while I manoeuvred myself onto the next tree which was a little taller and with more solid branches. Once I was stable, with one hand holding onto the tree, I reached out the other hand and told the man to grab it. The man struggled a bit but eventually grabbed my hand. In an instant he disappeared under water but I pulled him with all my might and brought him to the tree I was holding onto. Once he was securely holding onto this tree, I let go of him and inched myself closer to the tallest tree.

I managed to work myself into position where I could reach the trunk of this tall, sturdy tree. I grabbed for a knot on the bark to get a sure hold. Using any form of roughness on the outer surface of the tree to cling onto, I managed to get myself around to the side of the trunk that was resisting the flow of the water and use this to hold me steady against the trunk. Eventually I was able to brace myself against the trunk of the tree. I then yelled to the man to try and manoeuvre himself to be in a position where I could grab his hand. The man struggled for some time, trying to move around the trunk of this small tree. Eventually he was in a position where he could hold onto the tree with one hand and reach out with the other and in so doing I grabbed the man and pulled him over to me.

The man then reached out, grabbed at the trunk and then held with two hands onto the rough surface of the tall tree while I held a handful of his upper tunic to stop him from drifting off with the current. Once I felt that he was stable, I told the man to try and climb up. There were enough knots and rough surfaces in the bark to provide places to grab onto to climb up out of the water. But the man just held onto the trunk. To assist him, I released my grip on the back of his tunic and went to grab an area near his shoulder to drag him up out of the water. By doing so, I felt what seemed like a rope or strap. When I pulled it, it partly came out of the water and I could tell it was some sort of shoulder bag.

"What's over your shoulder?" I asked him.

"It's a carry case I carry the Koran and some other books in."

"Let me pull it over your head," I suggested. "It's weighing you down and is pulling you into the current."

As I pulled on it, I noticed how heavy it was. I was surprised that he hadn't drowned with this excess weight.

The man held with both hands onto the trunk and allowed me to hoist the carry bag over his head. The strap was now over his right shoulder. I noticed a buckle along the strap. I realised that if I unclasped the buckle, I could remove the bag from the man without him having to lose his grip of both hands on the trunk. While keeping myself braced to the trunk of the tree with my legs and torso flattened against it and the current keeping me in place, I was able to use both hands to finally unclasp the buckle and then remove the shoulder bag away from the man. Once it was away from him, I began trying to reclasp the buckle.

"What are you doing?" the man yelled.

"I'm just clasping the strap back together so I can hang your shoulder bag onto one of the knots in the trunk until you are safe up and out of the water."

The man gave me a strange, angry look and then yelled at me as a retort, "Just let go of it! There are only books in it!"

"But, you said you had the Koran in there," I called back.

"Yes, and so what?" the man snapped. "Which is more important? To save these lifeless books or to save our lives?"

I was stunned by the comment. I hesitated for a moment. But then as I noticed the man struggling to keep a grip on the trunk, I did what he said, let go of the carry case and then attended to helping the man.

With a few heaves, I had the man climbing up on the trunk. The lowest branch was barely a metre above the surface of the water. Once he was finally settled on the first branch, I then followed and sat on a branch on the opposite side of the trunk and a little higher out of the water than what this stranger was sitting on.

Once this man was out of the water, his clothes clinging dampeningly to his body, I could tell he was wearing a *kameez*, the long shirt that came down to the knees, what was typical of our traditional clothing, but with his beard he looked like a Mulvi or a Mufti. He was now definitely a drenched one.

"Thank you," the man said once he had settled. "Thank you for saving me."

"That's okay, sir," I replied respectfully.

The man looked at me and then smiled.

"My name's Muhammad."

"Mustafa," I replied. "Mustafa Faakhtaa."

"Mustafa Faakhtaa," Muhammad then echoed. He then had a deep furrow in his forehead. "Mustafa Faakhtaa from Karachi?"

I thought I was going to fall off my branch.

"Are you a prophet or something?" I asked perplexed.

Muhammad laughed.

"Quite the contrary," he replied. "You're a friend of Maaz Faydakh from Yemuhamvar."

I remained speechless for a moment. Then as I looked carefully into Muhammad's face, I noticed the unusually bushy eyebrows that met at the middle and pointed up at the dark freckle in the centre of his forehead. That's when I realised where I had earlier seen him.

"Yes, I remember you. We met once in Vokyalesh."

Muhammad looked at me intently, trying to work out my features.

"Mmmmmm. I don't rightly remember you. But then you were probably a lot less waterlogged at the time," he replied.

We both looked out across the water and could see in the distance more trees and a small agglomeration of houses so we must have been somewhat close to a farming village. We started yelling towards the houses to get people's attention but it became obvious that the sound of the water rushing by was drowning out our calls for help. We could see people sitting on the roofs of these partly submerged homes. We began waving in their direction. Soon a few people on the roofs waved back which indicated that they were aware that we were here in the trees. But there was no way that they could come to us or we could get to them. At least they were aware we were in these trees because once the rescue helicopters eventually came to save them, these people could also direct the helicopters to come and get us as well. So now we realised that there was nothing else we could do but wait.

"So, are you a Mulvi?" I asked.

Muhammad laughed.

"No, but I'm a Mulvi's son. What made you ask?"

"You're dressed like a Mulvi," I replied. "And you were carrying religious books like a Mulvi."

Muhammad looked down at his drenched and now dirt stained clothes.

"I thought I was dressed pretty normally for a Pakistani," he replied.

There was something familiar in Muhammad's face and voice which drove me to ask more about him.

"What's your family name?" I asked.

"Nashrooyarth."

Once he had told me his surname, I realised why he looked so familiar. From our conversation at Vokyalesh, he had said he lived near my suburb of Alekh-Jahan. There was only one Mulvi I knew with this surname in my home suburb.

"Oh...my...God!" I exclaimed. "You're *my* Mulvi's son."

I thought about my Mulvi telling me about his son, Muhammad, often coming to this area because of his work.

Muhammad laughed at my statement.

"So," he then said. "Are you a diligent student of my father? Or did you become a doubter like Maaz?"

Muhammad then looked back at me with a cheeky grin on his face once he had said this.

I didn't dare answer Muhammad's question.

"Don't worry," Muhammad laughed and then continued. "I can tell from your silence to my question that I'm in good company. Maaz told me that he had told you about the lack of mention of the traditional Islamic Muhammad in the Koran and how the Muhammad in the Koran is most likely Issa, although not the Issa of Christianity where the Christians claim that Issa is both the Son of God and God Himself."

I felt a flush in my face when he mentioned this. For a second time I didn't know what to say.

Muhammad laughed again.

"Yes, Maaz told me a lot about you," he continued, "how you were also searching for answers from the Koran. I was the one who pointed out to him the real identity of the Muhammad in the Koran."

"So, that was you?" I asked in surprise. "So, are you a Christian?"

Muhammad laughed yet again.

"Of course not!" he replied. "The Koran is right when it says that God cannot have a son like the Christians say. It makes absolutely no sense that God can be eternal and then have a son who is also supposed to be eternal. If Issa were truly God's son, then Issa could not be God and definitely could not be the eternal God because being a son means that he had to have had a beginning which therefore doesn't make him eternal."

"But you still believe the Koran is the Word of Allah, then?" I asked.

Muhammad adjusted himself on his branch.

"What do you think?" Muhammad then asked me.

I shrugged my shoulders.

"Well," Muhammad then said by way of answering my nonverbal response. "Let's let the Koran itself tell us whether or not it is from Allah. Doesn't the Koran say in Surah An-Nisaa 4:82 'Do they not ponder on the Koran? If it had been from other than Allah, surely they would have found much contradiction in it'. The Koran itself puts us to the test to see whether or not it was from Allah or from someone else. So, let's test it."

I felt a shiver go straight up my spine. In the past I had questioned internally the veracity of the Koran. Also, my discussions which had caused doubt were more over interpretations of what the Koran said. But this was now the first time that I had spoken openly with someone else, challenging the veracity of the Koran as the book from Allah. However, Muhammad seemed quite relaxed discussing this openly with me.

"So, according to Muslims," Muhammad began, "who is the greatest prophet? And if you're not sure of the answer, just quote to me the Shahada."

To this last statement, he laughed.

The Shahada went through my mind.

"Naturally, it's Muhammad," I replied.

"Then why," Muhammad continued, "is it that Muslims say 'We believe in Allah and Muhammad is the Messenger of Allah' when such a statement does not come from the Koran? You will find the statement 'There is no god but Allah' mentioned over 30 times throughout the Koran yet not one verse in the Koran adds to this the last piece of the Shahada that Muhammad is the Messenger of Allah. Yet the Koran clearly states in Al-Baqarah 2:136 as well as in a few other verses in the Koran that 'We believe in Allah and what is revealed to us and what was revealed to Ibrahim and Ismail and Isaac and Jacob and the descendants, and what was given to Moses and Issa and what was given to the Prophets from their Lord. We make no distinction between any of them.' If Muslims truly believe the Koran as they say they do, the Shahada should make a claim similar to this, that all the Messengers are Messengers of Allah and not just Muhammad."

My furrow deepened.

"But that isn't a contradiction in the Koran. That's just a contradiction between the Shahada and the Koran."

"Very good observation," Muhammad replied. "Let me now get to the point. If the Koran says in this verse in Al-Baqarah not to make a distinction between the Messengers, why does it say later in Al-Baqarah 2:253 'These Messengers! We preferred some over others. Among them were those with whom Allah spoke, and He raised some of them in degrees'. Why is it that Allah says in one verse that He preferred some prophets over others yet in another that we are required not to make any distinctions between them? The Koran repeats this preference for some prophets over others in Bani-Israel 17:55 where it says 'And your Lord is most knowing of whoever is in the heavens and the earth. We have preferred some of the Prophets to others'. If we are to make no distinction between the prophets, how can there be those prophets who are preferable to others?"

I just stared down at Muhammad. I had already been familiar with this contradiction but had pushed it to the back of my mind. Muhammad had once again brought it back into my consciousness. Yes, this was a contradiction and for the first time I felt that I didn't have to try and explain it away. I agreed with Muhammad that this was a blatant contradiction but I gave a noncommittal shrug of the shoulders as my answer to his question.

"Have you also noticed," Muhammad continued, "that in this verse from Al-Baqarah that Allah preferred some prophets over others and those prophets He preferred were those prophets to whom Allah spoke directly? If this is the case, and as it says in Surah Al-Imran 4:164 that 'Allah spoke to Moses directly', this makes Moses greater than Muhammad because we have been told, but this is not found in the Koran, that Allah didn't speak to Muhammad directly but sent the angel Gabriel to speak to him."

For the first time, instead of a shudder at the discovery of a contradiction in the Koran, I felt a relieving sensation that my final rejection of the Koran as perfect had a solid foundation. Further, for the first time, I could openly admit it. I no longer had to deny it. I paused for a moment and then, like opening the blow-hole of a balloon and letting the air out, I felt I could also relieve myself of the pressure inside me.

"And not only does the Koran say that Allah spoke directly to Moses," I replied, "it says that Allah spoke directly to Issa as well. This is a contradiction in the whole Islamic faith, not just within the Koran but in the entire belief. Muhammad may have been the last prophet, but if prophets who had spoken directly with Allah are greater than those who had received revelations indirectly through a mediator, this means that according to the Koran, Muhammad is in a lower degree to Moses and Issa. The verse you quoted indicates that it is not the chronology of the advent of the prophets that makes one prophet greater than another but the means of communication Allah has with them."

"Yes," Muhammad said to that comment. "Very insightful. I can see why Maaz spoke so highly about you!"

Muhammad then moved on the branch to make himself more comfortable.

"As for the Koran itself," Muhammad continued, "did the Koran come to Muhammad all at once?"

"No," I replied. "The Koran was revealed in stages over the lifetime of Muhammad."

"So the Koran tells us," Muhammad replied, "at least in Surah Al-Furqan 25:32 where it says 'And those who disbelieve say, 'Why was not the Koran revealed to him all at once?'' and later in Surah Al-Insan 76:23 where it says 'Indeed, We revealed to you the Koran progressively'. However, in Surah Ad-Dukhan 44:2, 3 it says 'By the clear Book, Indeed, We revealed it in a Blessed night'. Assuming that this 'clear Book' is the Koran, then was the Koran revealed all in one night as it says in Ad-Dukhan, or in stages as it says in the other verses?"

I just smiled and nodded. There was something relieving about being able to openly air the problems with the Koran without the threat to our safety and even our lives. But at this point it was more Muhammad than I who was doing all the expressing.

"Shaitaan makes us see there are contradictions in the Koran," Muhammad then said and there was a lot of mocking contempt in his voice. I could appreciate why he reacted in this way because this was what we had been told. "But don't you think," Muhammad then continued, "that it's strange that Shaitaan, or Iblis, or Satan, or whatever we want to call him refuses to worship and obey Allah? After all, it says in Surah An-Nisaa 4:172 that 'Christ disdains not to serve and worship Allah, nor do the angels' and again in

481

Surah Ar-Rad 13:13 'And the thunder glorifies His praises and so do the Angels' and again in Surah An-Nahl 16:49 'And to Allah prostrate whatever is in the heavens and whatever is on earth of the moving creatures and the Angels, and they are not arrogant'. So the Koran clearly states, and we are often told, that all the angels obey Allah, they are unable to disobey Allah, and further they are not arrogant. Yet then the Koran says that Shaitaan is an angel and then says he was arrogant and refused to obey Allah when Allah told the angels to prostrate to Adam once Adam was created as it says in various places in the Koran, in Surah Al-Baqarah 2:34, in Surah Saad 38:73 & 74, and elsewhere."

I nodded in reply to Muhammad's analysis. Muhammad continued.

"And it's not only the angel Shaitaan who disobeyed Allah. In Al-Baqarah 2:102 we read about the two angels, Harut and Marut, who taught magic contrary to the wishes of Allah. So, what are we supposed to believe from the Koran? All the angels obey Allah or there are some who don't?"

"The problem goes a lot deeper," I replied. "The very nature of Shaitaan according to the Koran is contradictory. As you've just stated, Shaitaan in Surah Al-Baqarah and Surah Saad is an angel. However, in Surah Al-Kahf 18:50 the Koran says that Shaitaan is a jinn."

"But aren't jinns angels?" Muhammad then asked. At first I wasn't sure if he was joking or serious. I screwed up my face as an expression of misunderstanding and this gave Muhammad the signal to explain himself.

"It says in Surah Saad 38:76 that the reason why Shaitaan refused to prostrate before Adam was because the humans were made from clay but he, Shaitaan, an angel, was made from fire. But then in Surah Ar-Rahman 55:15 it says that Allah made the jinn from fire. Which then raises the question about the difference between angels and jinns. Are angels and jinns the same thing or are they different?"

I thought just how correct Muhammad was with his analysis. Muhammad gave me a wry smile.

"Well," he then added, "we could say they are different because in Surah Saad 38:76 it simply says that Shaitaan, as an angel, was made from fire whereas in Ar-Rahman 55:15 it says that jinns are made of *smokeless* fire, and that makes all the difference."

I just burst out laughing when Muhammad said that.

"You know," I then replied. "I've never thought about this before. But when you think about it, you can't make anything from fire. Fire is energy. It's just the energy given off during the combustion of carbon and oxygen, energy in the form of light and heat. And smokeless fire is simply complete combustion because all the carbon gets bound up with oxygen to make carbon dioxide, which is an invisible gas. When we get smoke from fire, the combustion between carbon and oxygen is not complete, that is, not all of it forms carbon dioxide. Some of the products of the combustion process form other carbon compounds that we can see and sometimes we see pure carbon itself being formed when we see the intensely black soot from a flame."

I thought a little more and then added, "And to get fire in the first place, you have to have something in the form of fuel. So if angels and jinns were made from fire, they were indirectly made from the substance that fueled the fire in the first place."

Muhammad just humphed, smiled wryly and shook his head.

There was a moment of silence and then Muhammad added, "And, I mean, how is fire a superior material to create anything anyway, better than clay, which caused Shaitaan to think he was a better creation than humans? What was Shaitaan's justification for claiming that he was a better creature than Adam apart from his simple claim that he was made of a different raw material? How does fire as the base material create a better finished product than something made from clay? Was that the best argument Shaitaan could come up with in his arrogance? This just makes Shaitaan dumb. And if he's so dumb to make such a claim, how is it that at the same time this same Shaitaan can be so brilliantly cunning to mislead humanity in the clever way that he supposedly does?"

With that, I just leant back and laughed. I had to hold onto the trunk of the tree to prevent myself from falling into the water. When we began to analyze this story in detail, I realized just how implausible and absurd it all sounded. Muhammad looked up at me, smiled, shrugged his shoulders and then shook his head. It took a moment before I could calm down enough to talk.

"However," I then said, "That's not a contradiction!"

"Ah, yes," Muhammad then stated, "we got off topic. We were talking about contradictions. Okay, here's another one. How long will the unbelievers reside in Jahannam and believers reside in paradise?"

I shrugged my shoulders.

"Forever," I replied.

"Yes," Muhammad replied, "that's what the Koran says in verses like Al-Baqarah 2:25 & 39. But in Hud 11:106 - 108 it says the unbelievers will reside in Jahannam and the righteous will reside in paradise 'as long as the heavens and the earth remain.' And as it says in Bani Israil 17:99 that Allah has appointed the heavens and the earth a term, and the Koran looks to the future, as it says in Al-Infatar 82:2 'when the sky is cleft asunder' and in Al-Fajr 89:21, 'When the earth is levelled, pounded and crushed', that's good news for the unbelievers, but not terribly good news for the believers."

Once again, I burst out laughing. But it was also an interesting point. Jahannam and paradise were not necessary the abodes of eternity if the verse from Surah Hud was correct.

"Speaking of the heaven and the earth," Muhammad continued, "Which was created first?"

I stared up at the top of the tree as if the answer were stealthily written somewhere high above me, the pages of the Koran in my mind flicking over while I tried to provide Muhammad an answer.

"It all depends," Muhammad said answering his own question, "which part of the Koran you read from. In Al-Baqarah 2:29 and Fussilat 41:9 - 11, Allah created the earth first and then turned to the heaven and created this afterwards. However, in Al-Anbiya 21:30 heaven and earth started out as one substance, and then Allah split this mass in two, one forming the heaven and the other the earth, the implication being that heaven and earth originally were created as one entity."

"And it's not only which one was created first and which second," I added. "It's also how many days it took to create. In that same passage in Surah Fussilat it says that Allah created the heaven and the earth in eight days but in Surah Al-Araf 7:54 it says that Allah created the heaven and the earth in six days."

"Speaking of numbers," Muhammad then added, "the Koran in these verses says that there is only one heaven. But then in Al-Baqarah 2:29 it says that Allah created seven heavens. God only knows why!"

I had to laugh at that last comment Muhammad made. I knew he meant it as sarcasm but that was the type of answer our religious leaders would give us if we ever questioned anything that didn't make sense from the Koran. I wasn't sure if Muhammad had deliberately chosen to make this statement as a play on words or he was just speaking exasperatingly.

"Not only did He create seven heavens," I continued, "there are those out there who claim that Allah means that He created seven parts of our atmosphere. But this doesn't fit the description in the Koran because it says in As-Saffat

485

37:6 that the lowest heaven is where we find the stars. We now know that the stars are well beyond the earth's atmosphere so this argument doesn't fit."

"And what were the stars created for?" Muhammad asked with a sarcastic tone in his voice. "As it says in the verses which follow this verse, the stars were made to be projectiles to cast at Shaitaan and his followers to prevent them from being able to hear what Allah is talking about while He is in the Exalted Assembly. Whatever that means!"

When Muhammad said that, I realized the inconsistency of this verse on so many levels. For a start, what was this Exalted Assembly that the Shaitaans wanted to get access to and listen in on? Who does Allah have an assembly with? This once again showed that the Islamic belief had not completely disposed of the idea of polytheism. For there to be an assembly required a group of people. That there was an Exalted Assembly implied that this assembly was much greater than any normal assembly, and because it was talking about God, it was a divine assembly. But if there is only one God, Allah, how could there be an Exalted Assembly? Unless there were other exalted beings in this Exalted Assembly. The other beings can't be angels because Allah doesn't discuss with angels, He simply tells angels what to do and they obey. If He discussed anything with the angels, this implied that the All-Knowing Allah listened to the advice proposed by the angels which raises the question as to why Allah would consult anybody for advice if He knew everything. So these beings with whom Allah schemes and plans in the Exalted Assembly have to be beings Allah considers His equals, highly exalted above humans and angels, and hence, by implication, other gods.

But further, what would Allah be discussing in the Exalted Assembly? That the Shaitaans wanted to listen in to what was discussed in this Exalted Assembly implied that the Shaitaans wanted to find out what Allah planned in His next move to defeat the Shaitaans, and the Shaitaans wanted to be pre-warned and therefore pre-armed. But that didn't make sense when we considered Allah's nature. Allah was omniscient and omnitemporal, knowing all of time from the beginning to end, but also existing in all time from beginning to end. So what would the omniscient Allah be discussing in the Exalted Assembly and who was He discussing with?

This also made Allah finite in space and time. But the Koran was clear that He was everywhere, occupying all the universe and even being closer to us than our jugular veins. So if there were an Exalted Assembly in which Allah resides to discuss tactical manoeuvres against the Shaitaans, does He only do this in this finite space? Why doesn't He have these discussions in all the corners of the universe in which He resides?

"These same heavens," Muhammad said which broke me out of my thoughts, "so it says in Surah Az-Zumar 39:67 'will be folded in His right hand'. This only makes sense if the heavens are made of solid material when we now know that what is outside earth is empty space."

There was a slight pause and then Muhammad added, "This is why Pakistan doesn't have a space program."

This brought to mind what Taheer had told me about the motions of the heavenly bodies as described in the Koran versus what we had learnt at school. I then thought of what Taheer had said, how that what we were taught about the makeup of the heavens and the movement of the heavenly bodies as it was discovered from scientific observation and measurement contradicts the koranic description of the universe, which ultimately meant that science teachers were in reality contravening our blasphemy laws.

Muhammad then talked about how the Koran talks of a flat earth and a moving sun, things that Taheer had made me aware of. But Muhammad added that according to Surah 55:17 Allah is the "Lord of the two easts and the two wests" when it was quite obvious that there was only one of each.

Muhammad then made the counterclaim against those who said that we should look at these unusual verses as metaphors. He said we should remind ourselves of the verse in Al-Imran 3:7 which says "Then as for those in whose hearts is perversity, they follow what is allegorical from the Book". While this verse works in favour of those who want to follow the literal commands of the Koran, it then puts these people in an awkward situation when they are required to believe the literal understanding of all these verses which describe the structure and movement of the universe.

I nodded my head in agreement when Muhammad had finished.

"But these are not contradictions in the Koran, either" I stated.

Muhammad pointed at me with an index finger and smiled.

"Yes, you're right," Muhammad then stated and once again adjusted himself on the branch. "Okay, getting back to Creation, have you ever pondered on this? The Koran says on several occasions that Allah created us in pairs, that is, one man and one woman, such as in Surah Ar-Rum 30:21, Surah Ya-Sin 36:36, Surah Ash-Shura 42:11, Surah Adh-Dhariyaat 51:49 and Surah An-Najm 53:45. Yet in Surah An-Nisaa 4:3, the Koran says that a man can have four wives. If a man can have four wives, then all things were not created in pairs."

This took me into deep thought. This was yet something else I had actually never thought of before. It was true that I had read these verses about being created in pairs and the other verse about having up to four wives but this was the first time that they were put together. And then I remembered something I had read in the Kitab-e-Hidayat.

"You know," I then said, "what is really strange with that contradiction is that the verse in An-Nisaa 4:3 which says that a man can have four wives is only two verses down from the verse which says that Allah created us from a single soul and then created a mate from this soul, the implication is as the rest of the verse says that men and women were supposed to be paired up, one man with one woman."

"Mmmmmmmm! A very good point," Muhammad replied.

There was a moment of silence while we looked out on the scene of this vast ocean of brown water. Then Muhammad once again spoke.

"I think," Muhammad then said, "that we've established that the Koran has enough contradictions to answer the challenge in An-Nisaa 4:82 that if we find many contradictions we know that the Koran is not from Allah."

Muhammad paused and then sighed. "Another difficulty, and what I find embarrassing, is that we are forced to accept as divine truth empty claims or pure nonsense."

Muhammad looked up at me. I stared back at him in expectation.

"I mean," Muhammad continued, "in Surah Ad-Dukhan 44:4 the Koran boasts that in it 'every wise affair is made distinct'. Yet much of what is written in the Koran is obscure, the stark evidence being the rise of the Hadiths, these copious collections of literature supposedly out there to explain what it is this supposedly clear book is saying. But, I mean, what wise affairs are made distinct or are even mentioned in the Koran? Is there anything in this book which gives advice to young school leavers about making the right career choices? Is there anything in the Koran which explains how to maintain one's physical health? Is there anything in the Koran which explains how to avoid serious illness, how to cure serious diseases, how to avoid and/or cure the plethora of ailments floating about in the world? Is there anything in the Koran which gives helpful instruction as to how to create a sustainable recycling system of goods so that humans don't create the amount of pollution they do? Does the Koran provide the blueprint on how to create a clean energy source that doesn't have the harmful side effects that fossil fuels currently have?"

Muhammad gave out another sigh of frustration while I contemplated on what he had just said. What came out of his argument to me was that throughout all my university studies, not once did any of my lecturers mention the Koran. It was not one of our recommended textbooks and there was nothing in the Koran which helped me with the learning I was gaining about this branch of science. The only conclusions that we could draw from this verse from Ad-Dukhan was that either this verse was wrong or there was nothing wise in anything I had learnt up to now in my degree. So did this mean that because chemical engineering was not mentioned in the Koran, all that I had learned of chemical engineering was foolishness?

"It's also the nonsense in the Koran," Muhammad then said which broke me out of my thoughts. "Have you ever wondered about this verse from Al-Baqarah 2:138 where it says 'The colour of Allah! And who is better than Allah at colouring?' And that's it. I mean, what in God's name does this verse actually mean? And what do we gain from this verse? How many a scholar has read this verse and then walked away totally dazzled and amazed, exclaiming something like, 'Wow! Yes! How profound is this verse! All the greatest scientists put together could never have come up with something as profound as this!'"

Once again, I laughed. Muhammad's sarcasm was humorous. Muhammad raised his bushy eyebrows and a smarmy look crossed his face.

"And what about this verse from Surah An-Noor 24:61," he continued, "where it says, 'There is no blame on the blind nor the sick nor on yourselves, if you eat in your houses or the houses of your fathers, or the houses of your mothers, or the houses of your brothers, or the houses of your sisters, or the houses of your paternal uncles, or the houses of your maternal uncles, or the houses of your maternal aunts, or whose keys you possess, or of a friend. There is no blame on you whether you eat together or separately.' Look at how lengthy this verse is and yet it tells us absolutely nothing. I mean, have there been people in society at any time in history full of anguish wondering whether or not they were about to commit a misdemeanour if they went and ate at one of their relatives' homes? Or were there those, blind, sick or healthy, who had been uncertain about whether or not they should eat together with people or eat alone? The picture that forms in my mind when I read this verse is of someone sitting down at home, rubbing their hands together full of anguish saying to themselves, 'Gee, my father just rang to ask if I wanted to come over and have lunch at his place, and I'm wondering if I would be committing a sin if I did such a thing. Worse, would I be committing a sin if I ate together with my father?'"

Again, I had to laugh. The way he presented the verse and his explanation of it was just so true.

"And," he continued, "what about what we read in Surah An-Naml 27:18 where it says that 'when they came to the valley of the ants, an ant said, 'O ants! Enter your dwellings so that Sulaiman and his hosts may not crush you while they do not perceive'.' Seriously! Ants talk? This sounds more like cartoons we watch when we are children and the animals in the cartoons are personified. And, what do they talk about? The daily news? The weather? And in what language? It can't be Arabic because ants don't have mouths like humans to frame the sounds we make. And speaking of languages, according to the same surah, only two verses before this one, it says, 'And Sulaiman inherited Dawood. And he said, 'O people! We have been taught the language of birds'.' I mean, seriously? Which birds? All of them? The language of pigeons, sparrows, bulbuls, penguins, ostriches, emus? And who are these people who with Sulaiman have been taught the language of birds? All humanity? Muslims? And what type of philosophical discussion could we have with birds? Why would anyone want to talk to birds anyway? Have you ever wanted to have a philosophical conversation with a pigeon?"

Once again, I just burst out laughing. I couldn't help the picture forming in my mind of me sitting in a park, throwing breadcrumbs to the pigeons and at the same time asking the pigeons their opinions about the current political situation in Pakistan.

Muhammad looked down at the water beneath us and then continued. "And why is it that Allah was happy for Sulaiman and these unknown people to learn all the different bird languages, but insists that Muslims who speak different human languages must learn Arabic and only read the Koran and pray to Allah in Arabic? Why didn't Allah do what He does to humans and make the birds speak Arabic and be done with it?"

I nodded and smiled at him. It was funny how I had read these verses before but hadn't actually registered what Muhammad was pointing out to me. But once he had done so, it was impossible to unsee it.

Muhammad then turned his head towards the canopy of the tree above us and then turned to me.

"But think of it this way as well. As it is with ants and birds, the Koran says that Allah talks. But what does this mean? Does Allah talk like humans? And if so, this means that there has to be air in heaven because human speech relies on the movement of air through the respiratory system and the movement of the tongue and the glottis. But we know there is no air outside our atmosphere."

Muhammad then went quiet for a moment. And when he spoke again he had become quite serious.

"What is annoying and frustrating is that not only is it oppressive that we have to live under the Koran and that people are imprisoned for criticizing the Koran, once people outside the religion read what the Koran actually says, it makes us look ridiculous for having such blasphemy laws in the first place. Not only are there concepts in the Koran that are childish, it's embarrassing that we are told to believe that they are true. For all those countries like Pakistan which have blasphemy laws for criticizing the Koran, this must make us look like a laughing stock to other nations when they finally discover these childish stories are in the Koran but the very leaders of our countries insist they are true and we could go to prison or be executed for showing how childish these stories really are. I mean, you think about it. Imagine a society where the ruling authorities insist that a children's book like *A Jungle Book* or *Jasmine and Aladdin* is perfect, a book that has animals talking in it like in the Koran, and anyone who finds fault with this book should be imprisoned. It is embarrassing that adults, especially well-educated adults who run the country, believe wholeheartedly that these stories are unquestioningly true when we know that animals simply don't talk."

We soon heard the sound of a helicopter. We both looked up and saw over in the distance a helicopter come to the houses and start picking up people from the rooftops, ascend back into the sky and then disappear.

There was something symbolic about looking at the tumult and turmoil flowing under us which reflected the emotional turmoil that I had gone through while trying to make sense of the Koran and the Islamic religion with all its varied sects. Pulling myself out of this maelstrom enabled me to feel safe and secure as I did while sitting on this branch but my movements were limited. I not only had to be out of the turmoil, somehow I had to get completely away from it.

But I had to ask something from Muhammad.

493

"So, who do you think wrote the Koran?"

Muhammad screwed up his face.

"I don't know for certain. But the Koran itself gives clues. For a start, look at its structure. Each surah is an agglomeration of verses. In much of the Koran there is no flow of thought from one verse to the next. Compare this with the Torah and the Injeel. The Torah and the Injeel have a logical flow. Muslims criticize the Torah and the Injeel saying they have been corrupted. But it would be difficult to make alterations in the Torah and the Injeel without it being obvious. I'm not saying it's impossible, just that it's difficult. By contrast, the Koran is a haphazardly put-together collection of verses. This therefore makes it easy to substitute one verse with another. And there are hints in the Koran itself as well as in the Hadiths that this is in fact what happened over the course of the time that the Koran was composed. As it says in An-Nahl 16:101 'And when we substitute a Verse in place of a Verse', this must have been going on throughout its development. And having the Koran structured the way it is makes it easy to substitute verses with other verses without making any changes to the verses which precede or follow.

As for what the original writers of the Koran first believed, to me it is obvious that they believed that Issa was a great prophet, in fact, *the* great prophet, the chosen one, the praised one, the Muhammad. However, these people weren't Christians, at least, not in the sense of Christians we know today who believe that Jesus is not only the Messenger of Allah but also Allah Himself. Needless to say, they had some connection and affinity with the Jews and the Christians because they also believed in their holy books, the Torah and the Injeel, and most probably the entire Old Testament and New Testament alike. But as time developed, they began to separate themselves from the Jews and Christians and indeed become hostile towards them. So they needed their own Scripture and they needed their own prophet. Seeing Muhammad is identified as Issa in the Koran, then the other mentions of the Prophet which don't match up with the life of Issa in the Injeel most probably refer to this new prophet that was forming. No doubt this new prophet eventually took on the name of Muhammad and this became a popular name. After all, my name is Muhammad and look at all the men throughout the Islamic world whose names are Muhammad.

What was also important for those who composed the Koran was that they had some sort of Holy Book. Originally they wanted to have the sanction of the Torah and the Injeel but once they had gained power, they wanted the Koran to replace the Torah and the Injeel. While the Bible still held authority, Jews and Christians in the West still had some power over the Arabian Empire. We see this change in thought process where the Torah and the Injeel are given great authority in the Koran itself and the Koran acknowledges that it is confirming the previous holy books. But then later we see that the focus changes from the Koran being an extension of the Torah and the Injeel to being *the* Book and then the *only* Book, which is in itself a contradiction."

We could hear the helicopter in the distance and there was a feeling of relief that it would soon be coming over to rescue us.

"What about you? So what do you believe?" I then asked.

Muhammad laughed. "I don't know yet. This is as far along the road as I have come." Muhammad then paused before continuing. "You know? Muslims criticise the Hindus because of their polytheism. But I've started reading about Hinduism and talking to local Hindus. The concept of polytheism I find somewhat absurd but the more you look into the religion, there is a lot of depth to it."

Muhammad looked up at me.

"Muslims criticise Hindus for their absurd beliefs. But when we criticise the Koran with its absurdities, the religious authorities, such as my father, claim that there is something deep and mysterious there which makes these absurdities somehow profound. But they don't do the same thing for Hinduism. Yet, I think there are things in the Hindu religion which may have some credit. I don't have any firm beliefs as yet. I'm still searching."

The helicopter kept coming in our direction which stopped the conversation. Both Muhammad and I decided to stand up and wave so that the helicopter pilot could see where we were. It took some time for the helicopter to remain in a safe, stationary position above us and then let down the rescue cord to pull us out of the tree. I let Muhammad go first and soon I followed, being plucked well out of the tree and up above the water to the safety of the helicopter. The rescue team inside asked us if we knew of any other people in the trees around where we were but we said we didn't know and couldn't see from where we were.

There was something even further symbolic about being flown away from the tumultuous waters below us. It was like a message from Allah that I needed to do the same. I could no longer continue to live in Pakistan simply because I no longer believed in the Koran and probably even moreso because I knew I could no longer live here as a gay man.

Chapter 21

After my graduation, which was held at Vokyalesh University, my parents, who had attended, flew together with me back to Karachi. My parents told me how proud they were that I had completed my degree which would enable me to get a good, well-paid job. They also commented on how well I looked, obviously because I had looked so sick the time they had come to Vokyalesh University when I was taken seriously ill but also from the exercise regime that I had taken up while at the university which concluded with me having a much better shaped body than I had before I left Karachi. A good-looking young man with a good job meant that I had all the chances of marrying well, which no doubt was the next event on my life's agenda according to my parents' thinking and which was the common thought in our entire society.

This was one of those moments I thought of Maaz, especially at night while I was alone in my bed and I reflected on the nights Maaz and I had spent together intimately. I wondered if he was already married. I also therefore wondered if he was lying in bed with his new wife. To this I thought once again about the cruelty inflicted on homosexuals by the leading authorities and our entire society, forcing us to be intimate with someone we were sexually repulsed by. Maaz no doubt had to somehow bring himself to actually make love to his wife when the physical appearance of his wife naked would cause him to gag or make him feel as if he wanted to vomit. Yet, it was a requirement in our society not only to marry but also to sire children and his parents no doubt would be in expectation of their anticipated grandchildren.

And now my parents were making the same plans for me. I at least had one trump card, or at least something that would buy me time. Unlike the situation with Maaz, there were no female friends of my acquaintance that my parents had their eye on in order to machinate the events of our eventual marriage. After the event with Rubasha, my parents knew not to apply too much pressure on me.

The other difficulty was the view of my religion. I had finally accepted within myself that I no longer believed that the Koran was the perfect Word of Allah. In fact, it wasn't merely a belief. All that had transpired in my past together with my long discussion with Muhammad while stranded in the tree over the deluge demonstrated that there was overwhelming evidence which supported this. But there was no way I could admit this openly. To be open about my apostasy would cause so many problems. For a start, recanting the religion in Pakistan was a death sentence so I couldn't be open about it to the general public. It could also cause total disownment from my parents and all my extended family. But also, it was impossible to disentangle the intertwined relationship between my religion and my parents. My parents would never be able to understand that my leaving the religion did not equate with me not loving them. They were still my parents and I loved them, but I knew as I had seen in other situations that parents cannot disassociate a failure to love one's religion from a failure to love one's parents.

Fortunately I had Muhammad. Muhammad was back in Karachi and he was my lifeline to sanity. As bizarre as the coincidence was, because he was the son of my Mulvi, my parents were pleased and further encouraged the friendship that had developed between Muhammad and me seeing Muhammad in their eyes was a religious friend.

The beauty about Muhammad was that he knew everything about me. Not only did he know about my apostasy, he was aware of my homosexuality, seeing he had worked out what had really been going on between Maaz and me. This in itself was extremely comforting. For the first time in my life I could talk to someone openly about my sexuality, and further with Muhammad who was heterosexual. I was amazed how sympathetic and understanding he was about the phenomenon and how he didn't recoil in horror, afraid that I would use every opportunity to rape him as the men of Sodom and Gomorrah apparently were supposed to have wanted to do to any male strangers who wandered into their cities. Muhammad told me that he had come to the realisation that homosexuality is not the problem that our society made out that it was and from information he had gleaned on internet, it was a natural phenomenon, not only among the human species but also within the animal kingdom. If homosexuality expressed itself in nature, it obviously was a natural phenomenon. He also discovered that one of his brothers and his only sister were both homosexual. Each of them had revealed this secretly to Muhammad, so secretly that neither sibling was aware of the other sibling's same-sex sexual orientation. However, unlike Muhammad, this homosexual brother and his homosexual sister still believe fervently in the Islamic religion and are trying their best to change their sexuality to be in line with the teachings of the Koran. Muhammad realises that there is nothing he can do to help them because this would mean he would have to confess his lack of faith and this is too dangerous, especially with a father who was a reputable Mulvi.

"So, what are you going to do?" I asked him.

Muhammad just laughed.

"There's little I can do. I am in contact with other people in Pakistan who say that they no longer believe in the Koran and in Allah. But on the outside I have to continue the pretence that I am still a devout Muslim."

Muhammad then paused for a moment before adding.

"It's not too hard for me, really. In some ways it's inconvenient but I can get around it."

Muhammad then looked at me.

"But not for you. Unlike you, I like women and so eventually I'll get married. I'm happy to comply with this social obligation. The difficulty I face, however, is that when I do get married and have children, if my wife or my wife's family find out that I no longer believe in Islam, I could lose my wife and children. I don't want to get emotionally involved with someone and have this happen. So, I have to choose my wife wisely. I'm hoping I will meet a woman who is also secretly a non-believer but who can at least reveal to me her disbelief."

There was a pause.

"However," Muhammad continued, "if I don't find a wife soon, my father may organise one for me and then I will be in somewhat of a similar situation as you are."

Muhammad stared outside, took a sip of tea and then placed his cup on the table.

"As for you, my friend," Muhammad then said, "I really don't see much future for you in Pakistan. If I were you, I would get out of here."

"What about you?" I asked. "Why do you stay?"

Muhammad laughed.

"I have no idea of how I can get out of Pakistan. I've tried to think of ways of getting out of here. I even thought of trying to get into another country, maybe the UK, as a refugee."

Muhammad pulled a strange face.

"Perhaps I could give that a go. But I have nothing to convince my father as to why I need to leave the country and go overseas, especially to a country in the West. But apart from my apostasy, I really don't mind living here in Pakistan. It's difficult pretending to believe in all of this when I don't. But I also love my father and my family even though they believe wholeheartedly in the faith. And in any case, I've been living this charade for a long time now. I guess I always will."

I felt for Muhammad. It's difficult when you realise you no longer believe in Islam at the best of times, so it would be worse with a father who is extremely religious. I did appreciate Muhammad's comment that he still loved his father. He had been a good man to me throughout my religious instruction. I could only guess that he had been a good father. But I totally appreciated the complexity of the situation that Muhammad was in. It's difficult to disentangle the love for one's religion from the love of one's family members.

But as Muhammad had told me, I needed to find a way out of the country. Unlike Muhammad, I did have an avenue out of Pakistan. I had been in contact with my cousin, Muzammil. Muzammil was an Australian of Pakistani heritage. My mother's sister, my aunt, had married a Pakistani man who had earlier immigrated to Australia and become an Australian citizen. They were living in Melbourne. Muzammil, their second son, had moved to Sydney to study.

I had been in contact with Muzammil through Facebook. Muzammil's tone on Facebook had begun to change once he had left Melbourne to reside in Sydney. He had become critical of Islam and posted a lot of links to Youtube, clips which criticised Islam, in particular *The Apostate Prophet, The Masked Arab, Abdul Sameer* and *Atheist Nation*. This created a lot of flak from other members of the family but it appeared that the worst they could do to him was get angry. I could only guess that he had the freedom to be open about his apostasy because he was an Australian citizen and the worst one could do in Australia was get angry at him. However, it was impossible for me to tell him that I agreed with him because if anyone got wind of this in my family in Pakistan, there would be terrible reprisals. But there was something comforting in knowing that there was a family member in

Australia with whom I could reside and with whom I could confide. This seemed to be my ticket out of Pakistan.

One evening, while we were around the dinner table, my father asked me how I was going looking for a job.

"Father," I said, "I've been thinking. I'd like to pursue further studies."

I took a gulp of food before adding my next statement.

"But not in a Pakistani university. I'd like to study overseas."

My father and mother stopped eating for a moment and looked at each other.

"I have it all figured out," I continued. "If I study in an overseas university doing a postgraduate degree, when I return, I will be able to get an even better job."

My father resumed eating.

"I think that's a great idea, son," my father replied.

I couldn't believe my luck when he said that. I was sure I was going to have to put up a fight to convince him.

However, my mother wasn't as pleased.

"You already have a degree," my mother replied. "And anyway, you can pursue further studies here in Pakistan."

My father looked up at my mother but he didn't say anything to contradict what she said. So I had to come up with something.

"There are offerings in universities in Sydney, especially near where Muzammil lives. He said that if I went to Sydney, I could live with him so I wouldn't have to worry about accommodation."

There was further silence while my parents continued eating.

"I can pay for it," I continued. "In Australia, I can work 20 hours a week and therefore you needn't pay for my university fees."

"Son, there's no need to worry about that," my father replied. "I can afford to send you there if you so desire." My father then looked at my mother. "Do remember, dear, that

I also studied overseas, in the UK, and this helped me to get in the high paid position I am in now." There was a slight pause and then my father added, "Also, remember that the Prophet said in one of the Hadiths to search for knowledge, even if you have to go to China to get it. And Australia is a lot further from Pakistan than China is."

What was amazing about this was this was the first time that the Hadiths actually said something in my favour. I couldn't believe it that at a time when I no longer believed in the religion, it was at this time that the religion actually worked for me.

Muzammil was very helpful in finding out information about the various universities I could get into and I finally got into one doing a postgraduate degree. There were a lot of forms to fill out and formalities to go through, and of course, a lot of handing over of money, but eventually I had all the paperwork required and the appropriate travel documents.

My parents decided to throw a large party for my departure. At one stage my mother burst into tears because her only son was leaving for another country. My father wished me the best of luck on my journey and asked for Allah's blessing on me wherever I went. There were more tears at the airport as I left them and passed through immigration.

It was sad leaving my parents, my grandparents, my sister, my brother-in-law, and all my friends. On the plane I realized I was torn between two, the love for my family and friends in Pakistan on the one hand, and the need to get out of Pakistan and breathe the air of freedom of being both ex-Muslim and gay on the other.

Muzammil picked me up from Kingsford Smith Airport, Sydney's International Airport. This was the second time I had seen him, the first time being only once during my childhood when he had accompanied his parents to Pakistan on vacation. Although I could recognise certain traits from what I remembered of his childhood face, he still looked very different as an adult that it was like meeting someone for the first time.

It was a very long drive from the airport. Muzammil lived in Penrith, a suburb about 60 kilometres west of the centre of Sydney. It is a suburb of Sydney and located at the western extremity of the Sydney Metropolitan Area.

Muzammil lived in a set of apartments to the south of the centre of Penrith. It was a large, brick building, something different to what I was used to because buildings in Pakistan are made mainly of concrete. Muzammil's apartment certainly wasn't flash or luxurious looking on the outside although it was a little better on the inside.

Muzammil didn't have to be a genius as to why I willingly and enthusiastically wanted to reside with him. It had become quite obvious from his Facebook page where he sat with regards to Islam and so for me to have left Pakistan and chosen to reside with him was correctly interpreted as my way of having someone with whom I could vent my feelings.

What struck me about Muzammil, however, was that he said that he was an atheist. I hadn't ruled out the idea that there was a deity, I had simply realised that the Koran was not perfect and if there were a god or gods, these divine beings certainly were not involved in the composition of the Koran. However, religious matters weren't Muzammil's first concern when I first arrived. Muzammil knew that in Pakistan, sex was restricted to within marriage but in Australia it was definitely an open pastime to all who wanted to enjoy it. Muzammil had a girlfriend, although to his frustration she was a Christian and therefore believed in a deity. What I discovered was that she defined herself as a born-again Christian and sometimes she said she was a Bible Christian, something I wasn't familiar with. In Pakistan, the only Christians I knew were Catholic Christians and I had assumed that that's what all Christians were. How sincere she was in her faith was difficult to ascertain. I had thought that Christians, like Muslims, had a strict view of sex as being something adults only indulged in after they were married. From the relationship she had with Muzammil, I simply guessed that Bible Christians weren't as strict in their adherence to the faith as Muslims were supposed to be. I did find out later that Bible Christians actually do have the same strict code of sexual conduct that we have in Pakistan where sex is only allowed between couples after they were married. How Muzammil's girlfriend got around this I never found out nor did I care to know.

Muzammil introduced me to life in the West in a big way. He took me into the city where I had my first taste of alcohol and soon learned why the writers of the Koran stated that there was as much sin in alcohol as there was a benefit when I had my first hangover. Muzammil tried to get me interested in girls and have a bit of pleasure of the flesh. I didn't know how to tell Muzammil that I wasn't interested in women and I seemed to frustrate him when I refused to lose my virginity with any of them.

One night Muzammil took me to a suburb called Darlinghurst. There was a street called Oxford Street which had a number of different bars and pubs. While walking down this street, a rather effeminate man stopped and greeted Muzammil. He had all the hallmarks of a heejrah, the way he walked, the lisp in his speech, what he was wearing and the way he had dressed his hair. My initial reaction was to avoid him but Muzammil spoke to him as civilly as he would to another human being. It was obvious that they knew each other.

But I didn't feel comfortable at first. Even though I knew I was gay, the idea of men who walked and talked like women still carried the negativity we held towards such people in Pakistan. It was therefore perplexing that Muzammil took the time to stop and talk to this man as if he were a worthwhile human being.

It was this fortuitous incident, however, that enabled me to open up to Muzammil. The following day I raked up the courage to ask about this guy Muzammil had greeted the evening before and what he felt about him. Muzammil went on the defensive, explaining that we should respect such people, that homosexuality is simply a part of nature and gay men and women do not choose to be this way.

There was a pause for a moment after Muzammil stated his argument before I could muster up enough courage to confess to him that I realised that I also was gay. Muzammil chuckled with some hesitancy which began to worry me that maybe he wasn't as open-minded as he earlier had appeared to be.

"So, my little cousin is gay?" he eventually said after a slight pause.

He then gave me a hug as reassurance. Wow! I couldn't believe it. For the first time in my life, I had actually confessed openly to a family member that I was gay and the reaction wasn't violence against me but the show of affection.

"So, do your parents know?" he then asked.

"No!" I replied emphatically. "Nobody knows. Except Muhammad and Maaz."

I then explained to him the entire story about what had happened between Maaz and me. Muzammil listened but throughout the whole time with a big Cheshire grin on his face.

"No wonder you had to leave Pakistan," Muzammil said. "And, so where is this Maaz?"

I explained what happened to Maaz, how we had separated when Maaz finished his last year and how that he had returned to Yemuhamvar with the prospect of marriage already hanging over his head. I explained how he probably was now already married.

Muzammil shook his head with a grave expression on his face. He responded to what I had just told him by telling me that this was just so cruel of Pakistan both because of societal expectations and what was required of the religion. He exclaimed that Pakistan, its society and its religion really needed an honest look at itself and open up to the realities of life.

"What about you?" I asked. "Have you told your parents you no longer believe?"

Muzammil smiled a cheeky smile.

"Oh, yes!" he replied. "Which is why I decided to leave Melbourne and come to Sydney. I miss Melbourne. But there was no way I could continue to remain in the vicinity of my parents. You might think it's dangerous in Pakistan to say you no longer believe in Islam. But it's also not terribly safe here either, although we have a lot more latitude here when we do proclaim our apostasy."

"Wow!" I exclaimed. "So, what happened when you told them you didn't believe in Islam anymore?"

Muzammil sat back in his chair.

"Well, I didn't come straight out and say it like that. It was a slow process, deliberately on my part. I began asking questions that my father had difficulty answering but he simply thought I was asking questions seriously about the faith. My father eventually realised that my questions were not the innocent questions of a faithful Muslim trying to find consistency in the faith but they were direct attacks at the religion. Whereas earlier we had long discussions where my father found himself in the embarrassing situation that he could not answer my questions, soon the civil discussions turned into heated arguments that ended with my father verbally abusing me, cursing me with threats of violence in this life and in the life to come."

This was ghastly news.

"Did your father ever attack you violently?" I gasped.

"No," Muzammil replied with an evasive air swipe with his hand. "My father is not a violent man. He never laid a hand on me. Probably because he knew he would get in trouble with the law here in Australia. But also, I have the suspicion that my father also has doubts about the faith but he just can't admit it. He would get angry at me, yelling and threatening, and then an hour later he would come into my bedroom and apologise, saying he could understand my questions but that I simply needed to have faith. He told me that he also could see the problems with the religion but he could not give up on his faith as he was sure that Islam was the true and perfect religion. He said that he knew in the end that these questions I raised would eventually be ironed out and I would also be convinced of the veracity of the faith. He said that he was afraid that I would end up in Jahannam for the rest of eternity if I doubted and left the faith completely.

That really was the great unravelling for me. That's when I questioned my father about the faith. 'Who is going to Jahannam?' I asked him. I went on to say that when you read the Koran, Jahannam is reserved for people who don't believe. That's it. It doesn't matter if these people led exemplary lives, simply if they don't believe in Allah, they're going to Jahannam. The whole concept to me became completely absurd and no longer made any sense. By contrast, people who kill will still make it into paradise. It says in the Koran, in Al-Baqarah 2:191 'And kill them wherever you find them' and that 'oppression is worse than killing', and then how it is a good thing to kill unbelievers simply because they don't believe for 'such is the reward of the disbelievers'. Further, in Surah An-Nisaa 4:89 it says to 'kill them wherever you find them'. In Surah Al-Taubah 9:5 it says 'kill the polytheists wherever you find them' but if they become Muslims, then they can be spared. We had been told that the people living in Arabia at the time were polytheists and these are the polytheists the Koran is talking about. But at the same time we are told that the Koran is eternal so this verse applies to all polytheists. This means as Muslims, we could read this verse as 'kill the

Hindus wherever you find them', or even here in Australia where the Australian Aboriginals believe in many gods, we could say 'kill the Australian Aboriginals wherever you find them', not because they have done anything wrong but simply because they are not Muslims. There is nothing in the Koran that says something to the effect of, 'go out and convince by good, solid, convincing evidence-based argument that Islam is the perfect religion of Allah so that they can avoid Jahannam'. In fact, if we are to believe the Koran, Allah knew even before He created the universe that He intended to create a large number of humans and jinns so that the majority of them could be thrown into Jahannam. As Allah says in Surah As-Sajdah 32:13, 'the Word from Me will come true, 'I will fill Hell with jinn and men together'.' Allah's whole starting point was to create enough humans and jinns so He could fulfil His own prophecy of filling Jahannam with them. This makes an absolute mockery of the opening verse of many of the surahs which say 'In the name of Allah, the Compassionate, the Merciful'. Further, because Allah made a promise that He would fill Jahannam with humans, who's to say that He won't take those who were originally destined for paradise and put them in Jahannam simply to ensure that His original promise to fill Jahannam is fulfilled? There is no promise that Allah will fill paradise."

I looked on in aghastness. I was surprised Muzammil was still alive when he said that. Muzammil told me that his father did get disturbingly enraged by the comment and hit the wall, putting a hole through the gyprock. That's when Muzammil realised that maybe it was time to get away from his family, especially his father, until his father could deal with the cognitive dissonance that was being aroused by Muzammil's argumentation.

Muzammil fortunately enough was living in Australia and he was after all an Australian citizen, having been born in the country and by birth able to gain the right to be a citizen of this country. Children of Muslim parents, even in Australia, however, are still under threat when they tell their parents one day that they no longer believe in Allah and the Koran. But there are still places of refuge.

But not in Pakistan. I could only imagine what would have happened to me had my parents discovered that I no longer believed in the Koran and further that I was gay. It is difficult to know which of the two would be more shameful to them. And there would be nowhere to run. My father was an extremely religious man and had been quite strict. I wasn't sure how far he would go if he became fully aware of these two aspects of me. But even if he didn't kill me, there was the State, and I could be killed lawfully.

In Australia, and with Muzammil, I was free to be myself. Eventually I discovered through various social media contacts that there were many other Pakistanis who were now in Australia and who also were gay. However, I was quite surprised to find out that some of them still maintained that they were Muslim and continued to believe in the truth of the faith and became quite hostile towards me for questioning it. When I pointed out that the Koran is extremely hostile towards homosexuals, in particular with regards to the inhabitants of Sodom and Gomorrah, these Pakistanis came up with explanations to excuse this. I didn't quite get it. Weren't they aware that Pakistan had laws against homosexuals because of what it said in the Koran?

As for the nature of sexuality, what intrigued me was how international homosexuality was. Because Australia is a multicultural country and Sydney has a large agglomeration of people from just about all the countries of the world, I was amazed to discover that homosexuals were found in all people of different nationalities. And along with their international background was also the wide ranging background in beliefs. There were homosexuals who had backgrounds in Christianity, Judaism, Hinduism,

Buddhism, and Zoroastrianism. Even some Australian Aboriginals were gay and their religious background was specific and unique to their communities that had evolved over the millennia inside Australia independently from outside influence. Arguments that I had heard that homosexuality was given as a curse to unbelievers or as a trial to extremely good Muslims simply did not fit the evidence. Rather, the evidence strongly suggested that homosexuality was simply one subset of general human sexuality.

But one thing they all experienced in Australia was the freedom of their sexual expression. And contrary to what we had been told in the mosque, homosexuality was not the cause of the downfall of society.

But what was even striking for me was the freedom of thought. At least in the presence of Muzammil, but also with the new friends that I was making in Sydney, I could be openly friends with fellow atheists and we could walk around without the fear of persecution or death.

What Muhammad had told me while we sat stranded on the branches above the flood waters was right. I needed to get out of Pakistan. Now I was out temporarily. And I knew I needed to make the exit from my country permanent.

Chapter 22

Leaving Pakistan and my family was a bitter-sweet experience. Pakistan was my country in which I had been born and grown up, and along with my parents and grandparents, my sister and all my extended family, it gave me my identity.

But at the same time, like a caterpillar that goes into its cocoon in one form and comes out another, I could feel that I had also completely changed from a Pakistani who is completely immersed in the Islamic religion to a new person with a completely different outlook in life. This didn't mean that I wanted to completely disconnect from everything in my past, but I did know that there was some disconnect whether I liked it or not.

Muzammil was a family member who was a part of the new person I had become. Muzammil was also a member of a new community and a new way of viewing the world. It actually gave me comfort that I had in the end one family member with whom I could relate and with whom I could speak openly both about my apostasy and my homosexuality.

Muzammil was a complete atheist. On first contemplation, I didn't like this. His arguments against the existence of a god I felt were simply directed at the absurdity of the existence of Allah who is a contradiction on many levels which therefore makes it impossible for Him to exist at all. Of all the contradictions about Allah that make it impossible for Him to exist is that on the one hand He is the Compassionate and the Merciful, yet on the other He has planned to "fill Hell with Jinns and men all together" as He Himself prophesied in As-Sajdah 32:13, sadistically forcing them to suffer unimaginable torture and horror for the rest of eternity as it is so detailed in various parts of the Koran. And the reason He will cause so many jinns and people to suffer cruelty in hell is because, as it says in Al-Hijr 15:33 – 39, He gave tacit approval to Satan, an extremely powerful and quasi godlike creature, to mislead humanity.

With all these passages of the Koran put together, the picture this creates of Allah is this. Right at the beginning of time, when Allah was about to create the universe, He said to Himself, "What I need to create is a place for Me to reside, and a platform, which I'll call earth, on which those I create can live. But also, before I create any beings, I need to ensure that I have also created a large waste disposal area which I will call Jahannam in which I can throw those creatures I create with defects and imperfections – which seems strange even to Me because I am the Almighty and I'm perfect hence it is impossible for Me to create any beings with imperfections – and I need to make this Jahannam really, really big because I have made a promise to Myself that I will fill Jahannam, which further means I really need to create multitudes upon multitudes of creatures with defects and imperfections in order to fulfil this promise I have made to Myself. I will create these creatures of a material that only ensures them a short lifespan during which time they will experience good and bad moments, and they will be completely blind to My existence and the existence of Shaitaan but I will still demand of them to believe I exist and I will allow Shaitaan to mislead as many people as he can to not believe in My existence. But after they die I will repair them so that they are immortal so that they will be forced to experience only good times forever or bad times forever. I will also create them with new eyes that enable them to see Me for real, not that it will do them any good because they will already be condemned to their respective destinies anyway. In this latter state, after I have repaired them, I will use most of them as fuel for Jahannam because

I created Jahannam and for some reason I want Jahannam to exist forever and I need fuel to keep it alive so why not use the bodies of the humans and jinns I created to fuel it? I will also create in parallel another place I will call paradise which is specifically made for those creatures I managed to create perfect – and what I mean by perfect is those who explicitly obey everything I tell them to do – which is impossible anyway because no-one will ever be able to obey everything I command so there will be those created humans still with defects that I will allow into paradise and I'll simply overlook these people's defects. Of course, why I can't or don't create perfect creatures now and an eternal paradise in which we can all live happily together is really up to Me to decide and no-one should question Me for doing things the way I choose to do them."

This really would be the way we would have to understand Allah if the Koran was our source of information about God.

One of the beauties of Australia that Australians take so much for granted is the local council library. In Pakistan, there are libraries only in universities, and even these are limited to holding books only related to subjects being studied at university, with only the rare novel or two purely for leisure. There are no local libraries containing books on a wide range of topics for people to freely read and from this open their minds about life and the universe. The only recourse to knowledge is through the internet and yet this is also tightly controlled.

In fact, these two aspects more than anything else made me see a creepy similarity to what George Orwell writes in his book, *Nineteen Eighty-Four*, and the reality of countries like my own. In the dystopic world of this fiction I could see parallels in the reality of Pakistan. Any form of knowledge whether books or websites which said anything against Islam were simply banned. And information control by the government in Orwell's novel to some degree finds its cognate in the government getting rid of general local libraries and controlling what information is allowed to flow through into the households from the World Wide Web.

Even the concept of doublethink and the thought police finds its cognates. The current blasphemy laws in essence mean any criticism of the Koran is a criminal offence which put people in prison or even get them the death penalty. So people are not even allowed to think about the errors in the Koran in order not to risk their thoughts being exposed and these people being killed as a result. What was particularly troubling and eerie about Orwell's book was the parallel between what happens in Pakistan and what happened to Winston Smith in the latter part of the book. Smith was held down in some sort of contraption in which he couldn't move, a machine which caused excruciating pain whenever O'Brien turned a dial. When O'Brien held up four fingers and asked Smith how many fingers he was holding up, when Smith answered that there were four because this was what he could see and hence this is what the evidence suggested, O'Brien set the machine in motion and Smith was dealt severe physical pain. What Smith eventually discovered was that the answer he was supposed to give O'Brien was that there were as many fingers that O'Brien was holding up as O'Brien told Smith that there were, even when the evidence before Smith's eyes was that there were four. In the same way, our blasphemy laws require us to do exactly the same thing. We have to say, in fear of pain and death, that whatever the Koran tells us is the reality, this is the reality, even when the evidence before our eyes clearly indicates otherwise.

In fact, the entire irony of the the blasphemy laws is that they are evidence in themselves that the Koran is not perfect. If the Koran were perfect, it would be impossible to find fault with it. So it makes no sense to put in place a law which prohibits finding fault in something that is supposed to be by its very nature impossible to find fault with.

In Australia, I had access to alternate knowledge and my mind was free to roam. I appreciated that Muzammil no longer believed in the existence of any god but I wanted to prove him wrong. The Muslim God didn't exist but this didn't mean that there wasn't a much more humane God guiding humans. Because of my freedom of thought, I began to ponder about Pakistan and its connection to its southern neighbour, India. We Pakistanis belonged to a separate state from India but this had been for only a short time, since 1947. Before then, and for the millennia before then, Indians and Pakistanis shared a common cultural and religious heritage. Islam, so I reasoned, was an Arabic religion, which is testified in the Koran itself. But the religion of the people of the subcontinent was Hinduism. Now that I was unleashed from the binds of Islam over my mind, I began to contemplate Hinduism, especially as Muhammad had begun to talk about Hinduism in a positive light. And like Muhammad said, I could no longer see polytheism as the great sin as it is portrayed in the Koran, but also I could understand that as Muhammad explained it, there may be something deeper in this concept of the divine.

A friend of mine from university who was himself a Hindu one day took me to one of the local Hindu temples in Sydney. This was a wonderful and imposing structure. The colourful decoration of the place and the larger than life size statues of the gods and goddesses were impressive.

This particular aspect of Hinduism, and of idolatry in general, and the criticism Islam makes against idols actually struck me. Muslims forbid the replication of anything divine, in particular Allah and the angels, and even the Prophet himself. But I could see that Muslims were doing the exact same thing with the Koran. Muslims say that there is a divine Koran written on divine tablets which co-exist eternally with Allah and the Korans that we have in our possession are simply replicas of this eternal Koran. So how was this different to religions which make idols as replicas of objects of the divine? And the way many Muslims treat their Korans was no different to the way those of other religions treat their holy relics. In fact, many Muslims I know treat their Korans with absolute veneration, they dust them, they kiss them, they place them in special places in their rooms and they would almost kill anyone who damaged them or even stepped on them unintentionally, in exactly the same way as those of other religions treat their holy relics and those who desecrate them.

However, it didn't take long for me to become skeptical of Hinduism. In a way, I could appreciate that although Hindus created grand statues, they stated that they didn't believe that the statues were the gods they were supposed to represent. However, it became obvious that many Hindus actually did treat the statues as the very gods themselves and not as mere reflections of the gods. What further troubled me was that many Hindus treated these nonliving statues of metal and concrete much better than they did their fellow human beings.

I then came across the *Satyartha Prakash*, a book containing the philosophy, or rightly said, the version of Hinduism purported by Swami Dayananda. Dayananda presented a new and modern version of Hinduism which fit more in accord with my view of God, that God does not dwell in statues and temples but lives all around us.

But while Dayananda's philosophy was in accordance with how I thought God should be, it shared certain aspects of the portrayal of God in Islam, Christianity and Judaism, that is, God is everywhere. And suddenly the thought struck me: if God is everywhere, isn't He right here with me at the very place I am in? The Koran says that Allah is closer to us than our jugular veins. If this is the case, then I can call out to Him right where I am and Allah should be able to hear me and respond. Yet, when I call out to Him,

517

He doesn't reply. Which raised the question: Why is it that according to Islam, even though Allah is right next to me and even inside me, rather than speaking directly to me, He spoke to a 7th Century human, Muhammad, who Allah knew would die in the end and it was through Muhammad that He spoke to humanity? Why doesn't God speak to all of us directly right here and right now?

This then set my thoughts running. Not only did every religion I was familiar with claim that God is everywhere, they claimed that this God did not speak to people directly but only through special people called prophets. The prophets are supposed to be only messengers who speak on God's behalf. More problems, however, came out of this.

One is that, if God speaks through messengers, these messengers don't come and tell us their own personal ideas. Messengers simply relay what God has said to them. This makes the messenger nothing more than a means for communicating God's message. So why do the different religions venerate their messengers? To me, it was the same as if God spoke to us through our smartphones and then people started praising their smartphones for passing on God's message when the only function of the smartphone was the means through which God spoke to us. Yet the way religious people venerate their prophets, and in particular, the way Muslims venerate Muhammad, it was almost difficult to separate veneration for the Prophet and veneration for God. In fact, the preservation of the Hadiths made this point even more pronounced. I had for a long time recognised that when Muslims say, "The Prophet said this" or "The Prophet did that" in the Hadiths, and this entire idea of sunna, all this made it sound as if the Prophet were God Himself. If the Prophet were merely a messenger, what the Prophet said was not something that came from his own mind, it had simply come from God, and the Prophet had simply relayed it, so why should there be any veneration for the Prophet? Further, Muhammad, according to what we had been taught, was only one within the chain of transmission. Allah spoke to Gabriel and then Gabriel spoke to Muhammad and then Muhammad spoke to humans, and eventually these humans spoke to us. I didn't get the Koran directly from Muhammad but from other people, such as my father and my Mulvi. Gabriel and all the humans involved in relaying Allah's Koran to us were just as much passing on information from Allah as was Muhammad, so why don't Muslims give the same veneration towards Gabriel and all the other people as they do towards Muhammad?

In fact, when I thought about it more, I noticed much more that the veneration for Muhammad is exactly the same as the veneration that Christians have for Christ. The difference is that Christians say that Christ is God. I could see that the Christian veneration for Christ actually had a sound basis. Christians not only claim that Christ was the messenger of Allah, Christians say that Christ is God. Therefore, Christians are not venerating a created being over and above their veneration for God, for their veneration for Christ is simply their veneration for God, for Christ to them is God. The Muslim veneration for Muhammad did not have the same justification. What was worse was that the veneration Muslims have of Muhammad is simply sheerk.

Another was that for the first time, I realised that removing the prophet was almost like removing God Himself. And once we put to one side those who are supposed to be messengers of God such as Moses, Zoroaster, Jesus and Muhammad, we are left with the stark reality: without these messengers, there is a terrible silence from the world of the divine. In fact, the more I thought about it, the more I realised that the need to have prophets was indirect evidence that there is no god because the need to cling to the words of those who claimed to have been prophets and spoken on God's behalf covers the pain of the reality that there is no-one in the divine who speaks to us.

I tried to think of a satisfactory explanation as to why God would speak to prophets and not to all of us directly. I remembered a story I had been told that when Muhammad was young and living with his foster mother in the desert, the angel Gabriel came down, opened his heart, cleaned it and purified it with a holy aroma, and then replaced his heart back into his chest. This then made him perfect enough for Allah to speak to him. But I then thought, if Allah needs humans to be perfect in order for Him to speak to them directly, isn't He the Almighty and can't He purify everyone's hearts so all of us can have direct communication with Him and not have indirect communication via an intermediary?

This then gave rise to more doubts about the existence of a god. But what was still holding me to the belief in an intelligence and power greater than us was the world around us and in particular the complex functions of the human body. The universe in all its glory just seemed too big and too organized for there not to be an intelligence greater than us who created all this in the first place.

But again, the more I thought about it, the more I realised the flaw in this idea. I had heard so many Muslims, and then later Christians, say that it was impossible that we arrived here by the long process of evolution. Among the many pieces of evidence presented to us was the human eye. The eye, so it was claimed, is perfect. How could the eye be something that developed over time without a greater intelligence behind it? However, when I thought more about it, I realized that the eye is not, in fact, perfect. For most of us, our eyes function very well. However, as we get older, our eyes fail us and when we reach a certain age, we have to wear glasses. This is a defect in this not-so-perfect eye. Not only so, there are many people who have to start wearing glasses at an early age, and I am one of these people. There are also people who are born colour-blind and cannot distinguish between red and green, or blue and yellow. Then there are people who go blind later in life and others who are born blind. And some people develop cataracts which cloud their vision. This means that not all eyes are perfect but many of them succumb to defects or simply do not work. Not only so, when the eye becomes defective, it is humans who help to fix the imperfections so that the eye can see normally again or at least function adequately. Humans make glasses so that people can once again see properly and humans have operations carried out by humans to have cataracts removed. If God made the eye, why does He allow these defects? And further He doesn't correct the defects but doesn't seem to mind or care whether or not humans do.

The picture this created in my head was God looking down on earth and commenting to Himself, "These are my creatures. And I created their eyes to be perfect. Oh! Oops! Look at that poor boy in the classroom. He can't see the board. Oh, look! The teacher is reprimanding him because he gave a wrong answer because his eyes have a defect and he can't see the board! Oh, look! There he is, going with his parents to the optometrist and this human is making glasses for him to adjust the defect. I mean, I could fix the eye because I created the eye to be perfect although it's unfortunately not perfect in this poor boy but I'd rather just sit here on the clouds and watch what happens. Oh, look over there! That poor old woman. She's walking around bumping into things. Oh, dear! She's got cataracts in my perfect eye which I created to be perfect. Oh, my! That must be so inconvenient and quite painful to bump into things all the time. Oh, look! Her daughter is taking her to see the doctor and now the doctor is carrying out the operation to remove the cataracts. Oh, wow! Now she can see properly again. I mean, I could have fixed the eye and removed the cataracts because I'm God and I can do everything, but I'd rather just sit back and do nothing and let the humans work it all out by themselves." This would be the picture of God that we would have to create if we took in all that we observed around us. It was at this time that I seriously started to consider the Theory of Evolution by natural selection and for the first time began to appreciate what the theory entailed and how it fit the evidence so well.

When putting all this together, it was becoming more and more obvious to me that the idea of God or gods just didn't fit the evidence. I went through a time of depression. But it was great having Muzammil with me because he was there and he had already gone through this time of reflection, rejection, depression and finally a rebirth into accepting reality for what it was.

My discussions with Muzammil helped me to see the appeal of religion. Religions provided a meaning to life, answering the questions as to why we were here, where the universe had come from, what was our purpose in life, and of course supposed evidence of an eternity to our existence. Religion provided comfort to those who went through distressing times, suffering terrible illnesses or when loved ones died. Take God away from religious people and their lives become somehow meaningless and the thought of no life after death inconceivable.

However, this need for the existence of a god was a powerful tool in the hands of the unscrupulous and controlling. This was particularly the case for the Abrahamic religions. Muzammil believed that religions actually start out with a noble purpose but eventually people in power use it for their own ends. Because Muzammil had a Christian girlfriend, this forced him to study up about Christianity. He noticed that Christianity started out as a way to unite the Jews of Palestine with the rest of the Roman world because the New Testament actually contains a mixture of ideas coming from both the Old Testament and the Classical Greek writers. While it began as a liberating principle to make Jews realize that they could connect with non-Jews, eventually the Roman Emperors saw this as a means of control and hence Christianity, instead of being a liberator of thought, it became a shackle over the minds of the people for centuries until the Enlightenment.

When Muzammil said that, this made me reflect on what was possibly the true source of Islam, especially in light of what Maaz had told me when he discovered the true identity of the Muhammad in the Koran. It would appear with the continual references to Issa coupled with the condemnations made against those who claimed that Issa was God and how it says that it is illogical that Allah could have a son, Islam began as a rival religion to Trinitarian Christianity but still focusing on Jesus, the Muhammad of the Koran. However, at its inception, the early form of Islam was an attempt to find harmony among the other believers of other religions, at least monotheistic religions, when the Koran explicitly states that Jews, Christians and Sabeans will make it into paradise. Also, the adoption of practices of other faiths and philosophies, such as the five prayers a day from Zoroastrianism and the philosophy of Taoism or the straight way to God implied an initial universal embrace and acceptance of the many religions and philosophies of the day. Possibly the genesis of Islam was actually to develop an all-embracing religion that found peace with all others of different religions but also attempted to iron out those things that were considered as absurdities, such as Allah having a son.

How, then, did Islam develop and finally morph into the religion we know it today? Two sources provided me with information that helped me to actually see what most probably was the development of the religion.

One of them was from a book I borrowed from the library, Robert Spencer's book, *Did Muhammad Exist?* As I read through the book, I was amazed at the evidence that Spencer provided which further concreted to me the evidence that Muhammad, the Arabian prophet, most probably was a creation. Spencer touched on some of the arguments about the paucity of mention of the prophet Muhammad in the Koran and in contrast with the copious mentions of other prophets, in particular, the prophets of the Christian Bible. Spencer also reinforced what Maaz had explained to me, how that the original Muhammad in the Koran was better identified as Issa or Jesus, but by a sect of Christians who did not recognize that Jesus was God or the Son of God, but that Jesus was simply a prophet. Spencer, however, went further by presenting evidence from other sources. The particular source that intrigued me was the evidence from the Dome of the Rock in Jerusalem. Once again, there is a paucity of mention of Muhammad in all the passages cited on the Dome of the Rock and much of these passages are directed at pointing out the true identity of Jesus.

It was also the issue of the Dome of the Rock that also brought this point out even further. In the Youtube clip, *Archaeological Evidence: Mecca was Petra – the Pagan Origin of Islam*[*], the author of all this research, Dan Gibson, shows through undeniable evidence that the original qibla was in fact towards Petra in Jordan and was not towards Jerusalem as we had been told. Further, according to this clip, Al-Masjid Al-Aqsa was not built until 706 AD. This then meant that the servant in Surah Bani-Israel 17:1 was someone who lived in the early eighth century and could not have been referring to Muhammad as Muhammad was purported to have died in 632 AD, almost one hundred years before the Al-Aqsa Mosque was built. Putting all this together, if what Maaz had said and which Spencer also strongly suggests that the Muhammad in the Koran is in fact Issa, then all the other mentions of "Prophet" or "Messenger" could refer to anyone. And if the qibla was changed after 724 AD as Gibson's research illustrates, then the timing of the verse in Al-Baqarah 2:142-144 which talks about the changing

---

[*]   https://www.youtube.com/watch?v=AbAkExcItlo

of the qibla was written well over one hundred years after Muhammad had died, which meant that this part of the Koran was not a revelation to Muhammad but to someone else. Who this revelation was given to remains unknown as the verse simply says, "We will turn you to a direction of prayer that pleases you" and who this "you" is remains a mystery.

There was another question that was raised in my mind: why create Muhammad as an Arabian prophet and not continue to believe in Issa as the Muhammad? The question, however, was not too difficult to answer. The Arabs had begun to create a large empire and one of its rivals was the Roman Empire. The Romans recognized Jesus as their prophet and this caused a problem. The Arabian Empire was politically opposing Rome yet in a way was religiously united with Rome because both empires shared the same prophet. Further, both the Roman Empire and the nascent Arabian Empire recognized the same Holy Scriptures, the Torah and the Injeel, these books, particularly the latter, giving foundation to the Romans. If the Arabians continued to acknowledge Issa and the Bible, they would continue to be religiously subservient to Rome. The Arabs needed a prophet from their own people and a holy book in their own language. I could see the development. Because of the great veneration given to the Christian Bible, for the Koran to gain any credence, it needed to show that it was justified by the Bible. But when the Arabian Empire had become strong and needed to distance itself away from Rome and its holy book, there needed to be an explanation for no longer following the Bible and only using the Koran alone as the revelation from God. This evolution of thought was evident in the Koran when we read the verses which first state that the Koran is simply a confirmation of what came before it and then we read other verses which talk about the Koran as a unique book from Allah.

Jesus, the central figure of the Injeel, and who is supposed to be the fulfilment of the promises in the Torah of the prophet who was to come, was a prophet who taught passive resistance in such teachings as "love your enemies" and "turn the other cheek". This would have caused cognitive dissonance in the warriors of the nascent Arabian Empire who went out fighting in the name of Allah and His meek-and-mild prophet. Further, while an earthly ruler could demand those under his authority to obey his decrees, it no doubt was recognized that there was greater and enduring power in saying that these decrees were not from the ruler of the empire but directly from Allah through Allah's Messenger. Thus a warrior Messenger was created. And this warrior Messenger as described in the Koran in places such as Surah Al-Anfal remained nameless so that it could refer to anyone as required. This also gave a further explanation as to why a ruling was made that the Prophet could not be depicted because at this point in time there was no prophet in existence to depict.

Eventually this Messenger needed a name and the name needed to come from the book that was claimed to have been the Arabic revelation, a name which would not become confused with other prophets from the Koran who had clear identifications. Hence the name Muhammad was chosen, especially as there was scant mention of the name Muhammad in the Koran and the vagueness of Muhammad's identity could readily be adapted as required. However, unlike the Torah and the Injeel, there was nothing in the Koran which talked about the biography of this Arabian prophet and so this is what led to the creation and canonization of the Hadiths, for without the Hadiths we know absolutely nothing of Muhammad. But the Hadiths further indicated to me that Muhammad was most possibly a creation because the Hadiths themselves do not agree on supposed historical details. As it comes out with the conflict between the Sunnis and the Shiites, such as the proclamation from Al-Ma'idah 5:3 that "This day have I perfected your religion for you", where one claims it was made at Mecca, the other at Ghadeer Khumm, it seems strange that details about significant events in the history of Muhammad can be so readily mistaken, but makes more sense if they were in fact simply made up. And if all this is made up, then life-threatening condemnations against those who disbelieve in these fabrications needs to stop so that we can finally move on and live in peace.

And it is these life-threatening condemnations which are the main problem. In Pakistan, no-one is allowed to form their own opinion from the evidence they gather about the Koran or Islam. But what is just as troubling are non-Muslims in countries of the West, like in Australia, who go on blissfully unaware of the oppression and the real physical threats ex-Muslims face on a daily basis, these unaware non-Muslims even assisting the abuse, oppression and threats against the lives of ex-Muslims by calling those who show up the contradictions of the Koran racists and Islamophobes. These unaware non-Muslims don't seem to understand that when we show up the inconsistencies and faults in the Koran, we do this in order to try and free Muslims from their mental slavery and allow them to expand their minds and live life to its full potential. By contrast, indirectly – and whether or not they realise this – these non-Muslims support the enslaving of Muslim minds to a repressive ideology and further the Muslim idea that ex-Muslims are not fit to live. These non-Muslims are totally ignorant that even in Sydney, like all other ex-Muslims, I am too frightened to go near a mosque or to walk around in suburbs with a significant number of Muslims living there because people assume that from my obvious physical features I am Pakistani and therefore I should be a Muslim. And if a Pakistani in these places recognizes me and further realizes that I am now ex-Muslim and gay, this information will eventually find its way back to Pakistan which will cause great problems with my parents. And if I am forced to return to Pakistan, I will be killed both for my homosexuality and for my apostasy.

My wish is that the world finally wakes up and looks at this situation for what it is. My wish is for those who are not familiar with what it's like living under the oppression of Islam to finally open their eyes to the reality and react in support of those whose freedom and very lives are threatened.

And so, I am Mustafa and this is my message, that the Koran is not the perfect revelation brought down from heaven to earth in one time in history. The Koran may have played an important role in the history of the Middle East, and later in the creation and establishment of my country of birth, and it may be considered by many as a book of inspiration. But like all great historical works of poetry, the Koran is still a human construct. Our reasoning should not be confined to this piece of seventh century literature. It is time for us to courageously and confidently embrace all knowledge and evidence at our disposal, using this to build a better, fairer and safer society for all of us to live in.